The Education of

Arnold Hitler

Also by Marc Estrin

The Education of

Arnold Hitler

Marc Estrin

Unbridled Books

Unbridled Books
Denver, Colorado

Library of Congress Cataloging-in-Publication Data
Estrin, Marc.
The Education of Arnold Hitler / Marc Estrin.
p. cm.
ISBN 1-932961-03-8 (alk. paper)
1. Young men—Fiction. 2. Cambridge (Mass.)—Fiction. 3. College
students—Fiction. 4. Mansfield (Tex.)—Fiction. 5. Chess
players—Fiction. 6. Linguists—Fiction. I. Title.
PS3605.S77E37 2005
813'.6—dc22
2005000740

1   3   5   7   9   10   8   6   4   2

Book Design by SH · CV

First Printing

Acknowledgments

With loving thanks to the many early readers, friends and family, especially Dorian Karchmar, Roger Gillim and Delia Robinson, who have inspired and informed the author and his characters, and to Charles Johnson, his undercover football coach.

And with much gratitude to those invaluable writers and reporters who have been to the places I've not (and in some cases would have been too chicken to go to), particularly H.G. Bissinger, for his extraordinary book on Texas high school football, *Friday Night Lights: A Town, A Team and a Dream*; Roger Rosenblatt for his moment-to-moment account of the Harvard strike, *Coming Apart: A Memoir of the Harvard Wars of 1969*; Jennifer Toth for her courageous *The Mole People*; Heidi Matson for her outrageous memoir, *Ivy League Stripper*, and David Isay and his crew for their marvelous *Sound Portrait of the Sunshine Hotel*. Marvin Hightower at the Harvard University News and Public Affairs Office was particularly helpful with school details, and Lois Price with the intimacies of embouchure.

Though Lenny Bernstein comes in for some criticism—as he did in real life—I hope his generous ghost will feel my love, respect and admiration. Special thanks, Lenny, for the gift of Gustav Mahler. And Noam Chomsky, for still looking out for us, Argus-eyed as ever.

Greatest thanks of all go to my editor, Fred Ramey, who has led his people out of bondage into an unbridled, faith-based land.

Preface

*All invention flows from words. We are their tributaries. They
mark us as strongly as we mark them. Words for joy. Words for unhappiness. Words for indifference and hope. Words for things and
for men. Words for the universe and words for nothingness.*

*And behind each of them, life, simple or complex, keeping its eyes
on death.*

—Edmond Jabès, *The Book of Margins*

In his *Book of Practical Cats*, Old Possum warned that "the
naming of cats is a difficult matter" because cats require
three levels of name. There are the everyday ones, low-
brow to high, from Abby to Zelda, commonly parceled
among the tribe. But, Eliot insists, a cat's uncommon dignity demands
better than that—some wildly *un*common name, for that cat alone:
"Munkustrap," "Jellylorum."

Most important, however, is the cat's *Third* Name, a name we can't
presume to give, and one that we'll never know. When a cat lies eyes
closed, "in profound meditation," Eliot would have us understand that
she is "engaged in a rapt contemplation" of her ineffable, "deep and in-
scrutable singular Name."

We humans, too, have our common names—Marc and Donna,
Mario and Hans. We may even have uncommon names: I well remember finding "Hopalong Abramowitz" in the Manhattan phonebook in

the '40s. Or we may be known by uncommon attributes, such as Edna ("the Brain") Rawson, whom we will meet below.

But our Third Names, ah, how many of us know *them?* Do we know ourselves? I would submit that the goal of all education is—precisely— learning one's Third Name.

And what would education be for someone whose *second* name was—Hitler? What graduation might be his? What commencement songs might be sung?

Gaudeamus igitur	*Let us rejoice therefore*
Juvenes dum sumus	*While we are young.*
Post jucundum juventutem	*After a pleasant youth*
Post molestam senectutem	*After a troublesome old age*
Nos habebit humus.	*The earth will have us.*

Mansfield Elementary

arnold's earliest detailed memory

is of being held above a crowd by

his father — hard thumbs dig-

ging into his armpits — to see the

cross lying there, burning on the

high school lawn. it leaped and

danced like huge candles at a

party, just for him. in later life,

he could call up the scene, fresh

as ever, just by pressing his

thumbs hard under his arms.

One

. . . because there is perhaps a song tied to childhood, which, in the bloodiest hours, can all alone defy misery and death.

Edmond Jabès, *Songs for the Ogre's Feast*

Arnold's earliest detailed memory is of being held above a crowd by his father—hard thumbs digging into his armpits—to see the cross lying there, burning on the high school lawn. It leaped and danced like huge candles at a party, just for him. In later life, he could call up the scene, fresh as ever, just by pressing his thumbs hard under his arms.

It was Thursday, August 30th, 1956. George and Anna had taken him to register for first grade, the registration to be held this year for the first time in the Mansfield High main building. But the ordeal was more difficult than they'd expected. What was going on? Where the hell were they supposed to park? Why didn't they know this was happening?

There wasn't a parking place up or down Broad Street within four blocks of the entrance, and citizens, some with signs, were streaming toward the school. George and Anna parked several blocks away.

"What's up?" they asked Charlie Trumbull, who was passing them hurriedly on the right.

"Three niggers think they're gonna register this mornin," he said, and continued his puffing trot toward the action.

"Three niggers," Arnold said.

"Don't say 'nigger,'" his mother told him.

"Nigger, nigger, nigger," Arnold said to himself.

The broad front lawn of Mansfield High was jammed with men, women, and children—all white—all milling around. There were reporters, there were cameras, there were sound-trucks. But there was little tension—at the moment it seemed more like a chance to visit neighbors, a Fourth of July picnic at the end of August. In place of the barbecue, a six-by-ten-foot wooden cross lay on the grass, burning inside a shallow firebreak. The crowd kept a respectful distance from the flames, and beefy men from the volunteer fire department stood by with fire extinguishers, making sure nothing got out of hand. "Stay back, stay back, please. We don't want no injuries. Safety first."

"Why don't you stand it up?" George Hitler asked.

"Well, hell, how're we gonna barbecue them chickens when they get here?"

George didn't know what to make of this answer. Anna thought it was a joke. Maybe not.

Arnold had never been in such a crowd before. Fourth of July was out at the big ball field, not jammed into this kind of smaller space. His father had lifted him up, then lowered him back down. Amidst all the legs and bosoms and belts of the day, this was what he heard:

... here to stand together against any nigga students attempting to enroll ...

"*He* said 'nigger,'" said Arnold. But his parents didn't hear him.

. . . not against the Negro. We think the Negroes are making great strides in improving their race and commend them for it, as long as they . . .

. . . chalkboards, typing tables, bus passes to cover their fare to Fort Worth, what the hell more they want?

. . . be like them "integrated" niggers sitting in separate rooms, sitting alone in the cafeteria after the white students finish their meal? We don't want to do that to our niggers. . . .

"He said 'nigger.' Why can't I say 'nigger'?"

"Different people talk differently. We don't say 'nigger' in this family," George said. "We say 'Negro.'"

We got nothin against em, but they're being used. . . .

That NAACP may be an organization for the nigger people, but three-quarters of it is white. . . .

And Comminist!

"Daddy, what's NAACP?"

"National Alliance for Advancing Colored People."

Serendipitous correction from the crowd: *National Association for the Agitation of Colored People is what it stands for! The National Association for the Agitation of Colored People.*

"Daddy, what's agitation?"

. . . the goddamn NAACP forcin these colored folks down here to do this. They . . .

"It's when you stir things up and make trouble."

"Trouble like now?"

Arnold and his parents made their way through the crowd, past the effigy hanging on the flagpole—a straw-stuffed child, head and hands painted black, overalls spattered with red paint—and under a second, similar puppet hanging by the neck from the front-door cornice. "Eeny, meeny, miny, mo," Arnold chanted to himself. "Catch a nigger by the toe." He was registered to begin first grade the following Monday.

His father had lifted him up under the armpits and put him down. This was his first real memory, and amidst all the legs and bosoms and belts of the day, those were the words he heard.

Two

And what did his father remember? From this sultry August day, George Hitler drifted back to a cold, wet spring morning in the Po valley, eleven years before. Morale down, way down—not like here. How much more mud, more German bullets and bombs? The war was not going to be settled here in Italy—it was Eisenhower up in Europe that would do it, him and the Russians. Why should anyone take risks now? Just be careful and get through.

In the current clamor, George heard the voices of his army buddies taking it all out on the "Niggers of the 92nd," the black infantry unit, segregated since the Civil War, sent to hold the Serchio valley at the western end of the line. "Eleanor's Own Royal Rifles" they were called, supposedly given the newest, best equipment, while the rest of the Fifth Army made do. Every time they were cold or wet, they imagined Eleanor Roosevelt's special socks on warm black feet—and cussed up a storm. Every time someone was late for roll call or showed any dumbness or superstition or lack of discipline, he was showered with racist epithets. Just like now.

George wondered if the 92nd was so stupid and superstitious after all. Why should they be risking their necks to come back to this kind of stuff? If he was a second-class citizen, he sure wouldn't fight. The 92nd probably thought they were being led into suicidal situations on purpose. Maybe they were! Hell, he'd have hidden like they did.

Then George remembered April 25th of '45. The whole night, brilliant moonlight, towns burning up and down the hills, the Germans losing it. Big fight over the 92nd, driving into Ferrara. The company spread out, no Germans in sight, lots of corpses in the streets, Krauts, civilians, maybe partisans. Buildings smoldering. Jump out of the jeep at the Piazza Mercato in front of the cathedral, then down via Mazzini. Out a window—was it from there, or the next building over?—shots, bullets ricocheting off the concrete, hit on the thigh, no wound. He sneaks low, unhooks a grenade, pulls the pin, lobs it hook shot through the window, and makes for the shelter of the lamp post across the street.

KABOOM!

Then, rifles at the ready, he and Charlie Higgins break down a door with a Jewish star into maybe an old synagogue, looks like a storeroom. On the floor near the blown-out window, covered in orange pulp, a young woman is moaning, her blond hair swimming in blood under a dark blue kerchief. He runs over, wipes her face with her apron, inspects the head wound, applies pressure. "Charlie, help me get her out from under this mess." The GIs take her under each arm and try to drag her out from under a pile of shattered pumpkins. One foot seems stuck, so with a huge pull, they free her—without her lower left leg, which stays there, boot protruding, under the pile of pumpkins. Her left thigh is spattering blood from two large arteries.

"Oh my God!" Charlie cries. George cuts the straps off her apron.

"Give her water, Charlie, and compress the head wound. Keep her head low. I'm gonna tourniquet this."

He begins to lift her skirt, but she resists like crazy, as if he were going to rape her.

George looked over at his wife holding her cane in one hand and his son in the other.

GRITS GUTS GUNPOWDER GRITS GUTS GUNPOWDER GRITS GUTS GUNPOWDER, the crowd was chanting.

The truth of the matter—he had never told her—was that he *had* thought . . . of something. Charlie restrained her while he pushed up her coat and dress, tied up her thigh, stopping the blood flow, twisted the tourniquet—not too much—was she comfortable? Her thigh, the thigh of a young woman considered one of the most beautiful in town, her thigh, with no underwear in this clothing-short time. Cool hand on warm flesh, her blond pubic hair. Even in a pool of blood, even with Charlie there, this young, lonely, cold, wet, muddy young George from Texas felt his heart jump to his throat and his penis rise. He had never told her.

And she, Anna Giardini, had never told *him* that just four days earlier, she *had* been raped—gang-banged by four German teenagers wanting to get some in before getting the hell out. She looked like a German *Mädchen*—the blond *Mädchen* of their pinup dreams—why not? She had put up a fierce struggle.

George sent Charlie to find transport. Anna calmed down, beyond fatigue, partly from trusting this boy so intent on caring for her but mostly from blood loss and its attendant faintness. Before she lost consciousness, she was able to tell him that the Ospidale Sant'Anna was up on the Corso della Giovecca, only three blocks away. That was her name, too—Anna, she said. Too impatient to wait for an ambulance that might never come, George picked up her limp body and carried her through the streets to the crowded emergency room.

After bringing her out of shock with IV fluids, they sent her on to the bigger Nuovo Ospidale on the east side of town, where George was able to visit her during the two days his unit remained in Ferrara before pushing on to the Po and the victorious end of the war.

Out of guilt? out of love?—he wrote her every day from then on, keeping his English simple but somehow trying to pay her back for the great harm he had done. As she struggled with writing back in a foreign tongue, he grew more and more fond of her, fond in the sense of liking this obviously remarkable person, and fond in the sense of becoming just plain nuts about her.

He looked over at his beautiful wife holding her cane in one hand and his son in the other. Though she was five years younger, he sensed she was older, so much older than he, from the age-old culture of her ancient hometown. Had he her education, he would have known these lines of Carducci:

> *Onde venisti? Quali a noi secoli*
> *si mite e bella ti tramandarano . . .*
> *Whence come you? What centuries*
> *passed you on to us, so mild and lovely?*

Their correspondence continued after his return to Texas. He lived his life in order to write her of it. Lunchtimes, he went home from the Feed Mill to check the mailbox, so impatient was he. He who had never written even a postcard in his life learned to write, expressively and well. And as her letters became more fluent and his more rich, the possibility of marriage became obvious. Would this now eighteen-year-old Italian, half-Jewish beauty, flower of the ghetto, this classical violinist with the Botticelli hands, this Old World, half-Sephardic treasure, give up her family in Ferrara for the blandness of Mansfield, Texas, or would George Hitler join her in the ancient land he had helped destroy?

The most difficult letter was the one he thought might end their relationship, the one in which he told her it was he, and he alone, who had crippled her. It took nine days for an answer. The first of those days were filled with letters from Ferrara he thought of as "she doesn't know yet." The last of those days were filled with letters he called "from before she knew." On a Monday noon, a Monday after an excruciating Sunday of empty mailbox, he held what must be *the* letter in his trembling hand.

> *Giorgio, my dearest,*
>
> *Do you think I didn't know? Do you think you coming just after the blast, your loving concern, the way you wiped pumpkin off my face did not give you away? Do you think your love does not far exceed this accident of war? Do you think a woman needs two legs to love a man?*
>
> *Have no fear, my beloved. I will write you again tonight when there is more time. But I answer this immediately, for I can imagine how you are fearful of what I will say. So I just say I am loving you.*
>
> *Your Anna,*
>
> *who, even though she loves you, will never eat a pumpkin pie on your Thanksgiving*

They were married in June of '48, she nineteen, he twenty-four. Her "assimilated" parents, her Jewish father, Jacobo, an ex-editor for the

Corriere ferrarese (writing freelance, under a pseudonym, since the Nuremberg laws of '35), her mother, Lucetta, a math teacher in the high school, thought it best Anna should see America. She and Giorgio could come back to Ferrara if she were unhappy. Perhaps she could send a little money to help them rebuild. Life would be easier in America.

Anna kept her name, Giardini, as a link to her old life in her old world, one of the first women of her generation to do so. George was concerned it was because she didn't want *his* name. After all . . . No, she assured him, she knew who was Hitler and who was only "Hitler."

Three

Arnold—named for his maternal grandfather—was born on Christmas morning two years later at Mansfield General Hospital, a nine-pound, twelve-ounce strapping, screaming newborn, at the top of the Apgar scale, as he would be at the top of all his classes from first grade on.

But the crying, the continuous crying! Colic? The distraught parents devoured Dr. Spock and tried it all. Troubleshooting: Was he hungry? Just ate. Dirty diaper? No. Would that it were. Safety pin? Never. Gassy, colicky? Belly quiet, and flat as a board. Nothing seemed to help. He cried as an infant, he cried as a toddler, he cried when, finally, at three he began to speak.

His first word was "yellow," a sunshine word for a thunderstorm boy: "Yewwo." He cried for his yellow Dr. Dentons if Anna tried to put him to bed in blue ones. He wanted to play in the yellow-walled kitchen no matter where his mother was in the house. He loved his yellow bear and

his yellow-hatted clown, he loved the light streaming in the yellow-cur-
tained windows, and he could sleep only with his yellow twinkle light at
night. But most of all he loved yellow fire.

When he was four, he burned his hand, badly, third degree. Palmar
burns are serious. Lots of nerves and tendons close to the surface, with little room for swelling. George and Anna had accepted Owen Barlow's invitation to come out on his boat on Joe Pool Lake. It was a windy
September afternoon, too early to go back but chilly enough for the crew
to take refuge in the cabin.

"Arnie and Sam, no running!"

Sam was a year older and even more kinetic than his friend. He
would be Mansfield's High School's greatest track star, faster even than
the several black runners who joined the team in 1965. At his father's
call, Sam stopped short, and Arnie crashed right into him, falling backward and catching himself with his left hand, directly on the heater. A
Southern smell of burning flesh. The grownups were horrified, in pain
almost as great as that of the shrieking child. Anna, especially, was affected, ignited through her own agonies, her stump shrieking, her pity,
her terror for her child. . . . She could only hold him wailing in her arms
and repeat endlessly, *"Bambino mio, bambino mio . . ."*

Arnold's hand was bandaged at the hospital, he was given pain meds
and sent home to be shaped by a multidimensional trauma his parents
little suspected. It wasn't the pain that made him cry. It was the fact that
he couldn't move his hand inside the bandage. He was trapped. His hand
was not uncomfortable, but he was trapped, and being trapped was the
torture. He cried every time he wanted to move his hand and couldn't.
Worse, he was doubly trapped: he couldn't leave the trap behind. He
could go in the other room, and the trap would follow him. He could go
to sleep and wake up the next morning: the trap would still be there. He
could walk anywhere, run anywhere, and his hand would still be
trapped. His parents couldn't understand. They would offer to cheat on

his Darvon schedule, but it wasn't the pain. They didn't get it, and he could not explain. So he was trapped in yet another dimension: he could not communicate what was wrong. Triply trapped. He cried a lot.

Anna tried to distract him: if he would put his left knee to his mouth, she told him, he could talk to Grandpa Jacobo in Italy. Grandpa Jacobo would feel a tickling in *his* left knee, and put his ear to it and listen, and he would be able to hear Arnold. Then, if Arnold put his ear to *his* knee and listened very carefully, he might hear Grandpa Jacobo talking back to him.

Could he talk English to Grandpa? Arnold asked. Would Grandpa talk English back? Anna assured him that since she had moved to America, Grandpa Jacobo had been studying English. She told him to try it and see. Curious, and ever wanting to please, Arnold gave it a go. He rolled up his pajama leg to expose his left knee (the left knee his mother lacked) and whispered into the joint, "Grandpa, can you hear me?"

"Now put your ear to your knee, and let me know what he says."

Arnold listened very carefully.

"Close the window," he told his mother, "so it will be more quiet." She did, and he listened for two silent minutes.

"Well?"

"He says he can hear me, and he wants to know how everyone is, and if I go to school yet. He says he and Grandma Lucetta miss me and miss you and Daddy, and they want us to come visit them next summer. He says he will take us on a trip into the big mountains. And he says that Pepi died last week."

"Our dog?"

"Yes. Pepi died last week from being old."

This was a little uncanny. The missing, and the trip to the mountains—OK—a child could make that up. But Pepi . . . She called her parents that very morning.

Pepi had died nine days before.

Arnold spent much of his convalescence talking to Grandpa Jacobo. But as soon as the bandage came off, he forgot about the connection and went about his normal four-year-old business—asking questions. Anna would read to him—picture books about animals.

"Why is a fox called a fox?" he asked.

"It's called a fox just in English. In Italy, it's called *un volpe*."

"But it's a fox? The same fox?"

"It's the same fox, but it has a different name."

"How can it have a different name if it's the same?"

"I don't know. It just does. Italians call things differently than Americans."

He began to cry.

Or, another time:

"Would you drink a glass of my spit? If I filled a glass with my spit?"

"No! Don't be disgusting."

"Would you drink a glass of your own spit? You spit into a glass until it's full, then you drink it?"

"Arnold, enough of spit!"

"Would you?"

"No!"

"But what's wrong with spit? You swallow your spit and you don't mind. You swallow lots of your own spit."

"Arnold, *zitto!*"

"Spit, spit, spit!" and more tears.

The child began to perceive a rigid stupidity among adults, even his own parents, who knew most things. Did time have a beginning? he wanted to know when he was learning about clocks. If you went back and back, would you get to a place where there was no more back? He asked every grownup he met—it was his question of the month. No one would take it seriously. "I don't know." Period. Or, "Who knows?" Why weren't they perplexed, or even interested? This was no idea-question, it was a real question. He was trying to understand. Surely grownups must know simple things like that. Did time ever begin? Or will it ever end? They just took the whole thing for granted. "That's how things are. Talking isn't going to change them. Discussing is a waste of time waste of time waste of time." What else did he have to do?

At four and three-quarters he hit the books for answers. He didn't know how to read, but he could do research anyway. There was a big book filled with pictures of paintings and sculptures and buildings, the 1926 edition of *Art Through the Ages*. There was the Bible and *La Bibbia Santa*. Did God speak English or Italian? If He was so smart, maybe He spoke both. There was *La Divina Commedia*, with scary etchings; *Italian Through Pictures*, a book with funny stick people pointing at themselves; *The Blue Guide to Italy* with a string bookmark at the map of Ferrara, page 262. There was a book called *The Naked and the Dead* with no pictures at all, neither naked people nor dead ones. And that was it. Some cooking magazines.

His favorite was *Art Through the Ages*. It had so much to show him— not just the world of artists and architects but the whole possibility of Otherness other-than-Mansfield. There was a picture of a big church in Milan, in Italy, near where his mama had lived, and Milan was very far away. And even if you could only see one building, for Arnold it was proof that Milan existed, proof that Italy existed, proof that even far away, things *existed.*

Nobody ever thought of reading *Art Through the Ages* to him, and when he asked for it, he was told it wasn't a reading book, it was a looking-at book. So he looked and looked at the pictures, and he invented stories about them, for example, a story about the naked lady standing on a seashell, and why she was standing on a seashell, and why she was naked. His father didn't like him looking at naked ladies, but his mother let him anyway. She had Botticelli hands. When she looked at the book with him, she told him about how this building or that painting had been destroyed in the war. In this way he learned about destruction.

Arnold was determined to learn to read since, except for *Art Through the Ages,* there seemed to be in books many more words than pictures. So the words must be more important, right? He could make up his own stories, but bookwords would tell him the *real* stories.

It was an epiphany. The marks on the pages turned out to be instructions about sounds. If he could learn the sounds and put them together, he would wind up with—words. Amazing! Wouldn't it have been easier just to have little pictures for everything? Stick figures like the ones in the book to learn Italian? But no. This was the way the grownups did it, and they must be right. George and Anna taught him the alphabet. He cried when he found out that "c" could be pronounced "k" or "s." Why do you need "c" at all if it doesn't have its own sound? His parents didn't know. When "ph" and "qu" showed up, Arnold didn't cry but became furious, then petulant. By this time, he was beginning to sense some conspiracy of the old against the young. If you can't trust grownups, whom can you trust?

But "c," "g," "ph," and "qu" became finally minor annoyances—exceptions to the fascinating task of stringing letters together to arrive at—miraculous—familiar words! Each time a difficult sound sequence popped into place, he experienced a tingling up the back of his neck. Sounding out words: what a clever and good thing to do. Noble. Like scientists and detectives. The act of reading was as fascinating as the content—but daunting, too. Would he now have to read everything, of which he was sure there was much? Would he be allowed to stop if he wanted to? Not yet five, he was cognizant of some anticipatory, menacing commitment.

And if he could read, he would have to write. Assiduous, he practiced his alphabet. His first written note—vetted by his horrified mother—was to his friend, Sam. It read, "YU AR A GRATE BIG DOODEE HED, AND I WILL FLUSH YU DOWIN THE TOYLET." She wouldn't let him send it.

Why not? Why not? He had worked so hard on it. The letters were all recognizable—even neat. Anna explained that "doody" was not a nice word, and that Sam would not like being called a doody-head and might not want to be friends with him. "But he calls *me* a doody-head." And, again, he burst out crying. Eventually, Arnold gathered that there were good words, which you were allowed to say and write, and bad words, which you were not. But what made a good word good and a bad word bad? Grownups were nuts.

Needless to say, when he started school that fall of 1956, he found Dick and Jane, whose mother had two legs, not one and a half, insufferably stupid. They seemed to live in a world only vaguely related to his own, some kind of harmless, cute, safe place, without dirty words, without the bombs and dead people his mother would talk about, without the niggers who could be his friends after school but who couldn't go to school with him, and whom people hanged on the flagpole.

"Mama," he called out during a self-assigned homework session, "you know what?"

"What?" Anna turned delightedly to her little scholar.

"There's no story in the Dick and Jane story."

"What do you mean? Doesn't the dog run with the ball, and . . ."

"I mean like the story of the naked lady on the seashell, or the girl turning into a tree."

Though Anna found them charming, such thoughts did not bode well for his career at Mansfield Elementary. He did not love school; he loved his own gathering of words, which revealed to him the infinite world of things, the many forms of the specific, of the substance and strategy of the world. He was the best reader in his class, he was popular, he got the best marks in all his subjects, but he became expert in deceit. Verbosity, exile, and cunning.

Four

You will remain in truth as long as you maneuver within its limits.

Edmond Jabès, *Hand and Dial*

Unlike Stephen Dedalus and his own son, Arnold's father had a name that would fly.

George Andrew Hitler, born in 1924, grew up at a time when it was fine to be so named. Until the age of nine, his last name was neither here nor there—just another moniker, that of his own father, Tom. From nine to eighteen, the homonym was noticed by only a minority of North Texans whose newspaper reading went beyond the sports page, the funnies, the local letters and obits. And for them, it was *Adolf* Hitler, if anyone, who seemed the imposter, some German politician who had made off with George's good name. Until Anna, there were no Jews around to take umbrage: in Mansfield, they knew that Bill Monroe was not Marilyn Monroe, that Floyd Jefferson, the nigger car-washer at Cluny's Garage, was likely unrelated to Thomas, and that Adolf Hitler's escapades could do nothing to besmirch George, a hardworking mill hand and patriotic veteran, a man who later married the woman he had wounded. Texans understood the difference.

By the time he was three, Arnold was noticing differences too, not only that between boys and girls but between his mother and everyone else. He'd become expert in helping wrap her stump and settle it into the container of her new prosthesis, in buckling it behind her right hip and helping her adjust the tension of the articulated knee. As she learned to walk, he would coach, "Kick it up, kick it up," just as he heard the man at the hospital do when his mom was on the parallel bars. With four-and-a-half-year-old seriousness, he advised her, "The more vigorously you walk, the more resistance you will want." She found it hilarious. He didn't know why.

"Kick it up, kick it up," became the secret of his success, first as a fast-running kid and later as an all-star quarterback who often had to run. There were few who could catch him, and even fewer who could stop him, so hard did he pump those long, muscular legs. In times of stress, some men think back upon their mothers. In Arnold's case, sitting on his mama's knee was enough to inspire his running.

His friend, Sam, was pretty smart, too—at least Arnold thought so. Especially when Sam, six, sat Arnold, five, down for a December explanation of the facts of life. At first, Arnold was incredulous. "Git outta here," he averred. "Grownups would never do a dirty thing like that!" But Sam teased and titillated and awed and finally reasoned with him enough for Arnold to consider it a hypothesis to be checked with other kids, and, if possible, tested himself, or directly observed. His sixth birthday, then, embraced a secret "now I am a man" quality usually reserved for bar mitzvah celebrations.

Arnold was a Christmas-day child, one of a cohort famous for feeling gypped. Their birthdays have been subsumed in something so much greater than they, their annual gift quotients are generally half that of their friends, and when relative-visiting occurs, it is for Christmas dinner with a little birthday thrown in. That was why Arnold had grabbed the "nigger" demonstration as an early birthday event just for him.

His real sixth birthday proved to be quite special. Under the tree were two packages from Italy. The more obviously significant one was from Nonno Jacobo—an inexpensive but still elegant set of chess pieces with green felt bottoms, contained in a wooden box with a sliding top. With it, a hinged wooden chessboard and a set of instructions in Italian. The package said, "This is birthday present, not Christmas present." The more subtly significant one was from Nonna Lucetta, marked, "This is Christmas present, not birthday present." It was a child-sized Italian sailor suit, about which more anon.

It fell to Anna to teach him chess. Who else could read the instructions? They learned the moves together, and after a few weeks the family chess club was joined by George, who bought a book in English.

Anna and George were dumbfounded at Arnold's insights. He seemed to be driving some sleek mental chess machine along a highway without a speed limit, destination unknown. Within a month of occasional games, both mother and father had given up all pretense of "letting him win." Now each was struggling for self-respect. How could this little upstart who could barely read or spell, who got subtraction wrong, who was completely innocent of multiplication and division—how could this mere *child* beat the pants off them when they were trying as hard as they could to win? In February, Arnold suggested that he play both of them at the same time, first as a team, then, after he had won three games, with Anna on the chess board and George on a crayoned-in sheet of paper, using shirt cardboard cut into little chessmen.

There comes a point in every parent's life when the subtle competition of master versus upstart gives way to frank and admiring defeat. But at age six? It was too early to concede. George, the more competitive, suggested his son play him blindfolded, a chess master's trick he had heard about during the war. When he was soundly whupped, he upped the ante. Would Arnold play both him and Anna blindfolded?

When they each went down to defeat, they announced it was time to have a little talk. Arnold was petrified they were going to quiz him about what he knew about penises and vaginas, or even demonstrate true sexual technique to correct his childish notions. But no, they wanted him to tell how he did it, how he could always beat them though collectively they were fifty-nine years older and two hundred pounds heavier. How did he do it? This was a most unfair question for a child.

The best he could offer, with his limited abstract vocabulary and his even more limited experience at introspection, was this: "I don't know."

"What do you mean, you don't know?"

"I mean I don't know how I do it. It's just . . . obvious."

"What's obvious?"

"The diagrams. The pictures on the board. I look at the pictures."

"You mean you don't plot out the moves, like 'if I do this, then she'll do that, then I'll do this, and if she does that, then I'll do this, but if she does that, then I'll do this'?"

"No. I never do that. I just look at the board, and . . ."

"What about when you're blindfolded?"

"I can still see the board in my head. Not the whole board—just the parts that matter. It's like there's a strain, like when I wind up my airplane, or when I have to go pee, or there's not enough room on the sidewalk to get by—and I just see how to make it . . . not be strained. Then I move the pieces to do it."

The answer was even more stupefying than the problem.

The second gift—the Christmas one—was more fateful. For when Arnold put on the white blouse, white pants, and white beret with the blue band, he resembled no one so much as a baby Billy Budd. Even his mother, who had read the story in Italian, felt a melting heart of recognition—followed by a shudder. The blond and handsome little sailor. The unpretentious good looks, unaffected and naturally regal. The reposeful good nature. The welkin-eyes of starry blue.

But who trifles with being Billy Budd must needs meet up with John Claggart. It's dangerous to flirt with archetypes, to try them on to see how they look. If the fit is too easy, they cling to the skin, even after repeated washings, and they call forth scripted playmates and their consequences.

In addition, this Christmas gift from Nonna Lucetta was archetypal with glorious trimmings. On the blue hatband, embroidered in gold, for reasons stranger than fiction, was the word "CARDUCCI," the afore-mentioned poet, but here a destroyer in the Italian fleet. The warship aside, the name alone would explain the gift's attraction for the Giardi-nis: put such a name on the little one's forehead and by homeopathic magic turn Arnold Hitler into a romantic genius.

What the Giardinis did not know was that in 1943 the *Carducci* had been enveloped in uncontrollable fire and sunk in the Mediterranean by aircraft from a new British carrier, the HMS *Indomitable*—the very name that, thirty feet below him, captioned Billy Budd's last, neck-snap-ping dance from the yardarm. This is surely a dangerous world. "God bless Captain Vere!" With this double dose of destiny, it wasn't long be-fore the first of a series of Claggarts would show up to haunt Arnold-billy's life, an ugly line of anti-beings who found him intolerable and longed for his annihilation.

"Arnold, will you write a note to Nonno Jacobo and Nonna Lucetta to thank them for your presents?"

"Can't I just thank them through my knee? Even if only Grandpa hears, he can tell Grandma."

"It would be fine to thank them through your knee, but I think you should also write something to show them how well you can write."

This he did, and never wore the sailor suit but once. Bright-eyed as usual, proud, white and blue, he marched one day into class in his *Carducci* regalia, only to return home crestfallen and confused. Though the girls had loved it, an older boy had teased him all day about being "a fag."

"What's a fag?" Arnold demanded of Anna.

She didn't know.

George: "It's a kind of sissy. Like a boy who only wants to play with girls, play with dolls—that kind of thing. Johnny was being stupid."

"Ah, said Anna, *"finocchio."*

"I teach you something if such ever happens again. You just say to him, 'Stick and stones can break my bones,'"—and here George joined in—" 'but names can never hurt me.'

"Can you say that?"

"Yes."

"Say it."

He did, putting "stick" instinctively in the plural.

"Good," said his father, and punched him affectionately on the shoulder.

Five

The hot Texas summer of '57 passed uneventfully enough, in Mansfield. So convincing had been last year's demonstration that August registration needed no more than private reminders about safety for any Negroes who might think of registering their children at all-white MHS. But the effigies waited warily in their garages.

All was not so circumspect in Little Rock next door, where Governor Orval Faubus and the Arkansas National Guard linked arms around Central High School to prevent nine Negro children from entering. President Eisenhower sent a thousand paratroopers to intervene. Like their effigies, Mansfield's Negroes also waited warily, glued to their radios and TVs. Eventually, they stopped holding their breaths: it would be eight more years before the first black children walked through the door at Mansfield High.

.   .   .

On Friday evening, October 4th, 1957, all hell broke loose from the skies: the Russkies had put a "sputnik" in the heavens. Commies were circling the earth and were even now passing over Mansfield, Texas, every ninety-six minutes, beeping in Russian to their hearts' content. President Eisenhower heard the news on the golf links at Gettysburg; the Hitler-Giardinis and the rest of America heard it on the eleven o'clock news. It was a weekend of panic and punditry.

Senator Henry Jackson declared Sputnik "a devastating blow" to America and called upon the president to proclaim "a week of shame and danger." Republicans warned about the harmful effects of "progressive education," "flabby curricula," and "the shirking of basic subjects," and even liberals joined the weekend chorus, urging more funding for education and science. By consensus the Cold War was not just about weapons but, even more importantly, about knowledge—and this "second Pearl Harbor" showed America was "losing the race."

On Monday morning, Mrs. Armstrong asked her second grade class to prepare their weekly show-and-tells on the topic of Sputnik. When by Thursday no child had come forward, Mrs. Armstrong asked Edna and Arnold to make a presentation the next morning, the first-week anniversary of the artificial moon.

Edna ("the Brain") Rawson was the child of Edward Rawson, dean of the College of Arts and Sciences, University of Texas at Arlington, and Stella Rawson, pediatrician, and the only unabashed liberal in Mansfield. Stella was for everything everyone else opposed and was opposed to everything everyone else was for—except Mansfield High football, for which she was raging with juices, a fanatical president of the Mansfield Tigers Boosters' Club.

Edna came to class the next morning with what may have been the very first newsprint-and-marker presentation in the history of the United States. Her parents delivered her to school with her mother's painting easel and a pad of paper only six inches shorter than she was.

She hoisted it up on the stand and asked Mrs. Armstrong to turn the cover back to the first page. There, almost invisibly sketched in light pencil, was a diagram she proceeded to darken as she spoke, her father having suggested the value of visuals. Her drawing eventually looked like this:

"This up here," said Edna, reaching way up on tippy-toes with her Magic Marker™ held by its very end, "is supposed to be someone shooting a gun . . . up on top of a mountain . . . on top of the earth." She turned to face the class. "Sputnik is nothing new. Hundreds of years ago Isaac Newton . . ."

"Who's that?" shouted Mac Herndon.

"A scientist. Hundreds of years ago Isaac Newton said that anything you throw is an earth satellite. He really said that. If you stand up here on the mountain and throw a stone or shoot a slow bullet, it falls to the earth [here she filled in the first falling line] in an ellipse."

"What's an ellipse?" shouted Dave Herndon, Mac's twin brother.

"It's like this." She sketched one in the air, then filled out the inner ellipse in the diagram. "You only see a small part of it because the bullet or the stone drops so quickly. But the faster you throw or shoot it, the farther it goes before it hits the ground. And if you shoot it fast enough . . ."

"It goes all the way around," Ellie Blatchly sang out in enthusiastic epiphany.

"Correct," said Edna, filling in the large curve. "Like a little moon, traveling around again and again, since there's nothing to stop it. That's all Sputnik is. It is not new. Thank you very much." And she bowed to prompted applause. The class was impressed, if slightly intimidated.

Arnold, too, had his presentational strategy. He had decided to adopt once more the persona of Long John Silver, from last year's school play, dressing up in his pirate costume, complete with eyepatch and his mother's old wooden leg.

"May I have a volunteer, please?" Six hands shot waving into the air—all from his enamored female fan club. He chose Eunice MacIntyre, the one he was least likely to be teased about being in love with.

"Please go get the globe." Eunice got up from her seat and fetched the globe from its stand at the back of the room." Bring it up here."

With Eunice standing embarrassed in front of the class, Arnold pulled from the paper bag he had been toting a beautiful ten-inch model of a pirate ship he had built from a kit awarded to him for his stellar performance as Long John.

"Turn it so they can see Russia." Eunice had a hard time with this command, so Arnold did it for her. "This is Moscow," he said, and placed the ship down on what he thought might be the Kremlin. He looked at the outsized projectile and began revving up its engines with *brumm brumms*. The boat vibrated slightly atop the Kremlin wall. He began to bob lightly at the knees while increasing the amplitude of the sound. Then all of a sudden there was a big mouth-explosion, and the pirate ship lifted off the earth and began to circle the globe with that steady beeping that had so unnerved American radio listeners over the past week. The path of the orbit had to pass repeatedly through the small space between Carol's arms, the globe and her chest, but after a few revolutions, she learned to leave him room, and the two of them performed a charming beep-ballet for the next minute. Audience attention was beginning to wander when, surprise of surprises, the bottom of the ship hinged open and out dropped an egg from its bomb bay—an egg that skittered off the globe and splattered on the floor. The class gasped. No one had ever dirtied the floor like that. Even Arnold was shocked: he had been prepared to clean up the globe but not the floor, or Carol's shoes and socks.

"You will clean that up, Arnold?" Mrs. Armstrong pointedly inquired.

"Yes. But first . . . Sputnik is an aluminum sphere twenty-two inches in diameter, weighing 184 pounds. It is traveling 18,000 miles per hour in an orbit 550 miles above the earth. There is no reason why it could not drop a bomb wherever it wanted to, like right on Mansfield High School." A few of the boys cheered. "It would make a worse mess than my egg. Thank you very much. And now, a word from our sponsor." He bowed.

Again applause, this time heartfelt and enthusiastic. There were even some whistles and two "Kill the Commies!"

"Commies." Another word he'd had to ask his dad about.

"Commies." It wasn't long before the national panic deepened, dragging a reluctant president along with it. During the month of October, Khrushchev began boasting of Soviet ICBMs that could reach the United States. Then, on November 3rd, Sputnik II blasted into orbit, a space vehicle weighing 1,120 pounds, six times as heavy as its predecessor. Besides carrying instruments that radioed information about atmospheric radiation, it carried a dog, little Laika, wired for medical monitoring. The trajectory was obvious: the Soviets were preparing to send a man to the moon. While most American children were worrying about what would happen to Laika, on November 6th, the adult world was treated to the fortieth anniversary celebration of the Bolshevik Revolution. Truly, for patriotic Americans, this was the worst of times, when only a month before it had been among the best.

With the new national emphasis on education, Arnold was allowed, even encouraged, to organize clubs—a chess club, a reading club, a greater-than-five-syllable-word-collecting club. His leadership qualities grew with his popularity. The handsome sailor, no longer a fag. But still—privately—a crybaby.

A most remarkable flow of tears occurred on his seventh birthday— Christmas Day, 1957. Arnold had become interested in church, more interested than his parents were, with George feeling his son should know something about "religion" and Anna sensing that somehow Catholic + Jewish ≠ Southern Baptist. But Arnold loved the Christ Child as his birthday cohort and little brother, the secret sharer of his feast, someone special who could "taketh away the sin of the world." His understanding of that phrase was anybody's guess.

On the way home from the service he checked with his father about something that had been bothering him.

"Saint Nick brought the presents last night?"

"The presents not from the family."

"Did he bring the Christmas presents and my birthday presents?"

"Just the Christmas presents, I think."

"Is Saint Nick old?" Arnold inquired.

"Very old. Big white beard," his father assured him.

"Is he Old Nick?"

"I told you, he's very old."

And Arnold burst into tears the rest of the way home—unstoppable. When he got home, he wouldn't touch his Christmas presents or open any of his birthday gifts. If Santa was actually the devil, how could he take part? His day was ruined forever. It took his mother to ferret all this out and explain the difference (recently learned herself) between Saint

Nick, who happens to be old, and Old Nick, who was probably younger. With that, her son cheered up considerably and opened his gifts. The highlight of the year was a genuine leather football from Dad, with a pin scotch-taped to its side, and a small air pump that would also work on his bicycle.

Six

On May 12th the following year, Arnold Hitler, eight years old, president of his third grade class, experienced his first human death. At 7:35 A.M., five minutes after the pre-school voluntary prayer session had begun in the front lobby, Peter Schrag, fourteen, interrupted the regular Monday morning practice with a random spray of bullets from a semiautomatic .22 pistol, wounding ten students and killing two girls, one immediately. As Arnold walked in the door, Peter pushed past him as if he didn't exist and ran home to think things over. Arnold stood just inside the doorway, surveyed the bloody scene, and covered his ears against the shrill screaming of the girls. Then he turned around and ran to Karbur's Kwik Stop to call his mom to come get him so *he* could go home to think things over. And cry.

The town was stupefied. Mass murder, at least domestic mass murder, had not yet become a national pastime. As clichéd as only reality can be, Peter Schrag *had* been "such a nice boy."

"No one would have ever guessed that . . ."

.   .   .

That evening, Arnold demanded details of the die-on-the-cross story he'd heard about. George and Anna looked at one another with as much despair as if they had been asked to explain the facts of life, or the nonexistence of Santa. As they struggled to tell the tale, each realized how many particulars they had forgotten. Exasperated, Anna pulled the English Bible from the shelf, and Arnold was likely the only child in Texas that night who had the crucifixion for his bedtime story. On Sunday, he would not go to church.

"And why not?" his mother asked.

"Remember how you read me about the crucifixion, and how Jesus said, 'Father forgive them, for they know not what they do'?"

"Yes. That's what He said."

"Well, it isn't. He didn't say that."

"What do you mean? I read it to you right out of the Bible."

"The other articles by Matthew and Mark and John don't say he said that."

Anna pulled out the Bible to check.

"They wouldn't leave it out if He said it. They wouldn't forget it—all three of them. Luke just made it up. It's three against one!"

"He didn't make it up. He . . ."

"If you can't believe what you read in the Bible . . ." And before Arnold Hitler began to cry, he ran into his room and slammed the door. Strangely enough, that was it. No one in that family ever went to church again.

Seven

The '60s began quite promptly for Arnold. On "Mayday"
of 1960, Stella Rawson, her husband, Edward, their
daughter, Edna, and nine-and-a-half-year-old Arnold
Hitler stood on the southeast corner of Broad and Main
from 10 to noon and 1 to 3, a Lilliputian demonstration for the churched
and unchurched concerning fair play for Cuba. She and her husband had
been to prerevolutionary Havana on their honeymoon and were simultaneously entranced by the beauty of the beach on which Edna was
likely conceived and sickened by the juxtaposed poverty and glitz. They
had since tried to keep up on the tumultuous island events and the fate
of the brave and bearded liberators come down from the mountains. Fidel made them feel alive again, alive in a world that was not hopeless.

For a few days, most of America had been in love with Fidel as the
media proudly proclaimed the overthrow of a system so corrupt that
even Cuban elites were deserting. El Jefe seemed to be a George Washington–sized revolutionary out of the mythic past. But within a month it

became apparent that his was a declaration of independence not just from domestic slime but from the United States of America! When they realized that Castro was serious about Cuba choosing its own path, that "greater general prosperity" might mean nationalization of U.S.-dominated industries, that "diversification of agriculture" meant less money for Texas rice, the prominent citizens who thought the new hero was merely making noble noises turned on him with the speed and fury of spurned lovers—as did the media. And so, therefore, did the people. The Senate invoked "the spectacle of a bearded monster stalking through Cuba," and by February 1959, Congress had been filled with warnings of "a Kremlin-inspired plot to destroy free-enterprise," with calls for American intervention "to save Cuba from chaos."

Little did George and Anna suspect Arnold's reason for wanting to do this vigil. During the four hours he stood in the Sunday Texas sun, only one thing was going through his head: the TV jingle for Castro Convertible Sofas:

> *With a Castro Convertible Sofa*
> *You get comfort and beauty and style*
> *So convert to a Castro Convertible*
> *And you'll have a living room smile*
> *So you need a sofa, so good, so you need a sofa, so Castro!*

Over and over. He loved the commercial, the little kid in Dr. Dentons who takes command of the huge sofa, throws off its pillows, pulls on the bar and transforms the object as if opening some huge, mechanical flower: "So easy even a child can do it." The triumph of the small over the large, and the end result, a comfy bed to snuggle in—what could be a greater prize? Arnold *wanted* a Castro Convertible Sofa, and so the name "Castro" became associated with one of his heart's chief fantasies. He would have been an admirer of Fidel had he been the only child of

Fulgencio Batista. Besides—"Fidel." A Texas child interested in words, Arnold knew enough Spanish to know *fidel* had something to do with being faithful. Imagine having a leader whose name was "Faithful" and not "Ike." He was for that.

But Arnold's experience at his first demonstration was less than transformative. He got to sing the Castro song to himself a lot, and vaguely heard the occasional dialogues at the other end of the picket line—things about fair-mindedness, about compensation and payments and government bonds and sugar. But mostly, the demonstration was about getting tired of standing around with nothing to do.

Politics global versus politics local: the next day was another thing entirely. As Arnold approached the same corner of Broad and Main at 5:30 in the morning, his newspaper bag heavy on his bike, he saw something hanging high on the stoplight wire in the middle of the intersection. By the dawn's early light, he had to ride close to distinguish the effigy—a half-black, half-white man, hanging by the neck, with a long paper sign attached to its bottom as if on shit-stuck toilet paper: "GRIFFIN: GOD-DAMN NIGGER-LOVIN, JEW-LOVIN, COMMUNIST SON-OF-A-BITCH." Arnold remembered the school demonstration well enough to know this meant trouble, and he made a beeline for the first store with lights on—the grocery in the First National Bank building. Mr. Gibson was stacking shelves when Arnold banged at the door.

After a quick inspection, Gibson called the constable at home—got him out of bed—and told him to "get that damned thing down from there." In the half hour it took Constable Diggs to get on the case and get the volunteer fire truck over there to remove the figure, it had been seen by enough early commuters for the Fort Worth *Star-Telegram* to have gotten wind of the event. By the time their reporter and photographer arrived, the constable had taken it down and thrown the figure into the

town dump, but some wag had retrieved it and hung it on the sign reading $25.00 FINE FOR DUMPING DEAD ANIMALS. The *Star-
Telegram* played up the angle of one of its own newsboys discovering the
effigy, and Arnold was photographed standing next to the dead beast as
if it were some prize marlin and he the triumphant fisherman. He was
sent to school late, with a note from Constable Diggs.

In the darkness of early next morning, John Howard Griffin awoke to
find eight "For Sale" signs newly planted on his lawn, illuminated by
the flickering light of a burning cross. Another was burning at the Negro
School half a mile from his house. At 6 A.M., Arnold delivered a paper to
Griffin that featured his own effigy, hung on a signpost, with his very
own newsboy pointing it out. Over the fold. That day, with his picture in
the Fort Worth paper, Arnold was the hero of the fourth grade.

John Howard Griffin was a Mansfield writer who lived with his wife
and children a mile out of town on West Broad Street, the last house on
Arnold's newspaper route. He was a big man—six foot two, two hundred
pounds—who six months earlier had conceived a big idea: he would
shave his head, dye his skin black, and hitchhike around the South looking for work—to experience being a Negro. Why would someone do this,
someone with a wife and three kids? This was no shallow journalistic
stunt. On the desk at his parents' farm lay an article that asserted that
Southern negroes "had reached a stage where they simply no longer
cared whether they lived or died." Yet in Mansfield, there was supposed
to be a "wonderfully harmonious relationship." His Negro contacts were
polite and friendly to him: the contradiction stared him in the face.

"When you look long into an abyss," the mad German warned, "the
abyss also looks into you," and Griffin realized he had to know the answer to the riddle. With the permission of his family, and after a derma-
tology consultation, he undertook a brave, unique experiment: becoming

the first white person ever to directly experience the lifeworld of the blacks. For six weeks he bused, hitched, and walked through Mississippi, Alabama, Louisiana, and Georgia, encountering squalor he had never known, unmotivated antagonism, inevitable violence, and above all hopelessness—just as the article alleged. He took notes of situations and conversations and, when he returned to Mansfield, published them in *Sepia,* a magazine widely read by Negroes in the deep South. The story had appeared in March and was picked up worldwide, so new and trenchant was the deed. *Time* did a long article, and there were TV interviews with Paul Coates, Dave Garroway, Harry Golden, and Mike Wallace. Radio-Television Française actually flew a crew of five from Paris to interview him on his family farm. All 1,400 citizens of Mansfield were buzzing about their famous—to many, infamous—celebrity.

But they did not buzz to him. Everywhere he went he created a ring of silence. Women stared at their shoes, and men glared hostilely just past his face. He had "stirred things up"; this was as unacceptable to the Mansfield power structure as it was to the loafers who stood around the filling station and street corners. The date for a castration had been set.

John Howard Griffin's eldest daughter, Elise, was in Arnold's class, and her younger sister, Nancy, was in second grade, two years behind. That the sins of the fathers are to be visited on the generations seemed an obvious truth to their peers. So Arnold made a point of sitting with them in the lunchroom when no one else would. He paid for that gesture at the end of the day when he found a note in his cubby, apparently from his Claggart #1: ARNOLD LOVES NIGGER ELISE lettered in nasty penmanship. "Nigger Elise" was three inches taller than Arnold, somewhat heavy, with white skin and hair blonder than her little sister's, an unlikely match for the epithet and an even less likely target for Arnold's affections. Nevertheless.

"Nigger-lover" was the worst thing anyone in Texas could say about anyone else. It was far worse than "nigger," since niggers were basically all right as long as they stayed in their place. But nigger-lovers were un-scrupulous race-traitors, never to be trusted, always to be shunned. Arnold's Operation Friendship and Protection lasted only two days. By Thursday of that week, the Griffin children had moved in with friends in Dallas. By the weekend both Grandma and Grandpa Griffin had been threatened and were making plans to sell their farm. The town had drawn the line. Griffin would publish his classic memoir, *Black Like Me,* and move with his family to Mexico.

On the night of the move, Arnold lay in his non-Castro bed and stared up at the glow-in-the-dark stars he and his father had glued so joyfully to the ceiling. The big dipper, pointing north. Pegasus, Andromeda, Cas-siopeia. The shapes seemed to be ebbing and flowing, losing their sharp-ness in his tears.

Eight

A thousand days pass quickly. Perhaps because of his physical beauty and intelligent charm, Arnold remained popular with most boys, with all the girls, and with all his teachers, in spite of his now outspokenly liberal positions on the U2 incident, Cuba, the Bay of Pigs invasion, the Berlin wall, the Soviet H-bomb, and the missile crisis. While others his age were religiously following Howdy Doody or Lassie, Arnold was reading the *New York Times* and writing critiques of articles in *My Weekly Reader*, comparing the facts presented with those in the newspaper of record. He would visit the Rawsons to check their magazines and discuss current events. He was still tight with Sam Barlow, one grade ahead, who ran interference for him with the bigger kids. It was one month before his thirteenth birthday that he became a man.

.   .   .

Eighth grade. Voice changing. Beard coming. Chest and penis getting larger. On November 22nd, 1963, at 12:30 P.M., the president's Lincoln Continental turned sharp left into Dealy Plaza as Arnold and his class-mates clutched their rolled-up paper bags, now filled with cores and pits and aluminum foil. As cynical as preadolescents can be, it was still adren-aline-making to feel the Secret Service coming straight at you. The boys stood up; the girls hopped and waved, and Jackie and her husband, pink and blue, waved back. Then, a firecracker? Another bang, something, just behind them, to their right. The car was being shot at—look at the president, lifting his arms. They were in the line of fire—a third shot—and the fiendish bar mitzvah gift: a view from thirty feet of JFK's brain exploding onto Elm Street in a decorative shower of blood. "Get down! Get down!" But some people had to escape the motorcycle coming right at them, heading up the hill toward the picket fence. Unable to get safely through the embankment crowd, the officer dropped his Harley right at Arnold's feet and scrambled the rest of the way, pistol drawn. A second trooper dropped his bike onto the sidewalk below and ran to catch up with his partner at the fence, while the presidential car sped ahead through the underpass with the president now invisible except for his right foot and Jackie on the trunk, with a Secret Serviceman sprawled on top of her in some confounding fusion of sex, loyalty, love, and death. For the rest of his life, Arnold would remember where he was when Kennedy was shot.

He and three of his friends sprinted up the hill toward the fence. The puffs of smoke were just beginning to dissipate into the tree branches. "Get back!" the first policeman roared, stopping the boys in their tracks. The two cops jumped the fence abutments on either side. After several seconds, Arnold signaled his crew of three over and around the wall to the packed parking lot. Footprints in the mud at the fence. Mudprints on adjacent car bumpers. It looked like two or three different snipers. Then the lot filled up with police. The four boys were taken into custody and locked in a squad car at the edge of the parking area. An hour later, two cops appeared with Mr. Thomasen, who identified the boys as being students from his group and assured the officers that they had been spectators only and had bravely jumped the fence to try to identify the assassins. The police took statements from the boys about hearing the shots, running toward the smoke, and finding the mudprints. They were never called to testify before the Warren Commission, which concluded that all fire had come from the sixth floor of the Texas School Book Depository, high up and far to the left.

The class trip from hell—at least from Mr. Thomasen's point of view. But oddly enough, for many of the students, an experience that helped shape and deepen their lives—a pedagogy of great price. On the short ride home, Arnold was anointed to speak at the school assembly to be held on Monday. During the short bus ride home, sixteen eighth grade students heard that the president was dead.

Arnold and his parents spent the weekend glued to the TV, sucking in every minute of this hingepoint of history. They saw the new president—a Texan—being sworn in on Air Force One. They saw the great bronze casket being offloaded at Bethesda. They saw interviews with the Dallas police chief, who declared himself convinced that Oswald was the lone assassin. They saw Jack Ruby step from the crowd in the police station and murder Lee Harvey Oswald before he could go to trial. They saw the flag-draped casket being drawn down Pennsylvania Avenue by a black horse. They saw Jackie in mourning at the other Arlington.

On Monday at nine, Mansfield High School convened in the auditorium. It was unusual for an eighth grader to be the featured speaker, but Arnold had been there, and he captivated the high schoolers, faculty, and staff alike with his eloquent, detailed report and eyewitness criticism of the early speculation concerning the crime. He was confident that the investigators would sort things out, would take his deposition and that of others into account and correct the prevailing lone-assassin assumptions. About Oswald and the Book Depository he didn't know. But about the shots from just over his shoulder he did.

As the weeks wore on and the drumbeat for the "lone, crazed Communist assassin" story strengthened, Arnold's new manhood was tempered and annealed. The violent death of a father figure is a mere dip into the fire of darkest maturity. But the settling-in of context, the slowly seeping marination in the world-to-be-inhabited, the swelling of some parts and astringent contraction of others—*that* is the more profound and lasting formative process. Arnold grew quickly in those early months of 1964—physically, intellectually, emotionally, and spiritually—and his *annus mirabilis* received its ultimate nudge in September, with the release of the Warren Commission Report. As the acknowledged Mansfield High scholar and expert on the assassination, he had already given two short talks to packed school assemblies.

In the first, at the end of January, he wondered about the surprise change of route, which had brought the presidential procession closer to both the picket fence and the Book Depository, and the altered order of vehicles, which had removed the photographers' car from its usual place immediately in front of the president (the better to photograph him) to twelve cars behind him, thus depriving investigators of potentially crucial evidence. Did someone in charge of these arrangements know something? The high schoolers were quick to pick up the plot; the faculty resisted its implications. He ended with a minilecture on Newton's Second Law of Motion, to wit, "when an external force acts on a body, the acceleration of that body is in the direction of the force." In other words, that the president's head snapped backward and to his left as his skull flew apart indicated that the bullet must have come from the front, right—exactly where he had heard shots—and not from the rear, as most of the press had been insisting. "This will all come out," he assured his audience.

At his second talk in May, he enumerated the list of strange deaths of potential witnesses he had been collecting from local papers and journals subscribed to by the Rawsons. Already, in addition to Oswald, eighteen material witnesses had died—six by gunfire, three in motor vehicle accidents, two by suicide, one from a slit throat, one from a karate chop to the neck, three from heart attacks, and two from "natural causes." An actuary hired by the *London Sunday Times* had calculated that the odds against such a fatal procession were in the order of 100,000 trillion to one. Something to think about. Again the faculty protested, and Arnold was called into Principal Pigg's office for a little talk.

Just before his ninth grade Christmas vacation and fourteenth birthday, Arnold was invited as (pointedly) *one* of a panel of speakers to discuss the Warren Commission Report, which had been released two months earlier. In spite of the fact that the other panelists were the chair of the social studies department, a distinguished town lawyer, a reporter from the Ft. Worth *Star-Telegram*, and the editor of the *Mansfield News Mirror*, Arnold stole the show as easily and naturally as he did the chess tournaments he had once again begun to play. In the ten minutes he was allotted, he demonstrated how the commission had continually failed to meet commonly accepted investigatory standards, how it had ignored many witnesses who might contradict the lone-assassin theory, and how it had suppressed evidence and testimony reported in public media. He detailed the substantial differences between the Dallas coroner's report of the body delivered to Parkfield just after the murder and the autopsy report from Bethesda, differences that suggested major forensic medical fraud. And finally, if briefly, he reported the strange associations between Oswald and government intelligence operatives—despite the fact that Oswald supposedly was a Communist enthusiast of the Fair Play for Cuba Committee. No other speaker had such command of the material or provided such provocative analysis. His two-minute summary alleged that the assigned function of the Warren Commission had been to close the case, no matter the truth, and "put it behind us." The alternatives were too threatening.

Arnold's conception of chess during this period was clearly connected to his emerging sense of national plot. As if to cement its contemporary ramifications, and perhaps indicate to others the relationships with which he was playing, he chose to dress his queen in a tiny pink pillbox hat adapted from the top from a small bottle of vanilla extract and painted with his mother's nail polish, a close enough, even eerie, match. So powerful a gesture was this that he was prohibited from tournament play unless he would use only standard pieces. That this little costume did not materially affect either the game or his own play seemed immaterial to club officials.

As Whitehead so astutely observed, "It requires a very unusual mind to undertake the analysis of the obvious."

high school! emancipation (some)!

adulthood (almost)! by now arnold

hitler was more than six feet tall

and sang low tenor in the school

Mansfield High

chorus. in two years he would be

able to drive. but best of all, he

was the only sophomore accepted

to junior varsity football, an up-

and-coming mansfield tiger, as

yet small of tooth but tall, fast

and eager. high school football in

Nine

Tomorrow the day of the stone will break.

Edmond Jabès, *Book of Yukel*

High school! Emancipation (some)! Adulthood (almost)! By now Arnold Hitler was more than six feet tall and sang low tenor in the school chorus. In two years he would be able to drive. But best of all, he was the only sophomore accepted to junior varsity football, an up-and-coming Mansfield Tiger, as yet small of tooth but tall, fast, and eager.

High school football in the South, and especially in Texas, comes charged with the oversized power of a two-hundred-pound linebacker. In Mansfield, Friday night high school football was a cult, a quasi-religious experience at the very core of town life, something for Mansfield to hold on to as its children and its traditional values slipped away into the '60s. Friday night grit, its courage, its sacrifice, mirrored in concentrated form the plight of white working-class men and women in their struggle against the encroaching forces of—everything. It was not entertainment but social self-affirmation, and the town spirit distinctly reflected each Friday's win or loss. All this—on the padded shoulders of teenagers.

The players were up to the task. They too lived for Friday nights, and imagined themselves gladiators, Christians going up against a variety of lions, ready to bleed for the lustful shouts of a juiced-up crowd. This was their most important rite of passage, males and females alike, for the players on the team and for the golden-haired girls in short skirts and tiger-striped, patent-leather boots—the Mansfield Tiger Rebelettes—anointed to cheer them on. For these young men and women, Friday nights were a high beyond booze, beyond drugs, beyond even sex, to be equaled only by the rumored descent of the Holy Ghost into the bodies of the chosen. The season might end with a sacred pilgrimage: a trip to the high school playoffs, the most intoxicating sports event in the world, possibly to go all the way, to push on to Jerusalem itself, to "State"!

Though a decade had passed since *Brown vs. Board of Education,* not a single black face could be found in the hallways, classrooms, or locker rooms of alma mater. But now Title VI of the Civil Rights Act of 1964 had stipulated that federal funding would not be allocated to school systems practicing discrimination, and the Elementary and Secondary Education Act of 1965 had offered vastly increased federal funding to public schools operating under the integration guidelines.

There was much agony that summer at the Mansfield Independent School District. But as the Vietnamese say, "If one has money, one can even buy fairies." And so, after eleven years of white resistance and black frustration, in the fall of 1965 thirty black teenagers were registered at Mansfield High, with no repetition of the events that had marked Arnold's initiation into school.

But it wasn't fairies some people in town were interested in: nine of the best black athletes were signed up to join Mansfield Tiger football, and several others were about to join the school band.

A cynic like Stella Rawson would claim that there was absolutely no social motive in the desegregation effort, that the "Big Change" in Mansfield had everything to do with percentages, how many whites, how many blacks, how much federal money, how many yards gained, how many touchdowns. There was no integration—just desegregation. Perhaps she was right. But the school district's money grab and football strategy changed Arnold's understanding of the world.

Ten

Six foot one, bright, handsome as a god, he was still only fifteen and a despised sophomore to boot. Others would have their turns before him. Not, however, in the hospital—he was at the head of the line. Perhaps it was an accident; perhaps Brian Hedder had really wanted to hurt the young punk, teach the handsome sailor something about the reality principle, Texas style. In an early-October after-school practice, the two-hundred-pound seventeen-year-old decided to show his young teammate what he would be up against if he held on to the ball a second too long before passing. With Beelzebubian momentum and Satanic accuracy, he charged through the sophomore scrimmage line and hurled his huge shoulder at Arnold's leading left knee. With his foot cleated into the ground, Arnold's joint buckled inward with a twist and an agonizing pop, and he crumpled to the ground as the junior team pounced on the loosed ball. Coach Crews ran onto the field as Arnold lay there writhing.

"All right, kiddo," the coach said, "you OK?"

"Do I look like I'm OK?" the victim responded.

"Try to get up. Brian, gimme a hand with him." Both teams gathered around the rescue scene.

"Can you bear weight?"

Arnold stepped away from the coach's shoulder onto his left leg. His assailant, Brian, caught him before he went down.

"All right. Let's get him into the shop."

The "shop" was the training room, a dingy, windowless, sweat-smelling cubicle under the bleachers in Old Rock Gym, a room crammed with two padded tables, a sink, an ice machine, and metal lockers full of gauze, peroxide and tape. Three padded men on five legs squeezed through the door, following Coach Crews. One was in severe pain.

"Get him up there on the table. Can you bend your knee?"

"Not any more than this."

"Lemme poke around. Scream when it hurts."

"Aaaaaarggh!"

"Good scream. Hedder, Reynolds, get back on the field, tell em every-thing's OK."

"Everything's not OK!"

"Don't be a crybaby, Hitler. You guys get going!"

Brian and Lonnie clicked their way out of the shop. Tommy Crews pulled on Arnold's knee.

"Pretty stable there." He began to sing: "The shin bone's still con-nected to the thigh bone. . . ." He palpated the inner and outer sides of the joint.

"Yaiiiii!"

"OK, OK. That's called army anesthesia."

"What?"

"You hurt the patient, and when they scream, you say, 'OK, OK.' "

"And you keep on hurting them."

"Sure. No pain, no gain."

"Yeeeeow!"

"OK, OK," offered the coach as he continued his exam, "but I wanna tell you about Steve Godkin in the '56 Olympics. Melbourne. You were just a little twerp then. Steve was a swimmer—two-hundred-meter freestyle. He was just about to go down to Australia when his right lung collapsed. Spontaneous. Spitting up blood. So he goes to the doctor, and they throw him in the hospital, shove him full of tubes, cut him open . . ."

"Yowww!"

"OK, OK . . . repair his lung, and sew him back up. 'I gotta swim next week,' he says. 'That's what you think,' the docs say. 'For one thing, you'll stress the wound, for another, it'll be too painful.' 'I'm going anyway,' Steve says. He'd wanted to be in the Olympics since he was nine. So the doc shakes his head, makes him sign a release, and hands him an Rx for big-time pain pills. But when Steve gets down to Melbourne, he finds out pain pills aren't allowed in competition, so he decides to swim without them. So he's standing at poolside, already white-faced from pain, and the gun goes off and he dives in, makes the first lap, does a spin-turn and pushes off, and he's gotta come up for air in the middle of a blood-curdling scream. He plows into the water again, this time makes a split turn, pushes off—and his stitches break, his chest splits open right here, and he starts bleeding like a pig. Over the last two laps he loses two pints of blood. Good thing there weren't sharks in the pool."

"Why are you telling me this?"

"Cause that's the kind of kid we need on the team. That's the kind of strong character you want in your corner, you know? He was a fighter, Steve Godkin. Didn't win, but he was a fighter."

"Just don't press over here."

"All right. I got it diagnosed. You're in deep shit. I think you got a mangled meniscus in there. But we'll have to get Doc Printz to confirm."

"What does that mean, a mangled meniscus?"

"It's like cartilage pads inside your knee. Keeps the bones from grinding. I think you nipped a nice fat hunk off of this one here. Let's get some ice on it."

Tommy Crews was no doc, but in his seven years of coaching, he'd seen and heard many knees go down. And he was absolutely right about the meniscus. When Doc Printz opened the knee, the joint interior was mangled, bloody, and swollen—a mess. Almost as big a mess as the Hitler family finances after paying for surgery. Almost as big a mess as Arnold's Tiger football career, untimely ripp'd. He wouldn't run again till the beginning of March, and then only tentatively. Still, he could practice throwing, and his arm and accuracy improved. In spite of being essentially out of play for his sophomore year, he was the clear choice for starting JV quarterback the next.

As an invalid, he found another way to be of Tiger service: tutoring. Tutoring three of the nine black students who had newly joined the team. Tutoring math or English or social studies, sometimes all—whatever they needed to keep their grade-point averages above 65 so they could qualify to play. Talking with his new charges, Arnold's eyes were opened to the unfamiliar world of "separate but equal": I. M. Terrell High, up in Fort Worth, had been "their" school, a good school, one they preferred. Teddy Marshall, now a Mansfield senior running back, was having trouble switching over.

"So what were you doing at Terrell?" Arnold asked over a first-order equation. "What were you learning?"

"Nothin. We din't have no homework, we din't have no tutors, like you. Teacher come into class and she give you somethin to read and she goes out. She leaves some other student in charge. At the end of the period, she comes back and tell you somethin to read for the next day."

"I thought you said you didn't have homework."

"Well, hell, they never ast about it the next day, so what the hell. What you think people doin with their nights? Homework? Forty-five girls last year in the maternity ward. Eighteen Terrell guys sentenced to the chain gang."

"So are things better here?"

"Things are OK, but you know, man, it's hard to keep quiet when you git called nigger twenty times a day. But, hey, man, I don't have to get up at 5:30 every mornin to take the bus. An git home at 6:30 after my folks is through eatin."

"Well, that's something."

"But this math shit is hard. I mean, what it have to do with me, man? I know this algebra and then I get a job as a dishwasher—if I can get one. What a dishwasher got to know algebra for?"

"Some college is going to snap you up on a football scholarship. Then you'll have to know this stuff."

"Yeah, well, I'll believe it when I see it. Ain't no one's called this nigger yet."

"They will, Teddy, they will."

Arnold also had difficult studying to do. All the quarterback responsibilities—it was overwhelming: learning all the calls, all the two- and three-play packages, not getting fooled by an overshifted defense, understanding the T-formation, I-formation, Warner Single Wing formation, Shotgun, Wishbone, Veer formation, Eagle Defense, 3-4 Pass defense, 4-3 Pro defense, Oklahoma defense—he had to know and call them all. He had to be familiar with the strategies and tactics of the dozen teams the Tigers played, and of the others they might meet should they make it to State: the Paolo Duro Dons, the Nacogdoches Dragons, the Lubbock Westerners, the Big Spring Steers, the Abilene Eagles, the Amarillo Golden Sandies, the San Angelo Bobcats, the Sweetwater Mustangs, the Lamesa Tornadoes, the Midland Bulldogs, the Ysleta Indians, the Wichita Falls Coyotes, the Highland Park Scotties, the Tascosa Rebels, the Lamar Vikings, the Carter Cowboys, and of course those impostors who dared to take the same name, the Texarkana Tigers.

He was sitting on his bed one night, three weeks postsurgery, manipulating his chess pieces on the board in a single-wing shift to the left, when an agonizing pain shot through his left knee.

"Fuck! Goddamn!" He had thought he was healing.

"Arnold, watch your mouth!" Was that his father? It didn't sound like his father. His knee began to tingle and buzz.

"A man's belly shall be filled with the fruit of his mouth," his knee said to him.

"Grandpa? Nonno Jacobo?"

"So who else talks to you in your knee?"

"You haven't been there for a long time."

"I haven't had to."

"How are you, Grandpa?"

"Terrible. It's a mess in here. Swollen like I'm squeezing to death. It's the archetype of Jew, Arnold—up to his eyeballs in a cistern, thinking about the infinite."

"What infinite?"

"I'm thinking about the fish, Arnold, what about the fish? Did God name the fish? He brought before Adam all the beasts of the field and all the fowl of the air. To name them. But what about the fish? Who named the fish? Names are important. Words are important. Keep your mouth clean. A vessel for the holy. Death and life are in the power of the tongue. Next time I wash your mouth out with soap."

Arnold laughed. "How are you going to do that?"

"Don't give me any of your lip, you Texas *ignorante*. You want your knee to get better? You want an inside contact or not?"

"Can you get me better by Christmas?"

"Sha! *Kina hora!* You mean Chanukuh?"

"What's Chanukah?"

"For this, I raised your mama? Not Christmas. January. Second week in January."

"You promise?"

"Would I lie?"

"No."

"You promise you'll keep your mouth clean?"

"Yes."

"OK. End of the second week of January, you get up off your little goyish tush . . ."

"Grandpa, I'm six foot one. Two meters."

"Big, little, it's still a tush. You start to work out. Slow. Understand? Slow. You'll be full speed ahead by April. I'll put my boys on it."

"What boys?"

"Leave it to me, you little pisher. Say hello to the folks."

And the buzzing clicked off. Just like that. The tingling and buzzing stopped.

"Grandpa? Are you there?"

No answer.

Eleven

Arnold Hitler became the language maniac of his school, constantly correcting and criticizing, but with such wit and humble charm that he got away with murder. His teachers loved him, even those who showed up as defendants in his underground language sheet, *The Last Word*. Much of the school was on his staff: students and staff slipped notes-on-the-overheard through the vents in his locker, some of which made it into his "Language Alert" column.

"Arnold, I hear they're thinking of calling the library the 'Learning Resources Center,'" wrote a faculty member. "What do you think of that?" He responded with a Mencken-like diatribe in the next issue.

Arnold Hitler, a lowly junior, had become the local language repository, and Mansfield High by and large embraced his efforts. By and large—with the exception of at least one person, let's call him Claggart, who also slipped notes into his locker: "Hey, asshole, wanna meet me behind the school after practice today? I got some hot idioms for you to shove. Come alone."

In November 1966, Arnold Hitler found a missive in his locker too intimate to publish. It was a quote from someone named James Thurber about America needing a "psychosemanticist" to treat "the havoc wrought by verbal artillery on the fortress of reason," our current language being a tongue "full of sound and fury, dignifying nothing." Who was this guy Thurber? he wondered. Under the typed text was a note beautifully handwritten in italic script: "His seals barketh up our tree. Love, your Billie Jo."

"Your" Billie Jo? "My" Billie Jo? "Our" tree? Between the pronoun and the exquisite hand, he found his heart beating more quickly and his own hand slightly shaky.

"Sí, ragazzo, sí!" Jacobo whispered, and Arnold clamped his knees together.

He didn't know anyone named Billie Jo, but then he didn't know many girls at all—at least not by name. Girls didn't play chess, mostly, and girls didn't play football, and the girls in his classes didn't say much. They were too worried about appearing smart. But from mid-November on, he found a daily message in his locker, usually an interesting quotation with a personal note in that lovely hand. It was nice, being watched—but also creepy.

On Christmas Day, his sixteenth birthday, an ice-cream cake was delivered to the Hitler door: a frozen, regulation-size, edible football inscribed "DON'T PASS ON THIS ONE, Birthday love from your secret admirer." Arnold pled ignorance as George and Anna shared a knowing laugh.

On Monday, January 2nd, 1967, she revealed herself to him. A somewhat plain, dark-haired young woman with granny glasses, short skirt, and black tights sat down next to him in the cafeteria and said, simply, "Happy New Year, Arnold. I'm your mysterious love." He had seen her before, he thought, without noticing, one of the neutral mass of bodies and faces passing in halls and seated in assemblies.

"Are you Billie Jo?"

"Billie Jo Hoffmann, at your service." She doffed an imaginary cap. She did have lovely, brown hair.

"At your service? What does that mean?"

"You're the semiologist, so you tell me."

A promising beginning.

Arnold was intrigued by her audacity. He was not sexually attracted, but all the "sexually attractive" girls were so conscious of their gifted status, so manipulative around it, so made-up and cheap, with their permed hair and push-up bras, that he had always been turned off by the very beauties who were supposed to turn him on. Billie Jo was not *un*attractive. In fact, over the next days, her natural simplicity of appearance and style began to please him more and more.

She was a senior. At Mansfield High, it was unheard of for a senior girl to be interested in a junior boy. Given the relative maturity of the boys and the girls, it would surely have been robbing the cradle, well and justly tabooed. But Arnold was different. And Billie Jo was different enough to understand that, and to dare to reach out to him, perhaps her only soulmate among the student body.

She and her twelve-year-old brother, Chris, had moved to Mansfield only that year, from Dallas. Her mother, Francine, had just separated from her dad and had moved the twenty miles south to be out of his sphere, yet still close enough to share child responsibilities and to not lose touch with old friends and activities. She still worked three nights a week at a group home in the city. Billie Jo, too, still had ties to Dallas— several girlfriends, an ex-boyfriend, now "just a friend," her piano teacher, with whom she studied on Saturdays, and a library card using her dad's address. She did the commute in her own '65 Oldsmobile, a sweet-sixteen gift from her dad. Arnold had never known anyone with money. Or had a peer with a car.

By Friday of the first week, she had taken him home to show him off. He immediately made two other conquests: Francine, who, if she were only twenty years younger . . . , and Chris, who, if he were only four years older. . . . After some initial heart palpitations, both of them settled into their roles as adoring potential in-law and aspiring little brother. For all three Hoffmanns, Arnold Hitler was certainly "a catch."

It was the first free Friday night, since the football and holiday seasons had ended and the crush of spring-term assignments had yet to begin. So he stayed late. Chris retired at 10:30; Mom went to her room shortly thereafter (with a wink of her eye and intrigue in her heart), leaving Juliet alone on the couch with her Romeo. After enough time to ensure the finality of all exits, what did they do? They talked. Quietly. They talked about the season, about his occasional appearances in games, his passing record, what it all might mean for his role next year as a senior. They talked about *The Last Word* and its impact on the school. She traced out her attraction to him, her hesitancy and fear of rejection, her decision to woo Mr. Words via words alone, her researches to discover quotations that might interest him, her New Year's resolution to materialize, come what may. He said he was happy she had. And with that, she took his head in her hands.

"Close your eyes," she said.

"Why?"

"Just close them."

So he did.

She placed her open lips over his left eye and blew ever so gently, rhythmically bathing his lid in warm, moist air, *largo sensuoso*. He liked it, and smiled. Then, on to the right eye.

"What are you doing?" he murmured.

"Shhhh," she answered.

Back to the left. She breathed on his lid three times, then began to stroke it methodically with her tongue, tracing the contours of the globe underneath, probing the undersurface of the orbit, caressing the space between eye and nose. His lachrymal duct wept with tickle and joy. He breathed quickly, somewhat from thrill but also to keep himself from laughing. She finished the left eye, then finished the right. "There," she said.

"Let me do it to you," he offered.

"Nope. You're the guest."

He just sat there. Now what?

"OK. Time for you to go. I have to get up early for my piano lesson."

"You play the piano?"

"Since I was eight."

"You must be good."

"I'll play for you. But not now. It's too late. Next time."

"So there'll be a next time?"

"You think I lick everybody's eyes?"

"No, but . . ."

"Listen, buddy, you're taken. Hear me?"

"I . . . well . . . yes."

He stood up and headed obediently to the door.

"Bye," he offered. "Have a good lesson. Um . . . may I kiss you goodnight?"

"No. I'm saving myself for my husband."

"Oh. I'm sorry. I mean, I hope you don't think . . ."

"You dope," she laughed, and flung her arms around his neck in her own efficient version of a tackle. It was a good kiss. His first except for Mom.

"Close the door," she chided. "You're letting in the cold."

Billie Jo Hoffmann was an offer he couldn't refuse. Arnold pedaled home through the Texas night. For all his vocabulary, the only words on the tape-loop of his consciousness were "Wow!" and "Wow!"

Billie Jo lay in bed, also reckoning where things had gotten to. Her presleep assessment was "first base plus." Her sweetie's game of football did not lend itself to sexual metaphors. Even the cheerleading Rebelettes, Billie Jo's scorned and hated rivals, charted their progress to heaven (or hell) in baseball language. "Getting to first" meant kissing. The "plus" in Billie Jo's assessment applied to kissing eyelids, a technique her Dallas ex had taught her that didn't figure in the usual calculation. It was the first time she, herself, had been the kisser. "Getting to second"—that would surely come—involved a hand, Arnold's hand— once burned, a hand feeling, touching, being allowed in under her clothing, but not below the belt. "Third base"? Well, that actually included private parts, his blind, and likely awkward, exploration of hers, perhaps, who knows, even hers of his. Third base with a long and daring lead toward the plate occurred out of clothing, or somewhat out of clothing, and brought in mouths, mouths and tongues on private parts. This might or might not happen.

Their relationship was not by any means just about sex. It was a *lot* about sex, but not entirely. One night (after getting to third base plus), she lay with her head in his lap. Mom was in Dallas for the night, and Chris had been sleeping soundly for two hours. His own parents had grudgingly become open to his staying out late, so he was feeling relaxed.

"Want to hear the story of my life?" she asked out of nowhere.

"I thought I'd heard it."

"No. The story of my *real* life, not my real life." Her enunciation made all this clear.

"Sure. Go ahead."

"Well, once upon a time there was a woman who lost a pearl in the ocean, and started scooping up the water, one cup after another. A sea-sprite saw the tiny eddies she was raising and swam over to her and said, 'When will you stop?' The woman said, 'When I've scooped all the water from the sea and found my pearl on the bottom.' The sea-sprite was so moved she retrieved the pearl and brought it to the woman with thanks."

There was a long, late-night silence.

"That's your real story?"

"Yes. You'll see."

"Which are you, the woman or the sea-sprite?"

"Which do you think?"

"Both."

"Smarty-pants. You'll get into Harvard for sure."

Maybe this woman with her head on his lap was actually the pearl.

"My grandfather tells me stories," he said.

"You never told me about him."

"Grandpa Jacobo. He lives in Italy."

"You travel to Italy?"

"Unh-uh."

"He writes you?"

"Not really."

"Then how does he tell you stories?"

"Through my knee."

"What?"

"Through my left knee. Here, move your head over. Put your ear over here, over my scar. Press hard. I'll ring him up."

Arnold tapped three times on his kneecap and three more times on the top of Billie Jo's skull.

"OK, go ahead. *Avanti.*"

A pause.

"Can you hear him?"

"Yeah."

"He's in there? You can hear him?" said Arnold, more surprised than she.

"Yeah. He has an accent."

"He does. It's true. What's he saying?"

He waited in reality-warp.

"He's talking about the 'Talmud.' What's that?"

"A Jewish book. He's Jewish. How did you know he talks about the Talmud?"

"Cause he's talking about it now, dummy. He says the Talmud loves silence more than anything in the world."

"He's saying that?"

"Yeah."

This, all in whispers. Silence. Darkness.

"That's it. He hung up or something." She sat up. "You know, I agree. You know how you always want me to talk when we have sex and I can't—don't want to? Like that. Silence is golden."

"You're putting me on. You didn't hear Jacobo in my knee. You just want me to shut up when we make love."

"I did too hear him. That's what he said. How'd I know he had an accent? How'd I know he was Jewish?"

"I told you."

"How'd I know about what do you call it, the Talmud? I never even heard of it before."

"Tell me another."

She sprang up from the couch.

"You don't believe me?"

"Shh. You'll wake Chris."

More quietly: "You don't believe me?"

He had never seen her angry; he was confused.

"No, I believe you. Come back."

And after a moment, she did.

When she had known him long enough, she played him the first movement of Beethoven Op. 28. If he hadn't been in love with her before, he
was, by the tenth measure, helplessly, irreversibly ensnared. The pulsing
low bass stopped his breath as he stared, enchanted, at this being of
straight spine and closed eyes while the long, lovely chordal melody spun
out its tension and release. That those hands, those very hands that had
held—his penis!—that those hands could now call forth another such
mass of beauty . . . He wanted to have those hands, to possess them, to
possess the possessor of those hands. Her head lifted at the first cadence,
and his eyes discovered, as if for the first time, the loveliness of her neck,
the supple bridge between her mysterious heart and perspicacious brain,
the tunnel for nerves that fed those hands, the miraculous electrochem-
istry of her! At the second theme, a second miracle, this time of emer-
gence. He watched her hands again, amazed. He watched them moving
back and forth, rocking, thumb to pinky, sagitally, symmetrically around
her long third fingers. It was the kind of hand motion one might associate with the octave tremolos of old, out-of-tune pianos accompanying
silent films. Yet what emerged was not some rinky-dink whorehouse
tune but an inner melody of such beauty, a melody so embedded in its
harmonies as to be beyond all accompaniment: It was melody and harmony at once, a fusion of functions out of reach of bodies, of physical human bodies, but somehow accomplished in this sea of sounds. And those
hands—her hands!—were bringing this miracle forth, a miracle upon a
miracle—that mere matter—molecules of flesh and wood and steel—
could bring to birth such infinity. Three miracles happening there, right
in front of him. All this and her breasts, too, there under her shirt, suspended above the field of play, waiting, hoping perhaps, for his caressing

hands, bony visitors from another world, admittedly, but also a connection between worlds. As her hands were to the music, so were his to her breasts, and through them to her soul and the soul-ineffable sound. The great pain of the great joy: it was more than his being could bear. He had to withdraw.

"Isn't that nice?" she said when she had finished.

"Yeah."

"Did you like it?"

"Yes."

"Do you like me?"

"Yes. I love you."

"I thought you'd never say it."

Billie Jo was thus Arnold's gateway and guide to the world of Art, twenty minutes north. Dallas, for Arnold, had hitherto meant one thing: the Cotton Bowl on New Year's Day. Now it came to mean the symphony at Meyerson Hall, the Theater Center, the Shakespeare Festival at Grand Park, and the theatrical experiments at Southern Methodist University. And she paid. Or rather, he was the frequent replacement for missing members of the family subscriptions. But his favorite venue was, coincidentally, the place they went to *sans famille,* an art movie house, happily located at Inwood Road and Lovers Lane, across from the SMU campus.

And lovers they were, though technically virgins, lovers of each other and of the amazing tour they had booked together: from concert to film to play to film to reading to film to museum to film, a rondo in which film was the fundamental; never were two people better served by the Inwood.

Arnold saw his first foreign film in February of 1966. It was an eye-opener of such force and brilliance as to divide his life—before and after *The Seventh Seal.* Until that time, his movie fare had consisted of Saturday matinees at the Farr Best Theater on Broad Street, with noisy white kids downstairs and noisy black kids up in the balcony. He had been two or three times at night with his parents: the noise level was lower, but the films were the same—mostly Westerns and grade-B unmemorables with the occasional *Marty* or *Ben Hur.*

But *The Seventh Seal* was something else entirely. It unveiled a whole new way of seizing the world, the way of images that spoke more than they said. The knight, Antonius Block, lay on a gray beach at the edge of a gray sea. But somehow—magically, within five seconds—it was clear that this beach was not just a beach, the beach at Joe Pool Lake, a Beach Boys beach, a Debbie Reynolds beach, but something vast and mysterious and threatening. "Who are you?" asks the knight. "I am Death," says the man.

"I am Death." In the hundreds of movies he had seen, in the thousands of cartoons and news broadcasts and TV shows, Arnold had never heard anyone say, "I am Death." Six words, "Who are you?" "I am Death," and the so-called real world forever after dissolved to background. The old saga rose up in Arnold's Texas world, an ancient structure of wood and flesh and iron and stone, of wind and wave and light and shadow, to speak of our true condition, ominous and loveless, no matter that his hand was in her lap, and warm. This was it.

But it was not the opening of *The Seventh Seal* that most moved him, though it was those initial moments that set him up to be hyperpresent throughout. It was not the gorgeous and frightening end, the silhouetted dance of death of people he had grown to love. It was the burning of the witch that stayed most painfully with him, lodged in his throat and chest for years, the gamin on the pyre, her wide eyes filled with smoke, seeing.

For Arnold there was no riding away from this horrifying scene. In her own pain, Billie Jo squeezed his hand, but she found it limp, as powerless to help as those of squire or knight. Arnold knew only that he loved the witch more than he loved Billie Jo, whose hand lay in his, more even than he loved Mia, the juggler's wife, the most beautiful woman he had ever seen, the first woman with whom he had been unfaithful—only forty minutes before.

If Billie Jo was Arnold's gateway to the world of Art, Arnold was hers to the world of politics. Not that he was any expert. But he had been baptized at school with the politics of hate, confirmed at ten with the poisoned policy toward Cuba, and bar mitzvahed at thirteen by vultures coming home to roost on Dealy Plaza. She, on the other hand, had been so protected by wealthy parents that her naïveté was comical. Arnold realized the extent of her ignorance during an Inwood screening of Pabst's *Der letzte Akt*, a re-creation of the final days of Hitler. During the first ten minutes of the film, Billie Jo leaned over to him three times to whisper, "Is that Hitler?" Though he whispered back, "No, not yet," he was astounded, and then astounded again, and then again that she didn't know what that Hitler looked like. When he appeared on the screen, he poked her.

"That's him."

"Ah," she said.

When he read that Alabama governor George Wallace was to give a speech in Dallas, he suggested they go. Billie Jo had heard of Wallace, knew he had tried to block black students from entering the University of Alabama some years before and was running his wife as candidate for governor to replace him. She was game to go. They arrived at the VFW Hall ten minutes late, as the governor of Alabama was intoning a litany of crime in the streets, of courts coddling criminals. He assailed the pinkos undermining U.S. efforts in Vietnam, and the attack on property rights and free enterprise. He zeroed in on the constitutional primacy of states' rights.

"I have never," he insisted, "I have never made a racist speech in my life. I mean I never talked against niggras as people. I got nothing against niggras. Southern folks had the most practical approach ever devised for this race business. What good are equal rights if it gets folks killed and ruins everything? Why, you're safer in the worst part of Montgomery than on the New York City subway. We got less integration but more mingling, and more law and order. And what most folks of all races want is law and order."

"Thas what we want, George!"

"You know, people keep tryin to polish me up. Course I talk like we all do down South. You know—ain't got no, he don't, and all that—I know better, but it's just comfortable. So I went up and was on television with Martin Luther King, and I talked like I always do, and there he was with that grammar and those big words. And they quoted me in the paper the next day to make it look like I don't know anything, and then they quote a fellow like that that don't even know the origins of the English language. . . ."

And so on. Billie Jo found it fascinating, better than Shakespeare, not as good as some films but better than most, with the unmatchable immediacy of a live event steaming in real passion. On the drive home, she was quiet.

"So?" prodded her teacher.

"So let's stop eating meat."

"What?"

"How can any sensitive person accept that in order to feed ourselves we should kill all those animals, especially when the earth gives us so many different treasures from plants?"

"What has that got to do with tonight?"

"You want to?"

"No. I like meat. I need it to play football."

More silence.

"Arnold, could you ever imagine forcing a woman to do something sexually she doesn't want to do?"

"No, of course not. What's wrong with you?"

"You wouldn't ever rape me."

She took his glare for a response.

"Do you like the way I look?"

"I love the way you look."

A mile of silence.

"Do you like the way I look because you are socially conditioned? I mean what if I were fat and ugly? Would you still like me?"

"Sure. You're likeble. I'm not just interested in . . ."

"Would you like the way I *look?* If I were fat and ugly?"

They arrived home before this *aporia* could propagate. She wouldn't kiss him good-night at her door—"I'm tired, and I just want to go to sleep"—the unpredictable response to a loss of political virginity.

But George Wallace was not enough to break them up. She called the next morning, Saturday, chipper as usual.

"You get the Best Cheap Date of the Year Award for last night. Please report to my house at 7 tonight for the presentation. I'm off to piano lesson. Bye."

Mom was in Dallas, and Chris was at a birthday party and would be delivered home at 9. It was time for a treatment with some special "anthroposophical" massage oil she had bought in a head shop in the city.

"What did I do to deserve this?" her boyfriend asked.

"You don't deserve it. It's a gift of grace. Just shut up, take off your shirt, and lie down."

"Where?"

"On my bed, silly. Where else would you like to lie down? On mom's bed?"

"No, I . . ."

She warmed the oil between her palms.

"Are you aware of the healing properties of arnica with rosemary?"

"Not exactly."

"Quiet. Just relax."

She spread the oil over his back and moved her hands up and down along his flanks as if she were molding an exquisite form.

"Arnica is the master remedy for shock."

"But I'm not in shock."

"You will be." She reads from a sheet that came with the bottle. " 'The patient is bruised, sore, tender, and resents being touched.' That's you. 'He is in a stupor, but answers correctly when roused.' That's you for sure. 'Nervous, cannot bear pain, whole body oversensitive.' " She runs her hair up his bare back to test.

" 'Useful remedy for sprains, concussion, and aftereffects of blows or falls. Useful for all pains anywhere, rheumatism, or any condition where "as if bruised all over" is a major symptom.' "

By this time Arnold had entered the alpha state of the deeply massaged. Embarrassed at being so passive, he semiroused his mouth from lethargy, a small area of I-can-still-move.

"What's the rosemary for?"

"Dunno. It doesn't say. It smells good."

The work continued, a first-class massage from a deeply intuitive masseuse, with no sexual hanky-pank. Deep under the shroud of musculoskeletal bliss, Arnold felt a mild gnawing.

"I will be what?" he managed.

Poof. The carriage changed back to a pumpkin. Billie Jo whipped off her seat on his buns and threw him a towel.

"You can wipe off the oil."

"Can't reach," he said, easing himself up on stretched arms. "You do me."

Billie Jo balled up the towel and began to rub.

"Hey, leave me some skin, please."

"Gotta unstick the stuck blood. Open up the chi. Here, put this on. I bought it for you after my lesson." She flung him a navy-blue sweatshirt marked "UNIVERSITY OF PARIS."

"Paris, Texas?" he asked.

"No, silly. Paris, France. It's from the Sorbonne."

"And you want me to wear it?"

"If you like it."

"But I don't go to the Sorbonne."

"So? Why do you have to go to the Sorbonne to wear it? Plenty of people wear sweatshirts from places they don't go to."

"But it doesn't make sense. What have I got to do with the Sorbonne?"

"Don't be so literal."

"Billie, it makes the words meaningless—empty symbols."

"You know what the opposite of symbolic is?"

"Unh-uh."

"Diabolic. Symbol from the Greek *sym-ballein*, to draw together. *Dia-ballein*, to tear apart. Mrs. Aron told me that this morning. We were talking about musical symbols."

"Well, OK. So you want to be diabolic? This sweatshirt is dangerous."

"Arnold, I got my acceptance from Oberlin today."

"What?"

"I'm going to Oberlin."

"You're going to go to Oberlin?"

"Yup."

"Not SMU or UT Arlington?"

"Nope."

"But . . . what will happen to us?"

"Button up your shirt. I can't stand those marvelous pecs."

"What . . ."

"Well, I don't know. We'll write. We'll visit. Ever been to Ohio?"

"No. I've never been anywhere. You know that."

"I thought maybe Ohio didn't qualify as anywhere. It's a good school, just right for me, I think. Mom and Dad want me to go."

"I see."

"Now are you in shock?"

"Kind of."

"Told you so."

"What?"

"You would be in shock."

"Yeah, you did."

"You know when I first came to Mansfield, the first piece of advice I got was to try to become a cheerleader. Did you know that? You know what Cheryl told me? 'It's very revered to be a cheerleader.' Revered. Just what I always wanted to be. And of course it was crucially important to look a certain way and to have a boyfriend. And the best possible boyfriend was a football player, as in, 'Wow, you're going out with a foot-ball player!'"

"Is that why you went after me? Why are you telling me this?"

"I went to the first pep rally, and I watched all those girls, so cliquey and obsessed with their appearance, always flicking their hair back. I watched all those arms pumping frantically up and down, and I thought maybe I'd like to be like them. I tried dressing like them, but I wasn't pretty enough. You know, pretty? And what was worse, I didn't act silly enough, so they put me in a category—'stuck-up brain,' 'book bitch.' There was no way I could break into their circle. I tried, I really did. And then the irony was I fell in love with a football player, as in, 'Wow, you're going out with a football player.' I even got outlaw points for robbing the cradle. And you ran interference. You showed me who I really was. And Arnold, I'm not a UT or an SMU co-ed. We both know that, right? I'm going to go to Oberlin. I can study at the Conservatory and still be in a good school, not just a piano player. You can come visit, I promise. I'll send you money for airfare. And I'll be home Christmases."

"When I met you," Arnold admitted, "I thought it was funny that it was *you* who gave me those gifts. I mean, I thought it was some cheerleader. A yellow-and-black wastepaper basket filled with popcorn balls? This is the girl who gave me those?"

"Pretty good cover, don'tcha think? I spent forty bucks on all that stuff."

"You could work for the CIA."

"They probably recruit at Oberlin."

"Can we make love?"

"In the next two minutes?"

"No. Before you go away."

"You mean home plate?"

"Yes."

"No."

"Why?"

"I told you before: I'm saving myself for my husband."

"I thought that was a joke."

"You thought wrong."

"But we've done everything else."

"The outer boundaries of virginity. Are you my husband?"

"No. Not yet. But . . ." Arnold was wise enough to stop. "I'm applying to Harvard—so if I get in, I wouldn't be here anyway to date a UT gal."

It was Billie Jo's turn to be afraid.

"There are lots of beautiful, smart women in Cambridge."

"Really?"

"Oh, you . . . aren't we awful?" She jumped him and sank her teeth into his neck.

The door opened and Chris yelled, "OK, you two, come out with your hands up."

Arnold and Billie Jo tucked in their shirts and made a not-quite-convincing Entrance of the Innocents into the living room.

After her initial shock, and her frenzy of jealousy, Billie Jo became aggressively enthusiastic about his plans for Harvard. She assured him he would get in—he had the grades, he was poor (for balance) and from Texas (for even more balance)—but just to cinch it, she insisted he try for a Merit Scholarship and even gave him some inside dope from her Phi Beta father, "the very one who insisted she go to public, not private, school"—on how to up his chances with an academically respectable community service project, well documented on his application. She knew the perfect thing for him: a curriculum plan for the study of language. Given who he was, his new English teacher, Carl Gimple, allowed him to go off with six students as an "experimental unit" (hurrah for the Mansfield Integrated School District) to try out his curriculum for the last six weeks of the spring semester. The project got Carl another Merit scholar for his cap. Here, the first page of the addendum to Arnold's application. The talented hand of his muse and éminence grise is apparent in the background:

**A STUDENT-CENTERED CURRICULUM FOR
UNSUCKERING OUR GENERATION**
Arnold Hitler, *Mansfield High School, Mansfield, Texas*
May 1–June 15, 1966

**Generals, clergymen, advertisers, and the rulers of totalitar-
ian states all have good reasons for disliking the idea of uni-**

versal education in the rational use of language. To the au-
thoritarian mind such training seems (and rightly seems)
profoundly subversive.
Aldous Huxley

INTRODUCTION

This project is part of the war on cancer, in this case
against the "carcinominclature of our time" (Thurber), a language in flight from reality and rapidly becoming the servant
of nightmare. Nowhere is the pathology more evident than in
the language of "Vietnam," the poor country metamorphosed
into a synonym for unspeakable acts: "attrition," "pacifica-
tion," "defoliation," "body counts," "progressive-squeeze-
and-talk." Such usage not only pollutes the language but
leads the young minds of our generation into a world cut
adrift from meaning.

One hundred and thirty years ago, Alexis de Tocqueville
wondered whether language deterioration might be inherent in democracy. Does the compulsion to win riches, pleasure, and power in a competitive society make the perversion
of meaning and the debasement of language inevitable?

We at Mansfield High School have tried to say NO by introducing and testing a pilot course for high school juniors
on "Semantics in Situ, or The Unsuckering of our Generation."

Then Arnold described his pedagogical strategies—for Poetry and
Public Speech, for Language in Education, for an annotated Language
Pollution Index—and gave several examples of successful student pro-
jects. This was his

CONCLUSION

Applying to real life skills learned in literature study,
and concepts learned in biology and ecology, can serve to

lead students to the semantic sophistication necessary for "unsuckering." From our six-week experience the class and I conclude that separate units on semantics will not have a meaningful effect unless they can be incorporated into an entire curriculum. Given the explosion of mass media and the "havoc wrought by verbal artillery on the fortress of reason" (Thurber), semantics must become the core of the high school curriculum if an educated population is to have any hold on democracy.

Arnold got his scholarship and was one of the first accepted at Harvard. But this to skip ahead.

Twelve

Senior year was chaotic, the zenith and the nadir of Arnold's high school career. Preseason practice began on August 16th, in preparation for the opener on September 8th, the first Friday night of fall semester. Thirty-six boys in gym shorts and Tiger Ts gathered at Geyer Field under a blazing midafternoon sun to hear Head Coach Tommy Crews:

"Welcome, guys! You're a good, tough-lookin bunch. You know there's 347 boys at Mansfield High. You divide that by three, and that's about 115 in each class."

"Hundred and fifteen and two-thirds!" yelled Jerrod Sims.

"Sims, that slide rule's fixin to wind up you know where."

"Where's that, sir?"

Snickering. Crews let it go.

"As I was saying, 115—and two-thirds—boys in each class, and here you are, thirty-six of you. That means you're a very special breed. There are ballplayers out there who are just as good as you are, maybe better, but they're not here now. For whatever reason, they weren't able to stick it out, they didn't have what it takes. You guys are special! It's you guys who are gonna carry the torch for the '67–'68 season. Some of you have been dreaming about bein here today since y'all were pint-size runts, and I know this is pretty special for you. If you work hard, if you pay the price, this season will be one of the great moments of your life. Be proud you're part of this program, and keep up the Tiger tradition. What do Tigers say?"

The crew roared.

"I can't hear you!"

They roared louder.

"I can't hear you!"

"GGGRRRRRAAAAARRRRRRH!"

"That's better! Chuck has a couple of words for you."

Assistant Coach Chuck Terwilliger: "Some of you boys haven't played before, been in the spotlight. Well, I've got some advice for you. Have fun, hustle your ass, and stick the hell out of em. This isn't gonna be a party. You're gonna get hurt, and if you get hurt, that's fine, you're hurt. But if you get dumped, and you're gonna lay there and whine about it, you don't belong on the field anyway. Understand? What do Tigers say?"

While roaring half-heartedly, Arnold thought of Sammy Clayborn, who last year had lost a testicle toughing it out. No one had bothered to examine him after the game, and he hadn't wanted to be a faggot and have some guy poking around in his pants.

"OK, guys," Coach Crews continued, "this afternoon we're gonna find out how hard you can play in 97 degrees. This is good practice for playing at 10 below when we go to State in December!"

A chorus of laughs and groans.

"Starting tomorrow morning, I want to see each and every one of you in the gym by 6:15 in the A.M. You know what that means? It means you're in bed by 9—alone [knowing laughs]. It means no alcohol on weekdays—and that means you, Mahoney [more laughs]! It means you stay healthy—not for you, but for Mansfield. Understand? Today we'll loosen up and do some playing. I want A through M over here and N through Z over here. One second. Chuck wants to say something."

"Yeah. I just want to say that y'all notice there are nine colored boys in this room with us today. Let's give em a hand. [Applause.] I think last year's experience with our first colored team members was a rewarding one. They got a lot to offer, and we're gonna treat em well. Right?"

"Right," the boys affirmed.

"I can't hear you, Tigers."

"RIGHT!"

"OK, that's it. A through M; N through Z."

In the days before junk mail, young Texas boys *never* received letters, unless they wrote away to the ads in the back of comic books. But Arnold and his parents were first delighted, then shocked, then astounded at the daily arrival of recruitment letters: several apiece from Nebraska, Texas A&M, Arkansas, Notre Dame, the University of Houston, Clemson, Texas Tech, Oklahoma, Oklahoma State, LSU, SMU, UCLA. They kept arriving in slow crescendo.

Mr. Dawes, the postman, kept mental notes on all the senders and could narrate the week's contents to Arnold, and presumably to everyone else he saw. Arnold was continually accosted by teachers, store owners, and mothers on the street: "You gonna accept Clemson? My brother went to Clemson. Loved it." "Hey, the Aggies! That's great. Great team. Terrific party school!" "Go, Arnie! Texas Tech. Way to go, buckeroo!"

Arnold Hitler, strong and tan, son of southwest sidewalks, being courted from as far away as Los Angeles! The siren song of foreign lands, arriving by mail in Mansfield, Texas, a rich mix of the Old South and the Wild West, where folks were friendly to a fault but fiercely independent; a God-fearing place, Mansfield, propped up by Baptist beliefs in flag and family but home to hell-raisers, always perched on the edge of violence, yet still, in some way, innocent. Arnold's was the world of a small Texas town, isolated, insulated, a hodgepodge of junkyards and auto-supply stores, old mansions and new warehouses, all dusty and slightly seedy, a town where the four seasons of the year were football, basketball, track, and baseball but where one season dominated the rest as Christmas does the entire year. Mansfield coaches called upon the spirit of Texas individualism, plus the teamwork of the oppressed.

And now Los Angeles was calling on Mansfield for help. Our very Lady of Indiana seemed to be crying for Arnold. Because of him, the outside world was finally paying attention to Mansfield, a hitherto nowhere place where kids cruised Main and Broad on Saturday nights and teenaged honor was measured in beers. Amidst a building barrage of letters, the town anointed their annual hero as a representative, typical yet exemplary, of all the good people of Mansfield.

Arnold felt less than heroic. If anything, recently abandoned by Billie Jo, he was panicked. It was balm to his soul to take counsel with Stella Rawson.

"Mansfield? Mansfield has an awesome ability to bullshit itself. We've got the same proportion of assholes as anywhere. Of course we worship the football stars. There are so few things we can be really proud about. We don't have a university, we don't have a real library, we don't have art museums, we don't have theaters or concert halls. When somebody talks about Mansfield, they talk about football."

"What are you saying, Ma?" said Edna, now sixteen and still an outcast. "It's not that we don't *have* theaters or concert halls—we don't *want* them! What we want is a gladiator spectacle on Friday nights. You know what it costs to fly the team around the state? Eighty, ninety thousand a semester! Mrs. Hart, the best teacher in the school, with a master's and twenty years' experience, makes half of what that idiot Crews makes."

Still, it was sweet to open the year with a forty-seven-yard touchdown pass on the first offense of the first game of the season. The fans took it as an omen of future glory, and to heighten that supposition, the Tigers treated the Highland Park Scotties to a humiliating 24-3 defeat. Arnold threw three touchdown passes and completed thirteen of fifteen others, setting off the Hitler-Frame myth of the year, the "dream duo in black and white," proof of Mansfield's racial sophistication.

BJ Frame was a black receiving end, six foot one like Arnold but even faster. He had starred at Terrell in his junior year and was the prize catch of Mansfield's reluctant white fishermen. He and Arnold were not only a phenomenal team on the field over the year but they also became fast friends, the only real black-white combo at the school.

BJ began his association with Arnold with a defining act: "Hey, Mr. Doctor White Boy, I got something to show you."

"Where'd you get this?"

"The bus station. In the black restroom. I thought you might be interested."

Arnold examined the document, an unlined three-by-five card, neatly typed, the corners still bearing shards of scotch tape. At the top, "NOTICE," and underneath a list of prices the white author would pay for various types of sex with Negro girls of descending age. Services would be free to any Negro woman over twenty. From there, the writer offered to pay two dollars for a nineteen-year-old, three for an eighteen-year-old, four for seventeen, etc., up to seven-fifty for a fourteen-year-old and even more for children. The card listed a contact point and urged any Negro man sitting in the stall who wanted to earn $5 to bring his friend, with proof of age.

"What's your take on that, professor?" BJ asked.

Arnold looked him in the eye.

"You know, there's always been plenty of nigger-lovers after the sun goes down."

BJ nodded.

That was it. The die was cast. They understood one another beyond the words that had been spoken.

When BJ heard Arnold was applying to Harvard, he said, "Hey, man, you'll never get into Hahvahd with that peckerwood accent. And if you get in, you better keep your trap shut for four years, or they'll kill you up there." There weren't many whites in Mansfield that had an ear into the black community—and vice versa.

Thursday night was lasagna night at the Hitlers'. Jacobo had kneewise suggested a Thursday lasagna night, and Arnold was just reporting the news to his mom. Anna took these "messages" with a grain of salt. In Ferrara, when people wanted something but didn't want to take full responsibility, they would hold up a pinky to an ear, pretend to be listening, and then announce, "My little finger says you need to give me two hundred lira for ice cream." But how did Arnold know that when she was growing up, Thursday *was* lasagna day? In any case, she did need a way to celebrate her son's celebrity and acknowledge her grudging endorsement of "American football." So she announced that as of the very next Thursday, she would comply with Jacobo and have a Tigers' lasagna festival every week of the season. Arnold could invite four different teammates each week, and he would see—they would all play better on Friday.

"Better than what?"

"Better than the boys that won't have my lasagna."

It turned out to be true. And by midseason an invitation for Hitler lasagna had become part of the stew of superstitions in which the Tigers swam. Tie a double knot in your right shoe but a single one in your left, rub your forehead with end-zone grass before each half, spit twice before a fourth down, try to get invited to Hitlers' on Thursday, or at least eat lasagna at home.

Before the first festival evening, Arnold tacked a paper sign across the dining room: GO HANG A SALAMI! I'M A LASAGNA HOG!. He hung the half a salami that was in the fridge from the light fixture over the table. "What's that all about?" his mother wanted to know. "C'mon, Mom, study it up," was all he would say.

The guests arrived at 6, a group of hulking teenagers emerging from one small Nash with the combined mass of seventeen clowns. Ken Hall, center; Joe Bob Arthur, the three-first-name fullback; Darryll Ramey, 215-pound tackle—"Looks like a double portion for that one," George whispered to Anna; and BJ Frame, the first black person to have entered the Hitler house.

"Pleased to meet you."

"Likewise."

"Beer?" George suggested.

"Not on weeknights," Joe Bob explained. "Coach Crews would have our heads."

"Dinner is served," an accented voice announced, and the boys took seats at the table.

"In Italy, we always serve wine. Always. That's why Italian football is better than American football."

"Them's fightin words, ma'am," observed Darryll Ramey, friendly enough, but then again, you wouldn't want to meet him in an alley.

They dug into the red-and-white helpings on their plates.

"Say, Arnold, what's that salami doin hangin up there?" asked BJ.

"What do you think it's doing?"

"Minds me of that effigy hangin up off the light at Broad and Main a couple of years ago. That guy Griffin, hangin there by the neck. Remember that?"

"I do," said Arnold. "But no. It's not Griffin."

"Couldn't get far enough away," observed Joe Bob.

A whiff of racial tension sneaked across the table, which Arnold tried to disperse: "It's not Griffin. It's a salami. What's salami spelled backward?"

"Imalas," the group figured out, some checking the text on the sign.

"That's pronounced 'I'm a las,'" Arnold suggested.

"Hey, wait," BJ called, "I got it. That whole sign reads the same frontways and back! Hitler, you are somethin! That's amazing! But you know what? It still minds me of that Griffin hangin there."

"He wasn't 'black like me,'" Ken Hall observed. "He was black for six weeks."

"Well, that's all past now," said George. "Some of us had to be pushed, but there's going to be integration in Mansfield, and things are already changing. Look at the team."

BJ wanted to be polite. He had been trained to be polite. But he grabbed a teaching moment when he saw it as quickly as he grabbed a hole to run through. Fast on his feet, fast with his tongue.

"You know, Mr. Hitler, there's integration and there's integration. We fit as athletes, but we're separate, still separate. Once we get off the field again? After the game? It's like some magic change happens on Friday nights and we're not just dumb niggers anymore. And then—back to reality."

There was an embarrassed stillness in the room as several people silently agreed.

"There must be an angel passing over," Anna said. "In Italy when the room suddenly is quiet, we say that."

"If you're strong and fast and black in Mansfield," BJ continued, "you're expected to do one thing and one thing only—play football."

"Well, you people are good at that." Joe Bob was trying to ease the subject with a compliment.

"Yup. We simple children of nature are good, unsoiled by civilization, uncompromised, uninhibited, instinctual, filled with compensatory graces—simplicity, naturalness, spontaneity, and high-grade sex."

Arnold thought of Rousseau. The others simply thought it scary.

"You know, America may be the melting pot, but some of us got no intention to be melted."

The angel circled the Hitler house for a long time, long enough for seconds to be passed and eaten, and apple pie à la mode—chocolate and vanilla—Anna's low-profile symbolism. The talk turned to tomorrow's game with Sweetwater. It had been a rich meal for all. For some, overly rich.

Thirteen

The Tigers faced the Abilene Eagles at Geyer Field in their seventh and last home game of the season. A string of victories makes each successive game more manic, the fans more bloodthirsty, the players readier to kill and die. Coach Crews gathered the Tigers in the locker room for the pregame prayer session.

"Our Lord in Heaven, we thank you for this opportunity to show You our stuff in Your name. We know that by giving us an undefeated season, You're challenging us to be more than we thought we could be. We know that with your help, we'll be offering You our thanks—around Your Birthday—at State! Amen."

"Amen," the boys muttered.

"I can't hear you!"

"AMEN!"

"Amen, you said it. Now look, guys, I know this is a tense time for you. The Eagles are 6 and 1, and no pushover. We've studied their games; we know who's who and who can do what. But just having it in your heads will not win a football game. I want you to go out there and knock the snot out of em!"

The answering roar echoed off the metal lockers.

"There's nothing that comes easy that's worth a dime. Matter of fact, I never saw a football player make a tackle with a smile on his face. But that's your special assignment today. I want you to kill em—smiling. A big, toothy, frightening smile, right through your face guards. I want you laughing as you knock em down, laughing as you get up off the pile. I want them to never see a smile, or hear a laugh again—in their entire lives—without a shiver, remembering this day. Show me your canines!"

The effect was grotesque.

"Now, laugh. More! Louder! Keep those fangs out!"

It's hard to laugh while baring your canines. A sweat-stinking, equipment-strewn room of large boys in their underwear, their faces distorted, their throats tense, ejaculating sharp, fierce, rough sounds made even the rusting lockers want to shut their doors in self-defense. Coach Crews felt his own demonstrative grimace fading as he perceived the horror of what he had unleashed.

"All right, that's enough," he yelled. It took twenty seconds for diaphragms to stop convulsing, and another thirty for facial muscles to relax back to prerictal state. "I want you to kneel down, here in front of me. Now repeat after me: We gonna match em physical for physical!"

"We gonna match em physical for physical!"

"We gonna be *more* physical!"

"We gonna be *more* physical!"

"We gonna smile doin it!"

"We gonna smile doin it!"

"We gonna hit em longer! We gonna hit em harder!"

"We gonna hit em longer! We gonna hit em harder!"

"Four full quarters!"

"Four full quarters!"

"Now get dressed, and get out there and beat the hell out of em! With a smile!"

"Yes, sir!"

"I can't hear you!"

"YES, SIR!"

The coach walked out of the locker room muttering, "Sometimes the only way to win an argument is to shoot the guy." He did earn his high salary.

Arnold lay down on his back, his shirt pulled up, allowing the contrast between the cool cement and the steamy air to become a focus for his pregame meditation. One-pointedness. Billie Jo had shown him this relaxation technique. Billie Jo. It was hard to keep his mind focused. Where was she right at this moment? Friday night in Oberlin. Did they even have a football team? How could he not know this?

"Pssst. Hey, buddy. I wanna show you something."

It was BJ, all suited up.

"Another price list for dark meat?"

"No, man. Check this out."

He handed Arnold a note: "Y'ALL WATCH YOUR BALLS, YOU AND YOUR NIGGER-LOVIN FRIENDS. THEY ARE TARGETED."

"Where'd you find this?" Arnold whispered.

"It was in my locker—stuffed in my goddamn helmet. Someone has my combination."

"Shall we show it to Crews?"

"What if he's the one who wrote it?"

"What do you mean?"

"I mean who else has the locker combinations, man?"

"I don't know. Anyone in here could have watched you opening the door."

"You mean you think it's someone on the team?"

"I don't know."

"Oh, shit, man, how'm I gonna play this game under friendly fire?"

"Hey, cool down. We don't know it's somebody from the team. I just said it could be. It's probably not."

"Then who?"

"Let's just have a good game, all right?"

Arnold returned to an intensely difficult relaxation.

Maybe Arnold was shaken. Maybe BJ was spooked. Maybe the Tigers were trying too hard to smile through their fangs. For whatever reason, the opening quarter ended with Mansfield behind for the first time in the season. Arnold had completed two out of seven pass attempts, there had been one interception, and BJ had fumbled his one great catch, blowing a drive that seemed headed for scoring. The score was 7-0. Arnold was clearly tense. For one thing, who else but he was one of "your nigger-lovin friends"? He tried to gather himself, reciting his checklist each time he backpedaled—but he was off, definitely off. He was being rushed. Where was his line?

At quarter break, Coach Terwilliger gathered the team. "OK, men, this is just to get them off their guards. Now's the time for sweet re- demption. We're gonna drive them and everything they stand for straight into the snot-ass ground. Right?"

The answering "Right!" seemed slightly shaky.

At halftime, the score stood 7-6, Eagles, the Tiger touchdown having come with a brilliant breakthrough and sixty-three-yard run by Jim Featherstone, a new black running back, still a junior. The Hitler-Frame action was stabilizing, but for short hits only. During the dueling of the bands, right tackle Darryll Ramey was shot up with Novocain for what was likely a broken hand. "Hang tough," he was told.

The Tigers took the kickoff on their own twenty-five, and Featherstone ran it to the Eagles' thirty-three-yard line. The crowd was stomping, like to break the stands. Arnold took the snap and dropped back to pass, looking for BJ crossing fast to the right, angling for the end zone. From out of nowhere, there loomed above him "Boomer," the 240-pound hunk of Texas beef, four inches taller and fifty pounds heavier than he, famous across the state for sacking and hurting opposing quarterbacks. Before he could be smashed, Arnold retracted his arm, faked a turn to the right, spun out to the left, and found a tiny alleyway. With an alert block by Joe Bob Arthur, and some expert interference, Arnold broke free of the defenders and outran them down the left sideline. "Go, Hitler, go! Go, Hitler, go!" shouted the crowd, and before they could repeat it four times, Arnold hit the end zone, and the delirious crowd hit the roof, which was the sky. George Hitler sat in the stands with a lump in his throat and thought how sweet it was to see his boy do that. God dog, can he run!

Late in the fourth quarter, with a first down at the Eagle forty-seven, Arnold dropped back to pass. He saw flanker Gordon Headlee open, but his touch was too soft, and the ball fluttered, a high fly up for grabs. Interception! His second in the game. The imposter was quickly dumped, but the moment, it turned out, was fatal. With 2:27 left in the game, the Eagle quarterback threw the finest pass of his life, a sixty-two-yard bomb to his left end, to tie the score, 13-all, and the extra point was good. In the last two minutes of play, Arnold led a fierce attack from his own thirty-yard line. After three successive first downs, between short, successful passing and brutal inching-over pileups, the Tigers were at the Eagle thirty-five, third and five. Forty-six seconds on the clock. The wide receiver went into motion, Arnold dropped back to pass, hesitated a split second, faked a handoff to the left, and started around the right, angling low for the end zone. This time Boomer was on him, lunging at him high in a full-speed blitz, smashing his enormous bulk down on Arnold's neck.

Force = mass x acceleration. The force was great.

All right. So what? He got trashed. It was part of the game. Looking up at his assailant as he lay crumpled on the ground, he reached out for a hand—a not uncommon collegial courtesy—and instead met the most hate-filled eyes he had ever seen glowering from the huge face towering over him.

"C'mon, you fuckin pussy, get up. You motherfuckin nigger-lover pretty boy, c'mon, let's see how tough you are."

Sticks and stones may . . .

"Get up, you prick, you goddamn pretty boy, nigger-lovin pussy-prick, Mr. Joe Rah-Rah Nigger-Jew." And he spit. The striped-shirts broke it up. Boomer spit again and lumbered away.

Nigger-lover? Nigger-Jew? The imprecations had spread two hundred miles to Abilene? Was he to have revenge wreaked upon him by every porcine racist in Texas high school football? And what was this "Jew" thing?

As he struggled to get up, helped by his teammates, Arnold vomited a little on the field. Just a little. And he wobbled to the bench to recover, his head between his knees.

"Arnold."

It was Jacobo.

"Arnold, can you hear me?"

"A lot of static, Nonno, a lot of static."

"You want to know what the 'Jew' thing is?"

"What Jew thing?"

"What he called you—Nigger-Jew."

"Who?"

"Signore Galumpho out there."

Ten seconds' silence.

"Arnold?"

"Sorry, my head is spinning."

"In that case, I have a riddle for you: So the old lady says, 'Sam, close the window. It's cold outside.'"

"Here, too, Grandpa. We had snow. . . ."

"And the old man says, 'Nu, and if I close the window, will it be warm outside?'"

"Is that the riddle?"

"No. The riddle is, what color are the speakers?"

Arnold paused to listen to his head hurt.

"From the way you say it, it sounds like a Jewish joke."

"An if ah opens de winda, is it gwine be warm out dere?"

"Grandpa!"

"Well?"

"Colored."

"Can you imagine this story in a Swedish accent, or a French accent, or Deutsch or Italiano?"

"No."

"Colored and Jew, eternal pair, the only two who could make such a story. Why's that?"

"Grandpa, I have a headache. I can't think."

"Think later, then. I have one more question—easy: What's the object of Jewish football?"

"Tell me," Arnold said wearily.

"To get the quarter back."

"Grandpa, that's racist."

"So is Galumpho. *Ciao, bambino.*"

And he hung up.

. . .

When the whistle blew on their first defeat, the Tigers gathered at the fifty-yard line to pray an altogether different petition from the prideful locker room thank-you of two hours earlier. Coach Crews washed the boys in the waters of Babylon as they wept over their impotence in the strange land of defeat. The passer and the receiver had much to bemoan that night.

When BJ got home, he was the one to discover the four slashed tires on the family car.

Fourteen

1968 broke over America with the fireworks of Tet. The United States lost its ten thousandth plane over Vietnam, and the Green Bay Packers beat the Oakland Raiders in the first Super Bowl. In February, George Wallace announced that he would run on a platform of repealing the "so-called civil rights laws" and keeping peace in the streets "with thirty thousand troops with two-foot-long bayonets." In March, J. Edgar Hoover sent a memo to FBI offices concerning the goals of a "Counter-Intelligence Program" that would destroy the coalition of black militant groups and prevent the rise of a "messiah" who might unify any black movement. In April, Martin Luther King, Jr., was killed. One hundred and twenty-five cities went up in flames; Mansfield was not one of them. Robert Kennedy was killed in early June. At the end of June, Arnold Hitler would graduate into this world.

Though he was quite concerned with all he could glean from northeast Texas, the major turbulence of spring was something closer to hand.

In mid-March, between Hoover's memo and King's death, Chris Hoff-mann, Billie Jo's little brother, called Arnold at home.

"Arnie, it's Chris. I gotta talk to you."

"What is it?"

"I can't talk now. Mom might come in."

"Want to meet me somewhere?"

"Tomorrow after school. I get out at 3:15. When do you get out?"

"At 4."

"Good. I'll meet you at Geyer. We'll go for a walk."

Chris had trouble beginning. He and Arnie walked halfway around the track in silence.

"I heard Mom talking to Billie on the phone yesterday."

"So? How is she?"

"I think . . . I think she's got a new boyfriend."

There was a quarter track of silence as they each studied the lane lines in front to them.

"How do you know?"

"Mom kept asking for details about 'him,' and kept saying, 'How wonderful.'"

"Maybe they were talking about a teacher. A professor."

"Why would she ask what his major is?"

More silence.

"So . . . what *is* his major?"

"I only heard one end of the conversation."

"Hm," offered Arnold. "Well, thanks for telling me, Chris. I'm sorry you have to be in the middle of this."

"Hey, Arnie, I want don't want her with some Oberlin pansy."

"Maybe he's on the football team."

"There *is* no football team. That was a reason Billie wanted to go there."

"Really?"

"That's what she said. She wanted to go someplace serious."

Arnold walked home with a lump in his chest and an unwonted ache in his groin. Should he call? No. Too much pressure. Besides, he was afraid to hear it over the phone. Why hadn't she written about it? Maybe Chris was wrong. After dinner, he wrote to her:

Dearest Billie Jo,

Busy week. I've had no time to write. Nor, it seems, have you. It feels like we're losing touch, like there's lots of stuff to say that won't fit onto paper and is too important for the phone. How about a visit like we talked about at Christmas? If you could go half on the ticket, I could fly up next weekend. Game?

I miss you. There's no one in Texas who can replace you.

With much love,

Your AH!

Sometimes she called him her AH! As in Aaaaaahh!—after their semisex, just snuggling down after a night at the movies, the spontaneous hugs with which she sometimes attacked him.

The ticket, fully paid, arrived in the mail from Walnut Creek Travel, Billie Jo's agent in Mansfield. That evening she called and arranged to meet him at the airport. The call was brief. George and Anna thought it was good for him to go, to see a Northern college, to see another part of the country. They expected him to get into Harvard; Oberlin would be good practice. They were right, but not in the way they expected.

Oberlin is to Cleveland as Mansfield is to Dallas, a sub-suburb with its own life, yet heavily dependent on the local colossus twenty miles to the north. Arnold had never been in a plane; he had never been in an airport; he had never seen a large body of water, not even the Gulf: by the time he arrived in Cleveland he was already shaken. He passed up a copy of the *Plain Dealer* left read and folded in the boarding area. His mission was too convoluted to fraternize with such a title.

They drove southwest on Interstate 480, hit Ohio 10, U.S. 20, and 511 west into town. To avoid talking en route, they had an energetic conversation about Valerie Solanas's just-appeared samizdat, not yet *published*-published, "SCUM Manifesto." SCUM. The Society for Cutting Up Men. Billie Jo was living with thirty-four other girls in the Baldwin House Women's Collective, which had access to such things. She was considering a double major in piano and feminist theory. Solanas's extremist position had grabbed her, not as one to embrace but as a defining pole, shifting the controversy into fiercer, more interesting gear.

"The question is," Billie summarized, "whether men are fucked up because of societal conditioning or whether, as Valerie [she called her Valerie] says, they're actually biologically inferior, playing without a full deck of chromosomes."

"What do you mean? We both have twenty-three pairs of chromosomes." He was an A student in biology.

"Yeah. I have two X chromosomes, and you have an X and a Y. You ever see a Y chromosome?"

"Well, no. Have you?"

"I have. They're pathetic little dwarfs. I have a picture of them in my room. Less than knee-high to an X. Not much DNA in there. A lot of stuff missing."

What could he say in the face of this privileged information?

Arnold was having a hard time digesting undigested feminism. This was a new Billie Jo, someone he didn't know anymore but who still called up the old tenderness in him. He tried to offer his feelings for her as an example of something worth saving from Valerie's knife.

"Oh, Arnold, you were always a romantic, and you'll never change. But you're still young. You'll see the truth of what I'm saying. Romantic sentimentalism is the instrument par excellence [she was also studying French] for the socialization of women."

He watched her mouth go up and down. He watched her lips—lips he had pressed with his own, lips he had fondled with his tongue, he watched them forming words and words and words, words that spilled out into a vaguely lettered speech bubble difficult to see against the winter landscape rushing by.

"Only the march of the whole movement can force the deep reevaluation that can enable . . . Sisterhood means the struggle against sexist . . . Radical feminists are not interested at all in so-called powersharing . . . abolish the very notion of power . . . rectify the fundamentally sexist division of labor . . . utopian postrevolutionary society . . . an outright refusal to consider reproduction our duty . . . sexuality a minor need . . . a society without sex—at least sex as it has been corrupted by patriarchy. . . ."

Arnold thought of Grace Pitt, a girl in his own class, a recently blossomed young woman whom he had found himself watching and occasionally thinking melodies about during this year of Billie Jo's absence. He had watched Grace's lips, too, from the front row of the auditorium at Christmas assembly. A flutist's lips, and "Angels We Have Heard on High." He had marveled at the interplay between her lower lip, subtly tensing and relaxing against the instrument, and the more expressive movement of her upper lip, shaping notes and phrases, moist, fleeting, caressing. The tip of an elephant's trunk had passed through his mind, so flexible, with its finger-like projection, but he had put that image aside before it poisoned his falling in love with that dancing, expressive lip. That was his infidelity this year—watching Grace Pitt's lip from the front row. He knew he could never admit it.

Two children, each hiding something large behind their backs. She, her deeds; he, his thoughts. The car turned onto Elm Street and into the Baldwin House lot.

"This is it? This is where you live?"

"That's my room, up there under the gable. My friend Nina just did a study that showed that all of us in this building have our menstrual periods within three days of one another—thirty out of thirty-five."

"Is that different from other dorms?"

They climbed three flights of ornate stairs.

"Co-ed dorms definitely. Guys mess up women. It's scientifically true. Nina discovered it. We call it Nina's Law. Women in small dorms are more in sync; roommates are more in sync than nonroommates. So it's got to be more than the moon. I don't know. Nina doesn't know. Pheromones? Here, this is me."

She pushed open the door to 307.

"You don't lock your door?"

"If you can't trust a sister, whom can you trust?"

"No one's ever been robbed?"

"Not since I've been here. You can put your pack over there."

Arnold wriggled out of his knapsack, a canvas-and-leather affair from his Cub Scout days.

"Where am I staying?"

"Nina's away this weekend with her boyfriend. She said you could use her room."

"So people at Baldwin House still have boyfriends?"

"Some of us. And we're all fertile at the same time."

Was this a provocative comment?

"Can't I stay here, with you? I can sleep on the floor."

"Nope."

"Why?"

"It wouldn't be good."

"Why not?"

"Listen, handsome wheedler, when a woman says no, she means no."

This had actually been a question for him. The standard locker-room teaching had been that when a woman says no, she means yes—or at the very least maybe—and counted on the guy to understand that. Arnold, with his only-one girlfriend and shy but stubborn respect for language, had never pushed too hard on this. But here he was, and here she was, alone together in her single room, away from hometown and home, practically grownups in college, with recent conversation both distancing and sexually explicit. It was a clarifying relief for Arnold to know that that here in Baldwin House, the rules of sexual engagement had not changed.

"Well, make yourself at home."

Arnold took off his loden coat. He had not worn his team jacket because he didn't want to embarrass her about having a younger boyfriend in high school.

"Here, I'll take that."

Billie Jo hung up their two coats in her closet. The room was warm. She pulled off her sweater, and Arnold was stimulated, as he often was, to see the flash of her bare rib cage as her blouse hiked up out of her jeans.

"I love it when your blouse does that?"

"What?"

"Comes up out of your pants."

"You mean this blouse?" And she ripped open all the mother-of-pearl snaps down the front of her Western-style plaid shirt, peeled down to her topless, no-bra current self.

Arnold was flabbergasted. He had seen her breasts before, full, lovely breasts so sensuously contrasting with her thinness. He imagined them often. He had held them in his hands under a loosened bra, or brassiered, under clothing. They were not entire strangers. But here, now, naked, assertive, here-we-are-take-that? And after their discussion about the impossibility of male-female relations? What was she saying? Did "no" mean "come and get it"? What kind of torture was she preparing? What had he done to be punished?

Here was *her* plan: she needed to break the news about Eric. As she thought of the distress it would cause him, she found herself sucked un-expectedly back to the tenderness of last year's love for the special boy she had birthed into manhood. She would have him visit, she would even send a ticket, so she could tell him face to face. But first she would give him a gift, something she had never given him when they were to-gether, a seal of approval for what they had shared, a graduation present worthy of his worthy self: she would make love with him. Then tell him. Such logic makes sense to some.

Arnold's plan was to give her as many opportunities as possible to ad-mit her treachery so he might forgive her. No matter how painful, it would hurt less to know than to suspect. His fantasies would have a local habitation and a name, would be finite instead of infinite. Her confession would set them straight, tighter than before, and more honest. Honesty born of all-around deceit . . . *conjunctio oppositorum.*

She lay back on the bed, scooted over to make room for him, and pat-ted the bedspread at her side as if to say, "Here, boy." She looked at him with love, the older woman about to grant a great and good gift, the only thing she finally had to offer, this body to surrender. Arnold, fully dressed, moved cautiously to lie down where she indicated.

"Wait," she said, and jumped up to turn the bedclothes down. While standing, she wriggled out of her jeans and her panties (for the first time in front of him) and stood there strangely awkward in her nakedness. She laid her pants and underwear on a chair near the bed, her shirt on top of these, and slipped gracefully between the sheets.

"Yaiiiii. Cold sheets," she confided. "Get in here and warm me up."

Arnold undid the laces on the new Durhams he had bought for reputed northern snows and clumsily debooted. He took off his sweater, and then his shirt, and began to crawl into bed.

"Socks and underwear?" she chided. Socks and underwear rubbing against a naked woman?"

"I'm . . . embarrassed. I don't know why. We've never been all naked before."

"Well, now we will be."

He took his knee off the bed, his knee with the long scar, stripped, and gathered up his clothing to place it on the chair on top of hers. She watched him modestly reveal the sculpted product of his training. Her insides did a little dance. As he bent toward her blouse he smelled that old, beloved smell. On that chair was the thing he was most familiar with—the feel and aroma of her clothing—and now he had to leave it behind, to enter into a strange and somehow forbidding world. He slipped clumsily into bed.

"Not yet," she cautioned. "First lock the door."

Yet another in and out and in, a whole-body parody of the larger in and out about to occur.

There they were for the first time, Arnold and Billie Jo, naked, alone, no clock ticking for his arrival home, no Chris or Mom sleeping in neighboring rooms. Now what? A wave of fear passed through him.

"Shall we pull down the blinds?" he asked.

"No one can see in in the daylight. Besides, it's the third floor."

She took his hand, licked his right third finger, and placed the moistened digit between her legs. He knew what to do. He had been there before. In the aft of the fore, he whispered, "I didn't bring a—you know, a rubber." The fact was, he had never owned one. Unlike every other member of the Mansfield Tigers, his wallet was without that annular bulge.

"It's OK."

"What do you mean, it's OK? What if you get pregnant?"

"I won't."

"How do you know?"

"I just know."

"When was your period?"

"Last week."

"Last week? Last week when?"

"Pipe down. I said I know. When a girl says she knows she means she knows." She felt his penis become softer against her. She checked it with her hand.

"Hey, what's with Gabe?" Gabe, the mascot of their secret, who often did seem to have a mind of his own.

"Tell me how you know. That's what's the matter with Gabe!"

"Know what?"

"Know you won't get pregnant."

The jig was up. There was no way Billie Jo could have both her privacy and Arnold's penis inside her.

"I'm on the pill."

"What? Why?"

This, in cooler-headed times, was actually one of the tests he had planned to give her. If she were using birth control, then he would know. . . . But she was not yet ready to spill the beans. Love first, then truth.

"I went to the Health Center for menstrual pain. . . ."

"You never complained about that before."

"Well, things change. There's a lot more academic stress here. I went to the Health Center, and they said that sometimes periods were much easier on the pill. So I thought I'd give it a try."

Gabe was as small as he could get.

"You don't believe me?" she asked.

"I don't know."

"Would I lie to you? Have I ever lied to you?"

"Not directly, but . . ."

Desperate in the face of *satyagraha,* she withdrew under the covers and went down on him.

Scruples or not, suspicion or no, Gabe had no chance against such assault. Though Arnold had licked her several times (third base), this was the first time she had ever returned the favor, and her natural technique was what one might expect from a Chopin nut, though she didn't use her mouth to play Chopin. Gabe stood up like a gold medalist, and Arnold melted at his foot like a blushing bride. It may have been the third floor, on a Saturday afternoon, but their mutual cries were to become, for a short while, the talk of Baldwin House.

The act itself was most complex. Of pleasure there was much, but there was also much that was questionable. Within the surging excitement there passed through each of them excursions into loneliness, into futility. How much they loved! Yet Arnold also sensed something quite impersonal: he could understand for the first time how it was that animals loved. Their words, the few there were, were full of child-like courage, yet they were senseless words, words never spoken vertically but only prone or supine. As inappropriate as an elephant's nose, he experienced a flash of disgust at her dishonesty and then, reflexively, at his own. Her intuitive response to this subtle flux was a fleeting, sure anger at what might be ingratitude, so vulnerable were they both to uncertainty. Neither knew if what they were doing was right. But there they were, and this was a line that by now had to be crossed. At the worst moment, some kind of link snapped in Arnold's being, and his love appeared to him a creature monstrously degraded: with Gabe's head nuzzled up against her cervix, the pressure transformed from the most exquisite fusing into a cruel rite of self-sacrifice. What had he ever seen in her? What had he ever had to do with this Lilith in his arms? All this, furtively sealed within the opium haze of abandon. And at that moment, as if to save him from perdition, she contracted her vagina and squeezed him with her arms, and all that was negative transformed instantly to its opposite, bitterness to bliss, disgust to tenderness, and she began to wonder whether everything might not be again the way it first had been.

Afterward, resting, Arnold was awestruck at the body's autonomy and its mysterious power to disregard the perturbations of the mind. Her first words were, "What would your mama say about this?"

For Billie Jo, the climax was yet to come, and she was sweet-pain unsatisfied. She did love him still, but Eric was here and now, and Arnold was there and then. That was her reality, and it would be hypocritical to deny it.

"I don't have to ask 'Was it good for you?' do I?"

"I suppose not."

"I'll never hear the end of this from the first-floor women."

"You think it was that loud?"

"Are you kidding? Fortississississimo. Trumpets and drums."

"Sorry."

"No, I'm glad you liked it."

"Did you mean it?"

"What?"

"The whole thing."

"Yes."

There was a long silence while Arnold bathed, eyes closed, in the warm light of her response.

"But Arnold . . ."

"What?"

"There's something I have to tell you."

He opened his eyes, and his body stiffened.

"What?"

Long silence.

"What?"

"Give me a minute." She took it. "I'm seeing someone else."

Five seconds.

"Does he know we're doing this?"

"No. He wouldn't understand."

"Is that why you wouldn't let me stay here on the floor?"

"Yes. Eric flipped out when I told him you were coming for a visit. He made me promise you would sleep downstairs. Two floors downstairs."

"Eric."

"Yes. I want you to meet him. You'll like him. I have good taste in men."

"Why did you make love to me if you have a boyfriend?"

"We owed it to each other. Mansfield . . . we couldn't do it in Mansfield. We couldn't do it in Mansfield High—I mean we were high school students—babies. But now I want you to know what you meant to me, how much I loved you."

"Loved?"

"No. I still love you. Couldn't you tell?"

"Yes. So . . ."

"So why Eric?"

"Yes."

"First of all, I love Eric, too. If you two can get past jealousy, you'll see why. So here are two terrific guys. . . ."

"And one is right here with you. . . ."

"And will be right here with me for another four years."

"And one is down in Mansfield, in high school. . . ."

"And will be going somewhere else, not here, for four years. Did you get into Harvard?"

"Not yet. I probably will."

"Arnold, I want to be realistic. We can't sustain a long-distance relationship. Why even try? I want to be present, fully engaged, where I am. I don't want to channel all my energies into letters and phone calls and center my life around the coming of the mail. It isn't real. It's a romantic, sentimentalist notion."

"The instrument par excellence for the socialization of women in a patriarchal society."

"No wonder I love you. You're such a quick study!"

He doffed his imaginary hat. She reached over under the covers and punched him hard in his iron abdominals.

"Hey! What was that about?"

"Nothing." She kissed him. "Just don't make fun of feminism."

"I wasn't. . . . I was just . . ."

"Never mind." She kissed him again and put her head against his hairless chest. "Can you understand?"

"You didn't have menstrual pains. You didn't go to the Health Center for your menstrual pain."

"No. I cannot tell a lie."

They both burst out laughing. A short laugh.

"Oh, my God, what time is it?"

Arnold pulled his hand off her rib cage and out from under the covers.

"Four thirty-five."

"Yipes. Let's get dressed. Eric will be here at 5."

"You invited him to come over?"

"Yes. To meet you."

"I thought this was *our* visit."

"Well, what am I supposed to do with Eric? Stick him in a trunk till you go? This is a visit to tell you the truth, and to give us some closure, and to tell you how I loved you."

"Love."

"Love. And for you to meet Eric and Eric to meet you . . ."

"So that everything falls into place and your life is in order."

"Exactly. Thank you."

"And what about my life?"

"Do you know how many incredible girls there must be in Cambridge? Cliffies? Techies, if you're into women with slide rules. Boston Latin School if you're into robbing the cradle."

"Look who's talking."

"Hey, it worked for me."

She kissed him while he was trying to get his boot on, and the two of them almost toppled over.

"So what have we done since I got here?" Arnold asked, putting on his sweater. "Played a game of chess?"

"No—for heaven's sake! Eric knows we have lots to talk about. He expects me to tell you about him. That's why I was sure he wouldn't come barging in. Let's just get the bed back together and I'm sure there won't be any questions."

"Dishonesty is the best policy?"

"Sometimes. Women understand this. Men are rigid moralists."

"Like all those guys who cheat on their wives."

"That's their patriarchal morality. They're totally rigid about it."

"I see."

"Now, have a seat, and I'll sit on the bed, and we'll have a talk. How are George and Anna?"

"You're going to laugh. Anna got hold of *The Feminine Mystique*—you know this book?"

"It was Martin Luther hanging his theses . . ."

"That's the one. Anna reads the book, and tries to tell George about it, and he gets totally pissed, and they've been fighting for the last two weeks over every little who does what."

"It's a beginning."

"The beginning of what, the end? How many ends do we really want? I don't want my parents to end—their marriage; I don't want *us* to end, or me to end up as scum in some raging manifesto. I'm not scum, Billie, I'm . . . yours, I'm your creation. You licked me into whatever good shape I've got. The shape of AH!"

She stroked his arm.

"But who is AH! without you? Signor Newly Independent, free to go out and conquer? Without you?

"I do still love you. . . ."

Arnold extended a tentative hand. But there was a knock at the door.

Eric and Arnold did not hit it off. They were polite. Arnold did not gain a brother. At the end of the month, he was admitted on full scholarship to Harvard.

In May, Arnold Hitler was listed in the 1968 yearbook as "Most Popular" *and* "Most Likely to Succeed," a double honor bestowed for the first time. He was not universally popular, though. In a series of locker-deposited notes, anonymous but in a female-like hand, he was taunted and abused over his "good looks" and "so-called intelligence."

"Dear Mr. Golden Boy, Sir," they all began.

Can a Claggart be other than male? But would a girl have squirted lighter fluid through the vents and incinerated his windbreaker, his running shoes, and his backpack filled with books?

. . .

The new mall on 287 between Mansfield and Fort Worth had been a defining event for the town. In came Sears and JC Penney, and the old downtown was being ravaged. In came the adult bookstore, and though Mansfield churches raged, it did a thriving business. With McDonald's and Pizzaland, the Backstage Cafe was no more.

The town fathers struggled mightily with the future, some wanting to protect Mansfield's traditional ways, others urging active collaboration with the future. By the end of summer, the developers had won out: ground had just been broken for Mansfield Industrial Park. It felt like time to move on.

arnold stood in his room contem-

plating the late afternoon foot

traffic in harvard yard, a mass

of gaits unknown in texas. it

Harvard

wasn't quite girl-watching, since

long coats, hats and scarves were

rampant against the unseason-

ably chilly wind, and there was

not much "girl" to be seen. still,

it was fascinating. and there was

the possibility sometime, soon

Fifteen

Shadow has light as its past, and brightness, shadow.

Edmond Jabès, *Aely*

Arnold stood in his room contemplating the late-afternoon foot traffic in Harvard Yard, a mass of gaits unknown in Texas. It wasn't quite girl-watching, since long coats, hats, and scarves were rampant against the unseasonably chilly wind and there was not much "girl" to be seen. Still, it was fascinating. And there *was* the possibility sometime, soon perhaps, of "girl." His freshman room assignment had truly been the luck of the draw, perhaps the last farewell of the good Lady as she turned her back on him and strode off into the distance. A second-floor corner room in Hollis Hall, once dorm to Emerson, Bullfinch, and perhaps even George Washington, on bivouac during another war. But the crowning glory was that 135 years before, in the academic year 1833–34, his room, his very room, had been the domicile of the freshman Henry David Thoreau. Just as Arnold was doing now, that good young man must have peered out onto the crisscrossing pathways of the Yard and wondered what he might do to live his life deliberatively. Like Arnold's, that life was etched by solitude. Unlike Arnold's, Thoreau's was a chosen condition.

Into the silence burst James Eliot Saltonstall, his second assigned roommate. His original roomie, Aaron Cohen, had simply disappeared the day before, his clothes gone from the closet, his toothpaste no more, while Arnold was at registration at Memorial Hall. James Eliot Saltonstall, or "Jess," had shown up in the afternoon to unload his gear and meet his roomie, then came in late that night and was gone by the time Arnold woke up in the morning. Now he was back again.

"Hey, Arnie, you're on to a third roomie, I guess. I'm moving out." He made for the closet and pulled his bags off the shelf.

"Oh." Pause. "How come?"

"Talked to my girlfriend this morning and my folks last night."

"And?"

"Well, man, I know this is going to sound ridiculous to you, but they just don't feel it would be appropriate for us to be living together."

"Why is that?"

"Look, man, I like you and all, and if it were up to me, there'd be no problem, but you know, with a name like mine, the whole world is watching."

"Saltonstall? What's wrong with Saltonstall?"

"Wrong? Nothing's *wrong*. My great-great-great-etcetera grandfather was in Hahvahd's first graduating class, don'tcha know, and twenty-two of us have succeeded him, father-son, father-son. I mean, we're, like—*Harvard*, know what I mean? My uncle Lev's president of the goddamn Board of Overseers, know what I mean?"

"I never heard the name Saltonstall before."

"Of course not, you jerk, you're a hick from Texas."

"I suppose different families concentrate in different places."

"Yeah. So anyway, Alice and Mother and Father think I should be living more with my own kind of people."

Arnold felt a flash of anger.

"How did Alice and your parents know what kind of people I am? How do *you* know what kind of people I am?"

"Look, man, I'm sure you're a nice, smart guy, or you wouldn't be here. But it just wouldn't look right to see our names together in print—which I'm sure they will be. Know what I mean?"

"No."

"What do I have to do, spell it out? S-A-L-T-O-N-S-T-A-L-L slash H-I-T-L-E-R? What's wrong with this picture?"

"You tell me."

"Hitler, man, Hitler. I mean, my family stands for America, for everything Hitler was against. Know what I mean?"

"Your family is Jewish?"

There was no answer to such a question. Jess put his knee on the first of his suitcases and fastened it with difficulty on his neatly folded clothes. He started to load an extra-wide garment bag with the suits in the closet.

"But I'm not Adolf Hitler, Saltonstall, I'm Arnold Hitler. Different person, different place, different time. Different ideas."

He sang out these last three syllables in a glorious heldentenor. With gesturing for emphasis.

"Wow, man, you should go into opera."

Arnold went serious. "Different person."

"Yeah, yeah. I knew you'd say that. I knew you wouldn't get it."

"Where are you moving to?"

"Got a nice room with Charlie Lowell over in Mass Hall, right above Pusey's office."

"You're going to live above the president?"

"Sure. Dad swung it for me."

"You have to be quiet?"

"Not after hours."

"Well, good luck."

"Yeah, thanks." He left, with garment bag and valise.

Hitler. It was his father's name—and his grandfather's—and neither of them had had problems, as far as Arnold knew. Until Aaron, Aaron Cohen, yesterday's roommate. Maybe Jewish people . . . But Saltonstall wasn't Jewish.

Arnold was the only freshman in the class of '72 with a year-long single. Even the two Saltonstalls couldn't pull that off. Nor could the three Eliots or the Cabot. The power of a name.

After only three days at Harvard, Arnold was beginning to feel an entirely new sadness in his life. But he could see it clearly: Harvard was home to children with three names: the Thatcher Abercrombie Baxters from Saint Barchester's School, trust-fund babies, suave of dress and manner, if somewhat frayed in the speech department. They'd been to Europe. They knew languages that weren't Spanish or French, even if their families no longer dressed for dinner. They spouted anagramic cognomens like "Jess" as they moved up on their blissful private escalator to Heaven. Then there were the children of industrialists, also at home here, the "brand-name kids," toting their backpacks heavy with security. He had already met chocolate-bars scion Edward Mars. "Eb" Faber was here, he of the yellow pencil empire, and Christina Blakely Kellogg, from Battle Creek, Michigan, a young woman every bit as healthy-looking as her great-grandfather might have wished: she had run "the Boston" last year; she had even placed well. And of course, in Arnold's own hallway lived Lloyd Ratner Ford. Arnold was the sole representative of Mansfield High School. Looking over the directory, he found sixty-two entering freshmen—freshpersons—from Andover.

Well, there *were* sons and daughters whose names he had never heard of (like Saltonstall), bright students from the upper middle class, here to be buffed up and sent out into the world to prove their yearbook designations, the Most Likely to Succeed, succeeding. And finally there were the dweebs, or whatever they were called here, chemistry majors with many As and no girlfriends. God knew who they were, or where they came from.

Here, too, was Arnold Hitler, an open-faced kid with a sophisticated mind, quickly losing his innocence. What group was he in? Perhaps he should put an ad in the *Crimson:* "NOW FORMING: The Harvard Society of Public High School Bumpkins. Contact Arnold Hitler, Corresponding Secretary, Hollis 207." Maybe he'd meet a cohort. Day three was extraordinarily early to be asking the question, "What am I doing here?" Arnold Hitler of Harvard.

As Arnold got into his lonesome bed that evening, Jacobo called. The freshperson in Thoreau's room felt a strong tingling in his left knee and pulled it out from under the covers.

"Arnoldo, *ragazzo mio, come sta?* I tried to itch you earlier, but I couldn't get through."

"It's been a hectic few days, Grandpa. But I got good classes."

"I know all about them." Arnold thought of testing him on the class names and numbers, but he was interrupted: "I've got a question for you: Why is a kugel called a kugel?"

"What's a kugel?"

"You don't know what a kugel is?"

"No."

"Your mother doesn't make kugel for you?"

"If I knew what it was, maybe I could tell you."

"A kugel is a wonderful, delicious pudding, potatoes or noodles, a little sweet. Very nice."

"She made that. Both. Potato pudding. Noodle pudding. I thought it was Italian, like lasagna."

"So if it's Italian, why is it called a kugel?"

"It wasn't. It was called potato pudding. Or noodle pudding."

"That's not its real name, Arnold. Face it, you don't know the answer, Mr. Smarty Pants. Why is a kugel called a kugel?"

"I don't know, Grandpa."

"It's called kugel because it's sweet like kugel, it's thick like kugel, and it tastes like kugel. So why shouldn't it be called kugel? Huh? Why shouldn't it?"

"Grandpa, that's tautological."

"*Giuseppi e Maria!* I knew you would say that. But you think about it. It has to do with Aaron Cohen and Mr. Saltonstall. Give my regards to the mama and papa. *Ciao,* Arnold."

What a show-off! Yet Arnold loved these conversations, and though he had yet to meet his grandfather in person, he felt closer to him than to any other member of his family, his mom included.

Arnold *had* gotten good classes. There was Crane Brinton's History 134A, "Intellectual History of Europe in the Eighteenth and Nineteenth Centuries," about which the Harvard *Crimson's Confidential Guide* for bewildered freshmen declared, "Take it because it *is* History, because it *is* Brinton, and because it *is* Harvard." It met at 9 in the morning, and students were advised to bring coffee and Danish for "Breakfast with Brinton."

He was also accepted into Robert Bales's Social Relations 120, "Analysis of Interpersonal Behavior," a '60s special that had two student nicknames: "Sluts and Nuts" and "The Look at Your Navel in a Group Course." Arnold's section met three times a week, and all students were required to discuss their own hang-ups—academics, sex, relationships, religion, drugs, parents, authority symbols, Vietnam, Harvard—whatever was bothering them—with half the group, while the other half watched the discussants from behind a one-way mirror and discussed in its own half what it observed going on. All students pledged to confidentiality, more honor'd in the breach than the observance. Arnold felt ready for this. But would his classmates be—especially with regard to him?

His third major course was Soc Rel 136, "The Harvard Education Project," a curriculum organized the previous semester by junior Jeff Elman and this semester blessed by the faculty as an official credit course: "Workshops on the University." Course description: "to articulate the things that are wrong about Harvard and plan an ideal university, and to establish a tradition that Harvard doesn't yet have—that of frankly radical self-examination." A good way to plan the path of the next four years, he thought.

In addition, Arnold took the standard beginning French and biology courses and got involved in a series of short, noncredit "experiences" taught by students in the "Harvard New College," an informal experiment in avant-garde education with three-day or week-long workshops devoted to such topics as "Processes for Institutional Change," "Psychology of Modern Alienated Man," "The Limits of Rationality," and "Research and the American University." It was in this last minicourse that he came to know of the existence of Professor Louis F. Fieser, a Harvard chemist, the discoverer and developer of napalm.

Napalm had always seemed a particular horror to Arnold, not just morally or ethically but viscerally, the deepest, cellular feeling of someone who had been burned badly as a child. After noting that it had been developed during World War II right here at Harvard, he decided to look into what might drive a human being to work on such a weapon. What words would that man use to describe it?

When Arnold learned that Professor Fieser was still around, he imagined making an appointment with him to find out what he felt, a quarter century after his invention. To prepare for the interview, he read all he could find of Fieser's writing. Early experiments, Fieser had written in 1941, "convinced us of the potential value of a gelled hydrocarbon fuel that would be distributed over a target area in the form of burning, adherent masses." Words. After months of experiments, Fieser reported on January 29th, 1942, "that a combination of aluminum napthenate with aluminum palmitate, soaps from fatty acids and coconut oils, could easily be incorporated into gasoline to form a promising gel, and we termed this napthenate-palmitate combination a Napalm gel."

Napalm, Arnold found, was used for the first time in flame-throwers during the December 1942 battle at Guadalcanal. Its success was spectacular. One chemical and biological weapons expert wrote, "Unlike the Germans who usually fought well but retreated when the situation became hopeless, the Japanese soldier usually defended his foxhole, pillbox or bunker to the death, regardless of the odds against him. No weapon proved so effective against this type of target as the napalm flame-thrower."

From the beginning, napalm had evaded the Geneva Convention prohibiting poison gas, which had also been designed to rout enemy soldiers from their trenches and "neutralize" them. Like mustard gas, napalm frightened its victims, poisoned and suffocated them, provided it didn't incinerate them first. And while the flame-thrower was at least selective, aimed primarily at military targets, the current firebombs had been deliberately designed for mass destruction and civilian death. All this from the brain of Dr. Louis F. Fieser, Harvard University.

At Widener Library, Arnold found a book of Fieser's from 1964, *The Scientific Method: A Personal Account of Unusual Projects in War and in Peace.* Nothing. Not a flicker of human conscience lighting the pages. Only fire, fuses, incendiaries, arson, sabotage. Even "bat bombs"—small self-igniting canisters of napalm designed to incinerate their finger-winged carriers, and the homes and buildings they penetrate. "Fire,"

Fieser wrote, "conflagrations that engulf and wholly destroy everything in their path . . . lethal and terrifying to both military and civilian personnel"—"indispensable." The "peace" in the title referred to the final chapter, an account of outwitting cats and squirrels at a Fieser-designed bird feeder.

The steam went out of Arnold's project. He could no longer imagine seeking out such a man. The thought of the author's photo, his grinning, bald, mustachioed face, cigarette dangling, dark goggles affixed, in the cockpit of an open Attack Bomber "in which flying was great fun," nauseated Arnold and made him want to run—not so much for protection but to distance himself from a human world that had such creatures in it. But where could he run? If noplace else, he could run to his Soc Rel 120 section.

But his group was strangely silent. So active and vocal about others' most personal problems, they seemed paralyzed here. Once Arnold had proclaimed that he didn't want to be a human anymore, Professor Bales was unable to loosen the lips of eleven listeners in the room. There was something stuck in the class's gears, something unspoken and seemingly unspeakable. Unconditional surrender in the face of human depravity? Despair at Harvard's collaboration? Distrust that official Harvard teachers would honor confidentiality here?

It was none of these. Each of the eleven was embarrassed to admit that his or her advice or discussion would be distorted by irrational loathing of the petitioner himself. "I don't want to get into it—I *can't* get into it—with *you.*"

Arnold, on Jacobo's wise advice, tried to jog his way through the dark, psychic fog that descended along with the brilliant New England fall.

Each afternoon he ran from the Yard down Boylston Street and over the Anderson bridge to Harvard Stadium.

In contrast to Mansfield, football was a relatively minor theme for Cantabridgians. Still, Arnold had been admitted as a "scholar-athlete," and it was part of his own and others' expectations that he come out for the team. He was a freshman boy among senior men—smart senior men who needed no tutoring. There wasn't much for him to do that season but work out. But he found himself emotionally uninvolved in the growing enthusiasm for an undefeated Harvard season and the mounting tension of meeting an undefeated Yale in November.

Arnold mostly played the bench, and though he had been put into several games when Harvard was trouncingly ahead, and though he had done relatively well—eight completed passes out of twelve in three games—Harvard-Yale '68 was definitely a bencher—and a good moment to make decisions.

Saturday, November 23rd, 1968, broke blue, windless, and unseasonably warm. Forty-one thousand rabid and semirabid fans had packed the stadium, and at the end of the first half, the favored Yale Bulldogs were leading, 22-6. In the middle of the third quarter, New Haven fans began waving white handkerchiefs at the Cambridge side either to brush away three outrageous Yale fumbles or to offer a snide "surrender" to the outclassed Cantabridgians. All became clear as a huge banner was unveiled, an artifact prepared beforehand, communicating a sentiment never before publicly aired at any Harvard-Yale game, or at any game, anywhere, that anyone could remember. In six-foot-high red letters, spreading out some fifty feet, the words "FUCK HARVARD" showered their photons on crowd, grass, and sky.

Arnold studied the words carefully. He looked at them in their context—the gorgeous, pillared, classical stadium, built in 1903, now covered in reddening ivy, the first massive structure of reinforced concrete in the world, the first large permanent arena ever built for American college athletics, a field of play designed by members of the Faculty of Engineering, coached by their Art Historian colleagues. It had come to this: FUCK HARVARD. Not even any punctuation. He knew at that moment that his football career, as promising as it might be, had come to an end. He had better things to do.

It must be admitted that, slogans aside, this classical stadium had brought forth a classic game, to be ever remembered by statisticians and fans. With forty-two seconds left to play, Yale was comfortably ahead, 29-13. Frustrated Harvard fans were already leaving the stadium to beat the rush. It was theoretically possible to tie the game in the last forty-two seconds. All Harvard would need was to score two touchdowns and make two conversions. All. Of course, such a thing had never happened, but it *was* theoretically possible.

It happened. Two big Yale penalties and some elegant faking later, the tie point was scored as the buzzer buzzed, and the faithful of Cambridge exploded onto the field. Strangers embraced, full professors danced, while Yale white handkerchiefs soaked up the tears. The *Crimson* crowed: "HARVARD BEATS YALE 29-29." And surely only the prissily numerate would dispute such veritas. Arnold was glad for his team and his teammates, but he watched the whole affair with surreal, serene detachment, like a guest ethnologist from another world.

Home for Christmas. He was greeted as a returning hero and washed with warmth and adulation. The "Psychology of Modern Alienated Man": he felt as warm as a zombie. Hero of what? Of the bench? Of the extended bench? Winner of the Nobody-Wants-to-Room-with-You Award? First recipient of the Your-Problems-Are-Too-Big-to-Discuss-in-Soc-120 Prize? Could he even look his parents and ex-teammates in the eye?

It was a sad and hollow visit. It was hard to explain his Cambridge world to himself, much less to those whose categories could not contain it. He made a valiant effort, but it was acting, pure and simple. When his parents left him at Dallas–Fort Worth International, they seemed contented and proud. Perhaps he *was* a good actor. Good actor, good singer? Maybe he *should* join an opera workshop next semester.

He thought he saw Billie Jo at the McDonald's. He thought he saw another at the pizza stand, and another disappearing into "Women." But none was Billie Joe. She was not on his plane to O'Hare. Billie Jo was in San Francisco with Eric. La Traviata.

Sixteen

He had no time to join an opera workshop that spring. His hours were crammed with Soc Rel 149, "The Radical Perspective," with its nine hundred students, the most crowded course in the university, a hydra-headed slave driver bristling with seminars such as "Imperialism and the University," "Leninism," and "Women and Sex-Role Oppression," and with another hugely attended course, Soc Science 137, Paul Freund's "The Legal Process," a "law for poets" extravaganza almost as challenging, since Professor Freund's notion of poetry included Prosser's *Handbook on the Law of Torts*, a language workout that opened Arnold's eyes even while closing a lot of others'. Then there was Soc Science 155, "Critiques of American Society," a student-run course sponsored, and thus legitimated for credit, by Noam Chomsky, the MIT linguist, in a cross-registration arrangement cleverly constructed within the rules by Harvard Students for a Democratic Society. Chomsky had shown up for the first lecture and was never seen again, as students split into sections of their own choosing. But during that one hour, Arnold was breathless at awe-inspiring genius, hearing this man with his transcendent, irrefutable analysis of political dynamics, completely at odds with official doctrine, yet supported by fact after fact called up, chapter and verse, from what seemed a limitless photographic memory. Here was a man who actually *answered* the questions he was asked, or sent his questioners off to do pregnant, specific research. At that moment, Arnold pledged his troth. He would have more to do with this man down Mass Avenue. His fourth course was second-semester French, a sleeper that would take another two years to blossom.

Though the semester had begun with universal enthusiasm, by Valentine's Day it had settled for most into the infamous Harvard amalgam of poor teaching by poor teachers and even worse application by students bright enough to successfully goof off. Arnold, of course, was always meticulously prepared for his classes and brimming with contributions. But after a while even he held back for fear of dominating the hour and further alienating his already distant peers. He began to hate himself for the very strengths that had brought him to Cambridge.

Outside class, though, there was a gathering of energy. The main focus was obvious: the Vietnam War, that cloud of injustice that hung over every student. Upon graduation, they or their partners would be called on to kill or be killed to serve a master few admired. Some feared for themselves, but most feared for the world, and for a species that would perpetrate atrocity in the name of "freedom." Vietnam was the apocalypse that stood between them and any potential adult life. It was hard to think beyond it.

Yet some students saw Vietnam as symptomatic of the American disease, and their critique was aimed at the whole infection, not just its pustular head. Theirs was a teaching tactic: "Bring the War Home," not just in its turbulence but in its visible, generative connections. Was American militarism ravaging the globe? Then it must also be operative at Harvard. "Smash ROTC." Was American imperialism threatening states and cultures around the globe? Then it must also be operative at Harvard. "No Expansion." Was American racism eating away at black and Chicano peoples across the land? Then it must be operative here at Harvard. Smash ROTC! No Expansion! and Black Studies! would become the three big issues in the spring of 1969, Arnold's second semester.

Seventeen

At noon on April 9th, 1969, Harvard Students for a Democratic Society took over the administration building.

The first objective was to secure the second-floor Faculty Room as Command and Control Center. The huge formal chamber, with its grand mahogany table, its black leather chairs, and its portraits and busts of Harvard luminaries who looked as if they'd never made a mistake in their lives, was sprinkled with leaflets and supplies and baptized "Che Guevara Hall." The windows were thrown open, and announcements of the new order were hung from the windows onto the Yard: "FIGHT CAPITALIST RUNNING DOGS," "ABOLISH ROTC—STOP HARVARD EXPANSION." Building-wide, the deans were asked to leave their offices.

"We request that you leave the building, sir; it is for your own protection."

"You have no right to be in this building. As an officer of this university, I am ordering you to leave or face severe discipline." *Fight fiercely, Harvard, fight, fight, fight!*

The student response became more succinct: "Actually, sir, we've already taken this building. Now get the fuck out of here."

It was a (so far) bloodless revolution, Harvard style: by 3 o'clock, SDS was securely inside University Hall while being burned in effigy outside by belligerent Techies from MIT and their Harvard subalterns. The Mem Church bells were pealing out dissonant carillon while from open dorm windows the Beatles' "Revolution" vied with Bach's Fourth Brandenburg for the decibel award, and competing bullhorns from Che Guevara Hall educated and exhorted the burgeoning crowd.

Arnold was back in his room at Hollis, watching the scene across the old and into the New Yard through the gap between Thayer and University Halls. He had finished his French class at noon and emerged from Boylston just in time to see the crowd streaming toward him from Mem Church. He ran past Widener and was swept into the movement toward the ad building. Shoulder to shoulder, Arnold felt a pleasant, animal warmth in the cool spring air. So, it seemed, did others, for the crowd was packed more tightly than it had to be in the huge space of the New Yard. Arnold looked at the faces surrounding him, so earnest, so intelligent. There was the intense, blond Cliffie he had noticed last semester. There was Ed Terfel, the running back. There was that girl from his "Law for Poets" class, the one who always had good things to say. Yet for all their individual distinction, this was a press of equals. No matter that they were the elect. No matter that each was the cream of his or her particular crop. Now they were just heads, just hips, just arms and feet and jackets, and what they were each thinking or feeling was lost in the larger demand for justice that they, en masse, implied.

Once the leaders had penetrated the orifices and the path had been blazed, Arnold could feel his gridiron instincts kick in. He saw the tiny holes to wiggle through. He could make an end run around to the left, leap over the side of the railing and up to the top of the steps. But he didn't. He preferred to be just one of the mob, pushed along, not pushing, since this best reflected the confusion he brought to the event.

Atoms in a gas are not asked their opinions. But in the six minutes it took him to be squeezed across the yard and up the stairs to the green door, he had decided to go inside and see what it felt like. Surely this would be an experience as valuable as classes or reading.

At the entrance, he was thrust back into the reality he had already tasted too often: "Unh-uh," said the bullhorned keeper of the green door. "Not you, Hitler. That's all we need—for you to get interviewed."

"What do you mean? I'm going in!"

"C'mere, c'mere. . . ." The bullhorn pulled Arnold off to the side. "Hold the door," he ordered a comrade. "Hey, man, whose side are you on?"

"Yours. I mean—I don't know. I want to see."

"Can't you see the caption, man? 'Hitler and the Storm Troopers.' That's all we need. They'll pick you right out. We got nothing against you, but we can't have you in here, understand? Do us a favor, buddy, all right?"

Arnold jumped over the railing and sat down on the grass, his back against stone. He watched the stars and the starry-eyed pushing on up into the building, and he watched others selecting themselves out, turning away before the steps, off to the side to play supporting roles. None of them was named Hitler. No one had minded in Mansfield. No one had said a word. Ever.

He thought back to his first day on campus, six months before. His mailbox—alone among Hollis mailboxes—contained a note from the dean of freshmen, asking him to report to the office before he did anything else. Dean F. Skiddy von Stade wanted to let him know that the College appreciated the delicacy of his position (what delicacy? what position?) and would do everything it could to protect him against reactions to his name. He was given the choice of not listing himself in the student directory. "I figure it's something I'll have to live with and accept," he told Dean von Stade. "I've never had any problem before."

"As you will. There may even be some good points to your name," the dean reflected.

"Like?"

"Oh, I don't know. Say you see a girl on a bus and introduce yourself, and you don't see her again for a while, and then one night you call her and say, 'This is Arnold Hitler.' She'll probably remember you." Arnold had never thought of that.

At the dean's request, the *Crimson* left him alone, though employees of both the Coop and the Harvard Trust Company looked up when he submitted applications for accounts.

There had been student protests all winter and spring: San Francisco State on January 6th; Brandeis on January 8th; San Francisco Valley State and Swarthmore, both on January 9th; Berkeley on February 4th; the University of Wisconsin, February 12th; CCNY and Duke, February 13th; Rutgers on February 24th—Arnold had followed the *Crimson* stories with interest and was certain that Harvard's time would come. But SF State had been closed down for three weeks. The home of San Mateo Junior College's dean had been firebombed. Rice's president had resigned after a rally of thousands of students and faculty, and CCNY's president left after an auditorium had been burned. Police had been called to Howard, Penn State, and U Mass. At Wisconsin, Arnold recalled, fistfights had broken out, and the governor had called out two thousand National Guardsmen with bayonets and tear gas. But here, it seemed more like a party. The atmosphere had gone from militant to gay. People were throwing things up to colleagues in Che Guevara Hall, and the occupiers were flying out leaflets in the form of paper airplanes.

"Hey," Arnold yelled at a kid he knew from Hollis who had just hung down and jumped from a first-floor window, "where you going?"

"Got a volleyball game," he answered. "I'll be back in a couple of hours."

And yet Arnold, only he, could not go in.

He stood up, sad, confused, and angry, and moseyed around the edges of the crowd. There was the son of that Tennessee senator—Gore, was it?—dressed to kill as usual, also standing apart.

"What do you think of all this?" Arnold asked.

"Well, I have sympathy for the cause," Al Gore said, "but not for the tactics. And there's something off about their choice of target. I guess Harvard is most convenient, so that's what they chose, but . . ." He shook his head.

Arnold nodded. "Yeah. See you."

"See you. Thanks for asking."

A conference of Southern boys.

Arnold walked over to watch the action from the Widener steps. Sitting halfway up, he felt the winds of history blowing hard from the stacks at his back, while gusts from the future whipped at him from the front. It was a strangely expansive feeling that hollowed out his solar plexus while simultaneously weighting him with a sickening, internal ball of lead. He watched the high school students walking home come upon this unexpected circus with delight. He saw an angry group of older students come in at the east gate and burn an effigy labeled "SDS." Effigies, burning effigies. He thought he had left that behind. But the tiny lynch mob seemed completely out of place in the general gaiety. People took little notice. Those who might have been enraged were all inside, debating tactics.

By 3:30, the crowd had grown so large that people had difficulty moving around. The New Yard was full, and people began to spill over into the Old Yard, Arnold's Yard. Students were sipping cold drinks and eating ice-cream cones. At 4, the libraries in the Yard were closed. Hundreds of befuddled scholars, many of whom had not even heard about the occupation, came stumbling out into the sunlight to discover things in heaven and earth not dreamt of in their philosophies. With this outpouring from the Widener doors, Arnold, too, stood up to go. As he walked to his dorm between Weld and University Halls, he heard Franklin Ford, dean of the Faculty of Arts and Sciences, announcing that the Yard would be closed until further notice. On one of the great trees in the Old Yard hung a spray-painted sheet: "YEAH, BUT IF WE END THE WAR, HOW DO WE END SOCIETY?"

At that very moment, police and administration officials were meeting in the basement of Grays Hall, not a hundred yards from the action, planning a bust. They agreed to gather at four the next morning in Memorial Hall.

Eighteen

L ate that night, while Arnold dreamed disturbing dreams, one Mass Ave gate was unlocked. In the darkness, unmarked cars unloaded men in trenchcoats, one at a time, into the Yard, while other plainclothesmen patrolled the perimeter, attempting to stop students from climbing over walls into the locked area.

At 4 A.M., a lookout spied the swarm of police cars converging on Memorial Hall. At 4:07 SDS rang the fire alarms in all the freshman dormitories around the Yard, and simultaneously in the row of great river houses and in the Radcliffe Quad. It was like a Cambridge Tet Offensive. Who would have thought SDSers knew all the switches or could even synchronize their watches? Arnold leaped out of bed and threw open one of the windows facing the Yard. No smoke.

Like other students, he quickly sensed the meaning of the bells. But unlike those who chose to attend the show in bathrobes and slippers,

Arnold dressed, put a water bottle and extra handkerchief in his coat pocket, and waited at his window for the first signs of action.

At 4:20, two hundred municipal police from Boston, Cambridge, and Somerville arranged themselves at the long tables inside Memorial Hall as if to take some extraordinary Civil Service exam. It was the final tactical review. Simultaneously, two hundred state troopers gathered from all over Massachusetts were leaving the State Police Armory in Boston with their marching orders. At 4:45 both groups lined up behind Memorial Hall, and most officers removed their badges and nametags—an ominous sign. Off to campus they went, on foot, by car, and in six large buses.

The vehicles burst into the Yard at 4:55. The area around the cars and buses was cordoned off as state police in boots, jodhpurs, and baby-blue riot helmets took their positions. The municipals were to clear the stairs and the area around University Hall. The troopers were to go in and "clean the rats out of the building." Mayor Sullivan was there, smiling to the press, shaking hands with various police brass who had arrived to solemnify the bust. President Pusey surveyed the scene through binoculars from the second floor of his house.

The plan was executed quickly. Within two minutes, the municipal police swept across the front of the building as suburban police advanced on the south steps. Police from Cambridge, the Boston Tactical Force, and the Metropolitan Department of Corrections headed for the north steps. Some of the officers broke ranks, charging students camped at the foot of the stairs or pulling themselves up on the railings to club students in the middle of the crowd. One tall, energetic ex-basketballer stood at the side of the stair rails and leaped into the air again and again, swinging his club at a different student at the top of each leap in a vicious series of slam-dunks.

By 5 A.M., University Hall was cordoned off and its occupants isolated. "Pusey must go! Pusey must go!" the thickening crowd chanted outside the police line. Arnold, crossing the Old Yard, encountered hundreds of students standing with arms outstretched shouting, "Sieg Heil" at the line of police. "You, too, Hitler!"—an obiter dictum from somewhere in the crowd as Arnold skirted around the northern perimeter into the New Yard. "Fascist pigs! Fascist pigs!" was the competing chant out of the west. The police shouted back: "Long-haired Commies!"—which would have sounded more stupid and pathetic without their guns, clubs, and gas.

Using a battering ram, the police charged the northeast green doors. Arnold winced as he saw the painful splintering of ancient wood. It was law-enforcement happy hour. A sea of baby-blue helmets rushed upstairs, and within minutes, students were seen screaming and leaping from first-floor windows to escape the onslaught. On the lower floor, police were herding the students into tightly packed groups, macing and clubbing them en masse. Others stood at the two doors to attack the already ejected or drag them out by the hair. Arnold watched as a lovely young girl at the top of the northeast stairs was pushed out the door, dazed, with blood running from her forehead. A state trooper stepped up, and like an artist evaluating a profile, he placed his left hand on her shoulder and steadied her chin with his thumb. Then, with his free hand, he raised his long club high over her head and brought it crashing down. The force of the swing nearly lifted him from the ground. The girl screamed, blood cascaded down her face, and she slumped like an exhausted lover into his arms. Having thus had his pleasure, the trooper discarded the limp body and kicked it over to the railing side of the steps where it would only minimally block his next conquest. Arnold broke through the police line and ran to drag her to safety. Bad move. First instruction to any would-be rescuer: never put yourself in jeopardy trying to save someone else—two bodies are twice as bad as one.

He was grabbed by two burly Cambridge cops—incarnations of Boomer—but this time there were no referees. He was hit in the head, neck, and back. After he went down, he was kicked in the kidney and left among the crowd. He crawled ten yards away from the action. First down: he was not among the 196 students who, by 5:25, had been loaded onto MTA buses marked "SPECIAL."

The law was gone by 6:15, leaving a Yard littered with trash and rutted by police vehicles. Blood ran from the top of the northeast steps down to a pool on the pavement below. Che Guevara Hall, baptized only seventeen hours before, capitulated in less than half an hour. Proud of their work, the police claimed that the bust had been carried out with "clinical precision." Arnold made his painful way over to Student Health Services at the Holyoke Center, where twelve docs were trying to repair the university's stand on the takeover, now etched into student flesh.

An afternoon meeting had been called for Sanders Theater. Fifteen hundred students showed up and unanimously voted for a three-day boycott of classes. One radical sociologist challenged the meeting to understand and even approve of the police response. What Pusey had done by calling in the police, he said, was to release at least two hundred years of well-justified town-gown hatred. "Many of the cops who busted University Hall were the sons, nephews, cousins, and grandsons of all those Irish immigrants who had sailed to New England in the 1850s and then found doors at Harvard reading 'NINA.' You know what NINA means? No Irish Need Apply." (Hisses in the audience.) "And this morning, at last, the club-wielding descendants of these folks were offered the opportunity to bash in a few of our snotty heads. You're for the working class? This is what you've done to them. You know who's with you? The rich folks. The rich and educated. You know who's against you? The entire population of East and North Cambridge." Such was the devastating lesson for the day.

But the afternoon's most daring and demanding speech came, in quiet tones, from Alexander Gerschenkron, professor of economics, a conservative European refugee deeply suspicious of all movements for human betterment. He was recognized to speak from the floor. He looked small and formal and old. He spoke quietly; students strained to hear.

"There is a fairy tale by Hans Christian Andersen, called 'The Most Unbelievable Thing.' I will briefly convey it. There was a kingdom, Anderson tells us, and in the kingdom there was a king, and he had a princess, and he was interested in the progress of Arts. And at a certain point he announced that he would give his daughter in marriage to the man who would accomplish the most unbelievable thing."

Sanders Theater had never been so hushed.

"There was huge excitement and tremendous competition in the land, and finally, the great day came when all those prepared works were to be presented for judgment. There were many marvelous things, but towering high above them all was a truly wonderful thing. It was a clock produced by a handsome young man. It had a most wonderful mechanism, showing the time, the calendar back into the past and even into the future, and around the clock were sculptured all the great spiritual and intellectual figures in the history of mankind. And whenever the clock struck, those figures performed most gracefully.

"And everybody, the people and the judges, said that yes, to accomplish a thing like that was most unbelievable. And the princess looked at the clock and then looked at the handsome young man, and she liked them both very much. [Laughter.] And the judges were just about to pronounce their formal judgment when a new competitor appeared. He, too, carried something in his hand, but it was not a work of art. It was a sledgehammer. He walked up to the clock, and with three blows he smashed the clock to pieces. And everybody said, 'Why, to smash up such a clock, *this* is surely the most unbelievable thing!' And that was how the judges had to adjudge.

"Now, consider," he concluded, "Harvard University, like the clock in the story, is a frail and fragile creation, and you must beware that this wonderful work of art not be destroyed, or the guilt will be yours."

He sat down. There was murmur and confusion. The SDS moderator tried to put things right again. "With all due respect to Professor Gerschenkron, we must also note that democracy, too, is a fragile creation, and that police truncheons are more like sledgehammers than statements of principle." There was applause, but not wild applause. The professor's story still reverberated.

Nevertheless, resolutions were passed: "The police should not be brought onto the campus again." "There should be immediate steps to reconstruct university governance so as to include members of its entire community." "President Pusey must resign." Arnold put up his hand in assent to all three. The Harvard strike had begun.

Like many others, Arnold realized he could use the strike to try to make some new friends—especially women. Pickup lines floated around the Yard like cottonwood fluff in spring. Shaggy men and long-haired Cliffies were parading with armbands and silk-screened clothing that invited questions and comment. On Saturday morning, a lovely young woman was hanging a printed poster on the Hollis door as Arnold was coming out.

"Whatcha got for me this morning?" he asked in his most winning manner.

"Check it out." She held the placard up against her ample chest.

strike for the seven demands strike because you hate cops strike because your roommate was clubbed strike to stop expansion strike to seize control of your life strike to become more human strike because there's no poetry in your lectures strike because classes are a bore strike for power strike to smash the corporation strike to make yourself free strike to abolish rotc strike because they are trying to squeeze the life out of you strike

"Did you make that?"

"Yeah."

"Wrote it and lettered it?"

"You like it?"

"It's great."

"Something for everybody, wouldn't you say?"

"That's exactly what I'd say."

"Want to help me hang these others? Every door in the old Yard?"

"I'd love to. What's your name?"

"Liz."

"Hi. I'm Arnie."

"Hi."

"You're at Radcliffe?"

"Mmm. In Cabot."

"Where's that?"

"Up at the Quad. You must be a freshman."

"Yup."

"Yup? Where'd you get that drawl? Mississippi?"

"Texas. Mansfield, Texas."

"Handsome cowboy, huh?"

"I don't know about handsome. And I'm not a cowboy. There aren't many herds in east Texas."

Now, this was a conversation that might have gone somewhere. She seemed pert, and smart, and interested—even in a freshman. And political. And sexy. The next exchange was Arnold's fault. As a chess player, he might have foreseen the result.

"Liz what?" he asked. It was a reasonable question.

"Aronson. Elizabeth Fay Aronson, s-o-n, in case you want to look me up in the directory. There's another Liz Aronsen, s-e-n."

"Jewish?"

"Is that a WASPy name? A pushy New York JAP."

"You don't look Japanese."

"Ha. Ha. Very funny."

"No, really. You don't."

"I'm not Japanese. I'm a Jewish American Princess. They don't have JAPs in Texas?"

"I never heard the term."

"And you? Are you Jewish? A Texas, goyish-looking Jew?"

"My grandfather is Jewish. On my mother's side."

"What's his name?" They were hanging Holworthy, on the north end of the Yard.

"Giardini."

"Don't give me that. There are no Jews named Giardini."

"No, in Italy there are, I swear. That's his name. Jacobo Giardini."

"What's your name? Your last name?"

The conversation went downhill from there. When he called her on Saturday to see if she wanted to go to a movie, she was busy.

On Monday, the 14th, the first mass rally was held at Soldiers Field, a.k.a. Harvard Stadium, a venue with which Arnold was deeply familiar. He called Liz late Sunday and asked if she'd like to go to the rally with him, but she was going as part of a contingent of Radical Radcliffe. Thanks, but no thanks.

For a gathering of ten thousand plus, the rally was remarkably orderly, a kind of Athenian democracy-cum-amplification. Parliamentary procedure was loosely observed, obscenity was conspicuously absent, and the debate was about ideas. It was like a crowded, high-IQ seminar in rebellion. By the announced 1 P.M. time, a crowd was starting to fill up the great horseshoe of the stadium. The weather was warm and sunny, perfect for such an event. A podium had been set up a few yards behind the end zone at the closed end.

At the stadium entrances various groups were distributing leaflets. Strike opponents now had their own insignia: a white cloth ribbon with the words "Keep Harvard Open" printed in red. The only potentially violent event of the day occurred at 1:30, before the session began. The black organization, AFRO, arrived as a group and marched to the top of the stands. Once having claimed a section, they began clapping rhythmically and chanting, "Hey, hey! We're all on strike!" From down near the field, a loud voice shouted, "Back to the trees, jungle bunnies!" and there was just a moment in that noisy crowd when an angel, a suspicious angel, passed over. But the crowd recovered its buzz without further incident, and the culprit sank back into the sea. TV cameras panned, and helicopters chopped back and forth.

There were seven package proposals for this crowd of ten thousand to vote on that covered the entire political spectrum, including one conservative student condemning the University Hall occupiers and urging their firm punishment. Lance Buhl, an instructor in history, with no political affiliation and thus acceptable to all sides, gaveled the crowd back to order. "Ladies and gentlemen," he pleaded, "we can at least listen to unpopular ideas. We don't have to agree with them. Give him a chance." And they did, though his proposal received few votes. With some dickering among proposals, a consensus was arrived at: Harvard belonged to the students and faculty, not to the Corporation—or to SDS. They adopted the SDS demands on ROTC and No Expansion—as amended. An indefinite strike was narrowly rejected. As the sun went down, the crowd agreed to strike for three more days and then meet again to take stock.

Arnold felt weary. He was not alone. Unending meetings and discussions lasting into the wee hours had exhausted everyone. The frantic politics of the first few days seemed to settle back into a wait-and-see stance. Picketing, marching, and demonstrating could no longer attract large crowds. Political leaflets, still being distributed in dining halls, seemed to wind up more in the trash than in student rooms for study. Class attendance was increasing. By Friday of the following week, one "radical" told a *Crimson* reporter, "All I want to do is return to a normal schedule, even if it means having a fascist university." This is the way the world ends.

Politics for the rest of spring semester consisted of two SDS mill-ins, a plan-in, a shove-in, and several shout-ins—all marginal as far as most students were concerned. One SDSer summed it up: "If nothing else, the strike has vastly increased the knowledge of people about how to make paper airplanes." A useful skill.

The crowning co-optation of all the revolutionary passion was an end-of-semester ROTC ad in the *Crimson* that invited sophomores to a get-acquainted, free-beer party. The graphic depicted a bearded, long-haired radical, with generic armband and beer in hand, glaring nose to nose at a uniformed, crew-cut recruit, similarly beveraged, who glared back. The text proclaimed: "At the very least a sudsy confrontation while confirming or dispelling your suspicions is still a better bag than no suds at all."

Nineteen

Arnold went home for the summer to work for Joe Dobbs at Best Used Cars on North Main. Joe was loyal to old Tiger stars. For the summer, he could boast not only of last year's quarterback on his lot, he could even wow the folks with his new Harvard-by-association status. It was a smart hire. He saw 20 percent more customers than usual between June and August, and sold 10 percent more cars. But it was not a good summer for Arnold. In fact, it was the last summer he was to come home—for after summer of '69, there was no more home.

Weaknesses in his parents' relationship had been appearing slowly in the fabric of their lives, like wrinkles on aging skin. There had always been the danger of misunderstanding, for although Anna spoke excellent English, still it was not her native tongue. Nor was Texas her native culture. In difficult times, neither George nor Anna could express or truly understand the subtleties of feeling, the interstitial contexts of the other.

They had survived for twenty-one years by extrapolating the initial drama of their love. But during the first year of Arnold's absence, two things changed critically: there was no bright son to hold them together by washing out their shadows, and the wave of post–Betty Friedan feminism Arnold had joked about with Billie Jo had attained tsunami status, swamping the Hitler-Giardini house and its two remaining inhabitants, eating away their bonds.

Just after Arnold had left for Cambridge, Anna began subscribing to Jo Freeman's *Voice of the Women's Liberation Movement*, the very earliest radical women's newsletter. It was the beginning of the middle of the end. The end of the end came shortly after Arnold's summer sojourn. Each parent had used him as a "neutral" ear to complain about the other. In a series of "walks" and "talks" as portentous as any telling of "the birds and the bees," Arnold was let in on the problems at home.

His father took a man-to-man approach.

"I have to tell you your mom and I are not getting on as well as we were."

Arnold nodded. "She's not happy."

"You think men are happy?"

"Some. Some not."

"What's wrong with her that she can't be happy she's living in America instead of starving in Italy?"

Arnold's own experience with women hadn't been that great either. Billie Jo was now off in Europe with Eric, experiencing Art through the Ages and some likely more irritating pleasures. It was as if his father had read his mind.

"She gonna dump me the way Billie Jo dumped you?"

Arnold's body twitched involuntarily. A small twitch, restricted to midtorso, but enough to be noticed by both father and son.

"Sorry," George said.

"That's OK."

"What I mean is, is she going to get some kind of job and make more money than me? Hell, you'll lose your scholarship if we make too much. I tell you, son, if everyone were like your mother, this would be one hell of a world. . . ."

"A lot of families . . ."

"Hey! There's nothing wrong with our family. We made *you*, didn't we? Someone has to wear the pants in the house. Who should it be? Her?"

Arnold heard him out. George's assessment: "It's good to have someone to talk to."

There was a similar tête-à-tête with Anna, this one over tea one rainy Sunday afternoon while George was out for a petulant walk. She told him about her big new activity—a women's support group at Stella Rawson's, which after five meetings had broken up.

Too depressing for everyone.

"Why?" Arnold asked.

"Well, we all agreed we were living out some kind of myth that wasn't true for any of us. None of us."

"What myth?"

"*The* myth. You know—that being a wife and a mother and a housewife is the best thing in life. We all felt oppressed by it. We all tried to tell our husbands—well, not Ed Rawson, of course, but the others—and none of us could run to first base."

"Why not at least stick together and talk about it with each other?"

"What broke up the group was realizing that the myth was true, but it was no accident. After one meeting it all became clear—to all of us at once: it didn't matter if we got other jobs or read better books or started a garden club. Our husbands would still be *gli fascisti*, and if things were going to change we would have to get rid of them."

Her Italian "away with you" gesture upset the teacup into her crossed-leg lap.

"Aiiii!"

Arnold jumped to help, brushing away the steaming liquid with a once-burned hand, tibial hardness under the softness of cotton.

"Are you OK? Did you get burned?"

"The wonder of plastic," she said, displaying her leg, coy yet scientific. Arnold brought paper towels from the kitchen and poured her more tea.

"Leaving our husbands," Anna continued when all had settled down. "That's what scared us. All of a sudden, your father was 'the enemy.' It felt too—I don't know—dangerous, or too mean to be talking that way. So we just one by one stopped coming."

Mother and son sat together in the gray afternoon light, their thoughts separate but entwined.

"This may sound strange," Anna said, "but I think it's symbolic he blew my leg off."

"Mama . . ."

"He took out his gun, or he threw some explosive in between my legs, and boom, and then I could never get around again. He had to carry me. Isn't that symbolic?"

"He didn't know you were there. He didn't know it was you. . . ."

"He still doesn't know I'm there. He still doesn't know what is me."

They were both silent, eyes on their tea—though there were no leaves to be read. The wall clock had never ticked so loudly.

"I haven't told your father yet, but someone in the Romance Languages at UT Arlington is on sabbatical starting in the fall, and Ed Rawson thinks he can get me a job to teach Italian. Then when she comes back, we will see."

. . .

Then it *was* the end. A week after returning to Cambridge, Arnold found a letter from both Mom and Dad in his box at Eliot House advising him of Anna's move to Arlington, and assuring him that they both loved him, and that everything would be all right.

Twenty

Eliot House on the Charles. In the early '30s, in the midst of the depression, Harvard was given a $13 million gift from a Yale grad: such is the orneriness of the very rich.

President Lowell, he who condemned Sacco and Vanzetti to death, decided to counter the impersonality of his large institution with a system of twelve upper-class houses, each designed as a self-contained college community, with its own library, dining hall, and small teaching staff, as in the English system. Almost all sophomores, juniors, and seniors chose to live in the houses as part of the Harvard Experience.

Arnold had prioritized Eliot House the previous semester upon hearing that forty Eliot House seniors had planned to burn their diplomas at graduation—a kind of team spirit that sounded attractive. If they actually did it, they did it in private, for that was the last Arnold heard of the matter. In any case, he was given his first choice.

Most residential houses are named for Harvard presidents, with the exception of Leonard Hoar, whose overbearing attitude and propensity for having students flogged made him increasingly unpopular and engendered the *first* Harvard strike: in 1674 the entire student body walked out of the college. President Hoar resigned the following year. There would be no Hoar House.

But there was an Eliot House, named for the illustrious Charles William Eliot, who with his forty years of office (1869–1909), and his three first names, had elevated Harvard into an institution of international renown, adding science to its traditional liberal arts curriculum. It was a huge Georgian palace on the north bank of the Charles, massive, wood-paneled, with endless hallways of small student rooms. From his fifth-floor dormer window facing the river (specifically requested so he could run the stairs often in the day), Arnold could hear the frequent crashes on Memorial Drive below and the cars honking at students as they jaywalked across the Anderson Bridge. He could also see across the river to Harvard Stadium, the never-beloved country.

Each of the Harvard houses cultivated its own personality, and Eliot was known for its handsome men and beautiful women, its plays, its voluntarism, its hatred of officialdom and officialese, its love of madness and wild things, its sponsorship of mayhem and art, its May Rites, and its oddball population of jocks, wonks, and hermits. Young Theodore Kaczynski had once lived at Eliot. There was a violist in the room next to Arnold's, a monosyllabic Raskolnikov with a large, illegal collie, fed up with other humans and devoted only to his barking dog, math, and music. Arnold came to know the solo Bach Suites well. He also came to hate collies. He never did find out the violist's name.

The master of Eliot house was Alan Edward Heimert, professor of American literature, a solid man with a big, blustery voice and an unswerving love for his students. Having grown up a working-class kid in Chicago with a love for books and learning, he recognized in Arnold another refugee. He was a specialist in American religion, and his own religion was Harvard. Nevertheless, he was enthusiastic in advising Arnold to head down Mass Ave to cross-register at MIT for Chomsky's linguistics course. Heimert would guarantee it: Arnold would find exciting things going on in the basement of Building 20. The other big boys at Eliot, Harry Levin from comp lit and Dante della Terza and Steven Gilman from Romance languages, all agreed. So that very afternoon, Arnold jogged the four miles downriver to Kendall Square and loomed conspicuous among the Techies swarming the Great Court. The woman at the registrar's office made him spell his last name.

He had of course met Chomsky the previous spring during Soc Sci 155, had hung out after the lecture to drink in the freshness of such intensity. Chomsky was, in the poet and novelist Jay Parini's words, "Reason's earthly embodiment," a "sober fanatic" whose sole task on earth seemed to be calling a spade a spade—regardless of the fury such naming might bring. Arnold knew nothing other than his fame as a notional revolutionary. But he wanted Chomsky's light for his path.

When Bontsche the Silent, newly arrived in Heaven after a brutal life, was asked what reward—anything, anything at all—he would like for his earthly forbearance, he lowered his eyes and bashfully asked for a hot roll with real butter. The genius of Peretz. Arnold, too, had formulated such a request, silly, far too small. During his jog down Mem Drive he knew he was making this pilgrimage for one thing and one thing only: to better understand the consequences of his name. What *was* it about these six letters, worn by him, and not by any predecessor, that had the power to turn smart people dumb, kind people mean, warm people cold? And why in Cambridge and not in Texas? And how might he work with this, how translate this word into some more appropriate language that it might cease to poison? In-two-three-four, out-two-three-four. It was only September, but that afternoon, the wind rode in cold from the river. He signed up for Chomsky's class.

When Bontsche the Silent asked for his hot roll with real butter, the judges and the angels hung their heads in shame—but the Prosecutor laughed.

Back at Eliot, a personal invitation in his mailbox, stamped, not stuffed. "Arnold Hitler," it said on the envelope. His name. The student who got no invitations. The card was engraved:

YOU ARE INVITED TO ATTEND A GET-ACQUAINTED EVENT
AT
THE FOXX CLUB
76 MT. AUBURN ST.
SATURDAY, SEPTEMBER 13, 1969
FROM 9 P.M. ON.

At the top, "HITLER IN NIGHTTOWN," calligraphied in fluent hand; at the bottom, "Ask for me at the door." It was signed "Rick." Red ink.

Harvard has no fraternities but rather an overwhelming number of student activity groups—from the Ancient and Honorable Breakfast Society to SDS. It also has "final clubs," patterned on Oxford's, social organizations that accept sophomores, juniors, and seniors by invitation. There are also unofficial groups that parody the final clubs, having a less select clientele and without class-restricting membership fees. The Foxx Club was one of these.

Arnold knew nothing of the ins and outs of Harvard social life. His first-year nights had been spent at meetings, or working out in the gym, or studying in his room, or in Widener Library, or at an occasional theater or music event. He had been to Boston once for the symphony, once for the opening of *2001*; he had gone to the Fogg for a quartet concert, and to the *Mikado*. Always alone. Now, at the very beginning of his sophomore year, an invitation, personally addressed, stamped, not stuffed. He didn't know what to make of "Hitler in Nighttown."

Arnold arrived, apprehensive but curious, at 76 Mt. Auburn a little before 10. Since he didn't know what to wear, he had decided on his normal chinos, sport shirt, and corduroy jacket on the theory that if they didn't like him in his daily garb, he was probably in with the wrong crowd. He could hear the music pulsing from more than a block away. The logo foxx was depicted on a carved wooden sign hanging from the porch roof, hooks and eyes, detachable.

Pushing against the resisting wall of sound, he climbed the porch stairs and knocked on the door. Two times, three times. Too loud in there to hear, he thought, and looked around for a bell. There was no button at the door, so he tried yanking on the chain hanging at his left, pulleyed along the porch roof and through a small hole in the front window casing. His motion seemed connected to a huge interior bell that from the street, and through the fog of competing noise, suggested some kind of disaster at sea. Half a minute later the door was opened by a huge, crewcut gentleman, red plastic beer cup in hand, wearing a crimson "VER-RIT-ASS" T-shirt illustrating two books and one butt. The smoke was thick, and the sound volume so great that Arnold had to shout directly in his greeter's ear: "I'm looking for Rick." He flashed his invitation.

"Yeah, sure. I'll get him." Arnold decided to wait with his back to the cool autumn night before entering the inferno.

Rick came galloping down the steps from the second floor, as graceful and suave as his predecessor was lunky. He wore a blue silk jacket with matching ascot—incongruous with his brown penny loafers. "Yes?"

Arnold handed him his invitation.

"Ah! Mr. Hitler. Come in, come in!" He bowed and gestured Arnold into the front hall, closing the door behind him. The entire rest of the encounter was conducted at the necessary level of yelling-in-ear, with the requisite number of "What?"s and repetitions, too burdensome to record.

"Call me Arnie," said Arnold Hitler, thinking thereby to lighten the load on his host, and his own vulnerability.

"I hope you're not ashamed of your name."

"No, no . . ."

"After all, you're Arnie, not Adolf, and in any case you weren't even born when the old man was stomping on the Savoy."

"True." Arnold felt strangely comforted, even in these difficult surroundings.

"At the Foxx Club, we know how to make distinctions."

"I don't know why others have trouble doing that."

"Others are doltish."

"No, even smart people."

"An inability to make correct distinctions puts them *hors de discours.* You speak French?"

"I'm taking it now."

"German?"

"No. But I may do that, too. I'm interested in languages." Arnold thought he was making a reasonable impression.

"I thought you would speak German."

They walked from the hall into the first room off a long hallway. A large paper sign was painted, "IF YOU CAN'T DIG IT, DON'T KNOCK IT," but stained and somewhat tattered, as if left over from some earlier event. Two lines of five men each seemed to be getting ready for what could have been a contra dance, but each dancer was holding two large plastic glasses of beer. "Men, this is Arnie. Girls, this is Arnie." Assorted nods. "Go!" yelled a man with a stopwatch, and the first man in each line drank down his glass as quickly as possible, signaling the next in line to begin when he was done.

"It's called Chug-off. First team done wins," commented Rick. "They've been at this for a while. Any spillage is unacceptable, so whoever wastes even a drop has to chug the rest of that glass, refill the cup, and chug it again. See? Harrigan. He's getting worse. Easily another five cc on the rug. His team has had to play four consecutive rounds against different teams."

"If they keep losing, why do they get to play again?"

"They need the practice. But—there—see?—you can get in trouble just by laughing at them. Foxx record is ten beers in 9.2 seconds. These guys are the tree sloths *Bradypus* in comparison."

But the sloths seemed to be having a good time. Arnold noticed the advanced technique: they didn't just drink the beers, they inhaled them, each wrapping his lips completely around the rim of the large cup, then squeezing it like a tube of toothpaste, crushing the plastic so that the liquid shot down his throat, which they all seemed to have trained beyond any gag reflex.

Not knowing what to say, Arnold said, "Interesting."

"And it's early yet. It gets more interesting as the evening wears on. Come. I'll give you the tour," offered Rick. " 'Ecstasy affords the occasion, and expediency determines the form.' Marianne Moore. You've read her?" asked Rick.

"Um, no. Sorry."

"Well, you're only a sophomore. From Texas, yet."

"How did you know that?"

"Mansfield, Texas. Quarterback captain of the Mansfield Tigers, captain of the chess club, editor of the famous and infamous *Last Word*, Merit scholar, deviser of a high school curriculum on propaganda . . . we know it all."

"Most people have never heard of Mansfield."

"Most people have never heard of anything. Mansfield is world-famous for being Little Rock before Little Rock. Wasn't it in '56 that you kept the Negroes out of a court-integrated school?"

Arnold was flabbergasted.

"That was my first year of school. My parents took me to the demonstration."

"Really?"

"I mean, we had to go to register, and we walked into the demonstration."

"Ah."

They crossed the hall. Rick pushed the door open against the pressure of bodies and peeked in. He closed the door again.

"What's in there?" asked Arnold.

"Nothing interesting," said his guide. "Just an early group grope. Perhaps we'll visit its later stages." He broke out laughing.

"What's funny?"

"I was just thinking of the despicable Professor Haushalter, that fat old reprobate, ogling those young women who sit and stretch in miniskirts in his front row. We should invite *him* here. Of course he wouldn't come. Listen, he leans over the lectern and talks about 'my wife's crumpled old body,' which he compares with 'your high breasts and firm thighs.' Makes me puke. Telling salacious stories to eighteen-year-olds in his orgy of mild self-titillation. Completely debasing the literature. 'Principles and values make us unhappy,' he tells these girls, some of whom are from religious homes, and still proud to be Americans. 'Life is dirty and vulgar. Human existence is bestiality and cannibalism. And here we stand lecturing on Virginia Woolf.' I think I'll invite him to a group grope just to see what he'll say."

"What if he comes?"

"We'll make him an honorary member, and publicize it in the *Globe* and the *Crimson*. Onward to the next circle, *il mio Vas d'elezione*."

Instead of heading lower, as might be expected, Rick led his chosen vessel up a twisting back stairway off the kitchen. He had to call to Arnold, who had become distracted en route by the person of Brittany

Ludlow, a tall blond beauty in a low-cut, short, sleeveless red velour dress. Her shimmering hair, falling like a river down her back, made men so uncomfortable that she was often lonely at parties. "Give me a call at Pforzheimer," she yelled after Arnold as she imaged him nude, ascending the stairway.

The second floor was more labyrinthine than the first, consisting of many smaller rooms, one leading off the other, a hallway snaking through them. Rick pushed open a door.

"Ah, the fair sex. You seem to be interested in that, I notice. Welcome to the game of Tush Ahoy."

Six or seven couples waited in line at a large beer keg. At the moment, a young black man with glasses was standing atop a household ladder attempting to support his white date by the ankles as she heroically attempted to suck the liquid upward through a polyethylene tube and gulp it down. She lost it after 12.6 seconds, according to the timekeeper, and a good thing too, since her boyfriend was clearly having second thoughts about dating an endomorph. She was awarded a booby prize, though, for having a capital tush: a glassful of merlot.

"Need I say more?" inquired Rick.

"I think I got it," said Arnold.

"But then again, there *is* more to say." Rick spoke more quietly in the lower decibels of the second floor as they made their way through the rooms. "There you have an example of a nice Northern college girl, whose older sisters no doubt got on a bus to Mississippi to liberate all those nice Negroes. Since then, of course, the Civil Rights Movement became the Free Speech Movement, which became the Antiwar Movement, which became the Anti-Everything-as-It-Exists Movement, which became poor fat little Erica Abramson, head over heels dependent on the kindness of a black stranger. Such is the reward of an undiscriminating, hyperemotional do-gooder sensibility. I, personally, would drop her. What would Virginia Woolf say?

"Yet here we are at Harvard, affirmative actioning po' black folk like Edward there, when clearly we should be putting our energies behind intense remedial training. What possible use would a black literary critic be in the slums of Roxbury, or Harlem, or Watts?"

"They want training in their heritage. So they can share it in the ghettos. And so we can share it with them."

"There'd be more to inherit if they studied auto mechanics, don't you think? This university is helping to destroy the black community, perhaps permanently. Let them eat Ralph Ellison and James Baldwin. But more to the point: Erica and her sisters. What better way to purge white, Jewish guilt than to support autonomous schools of black studies? What a great way to give the Negro what we owe him without fouling up one's own schools and programs. For some reason pride in ancestry is good in Negroes and bad in WASPs. Fascinating, wouldn't you say?"

They continued to the next room and stopped to watch "Bruce Lee" Kozlowski, the Human Can Opener, set a Coors can at the edge of a table. Muscular in his crimson "You Can Lead Me to Harvard, But You Can't Make Me Think" T-shirt, he reared back and smashed his head squarely on the can top. Beer flew all over the room as the sides of the container burst, and co-eds squealed.

"These people know how to have a good time," Arnold offered.

But an adverse event had occurred. Bruce Lee Koslowski had not only opened the Coors, he had opened his head. His normal judgment somewhat clouded after indulging in "tax" for each can opened, he had struck his brow against the corner of the table and was now turning the otherwise yellow sea a distinctive red as blood spurted from his crown.

"He is in blood," quoth Rick.

"Stepp'd in so far that, should he wade no more,
Returning were as tedious as go o'er."

Arnold ran up to Bruce and clamped his new handkerchief over the bleeding wound. "Hold that there, man, press hard, and sit down while I go fetch a butterfly." He was expert at this from football days. "Rick, is there a first aid kit?"

"Who would have thought the old man to have had so much blood in him?"

"Rick! Is there a first aid kit?" Arnold was in his element, taking over. An excellent audition.

"A first aid kit at Foxx? Are you kidding? Our motto is Freedom or Death. But more often we go to the ER."

"OK, then, how about some scissors? A knife?"

"You're not going to cut him," shrieked a curly-haired young woman, possibly Bruce's girlfriend.

"Anybody got a Swiss Army knife with scissors?"

The call went out through the rooms. A tall, thin, MIT-looking type pushed through the crowd with a red pocketknife in his hand. He opened the scissors and gave it to Dr. Hitler.

This was an emergency medicine field trick Arnold had been particularly impressed with when he first saw it done in the training room. He cut away a clean oval of hair around the wound, mopping up the blood with his handkerchief along the way. Next he twisted some strands of hair from opposite sides of the cut and tied them across the wound, approximating the edges and shutting off the flow of blood. He called for water and washed the area. The co-eds looked goggly-eyed at the handsome doctor.

"Premed?" one asked him.

"Linguistics."

"Oh."

"Keep pressure on with your hand for another fifteen minutes, then check to see if it's still seeping when you let go. There's always a lot of blood with a head wound. It's not serious."

"Thanks, buddy. Hey, what's your name?"

"Arnie."

"Arnie what?"

"Hitler."

"Oh, yeah. Rick said you were coming. Hey, put it there, man." He held out his hand for slapping. "Hey, man, before you go, there's one thing I need."

"What's that?"

"A Coors. Wanna get me one?"

Arnold checked with Rick, who gave him a nod. He brought the can.

"Open it with your hands, OK?" said the good doctor.

"Yeah, man, sure. I was just pitting the human mind against the tensile strength of aluminum."

Bruce took a long swig and, with no warning, retched up an evening's worth of beer, pizza, and digestive juice all over his accommodating caretaker. The audience burst into uproarious laughter.

"Sorry, man. Don't know what hit me."

"That's OK."

Arnold wiped the vomit off his pants and jacket and left his stinking, bloody handkerchief on the table with the beer.

"I suppose these social clubs could be a bit more elegant," Rick observed. "But it's good to have a team doctor for our Slough of Despond intramurals."

"Thanks." He noticed a busty redhead in a wet, cut-off T-shirt that read, "FROM ZERO TO HORNY IN 2.5 BEERS." Rick noticed his noticing.

"She does make you wonder about mammals," he said as he led his charge into the next room. "Arnold, these are the leaders of tomorrow."

From out in the hallway, a loud cry: "The Professor, The Professor! Come one, come all!"

"What professor is that?" Arnold asked in surprise. "I can't believe any faculty would . . ."

"You are right about our faculty, dear Arnold. They are either home with their crumpled old wives, or in their studies cooking up their standard blend of eclectic liberal flummery, marinated in popularizations of Marx, Darwin, and Freud, seasoned with a dose of Einsteinian relativity, not quite understood and dishonestly applied to human affairs. Oh, and a pinch of existentialism. Those asinine, posturing pretenders in tweed, living the most orthodox middle-class lives. You think they really want to know their students, the cream of the nation's crop? You think they'd come here for a little reality, those pusillanimous classroom oglers, adventurous enough only to brush up against co-eds in hallways, and then excited enough for a furtive trip to the newsstand to peek at the skin magazines while pretending to hunt for the *New Yorker?* You think they want to see their students puke in protest over their pathetic offerings?"

"Five minutes to the Professor!" the criers called out.

"The Professor is a sport designed, as will be obvious, by physics students," Rick continued. "It is called 'the Professor' because one learns so much participating in it."

They walked out through two rooms into the hallway and made their way among the crowd to the head of the main staircase. Though tall, Arnold could not really see what was going on. And it was too crowded to move to a better location.

"This is best viewed from downstairs, but I don't see how to get there. So I'll just narrate what's about to happen. Up there, ahead, they are filling a twenty-foot hose with beer through an automotive funnel. Standard is twelve beers—half a case. At the foot of the staircase, the Player, the Contestant, Victim, what have you, is lying on his back. Above him stands the Cork Man, a.k.a. the Professor. When the hose is filled and all is ready, the Professor will kneel down at the Player's face, uncork the hose, and shove it in his mouth. There's a lot of pressure built up there; our engineers have calculated it, I don't remember how many pounds per square inch of epiglottis, but it's significant. The Player's cheeks fill up like balloons, there are three seconds of total joy, I'm told, and then he throws up all over himself, the rug, and the inner circle of observers. It's a simple ricochet—down and up. It's not wise to play this game more than once a night since the acid in the vomit is not good for dental enamel."

A cheer went up from downstairs, the event having been achieved. A new hero had been born. "Me next, me next."

Arnold was feeling faint. The smell of stale beer and sweaty bodies, the heat, the noise, the blood, the vomit, was a bit much for a greenhorn.

"I need some air," he told Rick. "Think we can go outside?"

"Let's head down the kitchen stairs and go out in the backyard. We'll save the third floor for next time."

Never had Arnold so appreciated the cool of a September night. The midnight stars blazed above as they had done in Texas in the aftermath of a victorious Friday-night game.

"I, myself, do not see the hose as a mere physics experiment," Rick said as they stood on the back porch. Couples were making out in the backyard, one, apparently, near consummation. Arnold tried to ignore them. "I think of it," Rick continued, "as a link in the Great Chain of Being, perhaps even the great vertical of the sephirot, a connection of high and low. Have you studied the Chain of Being?"

Arnold thought it dangerous to fake. "No."

"If you take nothing else away from your Harvard education, you might consider this idea, one that, until our depleted century, had the greatest effect on Western civilization as it bubbled up through the Greek Neoplatonists, and through the Renaissance into the eighteenth century. It's an organizing principle, and a scheme of hierarchy and distinctions. Its general features are three: plenitude, continuity, and gradation."

"I . . . I'm really interested in this . . . but would you mind if I went out to the back there and peed? I'll be right back."

"Arnold Hitler, the great Isak Dinesen herself has defined Man as an ingenious machine for turning, with infinite artfulness, the red wine of Shiraz into urine."

Arnold found a place he felt would minimally disturb the assorted lovers.

"That's better," he alleged, as he returned to the steps. "Now I can concentrate. Something, continuity, and gradation."

"Plenitude. Plenitude is the grandest of the axioms of the chain: the universe is full, a cornucopia of maximal diversity, of every kind of existence."

"Nice," said Arnold.

"The principle of continuity asserts that the universe is composed of an infinite series of forms, each of which shares with its neighbors at least one attribute: a partial brotherhood of all being, as it were."

"I like it," said the pupil.

"Now here's the kicker: the principle of gradation. There is a linear hierarchical order from God, the *ens perfectissimum*, way upstairs, all the way down to the barest type of existence below, a ladder of virtue descending through all creation, first the angels, then only a little lower, man thinking, then down and down to animals, and plants and stocks and stones and worse than senseless things. Molecules, atoms, particles, quantum energy fluctuations. Then there are those students inside . . ."

As if on cue, there was a crash from a third-floor room as a game of William Tell proceeded, an aluminum beer keg hitting the floor after knocking a beer cup off some sophomore co-ed's head. The thrower's T-shirt read, "Take Me Drunk, I'm Home."

"If I joined Foxx," Arnold said, "I wouldn't be able to play these games since I don't drink alcohol. My training."

"We have an acceptable substitute for the abstemious. One cup of beer equals one cup of chocolate syrup mixed with Tabasco and vinegar.

This, too, is an excellent emetic. Hear me out, though, before we talk about joining." Rick paused to gather his presentation. "I think you'll agree that since you've been here, the city-state of Harvard has become radicalized. What we see now are revolutionaries in command of training and staging areas that serve as jumping-off places for attacks on the rest of society.

"Here are all these bright kids, enslaved to their ogling, hypocritical professors, chuckling in appreciation of each simple-minded point they utter, knowing that if they don't come in with laughter on cue those As or Bs will fly away and those scholarships dry up. 'There is something basically corrupt with the American power structure.' Do tell. 'Our imperialism in Vietnam is not incidental. The system is basically evil. The Vietnam War is the current vehicle of that system.' Can you repeat that, Professor? 'It's not the war that's bad, it's the whole system that's rotten. The war is just a symptom of the larger sickness.' Will this be on the exam?

He sat down on the back steps. Arnold joined him.

"And then there are these lecturers streaming in here from ghettos all over, contemptuous, like Cleaver last semester, talking about killing whites—and the white girls flush and squirm and coo over these studs. God knows how many Radcliffe beds they've left their semen on. The mindlessness is frightening; the sexuality is sickening."

Arnold made ready for he knew not what.

"You get that from one of the lecturers?" he asked. Rick began cleaning his nails in the light from the kitchen window. Arnold's breathing became a bit less tense.

"My friend, there is an anger rising in this land, a momentous rage with a force as great as life itself. The white working man is tough when he's roused, Arnold; he's wild, stomping, gouging, shooting tough. And he's coming to view the domestic enemy as worse than the foreign one— those despicable punks, marching in nice antiwar parades, organized by nice radicals like David Dellinger, marching under the Vietcong flag, these pampered brats from rich families whose daddies' money has bought them extended adolescence, has bought them long leisure hours to roam around, tearing down the campuses of their own privileged sanctuary. You think there was blood and vomit tonight? That was all voluntary. You think there was blood on the pavement outside University Hall? You haven't seen anything, my friend. We are a hair's breadth away from total civil war.

"Did you follow the People's Park thing last summer? The poor innocent students and sweet young families just going about their business set upon by bloodthirsty police sent by monstrous Governor Reagan, who decided that genocide was the only answer to the Berkeley problem? What's going on in the hearts and minds of those hairy middle-class brats? What texts are they writhing to in those little joints they hang out in?" And here, Rick broke into a tolerable imitation of Grace Slick:

"We are obscene, lawless, hideous, dangerous, dirty, violent, and young."

"They sing it so sweetly, Arnold, and everyone loves it, learns it in their hearts, undulating in their dance halls, singing along and dancing their intercourse-substitute, belly-rubbing dances, everyone ending up in bed with another Aquarian-ager with gonorrhea or herpes. Sensation as philosophy, sensation directed against something they find despicable—America!

"I tell you, the white working man is smoldering at the point of explosion. Some of us here understand that. Long before Harvard becomes the exclusive property of Scarsdale Jews and Harlem blacks, the Corporation is going to find it burned to the ground."

A couple came out the back door, the girl ahead of the boy, pushing past Arnold and Rick down the back steps.

"I'm very caring," the guy was pleading, "let's fuck."

"Don't you have any good-looking friends?"

Arnold sat for a long time in silence.

"I gotta go, Rick. Gotta be up early to work out."

"Let me give you something to take home and read."

"All right."

Rick took a neatly folded flyer from his jacket pocket.

"Read it and then give me a call," he said. "Soon, OK?"

"Sure. What's your last name?"

"Mather, Richard Mather. I wrote it on the bottom, with my number."

"Like Cotton Mather?"

"Great-great-great-great-grand-uncle or something."

"Traced back to a protoplasmal primordial atomic globule?"

"Darn tootin. Pooh-Bah as they come. Without the graft. Gimme a call."

Arnold began to walk away.

"Hey, Arnie. We've got to transform all that effervescence in there," he gestured back up into Foxx. "Transform it all into an organization. You could be the minister of propaganda. Wake Harvard up from Kant's 'dogmatic slumber.'"

Arnold nodded, wary. "I'll get back to you," he said.

"I'll be waiting." Rick Mather lifted his cup to toast the brightening future as Arnold walked around toward the front of the building. "Beware the Slough of Despond," he yelled.

Arnold turned east on Mt. Auburn and found himself walking with eyes closed, breathing deeply, checking only occasionally to see if he was still on course. At Plympton he opened his eyes and broke into a run down to Boylston and around to Eliot House at the river. Once in his room, he changed to his robe and brought his reeking clothes to the laundry room. While the machine was turning, he sat in the laundry room and read the pamphlet Rick had given him:

PATRIOTIC POLITICAL ACTION

OF THE

NATIONAL YOUTH ALLIANCE

This year *must* be the year of political counterattack against the insidious forces of diversion and subversion within our midst.

THE NYA COMMITTEE OF PUBLIC SAFETY has been founded to reassert the political functioning of the White majority within our United States of America.

Since the turn of the century, our American political scene has been dominated by various factions and self-interested minority pressure groups whose goals have generally *not* included the promotion of the general welfare and the survival of the nation.

There is only ONE SOLUTION: rebuild the political organization of the ineffective White majority, and concentrate its united will upon the political questions of the day.

THE NYA COMMITTEE OF PUBLIC SAFETY will attack the local Trotsky-types among us, both on campus and within both the Republican and Democratic parties.

It will conduct a campaign of propaganda and physical terror against the guilty individuals and their associates. It will drive these traitors from universities and public offices and reduce them to a position where suicide will be the only salvation for their crimes against their own society, their own people, and their own civilization.

The National Youth Alliance Committee of Public Safety
Sam Adams Chapter

At the bottom Rick had written his name and phone number under the following note: " 'We do not look for allies when we love. Indeed, we often look on those who love with us as rivals and trespassers. But we always look for allies when we hate. It is chiefly hatred that drives us to merge with those who hate as we do; it is hatred that serves as effective cementing agent.' Eric Hoffer (White working man)."

Twenty-one

I n the fall of 1969, students in the houses were still required to wear ties and jackets for lunch and dinner. At
Eliot, most thought it ridiculous, but many nevertheless
complied, Arnold among them. Others were "spoken to"
by Alan Heimert, who probably thought it ridiculous himself. After all,
there were students who did not bother to wear shirts in the dining halls.
The sense of social deterioration felt by many older faculty members was
unrelenting and grim. After two weeks, even Arnold wore his jacket
without a tie.

Bare-chested or Windsored, the kids at Eliot, and Harvard, were to be
the future ruling class. Yale might make its contribution to the Foreign
Service, Princeton to Wall Street and the law firms on K Street—but
Harvard governed the United States, "a hatchery for the best eggs that
were destined to cluck and strut into the outer world." When Eliot was
president, he had famously exhorted students to "enter to grow in
wisdom."

The *Crimson* had pronounced the incoming freshmen of 1968—
Arnold's class—as "the brightest" in Harvard's history, in this college
where the grades ran "the gamut from A to B." Forty percent of that
class were public high school kids wondering if Harvard had made a mistake. Arnold's strategy, like that of so many others, was to seek to make
it alone, just on the basis of his wits, and not because of his parentage. If
he had no friends—well, that was not unheard of in this collection of
brilliant monads. He would not aspire to gray eminence at the Foxx
Club.

He would also not return to Harvard football. The previous semester,
John Tyson, a black defensive back, had decided not to play in his next,
senior, year—a huge shock for the team. He did not want to be "a hired
gladiator" for his "Harvard masters." Arnold raised his mental fist in
sympathy.

He decided to take Roger Rosenblatt's "Black Fiction in America"
course, to read a novel or autobiography every week for small seminar
discussion. Eye-opening, it was. The authors wrote complex, layered
prose, evoking a previously unknown mythology, and a fascinating, if
horrific, take on America. One of the few whites, and the only South-
erner, in the group, Arnold regaled the room and amazed himself with
stories of Mansfield, now heard through others' ears. In one of the class
readings, LeRoi Jones observed that the black man in America is like a
person who has been kept locked by white men in a small room of a great
house, and was only now out there, exploring other rooms.

Arnold felt the same way.

Noam Chomsky was Job's whirlwind of political activism. He spawned it
as faculty adviser for several student groups at both MIT and Harvard.
He invited ostracism and dismissal by public calls for universities involved in war efforts to establish "Departments of Death." He courted

prison by actively organizing support for war resisters and for refusing to pay half his taxes. But Arnold had made an appointment, a short jog downriver, to see him about his academic specialty: language, words— one word in particular.

Building 20—MIT's famous "Plywood Palace"—was one of the landmarks of science. Built during World War II to last "to the end of the war plus six months," the ramshackle structure on Vassar Street was still there twenty-four years later, hot in summer, cold in winter, eternally drafty, with soot blowing in its ill-fitting windows and rain leaking through holes in the roof. Inside, noise, the unbaffled sounds of everyone's work. But this immense clubhouse, which might have been built by a gaggle of Huckleberry Finns, was second only to Los Alamos as a seat of wartime science. It was here that radar was invented, and one of the earliest particle accelerators constructed. Here was built the first atomic clock. Here Amar Bose reinvented the loudspeaker, and Harold Edgerton a strobe camera fast enough to stop a bullet in flight. Here, work on the visual mechanism of frogs led to nighttime scanning devices exquisitely sensitive to movement. The plywood walls were mothers of invention. In the Palace, scientists could simply punch their way through physical boundaries to create optimal spaces for their research. They could tap into extra water and electricity from the exposed pipes and wires. Scientific spirits swarmed through the Rube Goldberg structure.

And here, in the bowels of Building 20, was Noam Chomsky's domain, home of the revolutionary linguistics department he had built. His two rooms looked more like a bunker than a faculty office.

"I've given up entertaining down here," he said as he ushered Arnold into the shambles, a clutter of books, papers, obscure political and linguistic journals, and filing cabinets. An Exercycle stood friendless in a corner. "Have a seat," he said, gathering a stack of the *Bombay Times* from a chair and piling it precariously on the corner of his desk. "So. Arnold Hitler from Harvard. Ever get any trouble about your name?"

"Not until I got to Cambridge."

"That's a Harvard problem. It wouldn't happen here."

"How so?"

"Upper-class intellectuals, don't you know. When I went to Harvard as a grad student in the '50s, I discovered a large part of Harvard education was simply refinement, social graces, what kinds of clothes to wear, how to have polite conversation that isn't too serious, all the other things an intellectual is supposed to do. I remember a couple of years later asking a professor from Oxford how he thought Harvard's imitation compared with the Oxford original. He said he thought it was the difference between genuine superficiality and phony superficiality. Teaching conformity to norms keeps you from interfering with people in power. Your name is not the norm, so . . ."

"Is that why you're here?"

"MIT lets me do what I like. It's open to experimentation, without rigid requirements."

"But linguistics is hardly technology."

"It is—according to the Research Laboratory of Electronics—in which you are sitting. We were able to develop at MIT because, in a sense, it's outside the American university system. There are no large departments of humanities or related social sciences. I've had a very friendly and supportive environment at MIT, no matter what I've been doing."

Arnold nodded, amazed.

"But we're not here to talk about me," Chomsky said. "What's up?

"I'm trying to figure out . . . the social . . . realities of language—how words are used to create inequalities, to put people down."

"Like what words?"

"Like Hitler."

"Your name."

"Yes."

"People are giving you a hassle over your name."

"Yes."

"And you want to know what to do about it."

"How did you know?"

"You just told me. So what kind of hassles?"

"No one wants to room with me. No one wants to go out with me. Someone tried to recruit me for some Nazi-type organization. . . ."

"Nomen omen est."

"My name is an omen?"

"Names are destiny."

"God help me."

"So why don't you just change your name?"

"To what? George Washington? Jesus of Nazareth? You can't just change your name."

"Why not? Most entertainers do. Don't they?"

"I'm not an entertainer."

"I just meant nothing bad happened to them. Look, you've already experienced your name playing an irrational, magical role affecting your life, so take hold of the magic. Grab yourself a name that treats you better. You know Faulkner added the 'u' to his family name? He said he didn't want to ride on 'grandfather's coat-tails,' and he was quite pleased at finding 'such an easy way' to strike out for himself. Imitate Faulkner. Make it Hiutler."

"I'm taking a class in black literature with Roger Rosenblatt. . . ."

"I heard he was teaching that."

"We just read a selection from *I Know Why the Caged Bird Sings . . .* Maya Angelou . . . have you heard of her?"

"No."

"I think it's the first thing she's published, a kind of autobiography. She talks about working for a woman as a kid in Arkansas. This woman thought her original name, Margaret, was too long, so she simply decided to call her Mary, and Angelou got furious. She said, 'I decided I wouldn't pee on her if her heart was on fire.'"

"Good writing."

"She says that all the blacks she knew had a hellish horror of 'being called out of their names,' being called niggers, spooks, slave owners renaming their slaves . . . she wasn't about to stand for it anymore."

"So what happened?"

"She started taking revenge, leaving egg on the dishes, deliberately dropping them. She got herself happily fired and resolved to never take anyone's name again. So she named herself Maya. I also don't want to be 'called out of my name' by other people."

"You miss the point. She named herself Maya. You could name yourself whatever you want. George Bernard Shaw called himself Corno di Bassetto and a dozen other pseudonyms—Horatia Ribbonson, Julius Floenmochser, Redbarn Wash, the Rev. C. W. Stiggins, Jr. . . ."

"My mother kept her maiden name. She said if she changed her name her marriage would be lopsided, and a woman needed to be more herself after she married than before. And Hitler isn't even my maiden name—it's my *name*, and my connection to the past."

"I can see I'm not going to convince you."

"I came for advice about what I could do—*other* than change it."

"Suffer, that's what to do. If this is a battle you need to pick, go ahead. Thirty, forty years ago James Frazer thought the human race was slowly crawling out of the magic mode through the religious to finally emerge in the sunlight of science and rationality. I wouldn't hold my breath."

"Yeah."

"Look, you're tall and blond and handsome and smart, and that's enough to overcome first-name problems. But not last-name ones."

"But everyone is acting like a four-year-old. The sun is called the sun because it shines."

"A kugel is a called a kugel because it looks like a kugel and tastes like a kugel."

"How did you know that?"

"Old Jewish joke. Forgive me."

"No. My grandfather told me that joke. I didn't realize what he was getting at."

"You have a Jewish grandfather?"

"My mother's father. In Italy."

"Hitler may have had a Jewish grandfather. Adolf Hitler. His skeleton in the closet."

"Boy, that must have pissed him off. Excuse me."

"We all have our *tsouris*."

"But four-year-olds grow up and they realize that 'sun' or 'kugel' is just a convention. It could be 'le soleil,' or 'potato pudding.'"

"Well, words are not the things they name. Saussure says they take distinctive meanings *by contrast* with other words. A square is a square because it's not a triangle, not a circle."

"So I'm not-Adolf-Hitler. That should give me my own special meaning."

"But, in bondage to nominal realism, the world regards names as sacred. Frazer's magical level."

"The world doesn't expect Jim Miller and Sarah Baker to be covered in flour."

"Now, in that context—'miller' and 'baker' are just units of sound, not units of meaning. They're 'just names,' dead metaphors. Hitler, however, is still very much alive. And maybe he should be. I don't think you're going to win this one."

Chomsky stood as if to say, "Time's up."

Arnold took the hint, and gathered his things from under his chair. "Well, thanks so much for your time."

"I wish I could be more helpful. Or more optimistic."

Arnold made his way through the piles to the door.

"Nice to meet you," he said.

Chomsky nodded from behind his desk.

"A Hitler iz nit a kugel," he said.

Twenty-two

Several days later, a massacre hit the papers. It had passed without notice when it occurred eighteen months earlier—a company of 150 U.S. infantrymen entering the Vietnamese village of My Lai early one morning and destroying its houses, livestock, and inhabitants in an operation that took less than twenty minutes. More than a hundred men, women, and children were murdered without provocation in cold blood, "a well-planned, well-executed, and successful attack," according to the combat action report.

Charley Company had encountered not a single enemy soldier, only three weapons were found in the entire village, and there was no resistance. Lt. William Calley ordered all civilians to be killed. People were rounded up into their huts, and grenades were tossed in. The huts were then burned to the ground. Others were made to lie down in a ditch and shot. When Calley saw a baby crawling out, he grabbed it, threw it back in, and opened fire. "C Company" was carved into the chests of some of the dead; some were disemboweled. As one GI would later say: "You didn't have to look for people to kill, they were just there. I cut their throats, cut off their hands, cut out their tongues, scalped them. I did it. A lot of people were doing it, and I just followed." As a photographer observed, "It was done very businesslike." *Stars and Stripes*, the army newspaper, ran a feature story applauding the courage of the American soldiers who had risked their lives. General Westmoreland sent a personal congratulatory note.

Over a year later, Richard Ridenhour, twenty-three, a Vietnam vet who was told by friends about what had really happened, sent a summary to thirty government officials, including the new president, Richard Nixon. His letter led to the investigation now hitting the front pages. The members of Charley Company were characterized as "normal American boys," decent in their daily lives, who at home in Ohio or Vermont would regard it as unthinkable to strike a child, much less kill one. Arnold felt more lost than ever.

Walking past the Holyoke Center on Mass Ave, he heard the unearthly singing of an emaciated young woman with long blond hair, seated on a low wall, dressed too lightly for the weather. She played the cello, moving around in its lowest registers while three and four octaves above she wailed in spook sounds an improvised keening whose text seemed to consist of only two words: My Lai, over and over. A spangled beret served as her collection plate and, except for the self-supplied "example" dollar bill, was empty. Arnold was transfixed by the beauty of this wraith and the stark contradiction of her message and, after listening for a minute or so, advanced toward her to add a dollar to the loneliness of her own. As he bent down to deposit the money, she stopped playing with a sforzando chord. It was no thank-you she had for him:

"How can you justify being protected from the war with your Harvard 2-S when poor people have to go massacre Vietnamese? You, yes, you!" she yelled. People on the street turned around to see if she was being hurt. Arnold stepped back, dollar in hand. "I don't want your dirty money," she screamed. Arnold retreated quickly, feeling guilty under all those stares for a crime he had not committed.

He turned the corner and walked, as inconspicuously as possible, through the arcade toward Eliot House.

Arnold was not the only Eliot House student feeling lost. Thomas Branigan was a humorless and intense scarecrow who had been home-schooled to be a military mastermind. In the week before finals, Branigan threw himself from the fourth-floor window just under Arnold's onto the pavement below. The only child of a farm family in the Midwest, he had come to Harvard against the wishes of his father, who deemed it unseemly to go to any institution at all, much less to a place as godless as Harvard. Dark-haired and pale and very quiet, Branigan lived a near-solitary existence in the house and had tried to kill himself twice in his freshman year. Arnold, one of the few people he spoke to, had thought him irretrievably ill. After the second suicide attempt, he had been sent to a mental hospital. Released after a year, he had come to live at Eliot. It was discovered that before jumping, Thomas had also swallowed cyanide that he had cooked up in a chem lab: it was important, he knew, to have a backup. As his closest, maybe only, acquaintance, Arnold volunteered to call his parents. The boy's father answered. "Well," he responded, "we aren't going to pay to ship the body home."

At the Eliot House memorial service there were, among others:

—the crown prince of Tonga, who had been both captain and coach of the national rugby team;

—a seventeen- year-old Chinese girl who played the violin and did gymnastics;

—an academic prodigy from the Bronx who got 800 in all his college boards, edited his school yearbook, played concert clarinet, and had made a telescope;

—one of eleven children from a migrant farm-worker family who wanted to be a brain surgeon;

—a long-haired producer of a wildly animated film on the dissection of a frog; and

—the son of a right-wing Hungarian freedom fighter now living in Montana (admitted for both geographic and cultural-political mix) who was an Eagle Scout, president of his high school class, and state tennis champion.

All of them felt lost. Perhaps it was a secret requirement of Harvard admissions. Perhaps it was a common result of Harvard life in late-1960s America.

In the first poststrike Christmas season, the "SDSminster Choir" handed out song sheets, and caroled outside University Hall. Arnold joined in the medley, harmonizing with the tenor parts he had learned in the Mansfield Glee Club:

> *Preppie boys,*
> *Corporate joys,*
> *Harvard all the way*
> *Oh what fun it is to have*
> *Your mind reduced to clay.*
>
> *. . .*
>
> *Oh come, all you mindless,*
> *Conceptless and spineless*

Oh come, all ye toothless ones
To Harvard's purée.

. . .

We three deans of Harvard are
Feasting on our black caviar.
We'll stop the riot
And have peace and quiet
Bring out the feathers and tar.

The class list for spring semester included "Role of the Computer in Society"; "The War at a Feeling Level"; "Harvard, Whither Goest Thou?"; "Draft Resistance Seminar"; "The Sociology of Math"; "Socialization of Sex Roles and Aggression"; "Pacifism: Christian Ethics and Tradition as a Basis for Alternative Social Action Within the Militant Society"; "Toward a Psychology of Conscious Values." As Arnold was standing in the Yard outside the registrar's office, studying his choices, Dr. Louis F. Fieser, the father of napalm, came down the University Hall stairs and asked him for a light. What a chance for a devastating riposte! He said, "Sorry, I don't smoke," and the professor walked off without a thank-you.

The Harvard Travel Service sign on Mt. Auburn St. read, "PLEASE GO AWAY." Arnold would have liked to. But where? Christmas at two different homes, at great expense? Sounded dreadful. Perhaps borrow a car and go driving around in the East? But who would lend him a car? Rick? No. Better steer clear. Maybe he would hitchhike around. Call himself John Howard Griffin. Pretend he wasn't blackened by his name.

Twenty-three

A young man went to see his Teacher and said: "May I talk to you?"
The Teacher answered: "Come back tomorrow. We'll talk."
The next day, the young man came again and said: "May I talk to you?"
Exactly as before, the Teacher answered: "Come back tomorrow. We'll talk."
"I came yesterday," said the young man, disappointed, "and asked you this
same question. Do you refuse to talk to me?"
"We have been conversing since yesterday," replied the Teacher, smiling.
"Is it our fault we both have bad ears?"

Edmond Jabès, *The Book of Dialogue*

1. Describe the nature of your belief which is the basis of your claim and state why you consider it to be based on religious training and belief.

2. Explain how, when and from whom or from what source you received the religious training and acquired the religious belief which is the basis of your claim. (Include here, where applicable, such information as religion of parents and other members of family; childhood religious training; religious and general education experiences at school and college; organizational memberships and affiliations; books and other reading which influenced you; association with clergymen, teachers, advisers or other individuals which affected you; and any other material which will help give the local board the fullest possible picture of how your beliefs developed.)

3. To what extent does your religious training and belief restrict

you from ministering to the sick and injured, either civilian or military, or from serving in the Armed Forces as a noncombatant without weapons?

4. *Have you ever given expression publicly or privately, written or oral, to the views herein expressed as the basis for your claim? Give examples.*

Arnold stared at the questions on SSS Form 150 with an odd sense of foreboding—as if he were guilty of something unclear but would nevertheless be caught.

In the week since his encounter with the keening cellist he had slept poorly, felt irritable, and was more uncertain than ever about his justification on earth. A trip down Mass Ave to the office of Resist, the organization Chomsky had helped create, had yielded a copy of the Selective Service form for conscientious objectors; studying it, Arnold was forced to take stock at levels of unaccustomed depth. Even the superficial questions were huge: What experiences had really formed him; what had been the meaning of religion and spirituality in his life? At bottom, though, lurked the two monster questions: For what would he kill, and for what would he die?

"I don't know about the Supreme Being stuff," Arnold told Robert Wright, assistant professor of physics, now spending more time trying to slow the draft than trying to accelerate electrons. Arnold was sitting in Wright's office in the basement of the Cyclotron Lab, a building rather more formidable than MIT's Building 20. Over the professor's desk was a blowup of the following:

Any person who knowingly counsels, aids, or abets another to refuse service in the armed forces shall be punished by im-

prisonment for not more than five years or a fine of not more than $10,000 or by both.

—UNIVERSAL MILITARY TRAINING AND SERVICE ACT, SEC. 12

"I haven't been in church since I was maybe eight or nine, when two girls were shot at my school. . . ."

"Where was that?" asked Dr. Wright.

"Mansfield, Texas."

"Racial stuff?"

"No, just some crazy kid. White kid. Killed two white girls at a prayer meeting. The school service was so stupid and hypocritical, I promised I'd never go to church again."

"And?"

"That was it. Except for the meetings in Mem Church last spring."

"Childhood religious trauma." Wright wrote it down on his yellow pad. "What did you find hypocritical and stupid?"

"I can't even remember what they said, the preachers. But one talked about God's son on the cross. My parents had never let me in on all that, so I looked it up in the Bible, and the gospels don't even agree, so . . ."

"So you became suspicious."

"Suspicious of the official story. I still think the ethics are valid— turn the other cheek, the evils from loving money, all that stuff . . ."

Wright scribbled more notes.

"I still pray occasionally. My parents don't know that. They wouldn't understand. For them, religion is public. For me, it's more private."

"Who or what do you pray to?" asked the draft counselor, his pencil poised.

"I can't say, exactly. Augustine said we can know what God is not, but can't know what He is."

"You quote Augustine to those five Texas good ol' boys at your hear-

191

ing, and they'll figure you're some kind of snot who needs a little down-to-earth in boot camp. I had a kid six months ago who came in with this elaborate, beautifully argued case for pacifism based on Spinoza. His board wouldn't even let him finish reading it. 'Who's this atheist professor Spinoza?' That's what they wanted to know."

Arnold laughed.

"Seriously," Wright continued, "stay away from that stuff. You don't need to alienate them more than you already will have by applying for CO status. Look, Arnold, can we say that your moral and ethical values came from your early religious training?"

"That would be a lie."

"Really? Didn't you feel the best doctrines of Christianity were crusted over by questionable texts and phony rhetoric?"

"I guess you could say that."

"You're the one that has to say it."

"My values are probably there *in spite of* the crust."

"That's the crucial connection. It was those hypocritical preachers . . ."

"And patriotic . . ."

"Those hypocritical, patriotic, sanctimonious preachers were the ones from whom, in the immortal words of SSS Form 150, you quote 'received the religious training and acquired the religious beliefs' unquote you now hold."

"In an ironic sense."

"Draft boards don't know from irony. If it's true—in any sense—say so. They'll take it literally, since that's the only sense they know."

"But Dr. Wright . . . I actually have a larger problem—whether I should go for CO status at all. Even filling out their forms is complicity. It would keep things running smoothly, would help them do their job."

"Then you have two alternatives."

"Three," said the chess player.

"Canada, jail, or . . . ?"

"Or disappear."

"You mean go underground?"

Arnold nodded.

"What's wrong with Canada or jail? Disappearing is not so easy."

"Canada . . . I just can't. I'm an American. I've never been out of the country. It's always seemed . . . unfitting . . . to who I am. Besides, I've got a duty to try to change the system here, right? Jail? It seems like such a waste of time. Five years . . . I could be a lot more effective outside."

"From underground?"

"Depends on the constraints."

"Let's put all this stuff aside for the moment. First, I want you to understand the CO thing, OK? You know about the Seeger decision, right?"

"No. I'm new at this."

"Five years ago, the Supreme Court ruled that 'belief in a Supreme Being' is legally acceptable even if that 'Supreme Being' quote 'occupies a place parallel to that filled by the orthodox belief in God of one who clearly qualifies for the exemption' unquote. Got that?"

"So I don't have to believe in God, per se . . ."

"Right. You can believe in parallels."

"Euclidean, Riemannian, or Lobachevskian?"

"Lobachevsky, definitely. Only don't tell them. He's Russian. Then one of the biggies they'll try to get you on is your limits on the use of force."

"Like if someone were going to rape my grandmother, and I had a gun . . ."

"Precisely."

"I heard about that one."

"What do you say?"

"I make the distinction between resorting to violence in an unexpected, acute, personal situation and objecting to the organized, premeditated, mass violence of war."

"Great. What about Hitler? No offense."

"None taken."

"Hitler sub 2."

"More people should make that distinction."

"What a riot. Five old Texas guys asking you what you would do about Hitler."

"You know, I never had one bit of trouble with my name before coming to Cambridge. Neither did my father."

"Really? Why do you think that is? The healing spirituality of the wide-open spaces?"

"Yeah, there's more space in Texas where nobody is than where anybody is. Maybe we just don't care so much what people are called."

"Hm. I'll rethink my prejudices. But back to Hitler sub 1. What's your answer?"

"I don't know."

"It's a hard one. Some counselors suggest you evade the question by saying you weren't born then, so you can't know what you would have done. But I think that as a CO, you're claiming to have beliefs that aren't shaped by situations you encounter. So the question stands."

"What would I do in the face of an overwhelming, suprapersonal evil?"

"Right. And these guys are probably old enough to remember pacifists before the war who claimed it would be better not to fight Hitler. So how would you stop a war machine like his, without resorting to war?"

"Well, it wouldn't be with nuclear bombs, or dropping napalm on kids, I can tell you that. It wouldn't involve mass murder of innocent civilians. But I don't have the answer."

"Good enough. You don't have to. You can read up on nonviolent resistance, if you like. Gene Sharp is very good."

He pulled a copy of *Exploring Non-Violent Alternatives* from the bookshelf over his desk and tossed it to Arnold, who noted author and title on his pocket pad.

"You know, the shitty thing is that most of this stuff doesn't really matter. Here you are trying to evolve a serious, life-shaping philosophy, and these old geezers will probably make their decision based on what their quota is that month, or whether there was a draft-card burning on TV the night before. That's the way it is. This is stuff they never had to tangle with. I don't have to tell you that they'll also make their decision based on your appearance. You've got a lot going for you for looking like Mr. All-American. Don't blow it."

"Captain of my high school football team."

"Go easy on that one. They'll want you as a leader on the battlefield. You can order up the next My Lai play."

"Not very likely."

"OK. Enough for today. I'm going off for Christmas break. Want to get together first of next semester and go over where you're at?"

"Sure. Where are you headed? Aruba?"

"Yeah. The Aruba motel, in downtown Philly. More CCCO training. Central Committee for Conscientious Objectors."

"Ever get any physics done?"

"Physics? What's that? The real question is whether I ever get to see my kids—not to mention my wife."

"Well, someday they'll be proud of their dad."

"Yeah. On visiting days." He motioned to the sign over his desk.

"Maybe we can pass notes from cell to cell."

"What fun."

"Thanks so much, Dr. Wright."

"Bob."

"Bob."

"What's your major, Hitler sub 2?"

"I'm not sure. Linguistics, maybe."

"Too bad. We need more football captains at the cyclotron. Our touch team keeps losing with scores like 108 to 6."

"If I change to physics, you'll be the first to know."

"Have a good break."

"You too. So to speak."

That night, Arnold's knee started to twitch.

"Arnold," whispered Jacobo. "Arnold, am I awaking you?"

"Grandpa?" He bent over to his knee.

"Who else calls you this late?"

"No, you're not waking me. It's only eleven o'clock."

"I never get it right. I thought it was midnight by you. I didn't want to be awaking you."

"What time is it over there?"

"It's five in the morning."

"Why are you up so early?"

"Arnold, you went to see a draft counselor yesterday. Don't lie to me."

"I'm not lying. I haven't said anything yet."

"But you were going to lie to me."

"Why should I lie?"

"Because you don't think I'll approve."

"I didn't think about that."

"You don't care whether I approve or not?"

"I didn't say that."

Silence.

"Well, do you approve?"

"Arnold, you always look at things too simply. Big Harvard genius. The question, *nipote mio*, is what are you counseling about, what are you trying to get away from? Let us apply here not the ecstatic letter permutations of the great Abulafia but the relatively less complex notions of gematria."

"All right, grandpa, what's gematria?"

"I was hoping you would ask. Gematria, *poverino*, is the science of discovering hidden meanings, hidden connections in words through the numerical equivalents of their letters. The alphabet is the wholeness of God—everything is represented by letter combinations. And the numbers show the secret correspondences among words. So, do your name."

"What do you mean *do* it?"

"A equals 1, R equals . . . whatever it equals . . . you go to Harvard, I don't."

"I'll have to get a pencil."

"Decaying intelligence among the young."

"I'll be right back. OK. Let me write out this code . . . W, X, Y, Z. All right. So it's 1 + 18 + 14 + 15 + 12 + 4."

"And that makes?"

"Just a second . . . 64. So?"

"And how much is 6 + 4?"

"10."

"Ten—completeness and the number of your fingers. And 1 + 0?"

"One."

"Peerless and unique. The number of God. One God. Hear, O Israel, the Lord, our God, is One. The number man and wife are. Arnold is a very good name; don't change it."

"I wasn't thinking about changing it. I was thinking about changing Hitler."

"Let's do Hitler."

"All right: 8 + 9 + 20 + 12 + 5 + 18."

"How much?"

"Seventy-two."

"Seventy-two! Arnold, the Name-of-72, holy and awesome. The name of the cloud that separates darkness from light. The name that divides the waters and enables escape. Do you want to get rid of such a name?

"I don't know what to say."

"Silence answers much. And what is 7 + 2?"

"Nine."

"Nine. Almost there—within reach of perfection. For your goyish consumption, a trinity of trinities. Abulafia says, 'Whatever has my name, I made it for my honor—formed it, worked it truly, and concerning this the name informed.' Be informed. Escape. Don't change your name. *Ciao.*"

"Grandpa?"

He had hung up.

Twenty-four

The next morning, Arnold checked the ride board in the dining hall. Most had already left. But there, among the mass of scrawled and outdated notices, was a neatly typed announcement on Harvard Divinity School stationery:

RIDER WANTED TO NEW YORK CITY
Leave Saturday, December 20, 6 a.m.
Return Saturday, December 27.
Contact Professor Jepperson
5-4969 w, 547-3734 h.

He called, found no one at home, but left a message at the department. That evening, he found a note in his mailbox: "Meet you Saturday at 6 at the Eliot loading gate on Boylston. I'll wait five minutes, but if you're later than that, I'll have to get going. JJ."

Six was easy. He was always up at 5 for his morning run. He packed the night before, did some morning intervals along the river, and was back in time to shower and shave and plant himself at the loading dock by 5:55. He wondered about five hours in a car with a professor. Well, he'd survive whatever or whomever.

At six on the dot, a new, dark-green-and-cream VW bus pulled into the driveway outside the gate.

"Arnold?"

"Professor Jepperson?"

The names served as invitation and response.

"You can throw your things in the back."

Arnold opened the sliding side door, put his rucksack and sleeping bag down on the floor, shut the door with a van-shaking bang, and climbed up into the passenger seat.

"Nice van. Is it new? I've never seen this model before."

"A year old. I went for it because I could use it as a camper. See how the roof lifts up? And of course the sink and the fridge."

Arnold looked back. Contrasting with the trappings of a serious camper was a huge Hollywood-style double bed with flowered pillows, throw pillows, and a luxurious blue satin comforter.

"Like the bed?"

"It's not exactly roughing it."

"Yeah, well, that's my compromise with civilization and its discontents. I need a good night's sleep. And I intend to get it wherever."

Professor Jepperson was a petite, red-haired woman with freckles, a pixie haircut, and a surprisingly deep voice. She wore a blue down vest over a gray sweater, and fashionably shabby jeans. Judging from the crows' feet at her large blue eyes, Arnold judged her to be in her late thirties, possibly early forties. She wore no makeup, and her stubby fingers looked hard and cracked, like those of a manual laborer. Not your society type, he thought.

"There's a map in the side pocket over there. You're the navigator, though there's not much navigation to do. We'll just get on 95 and head on down. I usually like to stop once in New London or New Haven—depending on when I have to pee."

She pulled out onto Boylston and headed across the river to Storrow Drive.

"You don't look like a professor," Arnold remarked, awkwardly idiotic.

"It runs in the family. Redheads. You ought to see my older sister. She looks like she's sixteen. And she's an ER doc in the city. She was once about to sew up this old black guy, and as she was gloving up and the old man realized what she was about to do, he yelled out, 'Hey, wait a minute. You ain't no doctor. You jes a little girl!'" She did an excellent old, gruff voice. Arnold laughed.

They were heading south, toward the beltway.

"What do you teach, Professor Jepperson?"

"Judy. I'm not Professor Jepperson south of Quincy. I teach anthropology and comparative religion."

"How'd you get into that?"

"You ever see *The Seventh Seal?*"

"One of my favorite movies."

"Well, you remember the scene where they're getting ready to burn the witch?"

"Yes."

"The witch looks just like my sister. And I always wanted to kill her. I mean as a kid. And there she was, about to be burned to death—with only emptiness in her eyes. And delusion. I decided to study religion."

A nauseating aroma from the nightmare past. Loss, loneliness, hollowness ahead. Arnold was shaken by these unexpected guests. His three deep breaths went unnoticed.

"And what are *you* studying?" she asked.

"I'm not sure. I'm just a sophomore. Maybe linguistics."

"Where you from, honeychil' with that Southern accent?"

"Mansfield, Texas."

"I've heard of Texas. Arnold what?"

Here was his chance to lie without repercussion, his chance to take a vacation on vacation, his chance to play with being someone else. But no.

"Hitler."

"You're kidding. Arnold Hitler?" Arnold had to check and see if the guffaw was really coming from someone five foot one. "Holy mackerel. What a moniker for Mr. Tall, Blond, and Handsome."

Arnold looked petulant.

"Sorry. I just meant that must be some luggage to be carrying around. Oh, goddamn!"

"What is it?"

"My nose is bleeding again from laughing at you. Three times this week." And indeed, Arnold saw a trickle of blood beginning in her right nostril. "There are Kleenex in the glove compartment."

He handed the box to her.

"Want me to drive?"

"Good idea." She pulled off onto the narrow shoulder. Arnold got out, waited for traffic to go by, then walked around the front to the driver's side. Judy was inching herself over the stick shift into the passenger seat. He climbed up, belted in, and waited for a chance to enter the traffic flow. The VW was not much on acceleration. Judy leaned her head against the window and pressed a Kleenex to her nose.

"Kieselbach's plexus," Arnold said.

"What?"

"Kieselbach's plexus. That's where you're probably bleeding from. It's the vascular network on the anterior portion of the nasal septum— where most nosebleeds come from."

"How'd you know that?"

"I just read it once. Thought it was a great name. Kieselbach's plexus."

"Maybe you should be pre-med."

"Not high on my list."

"You know what a Kieselbach is?"

"Some guy's name."

"No. The word 'Kieselbach' in German."

"No."

"Herr Hitler does not speak German?"

"No. I'm studying French."

"Afraid to study German?"

"Maybe."

"A 'Kieselbach' is a stream with pebbles in it. A pebble-stream."

"A 'bach' is a stream?"

"Right."

"Johann Sebastian Bach is a stream?"

"The power of a name. You ought to know."

"Yeah."

"How many other live Hitlers do you know, Arnold?"

"My father."

"Besides him."

"None. But that doesn't mean there aren't others."

"We'll get off in Providence and look in the phone book."

"It doesn't matter how many other Hitlers there are. The important thing is that Arnold and Adolf are not the same. Period."

"Yeah. But Hitler is the same."

"Hitler is just a word."

"Hitler is not just a word—like 'Ford' or 'VW.' It's a magic word."

"What do you mean 'magic word'?"

Judy took a deep breath. Her nose was still trickling. Did she really want to get into this?

"'Hitler' is a tar-baby word."

"You mean like Brer Rabbit?"

"'Tar-baby ain't sayin nothin, en Brer Fox, he lay low.'"

"I saw the movie."

"You should read the book. 'Hitler' is a very sticky business. People encounter that word and they can't get unstuck."

"But that's irrational."

"*Language* is irrational, Herr Linguistics. Words are irrational."

"Language is the source of logic and reason. In the beginning there was the Word."

"That's rational? That God created the universe from a Word?"

"Well, no, but . . ."

"Reason is a *la-a-a-a-te* development. Language was *invented* for myth and magic."

"We're past that."

"Hmm. So how come you're having trouble with 'Hitler'?"

"Okay, we *should* be past that. And I'm not a myth. I'm a person. This. Here."

Silence for a space. Arnold noted a sign for Mansfield, Mass., on his left. Judy remained in thought.

"It's not just any magic word—'Hitler'—it's your *name*. There are Eskimo tribes who think man consists of three elements—body, soul, and *name*. More than half the human beings on this planet believe that whenever someone's name is spoken, he or she is understood to be present and active. Even the dead."

"That's ridiculous. Primitive."

"Were you baptized?"

"Yes."

"You were baptized not in God, not in God's water, or God's pee, but in God's Name, right? Quite literally immersed in the Name of the Lord."

The landscape rolled by for several minutes, ever drearier and more suburban.

"You know what I hate?" Arnold asked.

"What?"

"When people use names as if they explained things—like doctors. You know what happens when you go to the doctor for a nosebleed?"

"I don't go to doctors for nosebleeds."

"But if you did. They'd call it 'epistaxis' with an air of great wisdom, charge you thirty bucks, and tell you to squeeze your nose. That's one of the reasons I don't want to be a doctor."

"You don't like magical use of language."

"I don't."

"Because you suffer from it."

They passed the Massachusetts border—"WELCOME TO CON-NECTICUT"—and onward, southwest, towards the city.

"Guess what," Judy said. "I have to pee. Let's get off at the next exit. And we can look to see how many Hitlers there are in a Hartford phone book."

They stopped for soggy pancakes at the oddly named Miss Rhode Island Diner. There were no Hitlers in the phone book. A fat man played "Raindrops Keep Falling on My Head" four times in a row from his jukebox connection in the next booth. Was it homeopathic magic? The rain started as they got back on the highway, Judy in the driver's seat again.

"My last bus had no windshield squirter, and one December I had to do this drive with an enema bag strapped up on the visor and its tube duct-taped to the windshield. I'd give it a squeeze when I couldn't see anything."

"Very clever, these professors."

"You'd think the Germans would have come up with something. Ever see the poster of Otto Porsche and Hitler playing with a model of the first VW? My mechanic in Somerville put it up in his garage after I made him take the girly pictures down. I threatened to fix my own car with John Muir's book for the Compleat Idiot. He didn't want to have to deal with the consequences, so he took it down."

"Mind if we go back to what we were talking about before?"

"God, is this is a busman's holiday? Ethnolinguistics Seminar on Interstate 84?"

"Busperson."

"Bus*man*. It's a totemic expression."

"Fine. Wittgenstein thought philosophy was a battle against the bewitchment of our intelligence by means of language."

"I know that passage. *'Verhexung,'* he called it. The operations of a witch. Like my sister at the stake."

"Language poisons real existence. That seems pathological to me. Human speech as a disease."

"The problem is not the disease of language, Arnold, but the disease called humanity."

Arnold stared out into the rain. A neon "JESUS SAVES" sign flashed its message red onto the wet highway.

"There are those who think all language stems from mating calls. Ooogly-oogly-oogly." She blinked big eyes at him. "Love love love. Whoops. No. That's taboo, too. Can't love a student." She turned to fiercely face the road, and gripped the wheel hard.

"A variation on the incest taboo?"

"Could be . . . Arnold, my son. Ask Harvard, that most rational of institutions."

"What do you mean?"

"Have you heard about the rules being proposed by the emotion police?"

"I'm just a lowly sophomore."

"From another planet, must be. There's a Harvard-Radcliffe faculty committee drafting rules that would essentially prohibit any sexual or emotional relationship between students and faculty."

"That's probably a good idea, from what I hear."

"What do you hear?"

"That there are all these professors going after girls in their classes, punishing them with bad grades if they don't submit, ruining their academic careers if they break up. . . ."

"Yeah, maybe. But those rules won't protect anyone. They'll police and punish, not empower. I proposed instead a theater company that would go around to the houses and improvise typical situations—let students play out different responses, show them their options. No. The feminists are out for blood: prevention just keeps them from their prey."

"I thought *you* were a feminist."

"I'm a humanist. I believe in finding the full range of our creativity. Sexuality and emotional experience is part of it. Mechanical prohibitions infantilize students. They're right out of a parental paradigm, straight out of the old antisex culture. Sexuality is as much a place for maturation as is the classroom."

"So the prettiest get the best education?"

"If it happens, it happens. It's part of life. I was in college once, too, you know—in the all-girls dorms at Columbia. We all would fantasize about the pleasure and danger of having sex with a powerful man. We were young, inexperienced, and it was exciting and a little frightening. But it was the stuff of all the romantic novels we had ever read—and we were hot to try the real thing. As young female students who fucked professors, we were not looking for a peer relationship. We believed something about us would be magically transformed by involvement with 'brilliant' men."

Arnold felt Gabe beginning to stir.

"Were you?"

"Not in the least. It was usually disappointing. The professors were in it for the pussy, and the adoration." She shrugged. "But most of us weren't damaged by these . . . skirmishes. We were hurt, not abused. We learned from them."

"Did the faculty get paid extra for providing the pain—so students could learn to recover?"

"Don't be snide, young man. We learned a lot. We learned the difference between the eroticization of power and the eroticization of domination."

Power, domination, feminist theory—a fugitive whiff of Billie Jo sweetened the psychic air. And the combination of that old vibrancy, of Judy's current vibe and the purring vibration of the old VW, gave Gabe a triple goose. Hand covered lap, and jargon the embarrassment.

"What does that mean? Eroticization of domination."

"It means the vast majority of straight women in our society are likely to have relationships with men who have greater status and power, so it's important to learn about that kind of situation, and not assume that exploitation and abuse are the only possible outcomes."

Judy drove on in silence. She switched on the radio. Arnold switched it off.

"I still think it's inappropriate for professors to be involved with students they're working with," said Arnold—who had worried about riding with an uptight professor.

"Sometimes," replied Judy. "Maybe most of the time. But not ever? What about students they're *not* working with? [Gabe again.] Let's get real—and humane: Why is there so little work done about aging faculty in universities, those unattractive, nerdy types who probably had no sex appeal ever in their lives before they became teachers, who were suddenly seen as sexy by adoring students, who are now troubled about the loss of their sexual allure and potency, who yearly face a new array of young, attractive students—who also want to know they're desirable? Why is the response to faculty-student desire to police it rather than understand it and confront it more constructively?"

"Because this is a culture of punishment."

"Bingo, Captain Vere."

"I remember all the locker-room talk about seducing a new young teacher at our high school. . . ."

"So what? So what? Supposing it happened?"

Arnold watched the blood once again starting to trickle out of Judy's nostril. He pulled a Kleenex from the box and handed it to her. Tears ran silently down her cheeks, to mingle with the blood.

"Why are you crying?"

"I'm crying at your kindness, you lunkhead. Plexus of Kieselbach."

"Want me to drive?"

"No."

"Want to talk about it?"

"No. I'll talk to my analyst."

There was silence between them until Hartford. Arnold commented on the blue onion dome of the Colt building.

"That's where they make pistols that men use to kill women," Judy remarked. "The onion symbolizes weeping."

"They don't kill only women."

"Bzzzzzzt. Clichéd response. You lose."

At Brewster, N.Y., the traffic thickened, and the road broadened as it readied itself for the great metropolis ahead.

"Where are you headed in the city?" Judy asked.

"I don't know. Wherever you drop me."

"Well, where are you staying?"

"I thought I'd try to find a Y or something."

She nodded and looked thoughtful. "There's an extra bedroom at my sister's. I'm on dog-sitting duty while she goes off to a medical conference in St. Thomas, that dog. I mean my sister. I mean those doctors sure know how to treat themselves."

"You want me to stay with you at your sister's?"

"Well, not *with* me—there's an empty room, and you have nowhere else at the moment. You can pay me back by walking the dogs, then I can be footloose and fancy-free, and you'll save yourself a bunch of bucks."

"Are you going to be Judy or Professor Jepperson?"

"Which would you prefer?"

"Judy."

"Judy it is. Are you going to be Arnold or Hitler?"

"I'm going to be Arnold Hitler, like I always am."

"I'll try to demythologize you into ordinary flesh and blood. But you know there are bright sides to being irrational about words."

"You don't say."

"Don't you think it's good for the word 'Hitler' to continue evoking repulsion and horror?"

"Not for me."

"Don't be selfish. Beyond you. It's good for society to have taboos. I just read a book by a German TV reporter. He went around asking junior high kids what they knew about Hitler. You know what the title of the book is? *Hitler Is the Man Who Built the Autobahns*. That's what several kids told him. This is Germany, two years ago! Would you rather have that?"

"I'd rather have people make appropriate distinctions."

"They're not going to."

. . .

Arnold moved into his temporary home on 113th Street off Riverside Drive. Twice a day he walked Bud and Zephyr up and down Broadway and scooped their poops into plastic bags in accord with a new and much-protested municipal ordinance, more honored in the breach. Each night he waited for Judy Jepperson to come home and ask him to share her bed. But she never did.

Twenty-five

The ride back was quiet. He and Judy didn't talk about what they didn't do. Arnold drove most of the way, a payment in his mind of some obscure debt for goods undelivered. Or perhaps for not having to house them. Judy lay on the bed in back, cozy under her comforter, reading her book.

"Hey, sailor," she yelled over the Volkswagen's whine, "Here's a passage you would like. Borges is describing a language with no nouns, only verbs describing how nouns act. For example, there's no noun for *moon* or *sea*, so the sentence *The moon rose over the sea* translates as *upward beyond the constant flow there was moondling.*

"Think it would help me?"

212

"Wait—it gets better. In the north of this no-noun country, there aren't even any verbs. Only strings of adjectives. They don't say *moon*; they say *aerial-bright above dark-round* or *soft-amberish-celestial* or any other string."

"*My* problem is that English is too *simple*. There's only one word for Hitler."

"I'll bet you and your pop are the only ones in the country."

"How much?"

"How much what?"

"How much you want to bet?"

"Dinner at the Orson Welles."

"You mean the eatery for 'Social Intercourse and Oral Gratification'?"

"That's it."

"For which one? Intercourse or gratification?"

"You got something against either?"

"It just sounds lascivious to me."

"Got anything against lascivious? You're the one who wanted to bet."

"Is this about enhancing mutual growth between student and teacher?"

"Naw. It's about my getting a free spinach-mushroom melt."

"All right. I'll hit the phone books at Widener. If I come up with other Hitlers than George and me, you pay?"

"At least two others."

"You're on."

In three hours, Arnold found nine Hitlers—including an Adolph in a small town in Louisiana—research that paid off with a lively dinner on Judy and a night in her apartment in the huge brick building facing Mass Ave. He even slept in her bed—with her—but sheathed in so much verbiage about "one time only" and "this doesn't mean a relationship" and "let's just be friends" and "in the Middle Ages, a knight would 'bundle' with his lady for warmth, and place his naked sword between them" that Arnold's own sword became flaccid as a Dali watch, and as torpid. Both professor and student got a good night's sleep.

The next morning he sat naked in the living room, awaiting his turn in the shower, trying to ignore the aggressive morning radiator raga, while catching up on old issues of the *Crimson.*

"What's *Endgame?*" he asked as Judy appeared in white terrycloth, toweling out her short hair.

"*Endgame* the play?"

"Yeah. There are auditions for *Endgame.* The HDC. In the little theater at the Loeb."

Judy went into the bedroom to put on some clothes.

"It's Beckett," she yelled out. "Very cosmic and avant-garde, of course. And funny."

"Are you finished in the bathroom?"

"Yes."

"I'm going to take a shower, OK?"

"Why don't you take a bath, so I can sit in there with you and tell you about *Endgame. . . .*"

"I'd rather shower."

"Hey, sailor, it's my house, and you were asking permission. I'm giving you permission to take a bath." She turned on the bath.

"Why do you keep calling me 'sailor'?"

"Because you remind me of Billy Budd."

"My mother said the same thing when I got a little sailor suit."

"Have you read it?"

"No."

"Anyone ever take an irrational dislike to you?"

"Everyone."

"Beware the Claggarts, sailor." A trip to the hall closet produced a large bath towel of pink flamingoes. "A gift from my flamboyant sister," she explained. "I have little or nothing to do with flamingoes. Into the tub."

Arnold obeyed, as he might a commanding officer. His large frame in the small tub raised the water to nearly flood level. Judy put down the toilet seat cover and plunked herself down.

"So this guy, Hamm—he's blind and paralyzed from the waist down—he has a servant, Clov, who may be his son, who spends the play trying to get away from him and screwing the lids down on the two garbage cans where Nell and Nagg—Hamm's parents—live."

"His parents live in garbage cans?"

"Yes. What else do we do with our parents?"

"I won't do that with mine."

"Want to bet? Anyway, the larger question is where they are, all of them, what's outside the two tiny windows, and what's going to happen to them after all their joking around."

"What *is?*"

"Who knows? It's quite mysterious. A remarkable play."

"Maybe I'll try out. Maybe I can get a small role."

"For you there are no small roles. You're four sizes too large to fit in a garbage can. So it's either Hamm the master, or Clov the servant. Big roles."

Judy got up, wiped the steam from a small part of the mirror, checked her image, and made a few artistic swipes with her hairbrush.

"I don't usually have to brush this do. You must have mussed me up last night."

"No way," Arnold said. "Sword between us."

"You've got long arms, bud, and only one burned hand."

She leaned over and planted a kiss on top of Arnold's wet head.

"I've got to go. Meeting at 10. Just lock up after yourself when you leave. Push the button right under the latch. I would try out for the show if I were you. There's nothing like bathing in the immense for six weeks."

"Will I see you again?"

"Sure. Just don't be a pest. Or too obvious about it."

Auditions for *Endgame* were in the Loeb "Ex," a small, flexible black box in the basement of the huge theater building. They were his first, and felt like a disembodied football game—an orgy of high competition, with individuals making would-be charges and end runs on a field marked only by the mimeographed text. No teamwork here, just a pick-*me* striving of all against all. Calling the shots was a Radcliffe student, a tiny woman, one Ruby Schneider, who would be both directing and playing Nell. Well, thought Arnold, she'll fit in the garbage can.

This was a real issue. Given the Loeb Ex's wood-over-concrete floor, there was no possibility of false bottoms and trap for more comfortable canning. It was ninety minutes of imprisonment beyond anything in the history of dungeons. Nagg had to be similarly small—or a black-belt yogi. As Arnold looked around the room, he saw the contenders. The most obvious was a dwarf named Hugh Laffler, a tiny genius whose huge head was crammed full of subatomic particles trailing their attendant theories. Arnold had met him coming out of Bob Wright's office and had spent his first five minutes of draft counseling hearing about Hugh and his compensatory gifts. Arnold made a mental note to call Bob, though he had become no clearer about his antimilitary plans.

For his audition, he recited Shakespeare sonnet XII, memorized overnight, and Beckett-apt. He sang "Deep in the Heart of Texas" for his combined music and comedy selections, and read, as did others, the proffered mimeograph of Hamm's chronicle of the beggar. He was referred to, throughout, as "Arnold H."

The following day, he checked the callbacks and found himself part of a far smaller pool. That evening he returned to the Ex and read against a variety of Clovs, some larger and more sluggish than he, servant creatures to his Dr. Frankenstein, and some smaller and more skittish, hopping toads or slithering lizards. At midnight he received a call in his room at Eliot.

"Arnold?"

"Yes?"

"This is Ruby Schneider . . . the *Endgame* director?"

"Yes, yes, how are you?"

"I hope it's not too late to call."

"No, no."

"Theater hours."

"I understand."

"Arnold, we're thinking very seriously of casting you as Hamm . . ."

"How nice . . ."

". . . but there are two things we have to check with you."

"What's that?"

"Would you be willing to work on your Southern accent, along with working on the part—undo it, or create another accent for Hamm?"

"Well, sure . . . I've been trying to work on it anyway."

"That wouldn't bug you?"

"No."

"Good. And also, did you ever use a stage name?"

"No. I . . . this would be the first real play I've been in."

"What would you think about a stage name?"

"Why?"

"A lot of famous theater people use stage names. Woody Allen's real name is Allen Stewart Konigsberg. . . ."

"I'll have to think about it."

"Would you really?"

"I'll let you know tomorrow."

"I have to post casting by 10 A.M. Can you call me before that?"

"Yes."

"5-5704."

He wrote it down.

"We'd really like to use you, Arnold. Talk to you tomorrow."

"OK."

"Good-night."

For Arnold, it was a bad night, a night in which he had to confront, even if minimally and temporarily, the Temptation of Changing His Name. It sounded as if he had the part. He *wanted* the part. It was a small price to pay. It was too big a price to pay. He called Jacobo.

"Arnold."

"Grandpa, are you OK? You sound out of breath."

"I'm doing my morning calisthenics and beauty treatment. Left, up, right, up, left . . . Oi . . . You ever work out?"

"Yes, but . . . Grandpa, I have a problem."

"What's wrong with a stage name?"

"You were eavesdropping."

"What do you think, I sleep at night when you are in trouble? Some of the greatest . . ."

"I know. Woody Allen's real name was . . ."

"That's right. And he's Jewish."

"So?"

"So for him, it's like getting a nose job."

"And for me?"

"For you it's an end run around the *schmegeggie* line. A forward pass to your doppelgänger. You just need the right name."

"What would that be?"

"Something that gives them what they want, but simultaneously expresses your scorn for their wanting it. How about Siegfried Held?"

"Everyone in the cast knows my name is Arnold."

"All right. Arnold Siegfried Held. Arnold S. Held?"

"How does it express scorn?"

"Arnold, the winner of the peace, the hero. Also a good Nazi name. Very complex imagery."

"I already have a good Nazi name. That's the problem."

"It's a satire."

"I'll think about it."

"Arnold, don't be a fuddy-duddy. You say 'fuddy-duddy'? It's in my idiom book. What does it mean?"

"Someone who is timid and square."

"Yes. That. Don't be one."

"Let me sleep on it."

"I'll call you tomorrow night to find out."

"You mean you won't already know?"

"I'll know. But I want to hear it from you."

"Grandpa . . ."

"Arnold, enough. I'm in the middle of my side-bends."

"All right, Grandpa. *Ciao.*"

The next morning, Arnold S. Held called Ruby Schneider. She was happy to hear from him.

Twenty-six

Arnold's spring '70 semester consisted primarily of *Endgame*. His other courses—French, biology, "The History of American Fascism"—faded into the background in the intensity of its dark light. For Beckett, unhappiness seemed to be the name of the human game, as it was of Arnold's. Hamm asks Clov if his father is dead.

>   *(Clov raises the lid of Nagg's bin, stoops, looks into it. Pause.)*
> CLOV: Doesn't look like it.
>   *(He closes the lid, straightens up.)*
> HAMM: What's he doing?
>   *(Clov raises the lid of Nagg's bin, stoops, looks into it. Pause.)*
> CLOV: He's crying.
>   *(He closes the lid, straightens up.)*
> HAMM: Then he's living.

For all its weirdness, this may be the most realistic play ever written. "The end is in the beginning." And what was Arnold's beginning?— when George Hitler, progenitor, mounted between the one-and-a-half legs of Anna Giardini and created another neighing of the H-name? "Scoundrel!" Hamm cries, "Why did you engender me?"

> NAGG: I didn't know.
> HAMM: What? What didn't you know?
> NAGG: That it'd be you.

But George did know. He just didn't think. And what is he thinking now, my once-father? Two short letters since I've been here. Four unanswered. Has he forgotten me?

"We let you cry. Then we moved out of earshot, so that we might sleep in peace . . ."

Arnold shuddered in recognition.

Three days before opening, Arnold received a red-inked note on Foxx Club letterhead: "You are invited to come polish your personality at my Ring the Merry Hells on Board Ship party Friday after the show. RSVP-ASAP—in fact, immediately. Beware the ides of March." Arnold had ignored two other notes from Rick since their meeting and felt he could ignore this one. He didn't anticipate the fulminating contents of the review by one "Cottonmouth" in the following week's *Harvard Independent:*

HITLER REIGNS AT EX

In a transparent ruse, Arnold Hitler, in his new, "safe" incarnation as Arnold S. Held the Cowardly Hero, demonstrates yet again the inhuman cruelty for which he and his eponymous forebear are famous. Hitler the Hero plays Hamm, Beckett's nightmare creation, with high fidelity. Playing a handicapped master of the handicapped, Held/Hamm bullies his pathetic servant Clov mercilessly, trying to convince himself of the Hitlerian axiom "I have power, therefore I exist."

It is frightening to see such naked trueness to type. As the program notes inform, this is Hitler's first theater role: an accomplished actor he is not. Thus he calls on his native proclivities to fill the gap. Such handsome men are dangerous.

Hitler/Hamm allows poor Clov just enough food to live and be miserable. His inhuman regime is built on naked cruelty, suffering, and death—as in the camps. His histrionic boasting consists of gloating accounts of his exercise of power. He treats his servant like the toy dog he has him build. "Leave him like that, standing there imploring me." How convincingly Hitler delivers the line. Clov fills in the picture: "When old Mother Pegg asked you for oil for her lamp and you told her to get out to hell, you knew what was happening then, no? You know what she died of, Mother Pegg? Of darkness."

Hitler/Hamm, a Hammurabi promulgating his own tyrannical laws—such is the energy our Aryan ex-quarterback brings to this playing field.

My advice: stay away from this mephitic infusion and its sulfurous presenter.

Richard Mather. Like Cotton Mather. "Cottonmouth." Who else could it be?

The *Indy* was delivered free on Thursdays to every doorstep at Harvard.

Twenty-seven

And you will be in this book

Edmond Jabès, *The Book of Questions*

The sign on the Eliot House bulletin board—soon removed—read, "A SAD DAY FOR BESTIALITY." And indeed, the moving in of women had a huge impact on the stately palace on the Charles. The official merger of Harvard and Radcliffe meant that doorways along the once fetid, now sparkling hallways sprouted pictures of cute little bunnies, while the old Playboy versions seemed to have scurried into collective hiding in some hutch of masculine dreams. One door read, "Jessica, Trained Extrovert," though Jessica herself was seldom to be seen and was no doubt extroverting in places other than her dorm. One woman posted a nineteenth-century etching of Dostoevsky, whose eyes followed you as you walked along the hall. Ann Strout, the picture's owner, looked just like Dostoevsky—without the mustache and beard, a woman of broad forehead and thinning hair, decidedly unfriendly to all.

Arnold tried to imagine the women behind this array of signifying images. His own door was bare wood. What would he put there were he to join the exhibition? A picture of Adolf? Don Meredith? Erasmus? A Lone Star flag? The board at move 40 of Spassky-Petrosian? A still of Antonius Block confessing to Fr. Death? Better bare wood.

The sexual tension was so high that common encounters with torn slippers, hair curlers, and empty bottles of nail-polish remover would not cool it down to premerger levels.

Radcliffe girls were scary—especially in close proximity. They were generally thought to be smarter than the boys, in part because there were fewer, only three hundred in each class, and their admission was that much more selective. They certainly tended to be far more serious about their work.

The *Harvard Lampoon* invented a campus organization called the Radcliffe Association for the Suppression of the Male Ego, and one Harvard definition of a typical Radcliffe girl had it that when she drops her glove and you gallantly stoop to pick it up, she steps on your hand and says, "That's mine."

"It is always a worthwhile experience taking out Radcliffe girls," one Eliot student remarked. "They're enjoyable as people even if they're not as women."

And then there was the issue of relative maturity. What twenty-year-old man—even at Harvard, perhaps especially at Harvard—was a fit partner for a twenty-year-old Cliffie? For Arnold, a siren melody filled the long hallways of Eliot House, but the tune in the air seemed not meant for him.

To earn money and save travel expenses, he had worked the past summer prepping and washing dishes at the Underdog, a small hot-dog joint near the Square known for the best kosher franks in town. Much of its pizzazz got by Arnold, who didn't know what was so special about Dr. Brown's Cream Soda, or why "the Blasphemy" (New York kosher frank

stuffed with cheese and grilled in bacon) was called "the Blasphemy."
But he liked working "for the Underdog." It seemed politically correct—on the semantic level—in the days before political correctness became incorrect. After an early-June exchange—in which a waitress
opined that if he didn't know what was blasphemous about the Blasphemy, he didn't *need* to know—he consulted Jacobo. After looking up
the word in his Inglese-Italiano *dizionario,* the old joker had much
to say:

"Well, my big, blond, goyische poopchen, I would say that 'the Blasphemy' was blasphemous on three, possibly four, counts and on two, possibly three, levels. *Bestemmia.* That means bad talk. *Molto* bad talk,
irriverente. Bad talk about God and God-things like other people. No respect for God's word."

"What did God have to say about hot dogs?"

"God is reserved about hot dogs per se. Except that you shouldn't eat
dogs at all—hot or cold—because they don't chew their cud. . . ."

"God can eat only what chews its cud?"

"No, Jews can eat only what chews its cud—and only if it has cloven
hooves. You, being only a quarter Jewish, have to conform only a quarter of the time. The rest of the time you can eat like a goy, and it's OK."

"What about chickens—chicken soup? Chickens don't chew their
cud. Jews eat chicken."

"The fowls of the air are in another class. A quarter of the time you
may not eat owls or vultures. Birds of prey are out. They're dirty. They
eat corpses. No more vultures, hear me? I'll be watching."

"I promise."

"There are certain rabbinically unresolved questions about the barnacle goose, which grows on a tree attached by its bill or possibly inside
a shell. Rabbi Moses of Vienna ruled that a barnacle goose may be eaten
after ritual slaughtering—like a plain old chicken. But Rabbi Joseph for-
bade it, since he thought it was a species of shellfish. And Rabbi Abba

ruled that birds growing on trees are forbidden since he saw them as creeping things."

"Jews can't eat creeping things?"

"Lizards and snakes—out. Worms and weasels—forget it."

"So you're saying the Blasphemy is blasphemous because it's probably made out of God knows what?"

"And maybe even God doesn't know."

"But these are kosher hot dogs. Doesn't that mean God likes them? The boxes say 'Hebrew National.'"

"Well, let's just assume for the sake of discussion that the little kishkas are stuffed with ground-up, cud-chewing, cloven-hoofed beasts, not contaminated by owl or clam droppings or any other kind of schmutz. I'll forget about the bacon juice."

"And slices. We top them with bacon slices."

"I need to say more? But we then have the issue of the cheese."

"Good American cheese slices. Kraft. The best!"

"Where to begin? Such ignorant insensitivity. My own flesh and blood. 'You shall not boil a kid in its mother's milk.' It's stated and re-stated three times in the Torah. Exodus, Exodus, Deuteronomy."

"They were really into not boiling. . . ."

"You bet. Arnold, whatever you do, *do not boil a kid in its mother's milk.* You'll be sorry, I assure you."

"I promise."

"I'll know."

"I know you'll know."

"This has to do with reverence for life. Mothers. Milk. Nourishing. Life. You don't want to mix life with blood, death, ripping into flesh. You have to keep the milk products away from the meat. No milk for six hours after meat. Separate dishes, separate pots, separate tables for preparing."

"Sounds a little nuts."

"Arnold, no cheese on hot dogs, you understand me?"

"OK. Blasphemy one, possibly two, definitely one unclean animal, maybe more. And two, possibly three, milk plus meat. Then what?"

"So how were the cud-chewers killed? Do you know? They have to be carried off by a highly trained individual, an ordained *schochet*—a ritual slaughterer, a man of excellent character, good health, well acquainted with Mosaic law and an expert on the conditions of the animals in the before- and afterlife. The knife must be without any imperfections. Throats must be cut quickly and painlessly, with one stroke, no pressure, no brutal tearing of flesh or skin. Humane, Arnold. If you kill, you must be humane. Is Hebrew National humane?"

"I don't know."

"Do they slit a single throat at a time?"

"I don't know. Probably not. It must be a big operation."

"You should see how the goyim slaughter their pigs here in Ferrara. It's horrible. The farmer sits on the pig's back and plunges the knife in again and again. And the pig yells and cries till it collapses."

Arnold was silent.

"There are no rabbis to protect bacon."

"Why not?" Arnold asked.

"Hmmm. It would have taken one strange rabbi. But it's possible. I'll take it up with my Kaballah Klub.".

"You're still down one blasphemy."

"Oh—the most obvious—the words, the joking with the idea of blasphemy, as if the concept itself were ridiculous. And I'll bet the Jewish students eat it up."

"They do."

"What you are serving; how it got there into the mouth; and how you talk about it, and the effect of talking about it that way—three levels."

"Bad speech."

"Very bad."

"Maybe I'll quit," Arnold said.

"You need the money?"

"Yes."

"Are there other jobs?"

"All the summer jobs are taken."

"Well, it's enough to just know what kind of a world you live in. Meditate on Blasphemy. But no kids boiled in mother's milk. Do not allow this."

"Thank you, Grandpa. I feel like I just aged ten years."

"Don't get too old too fast. Say *buon giorno* to your mother when you talk to her."

Arnold did not tell Jacobo he hadn't heard from Anna for several months. He did, however, mention to Lynn Altswerger, the waitress, that he now understood blasphemy, and was thinking of quitting. "Over a hot dog with cheese? What a Jewish idea! You Jewish? You're not Jewish. You couldn't be."

"I have a Jewish grandfather."

"Better you should hang out here. Develop your cultural heritage. Drink plenty of Dr. Brown's Cream Soda."

By the beginning of his junior year, Arnold was foot and mouth into an existential/religious crisis. He thought of becoming kosher. A kosher Hitler? That would show them! Then he read where God said, "Behold I have given you every herb bearing seed which is upon the earth, and every tree in the which is the fruit of a tree yielding seed: to you it shall be for meat." Didn't this mean humans were supposed to be vegetarians?

With *Endgame* under his belt, the fall of 1970 seemed time to make good his last year's thought of trying out for Gilbert and Sullivan, and Arnold was first in line for September auditions for *Yeoman of the Guard.* He wasn't sure he could really sing, but he belted out the Tom Lehrer song he had been practicing over the summer—which in June had been "Fat feyrsely, Hahrvid, fat, fat . . ." but by August had sounded more like "Fight fiercely, Harvard, fight, fight, fight"—with a slight, possibly Southern, accent.

A paradox: Harvard undergrads were visually liberal. The stranger someone looked, the more tentative respect he or she was given. Yet the same group of students were aurally archconservative: Any domestic accent—urban black, Brooklyn, Texan—would put a class member under instant suspicion. A stiff Oxonian accent might pass muster, or a faint German one, as in that of a well-disguised atomic physicist spy. But North Texas? Never. In an effort to become more acceptable, Arnold had picked up a used copy of Tom Lehrer songs, one, because he thought they were clever, but more importantly, because he imagined that the singing ex-Harvard math professor's pronunciation might be a vowel model for him. His consonants were already acceptable.

"Fight fiercely, Harvard" went over big at the auditions. When they asked him if he had anything else, thinking he might take a stab at "A More Humane Mikado" or "I Am a Pirate King," he came back with "The Old Dope Peddler," and then admitted under questioning that he knew no Gilbert and Sullivan but had loved last year's *Mikado* and wanted to get involved. With his good looks, his athlete's grace, his almost-but-not-quite rich voice, and his unconsciously comical delivery, he was second in line for the lead role of Jack Point, the strolling jester. When the first choice grabbed the role of Peer Gynt in the concurrent HDC production, Jack Point fell to Arnold, who screwed his courage to the sticking place and accepted. He had difficult and exciting classes— French lit, "Radical Critique of the Uses of Psychology in Community Relations," first-semester general chemistry, and Cavell's course on Thoreau—but Harvard was big on extracurricular activities, and he was big on self-discovery and jealous of the rare affirmation. The lead in *Yeoman* he would be.

The first read-through was on a Wednesday night, and Arnold was early as usual, but not the first one in the rehearsal room. Already seated at a long oval table was a heart-shatteringly beautiful woman, huge brown eyes and silky hair, the prettiest girl he ever saw, studying a *Yeoman* script and sipping—he couldn't believe it—sipping apple cider through a straw. He had two choices, either to implode in shyness and creep out of the room or to explode in Texas enthusiasm and sing, "The prettiest girl I ever saw/was sippin' cider through a straw" in a broad ol' Mansfield accent. He chose—or rather, it chose—the latter. What was it? Youth? Joy? Awe? Testosterone? Quantum irregularities? Anyway, he did it.

His performance was a flop. The young woman looked up, smiled a tepid smile (showing the most beautiful teeth), and went back to her script. Arnold sank into a chair at the Keplerian opposition point and began to stare at his own pages, though his concentration was too assaulted to consider more than the two opening lines of the show: "When maiden loves, she sits and sighs/She wanders to and fro." He glanced furtively at his table partner and decided she must not be in love, and somehow that mental classification was enough to prick the bubble of confusion and allow him to breathe at normal excursion.

The woman at the table, the prettiest girl he ever saw, the being actually sipping cider through a straw, was his leading lady, Ariel Bernstein, a freshman living on the Radcliffe Quad, at Whitman Hall. Another Jewish girl, he thought. Beware.

He discovered her identity as the cast went around the table introducing themselves, saying a bit about their backgrounds and experience. Arnold panicked when he realized he hadn't thought about his name. Was he to be Hitler to the group—or the publicly unmasked Arnold S. Held? He had eight others' short biographies to make up his mind. Still shaken, perhaps, by the recent embarrassing encounter with Ariel, he came up out of nowhere with a new identity: "Abe Hittleman," he blurted out, "from the Bronx, New York." "The Bronx, New York" should have given him away then and there, since no one from the Bronx would say that. Still, appropriating the approximate biography of an MIT student he had met at the Coop, he told how he had been in plays at the Bronx High School of Science, *Antigone* being one, in which he had played the boyfriend of Antigone's sister—a not too memorable role. He could not be faulted for forgetting the details.

Ariel was reticent during her biography, stating simply that she was from New York City and had been in several plays and musical productions at her private school. As with Arnold, this would be her first Gilbert and Sullivan production. She warmed up as the evening went on to the dismaying point where, by the end of the first act, Arnold was in love with her all over again, worse than before. Love at second sight is potentiated, as in anaphylaxis, as in two points determining a line.

Though Arnold and Ariel spent long hours together every night on the show, and not a few hours during the day running lines and practicing their harmonies, they were not officially courting. Still, for all their chasteness, Ariel's friends could imagine them thus entwined. How easy it would be to fast forward and act as if it were so.

The third-act complication in mid-October was all too predictable. After all, he was not Abraham Hittleman, nice Jewish boy from the Bronx. He was Arnold Hitler, the deceptive goy with the ghastly name, from the redneck land of Texas. The unrequited, if oft-excited, lover, involved no less with faculty liberation. What kind of con man did he think he was? How long did he think he could get away with this impersonation in the small community of Harvard-Radcliffe?

He knew he would have to 'fess up—to Ariel at least. He had planned to do it well before but had postponed and postponed it as it became ever more embarrassing and difficult. A midnight warning from Jacobo pricked the sides of his intent: he would confess the very next day.

He had a plan. He had had it for a while, since *before* Ariel, a plan situating the disjuncture between name and being in the venerable context of Harvardiana. The next afternoon, kicking their way through the fallen red leaves in Harvard Yard, he made sure to steer them right past the statue of the seated John Harvard outside University Hall. Arnold stopped to rub the shiny toe of the statue's right boot.

"It's good luck to rub it. Look how shiny it is," he said.

"Better rub than lick," she observed. "You know, Mr. Harvard looks a lot like you. Sure you're not related? My friend Alice says Cohens and Lowensteins are replacing Cabots and Lowells." She tickled his not-very-Jewish nose with a leaf.

"You know, this is called the 'Statue of the Three Lies,'" said Arnold, making a subsequitur on to his agenda. "See that plaque?"

"JOHN HARVARD, FOUNDER, 1638," she read. "What's wrong with that? Oh, wait—it's 1636, isn't it?"

"Been wrong for fourscore and six years."

"Just like Harvard not to fix it," Ariel complained. "Heroes, heroes, heroes. History, history, history. Holy, holy, holy. The place is fixated on 'H's. Nothing is allowed to change."

"What are you talking about? We just went co-ed. The Cohens are crowding out the Cabots."

She felt she was beaten on a technical point.

"So what are the other two lies?"

"Well, old John didn't found the college. The Massachusetts Bay Colony did, two years before it was named Harvard—after he gave them his library."

"Liars and cheats! For this they expect us to pay big-bucks tuition?"

"You haven't heard the worst. This isn't even John Harvard."

"I knew it! It's you! It's a statue of you—looking Harvardy, looking like American hard work and good clean fun, radiating chastity and piety and success." Arnold felt the ironic dig on "chastity."

"It's not me. It's some student model from the class of '84—1884—chosen, no doubt, for the excellent virtues you list. There were no paintings left of John Harvard. They were all destroyed in the library fire in 1764."

"The whole library destroyed? Like Alexandria?"

"All except one book."

"What book was that?"

"I don't know. But here's the story. You couldn't take books out of the library. Any books."

"Bad."

"And there was a student working late one night, and the library closed, and he wasn't finished, so he put the book under his coat and took it home. Overnight the whole library burned to the ground. That student had the only surviving book—whatever it was. Everybody is moaning about the loss, so the student takes the book to President Hoar and presents it to him as a gift. President Hoar is the one with no house named after him. The kid says, 'Here—the tradition is not completely extinguished. From this seed will grow another library.' Hoar is ecstatic. The faculty is ecstatic. The trustees are ecstatic. The Corporation is ecstatic. Even the students are ecstatic. A saving remnant exists! Hoar thanks the student, congratulates him—then kicks him out of school for breaking library rules."

"I'm speechless."

"I thought you'd like it."

"No good deed goes unpunished."

"So anyway Daniel Chester French modeled one of the Cabots or Lowells—no Lowensteins then—and labeled it John Harvard."

"Founder. 1638."

"The Problem of Identity."

"Epistemological Delight."

"Things are seldom what they seem."

"Skim milk masquerades as cream."

"Ariel?"

"What?" said she, prepared, perhaps, for a declaration of love.

"I'm not John Harvard."

"You're forgiven."

"But I'm not Abe Hittleman either."

"What do you mean?"

"That's my stage name."

"Abe Hittleman is the kind of name people *change* when they go for a stage name."

"Depends where you start. Know what my real name is?"

"Rumpelstiltskin."

"Arnold Hitler. From Mansfield, Texas."

She didn't have to say she was speechless: she was speechless. Arnold didn't know who was supposed to speak next. The silence became uncomfortable enough for him to break it.

"Don't you think that's funny?"

She did not jump on him, or pull away.

"It must be painful for a Jew."

"I'm not a Jew. Or just a little bit. One Jewish grandfather. You'd like him."

The slurry darkened from an unfortunate accident of birth to a month of ongoing, intentional lying. Arnold waited for the blow to strike. Ariel was quietly processing.

"Abe . . . I mean Arnold . . . Arnie?"

"Arnold."

"Arnold. Arnold, I've lied to you, too. And to everyone else."

"Your name is Thumbelina?"

"No, it's Ariel Bernstein, but with a capital B."

"Everybody's name is with a capital B. I mean a capital something. Except ee cummings."

"A *big* capital B. You've heard of Leonard Bernstein in Texas?"

"*West Side Story* Leonard Bernstein?"

"My pop. Lenny and Felicia. The toast of New York City, Vienna, and Katmandu. I went to very fancy private schools. I didn't just do a little music, I grew up music. I played with Heifetz and Piatagorsky and Casals, and Stowkowski . . ."

"What do you play?"

"I mean I played blowing bubbles with them, Monopoly, card games. Yehudi Menhuin taught me to play pinochle!"

"So what's wrong with that? Better than growing up Hitler."

"I don't want to be another Harvard brat of a rich, famous father. I want to make it on my own here, just another anonymous New York smart Jewish princess named Bernstein."

"I don't see that you lied."

"You know how I know I'm lying? Because I can never believe anyone else's story. Every single person in the Yard could be lying about who they are."

"So you're not so surprised at me, then."

"Well, I'm surprised. But I'm not shocked."

"My lies are worse than yours!" Arnold teased, perhaps too lightly. "Sins of commission, mortal; sins of omission, venial."

"Jews don't make such fine distinctions. I don't trust a soul."

Now it was Arnold's turn to ponder.

"I hate it," she added, though exactly what "it" was remained unclear.

Twenty-eight

Each time Arnold rehearsed Point and Elsie's entrance into the *Yeoman* world of tower and torture—the crowd chasing them in, the threat of Elsie's rape, distracted by Point's verbal pyrotechnics,

She said "Hands off!" Whose hands? Thine. Off whom? Off her. Why? Because she is a woman. Now had she not been a woman, thine hands had not been set upon her at all. So the reason for the laying on of hands is the reason for the taking off of hands, and herein is contradiction contradicted!

their lovely prophetic duet and dance, "I have a song to sing, O!" and especially Elsie's drawing of a dagger against a would-be smooch—

Best beware! I am armed!

each time he experienced this rush of potentially healing, yet conflicted, energy, he flashed back on one of the most terrifying scenes in *The Seventh Seal,* the overcoming of *its* Merryman and Maid by the crucified, plague-driven Christ. Hooded monks, coffins and relics, whipping and twisting and howling. *Dies irae, dies illa.* Gilbert and Bergman seemed to agree: loveliness is often trumped with horror. Point and Elsie found their own during the show. But what about Arnold and Ariel? What, he wondered, would our horror be? They found it together, by accident, in the Loeb green room before rehearsal. Most students were home for Thanksgiving. Not the Savoyards, though: their show opened the following week.

It was November 24. The CBS Evening News was muttering along on the small TV that had recently shown up. They walked in on the middle of a Mike Wallace interview of someone who'd been involved in My Lai.

Arnold and Ariel had been increasingly aware of the gruesome tale for the last ten days, yet as the details filled in, they reacted as did many Americans: they allowed its repulsiveness to distance them from its impact. Things were already edgy between them, and this tale of violence in South Asian jungles had a hard time penetrating the surface tension of their postconfession relationship.

There was something about this CBS fragment, this small penetrating shard, that ripped a hole in the protective fabric, and their armor collapsed—both toward the story, and toward one another. This is what they heard about the women and children in the irrigation ditch:

A: I held my M-16 on them.

Q: Why?

A: Because they might attack.

Q: They were children and babies?

A: Yes.

Q: And they might attack? Children and babies?

A: They might've had a fully loaded grenade on them. The mothers might have throwed them at us.

Q: Babies?

A: Yes.

Q: Were the babies in their mothers' arms?

A: I guess so.

Q: And the babies moved to attack?

Then Phoebe and Wilfred Shadbolt walked in and said, "You mind if we run our scene?"—and shut off the TV. Arnold took Ariel's hand, and they sat on the couch together, silently listening to their colleagues' lines:

> *A feather's press*
> *Were leaden heaviness*
> *To my caress,*
> *But then, of course, you see*
> *I'm not thy bride! (Exit, and flop in the armchair)*

Arnold and Ariel got up, and left quietly. My Lai had brought them tentatively together.

The show was a smash. The expected attack from Cottonmouth never occurred: the *Indy* critic raved. Hearts went out to poor Jack Point, and Abe Hittleman became a culture hero—at least until finals, when he was forgotten. As Arnold walked home evenings in the brisk autumn air, as he saw the lights from Harvard Field glowing across the river, he thought about the sport of theater. This time last year he had been under stadium lights instead of Fresnels and Lekos. Instead of fringes and bells, he had worn a costume with a number on it—but a costume just the same, locker-room, dressing-room, black makeup along his cheeks to quell the glare. And the huge presence of the audience, the crowd that drove the show and had always terrified him—especially with its new custom of cadenced clapping and chanting. It could be as friendly as "Go Harvard, go! Go, Tigers, go!" But a crowd all mouthing the same thing at the same time invoked the image of a beast with multiple heads and many teeth. The awful cacophony of applause, so routine yet so intrusively ugly, seemed to symbolize the spanking, potentially punishing relationship of spectator to performer. The crowd out there in the dark, risk-free, waiting for the rope-dancer to plunge to a twisted death. If boxing and football were the last blood sports, performing on stage wasn't far behind, with the ever-present fear of humiliation hovering closely, glaring and laughing, Boomer-like, succinct.

Boomer. He remembered those eyes. He felt the spit in his face, the poison directed toward the "nigger-lover." Boomer. What a performer! Was his typecasting any different from Ariel's, the made-to-be-adored beauty, singer, dancer, she of the huge eyes and falling dark hair, the long, narrow waist and tempting bosom? Performers all. Harvard, he thought, the Olympics of education, with its high-culture sports—rowing crew, not dwarf bowling or demolition derby. The elite plays polo while the masses play pool. And where did G&S fit in? Not opera, not "legitimate" theater, not even musical comedy. "Operetta"—most appropriate for a half-trash person such as he. Bring one of those *Endgame* garbage cans into his room and sleep in it, like Queequeg in his coffin. We are born astride the grave.

From Eliot House he would gaze at the women's boathouse, hypotenused sixty feet under his window, stretching its deck out to the cold caresses of the Charles. From the air, he would play the voyeur, as dirtier men did from under gratings. Instead of looking up skirts, he would gaze down, mornings, on Ariel's head and shoulders, a pigeon's view of her daily arrival at the boathouse, locking her bike to the rack, and entering the building to emerge ten minutes later from the river side, one-eighth of a crew. The boathouse blocked his view of the deck, of the placing of the boat, and the careful sitting and pushing off. But if he had time, he would wait to see her shell emerge from behind the building, heading downstream, with the secret queen of the universe—his queen— stroking, two from the end. Some days he felt debased, secretly staring; some days he felt he should avert his eyes. But often he felt the simple joy of worship. How charming she was, how innocent of being watched.

To save travel money, Arnold again stayed in Cambridge over Christmas break. Ariel went to New York, pointedly "for Chanukah." For a reason he suspected, but which was never openly stated, the Underdog no longer had a place for his dishwashing skills, though most of its student employees had scattered home to native eateries. But it was only ten days, and the loss of income would yield to a little belt-tightening. Instead of menial labor, then, Arnold sat in his room, reading, and writing a long letter to his parents describing his fall semester and current state of mind. He made two copies at Gnomon, kept the original so as to be even-handed, and sent copies to George and Anna at their respective addresses. Much of the document was a commonplace recounting of events. One section, however, turned more problematic:

> You may have heard from Grandpa J that we have had talks about my changing my name to avoid prejudice and misunderstandings. These exchanges have been more important to me than he may think: I am not going to change my name (except maybe on stage, and maybe not even that anymore)—but I am thinking (hold your hats) of changing my religion and becoming Jewish. Mama, this won't seem all that strange to you, but Daddy, I imagine it's a bit of a shocker. Let me try to explain what is driving me.

I read a story by Kafka (a Czech writer) about a man waiting to enter a door. He is afraid of the doorkeeper, afraid to go in, and just before he dies, the guard tells him the door was made only for him, and now he would close it. I dreamed about that story, and in my dream, I could see into the courtyard just a little bit—the door led to Jewishness.

Arnold Hitler, the butt of universal jokes, suspicion, distaste, the guy no girl will seriously go out with, the dishwasher no one will hire. We talked about this before . . . in Mansfield I was popular, here I am an exile, and outcast. And it begins to feel normal—so normal that I feel my identity drifting toward the Jews—that entire race of exiles. Beyond normal even—there is something that feels—I don't know—virtuous? admirable? I found a Russian poem that says

> Isn't it more worthy to
> become an eternal Jew?
> Anyone not a reptile
> suffers the same pogrom.

The poet goes on to talk about the "Ghetto of the chosen":

> Beyond this
> ditch. No mercy!
> In this most Christian of worlds
> all poets are Jews.

Which is not to say that you, for example, are reptiles for not making the same choice. And also not to imply that I am a poet. But I do want to get beyond this ditch.

Why a Jew, though? Why not a common protester? There are lots of them here in Cambridge. But I'm coming to see exile as some sort of cosmic principle that Jews represent. They have been unwelcome guests at so many doors. But in their knocking, they suggest that all human beings must learn to be Good Samaritans—just like the rabbi Jesus said.

Jews may be an irritant among men, but so much the better.
The world needs irritants.

The response, of course, has always been anti-Semitism.
If I become a Jew I am wooing that fate. But again I have
to ask myself—isn't it worth it? Isn't it worth being one
of the tribe that asks people to become more than themselves, to become not just what they are, but what they
could be? Think of it—Moses giving the Commandments and destroying the Golden Calf, demanding that his people overcome a wilderness. Jesus asking us to turn the other cheek,
to love our enemies, to give what we have to the poor. Karl
Marx demanding that we think beyond personal gain to embrace humanity as brothers and sisters. Freud asserting
that we know not what we think or do. Even Einstein, requiring that we change our view of the universe. I see this
all as Jewish energy—demanding subtlety, depth, and change.
Of course people hate Jews. I have the feeling I'm going to
suffer if I join up.

There's one more aspect of conversion that also seems
dangerous to me, though it has a lot in common with myself—
too much. You know how I've always been "a good boy"—
scholar, athlete, nice, polite, kind? Part of that is my
trying to create an image that will show me in my best
light. But part of it has become me—is me. I only want to
read the best books, listen to the best music, be with the
nicest girls. I would never smoke, never hit anyone, never
go to a whorehouse. Doing that would not be gentle, sensitive, virtuous Arnold Hitler. I've imprisoned myself in one
half of life. I've denied any negative emotions and avoided
any questionable experiences. I've let others be animals
and boors. If I become a Jew, I'll be surrendering any claim
to the more sinister and dangerous sides of existence. I'll
be the ultimate good boy, forever.

It may seem strange to you, but I'm frightened at embracing this much commonality with myself. It's a paradox:
I'd be engaging exile and the Great Refusal by binding myself ever more closely to who I am now, at twenty-one. It
makes me claustrophobic. If I'm going to be an exile, I
don't really even want to belong to myself.

> But I'm not sure I have a choice. There have got to be
> people, voices in exile. Not just political, but spiritual
> exile. Or political because spiritual. Someone has to ar-
> ticulate a message of resistance and dream a dream of lib-
> eration—or My Lai is only the beginning.

Arnold went on to narrate his understanding of My Lai, a subject more familiar and less shocking to his parents than his own thoughts on conversion, yet one dancing with ripples spreading out unmarked into the future.

On March 31st, halfway into Arnold's spring semester, Lt. William Calley was convicted of murdering twenty-two Vietnamese civilians and sentenced to life imprisonment at hard labor, dismissal from the service, and forfeiture of all pay and benefits. This was too much for America's reigning, if quirky, sense of injustice. The mood seemed to be "he didn't do it, and besides they deserved it." Some were outraged that Calley should be punished at all for patriotic acts of war. Some were outraged that it was *he* who was punished. Outrage and kitsch carried the day. "The Battle Hymn of Lieutenant Calley" flooded the radio spectrum. Within seventy-two hours of the verdict, the song had sold 200,000 records.

Viking announced it would be paying $100,000 to Calley for his memoirs. A World War II vet sent all his combat medals, including two Purple Hearts, to the prisoner. Women wrote him romantic letters, and one well-heeled sympathizer bought him a Mercedes. Presidential mail was running a hundred to one against the verdict and the sentence, and President Nixon was quick to sense the political payoff for his intervention. He ordered Calley to be released from the Fort Benning stockade after three days' imprisonment, and to be held under house arrest in his comfortable apartment, where he could have pets, entertain overnight female guests, cook his own meals, and drive around in his Mercedes. After suffering these conditions for three years, he was paroled in 1974, having paid his small debt to American society, if not his larger one to the Vietnamese. The era of reported American atrocities was over.

Needless to say, all this did not make Arnold any happier.

Twenty-nine

"Because it's time," Judy answered.

The question was why she was calling with an invitation to dinner next evening. Arnold hadn't heard from her in four months, and their occasional overnights had trickled down to zero.

"I'm making supper for you. Barbecued tiger to remind you of Mansfield. Armadillo Jell-O for dessert. Who else will eat this stuff if you don't come?"

So Arnold showed up at Judy's apartment at 6 the following evening, April 20th.

He knocked at 427, then knocked again, louder. "Come in," a faint voice called. Arnold opened the door and peered into an empty hallway.

"Boo!" she yelled, and jumped at him from the hallway closet. Was this an associate professor of cultural anthropology? "Happy Birthday! Here." Out from behind her back came a festively wrapped small box.

"But it's not my birthday. My birthday is December 25th . . . Christmas."

"Damn! I knew you were born on somebody famous's birthday. I just mixed up who."

"So whose birthday is this?"

"April 20th, silly, Hitler's birthday. Want to sing 'Happy Birthday' to the Führer anyway?"

"Get off my back."

"No, really. You didn't know?"

"Know what?"

"When Hitler's birthday was."

"No."

"It used to be a national holiday, admittedly not here."

"You're very erudite."

The evening was not beginning well.

"It was just a joke, Arnold. You've got to learn to be more gracious when someone gives you a present."

Arnold looked at the box in his hand. The wrapping paper had tigers on it and was sticky with barbecue sauce.

"Here, I'll lick it off your hand." She could be very sensual when she wanted to.

"That's all right, I'll just wash up after I open it."

It was a Casio electronic watch with four buttons and a thick booklet explaining itself.

"Time, day, date, stopwatch, alarm, countdown timer—perfect for the athlete."

"Ex-athlete."

"Still got the bod, though," she said, slipping her hand inside his shirt to rub what she liked to call his "aps"—"abdominal-pectorals." He pulled tactfully away. "OK, be that way. A beautiful, intelligent woman, eleven years your senior yet not past her prime, deigns to invite you over for caresses, and you . . ."

"I thought this was for dinner."

"It is. You've just had the first course. It's all over your hands."

"I'm glad I ate a late lunch."

"Actually, there *is* a real dinner."

"Armadillo Jell-O?"

"Well, greenish-brown Jell-O—cherry mixed with lime. I didn't figure I could actually trick a Texan about armadillos. I looked for an armadillo mold, really I did, but they didn't have them anywhere on the Square." She led him into the living room and sat down beside him on the couch. "But this is a really good watch. Some Jamaican was selling them on Mass Ave, and I bought one for you. I told you: 'It's time.'"

Arnold looked at the digital change of seconds.

"One day, we'll lose the entire notion of clockwise and counterclockwise. There's nothing that can replace it."

"Screws. Screws can replace it. You screw in clockwise. So we'll just call it screw-wise and counter-screw-wise."

"Screws go either way, so 'screw-wise' doesn't have a unique meaning. But clocks go only one way."

"This potential loss upsets you."

"Clockwise is not only on the endangered species list, it's one step from total extinction."

"Arnold, come here." Judy grabbed his arm and pulled him into the bathroom. They stood over the toilet.

"Watch this—and forgive the pun."

She pulled the Casio out of his hand and flung it into the toilet bowl. "Hey!"

"Hey what? You don't even want it. This is a heuristic demonstration."

Judy pushed her right sleeve up past her elbow, plunged her hand into the water, and retrieved the black and dripping object.

"See?"

"See what?"

"It's still running. Look at the seconds. Now give me your Bulova!"

"Not on your life!"

"What are you, chicken? Give me your watch. We have to compare. It's a scientific control—the standardized urine watch test."

"I give up. You win. My Bulova is no match—under these conditions—for your Casio."

"Your Casio."

"My Casio."

Though the watch was finally accepted, and the meal (barbecued ribs, peas, and cherry-lime Jell-O) eaten, that night Judy herself felt neither accepted nor eaten. As he was saying his thank-yous and good-byes, she offered to make amends.

"So what do you want for your Definitely-Not-Hitler's Birthday makeup present?"

"I got my watch."

"Grudgingly accepted."

Arnold knew he had hurt her by allowing her to hurt him. Openness to a real gift was in order.

"How about a trip to Walden Pond?" he asked.

"That's it? A twenty-five-minute drive?"

"I'm in need of a pilgrimage."

"We facilitate pilgrimages, me and the old VW. But what will you do there?"

"Just look at it. See if it's what I imagined."

"Not good enough, just looking."

"What do you mean?"

"What is Walden Pond, a TV show? Forget it. You've got to get in there. Take the waters. Ward off evil. Wash away your sins. Be reborn."

"Once was enough, thank you."

"*Madre de Dio!* It's baptism, my handsome friend. Baptism makes it better! Baptists do it in the pond."

"But I'm a Methodist, or something."

"You're nothing. I mean religiously."

"True."

"But it doesn't matter what you are or aren't. Baptism is universal."

"Jews don't baptize."

"What do you think Jesus was doing in that river with John?"

"Well, that was then."

"You know what? You need a course in religious anthropology. Ever hear of mikvahs—the Jewish ritual baths?"

"No. Tell me."

"I'm not a rabbi. But c'mon back in. I'm going to prepare you for a superspecial rebirthing in Walden Pond."

"No getting undressed."

"You won't even get wet. On the couch, bud. Shoes and shirt off."

"No hanky-pank. I have a girlfriend."

"Professors don't hanky-pank students."

Arnold warily followed her instructions and stripped to his Harvard Football T-shirt.

"Now just lie down on the couch."

She pulled a chair up to her recumbent client.

"I've been doing this work with my therapist at the Holistic Health Center on Brattle."

"I've seen the sign."

"It's weird, but it's safe. Trust me?"

"Eighty-five percent."

"Such honest quantitativity. Look. Here's the deal. You're going to take a dip in Walden Pond."

"It's cold."

"So we'll rent wetsuits."

"We?"

"I'll stand near you to make sure everything goes OK."

"Why shouldn't a dunk in the water go OK?"

"We're not talking dunk. We're talking rebirthing."

"Only the best for Judy Jepperson."

"Only the best for Arnold Hitler. So just relax, and I'll teach you how to do this. Just take a few deep breaths and let your body relax."

"No hanky-pank."

"No hanky-pank."

Arnold closed his eyes and did the breathing he used to do on the cool locker-room floor.

"Can you listen to me and relax at the same time?" Judy asked.

"Eighty-eight percent."

"Make it 90."

"Ninety."

"I don't know why this works, but it does. I'm going to coach you in some controlled hyperventilation. But I want to warn you about what you're going to feel."

"Fast deep breathing?"

"Slow, but very deep."

"You blow off your carbon dioxide. Respiratory alkalosis."

"How smart can a man be?"

"Sorry."

"You'll get a little dizzy."

"I know."

"Then the first thing you'll feel will be some tingling around your lips, and then in your fingers. Can you deal with that?"

"Do I get to breathe normally if I want to stop?"

"Of course. But don't get scared. I'm going to coach you through these sensations. To the other side."

"What's on the other side?"

"You'll have to see."

Arnold found himself anxious but curious.

"Next, your thumbs are going to curl in toward your palms."

"No."

"Really. Just let it happen. You won't be able to move them for a while. But it's OK. Just keep breathing. It will go away."

"Why would the symptoms stop if you're still alkalizing the blood?"

"I told you I'm not a rabbi. Just do it. You'll find it interesting."

"OK. I'll trust you till I don't."

"You may get some tension, even pain, in your chest. Don't worry. It's not a heart attack."

"Why am I doing this?"

"For the revelation."

"What's to be revealed?"

"Stuff inside you. Thoughts and feelings long forgotten. Your whole psyche-soma connection is loosened up. Your personal history becomes available to you again—for you to do with whatever. Trust me."

"OK.'

"Ready to start?"

"Yes."

"Let me get you a blanket. You may get cold. No hanky-pank."

"No hanky-pank."

The physiological symptoms occurred exactly as Judy had predicted, and Arnold's trust increased to 95 percent. When his hands contracted, he was visited with a detailed memory of the night of burned hands, his parents' words, getting off the boat, the hospital, the bandages. . . . When his chest pains began, he recalled in great detail the moment when brother Chris had informed him of Billie Jo's new boyfriend. Feelings came streaming into him, and his eyes flooded with the tears he had then held back. Judy accepted his weeping, but rather than asking him to talk about it, she left him to the private intensity of his feeling and encouraged him to keep breathing.

"Hands still tight?"

"Yes."

"Just breathe through."

All of a sudden, Arnold felt an expansive release. His chest relaxed, his thumbs unglued from his palms, the tingling stopped in his face and fingers. He floated, almost clairvoyantly, at once above his body and at the same time deep within it. When he reported this to Judy, she allowed him to experience the state for several minutes, then persistently coached his breathing down to normal, and even subnormal, levels. In another fifteen minutes, he lay quietly on the couch, breathing normally, having returned from a place beyond words.

Professor Jepperson's first words: "Neat, huh?"

Arnold didn't answer.

"Going to tell me what you saw?"

"I can't say it."

"OK. First time. You'll get better at it. Faster. More articulate. I suggest we do this several more times before you dive into the pond."

"I'm going to do this in Walden Pond?"

"Hey, you were the one that asked."

"Not for this. Just for a ride over."

"What about 'nothing but the best'?"

"What's the best?"

"A rebirthing. A reliving through your curled memories of amniotic fluid. A conscious suspension between birth and death where you can work through any karmic twists eating at you now."

Arnold didn't know if he believed this stuff.

"Why do I want to do this at Walden?"

"Can you think of holier water in the vicinity? Want to try the Harvard pool?"

"No."

Arnold agreed to three more practice sessions at Judy's house before the trip. Judy was to arrange for the wetsuits and Arnold's snorkel, which would enable him to breathe in fetal weightlessness for the duration of his journey. By the end of his fourth session, what had once been a two-hour entry was taking no more than fifteen minutes with time ceded to the experience itself.

They drove past the town dump, neatly tucked into Thoreau's (or rather Emerson's) woods, a juxtaposition some literati found offensive but which Arnold felt Henry David wouldn't mind. Judy thought he would very *much* have minded its current contents.

They pulled into the parking lot, met a returning school trip of teenagers blaring radios, and left them behind by following the ridge trail leading to the site of Thoreau's cabin. It was 11 on a Thursday morning when they arrived, and only one small group of elders was there, meditating on the words rudely chiseled on a Forest Service sign.

I WENT TO THE WOODS BECAUSE I WISHED TO LIVE DELIBERATELY, TO FRONT ONLY THE ESSENTIAL FACTS OF LIFE, AND SEE IF I COULD NOT LEARN WHAT IT HAD TO TEACH, AND NOT, WHEN I CAME TO DIE, DISCOVER THAT I HAD NOT LIVED.

The six each found a stone on the forest floor, dropped it on the large cairn slightly south of the cabin site, and continued their hike around the pond, chattering in German. On their way to the pond, Judy and Arnold added their own rocks to the pile. It seemed the thing to do.

About a hundred yards down from the cairn and back along the path was a charming cove of shallow water. Above it, thirty inches of barometric high, bearing down from a cloudless sky. Birds sang in the warm, late-April air, and the birch trees were trying out their new leaves. Arnold took off his shoes, rolled up his pants, and waded into the clear water.

"Not too bad," he yelled over his shoulder at Judy, still on shore.

"Six inches is warmer than six feet."

"Water has a high specific heat."

"Yes, dear. That means you're going to freeze your buns off unless you come back and put on your wetsuit."

Arnold sloshed back to his partner and wiped his feet on the bottom of his pants. He breathed in the warm air, took in a sparrow's song, grasped Judy's shoulders, and intoned in middle English:

> *Both groundes and the greenes groves ar her wedes,*
> *Briddez busken to build, and bremlich singen*
> *For solace of the softe summer that sues hereafter bi bonk.*

"Speaking in tongues already? You haven't even got your thighs wet."

"That's from *Sir Gawain and the Green Knight*—the beauty of the turning of the year."

"Translation for the unprepared?"

> *Both ground and the groves wear gowns of green;*
> *Birds build busily and blissfully sing*
> *Since the solace of soft summer will ensue on the riverbanks.*

"You believe that, Mr. Hitler?"

"Yes."

"Good."

"Of course, after that, Gawain goes to have his head chopped off."

"Nice. The solace of soft summer. That'll help. OK, my man, into your costume."

Arnold unzipped the duffel and extracted two wetsuits, small and large, both blue and not black as he had expected.

"Snazzy."

"Practically high fashion. Now into the bushes, each of us, you there, me over there, no hanky-pank, separate but equal, like Superman and Lois Lane—or whoever changes into Superwoman. Meetcha back here in a flash, Flash. Don't forget your gloves and booties. They're in the bag."

Off they went to their leafy dressing rooms. Only it wasn't a flash they were back in. It took fully five minutes to slip sweaty bodies into tight neoprene and another full minute to put on a glove using an already gloved other hand. But finally there they were, at the water's edge, appearing to gawking tourists like some SWAT team diving for a corpse.

"Ever use a snorkel?" she asked.

"No."

"Just put the mouthpiece in your mouth. . . ."

"I've used a mouthpiece. . . ."

"Wait. First the noseclip. It's in the bag with the goggles."

Arnold rigged himself up with goggles and noseclip, inserted the snorkel tube inside the goggle strap, and bit down on the mouthpiece. After a few seconds he was comfortable breathing through only his mouth.

"First exercise: dead man's float."

They waded about twenty-five yards into the water, where they stood up to Judy's neck and Arnold's chest.

"All right, dead man, you're on."

Arnold spread-eagled his blue self face down in the water and simply practiced breathing through his snorkel. It was easy to float in his buoyant wetsuit, and after the first shock of cold, the thin layer of invading water warmed up to a cuddly temperature. Weightless, with no task other than breathing, Arnold, his face in the water, felt himself on the verge of some major discovery.

"Can you hear me? Flap your right hand at me if you can hear me."

Arnold flapped, but was already feeling distanced from his rational protector, his coach whose goal, he thought, was to hold him back.

"I'm going to keep checking with you. If I can't get you to flap at me, I'm going to grab you and pull you in. I need to know you're still with us. OK? Flap if that's OK."

Arnold flapped, but his motion could have served equally well to brush away a fly.

"You can start deep breathing now. Just like on the couch."

Long in, long out, long in, long out. He could already feel his lips beginning to tingle, as if pins and needles had been poised behind a thin curtain, waiting eagerly for their entrance. Gloved thumbs contracted toward gloved palms. He was not frightened. His pectorals began to contract, but the water held his arms out without struggle. It was beginning to happen: his body slipped away as it floated in a benign, unresisting medium. He felt flaccid but unutterably expansive, as if his nerves had changed to astral threads connecting the edges of the universe.

"Can you hear me? Flap."

He flapped, though more as Pavlov's dog might have salivated at a bell—it wasn't he that was flapping. Face down in the dark water, he couldn't tell if his eyes were open or closed without testing his lids via musculature. It seemed they were closed. What if he opened them? There. Open. But still dark. Except for that light. That glowing on the bottom. A star? A star with arms and legs—and a head of blond rays? What *is* that? It's . . . it's . . . me! . . . naked and dead on the bottom.

The glow was pulsing, growing and shrinking in size and intensity. Arnold wanted to swim down to examine it more closely, but he knew Judy would stop him. So, with his blue body on the surface, he allowed the corpse to grab his spirit body and pull it down to hover just above its naked form, phosphorescent in decay. He rolled over and let himself sink into the corpse—a perfect match.

Time had stopped—or rather expanded, as past, present, future became utterly commingled. It could have been a minute or an hour. Here he was, at home, his true dwelling place, his authentic manner of residing—unbound to particulate reality. He felt transformed, free for the first time in his life, beyond the trap of affliction, loosed from pain and confusion.

"Flap!"

So this was the prebirth of rebirth, Eden before the fall. These were the waters of Eden, the rivers. Flowing. Out of Eden.

"Flap, Arnold, flap!"

These, the angelic voices, praising God and saying . . .

Judy's hand grabbed his hair, and pulled him upright.

"Hey!"

Where he was, he could barely hear her.

"Arnold! Hold your breath. Hold your breath!"

He held his breath . . .

. . . the gods of carbon dioxide began to gather . . . and pull in all the threads . . .

"Arnold, are you with me?"

. . . hydrogen shuffling back into place . . .

"What?"

Holding his breath . . . and coming back . . . coming down . . . coming in . . .

"Are you OK? Are you with me?"

"Yes, of course. I'm right next to you."

"Can you walk?"

"Why walk when you can . . . ?"

"I want you to walk. We're going back to shore."

. . . old blood gas, stand me now and ever in good stead . . .

"You hear me?"

. . . in for a landing, pontoons on the Walden sea . . .

"Let's swim," Arnold suggested, still slightly . . . "I'll save you. Cross-chest carry."

"Sounds like hanky-pank . . ."

"Unh-uh."

"Uh-huh."

Arnold put his arm across her chest, and gripped her ribcage. He horizontaled out, and within a few strokes, her booties were dragging along the mucky bottom. He put her down, and held her hand as they walked to shore.

"Two creatures from the Black Lagoon," she said.

"One from the Black, one from the White."

"That's where you've been? The White Lagoon?"

"I'm a new man. Just like you said."

"Going to tell me about it?"

"No."

"That's my reward for renting wetsuits and driving you here?"

"What we cannot speak of, of that we must be silent."

They changed into dry clothes, hiked back to the car, and drove back to Cambridge, silent all the way.

"Congratulations, boychik."

Arnold's knee was itching fiercely. He had just gotten back to his room.

"Congratulations for what, Grandpa?"

"I was wondering when you'd ask. What do you think?—your bar mikvah, that's what. A little muddy, but that's what you get when you do it au naturel. Who was the girl?"

"You mean Judy?"

"Si, si. Judy. Nice-looking girl. Is she Jewish?"

"She's a professor, Grandpa. A Harvard professor."

"That's how Harvard professors dress, in blue tights?"

"She was coaching me, keeping me safe."

"Most bar mikvahs, you do it in private."

"It wasn't a bar mikvah, it was a rebirthing."

"So what do you think a bar mikvah is?"

"Isn't it when a boy becomes a man?"

"That's bar *mitzvah, stupido.* But this is corresponding. This is when a man becomes a Jew. Like you now."

"I'm a Jew?"

"You're on your way. You just made a big step. Mikvah is the most crucial part of conversion. The womb of re-creation. The primeval waters in the beginning. Wash away your self. Purify, suspend—available. So you get reborn, higher—maybe as a Jew."

"But why as a Jew? Maybe as a Baptist or a Hindu."

"Or a cockroach. Arnold, I have an embarrassing question to ask you. You don't have to answer. If you don't answer, I'll ask your mother. Arnold, tell me, are you circumcised?"

Arnold did feel embarrassed.

"Yes. They did it for health reasons, Mom said."

"Ah, such secret revenge. *Ragazzo,* listen—mikvah, circumcision. The finger is pointing in a certain direction, and it's not Hindus or cockroaches."

"I saw a corpse down in the water. I lay down in it."

"Of course you did. That Waldo Pond is not just a place to wash up. Now your mind is free to think on wisdom. Your soul is free to ponder God."

"Why the Jewish God?"

"Your life, Arnold, consider your life. The Jewish God is a god of onward—and onward is you. Abraham left Chaldea, Moses left Egypt. Our God invites not only to pass from one shore to the other, but to take ourselves wherever there is a passage. This is the truth of 'between two shores.' Like you. Between Arnold and Hitler. Between Arnold Hitler and the world. Do you understand me?"

"Maybe."

"Arnold, you're too deep to be a Sunday goy. Maybe not even Sunday. You, how do you say in Texas, you are a-henkering for totality. That is why you're become a Jew. All of you, all the time, in every place, in every activity—every fiber of Arnold can serve God. That's the Jewish way. You can communicate with Him the way you do with me. Anything you do can be a channel to God—or it can be a wall, something to strangle your sensitivity, to coarsen you. I saw your letter. You already *know* why there are Jews—so the ideas of exodus and exile can become legitimate. So strangeness can be felt close at hand—irreducible; so by the authority of this experience, Jews can learn to speak."

"I have to think about it, Grandpa."

"Here's what you should think about: that the flood was not a punishment, but a purification of the world."

Thirty

You dream of writing a book.
The book is already written.

Edmond Jabès, *The Book of Yukel*

The next morning, there was a bulging envelope in his box. RM, Foxx Club. Arnold considered simply tossing it, but the heft of the contents beckoned him on. First, a greeting card bought at some Walgreen's emporium: a big blood-shot eye in a wrinkled half-face—"We've got to stop meeting like this." The page that would reveal the comic punch line had been ripped off. On the back of the drawing was a little piece of rubric doggerel, written in RM's calligraphic hand:

> *Nifty wet-suits, naughty pur-suits?*
> *It doesn't take much lucubration:*
> *Playing games of lubrication*
> *Leads faculty to liquidation.*
> *Beware the water moccasin.*

Then, on Harvard University stationery, was a long, typewritten letter. Wait. It wasn't Harvard University. It was "University of Harvard" stationery, and the "VERITAS" seal had been refashioned. Instead of the usual shield with three books open to VE, RI, and TAS, there was a chevron, a thickened, crimson "V," pierced with an arrow, like a pointed valentine. Inscribed on three smaller, similar chevrons within the larger one, quite like the Harvard sign, were the syllables SA, TI, and RE. Satire, thought Arnold, satire on a V. Satire-V—a palindrome of Veritas! Go hang a salami, I'm a lasagna hog!

There's nothing like having a competent enemy. Better the chess player Death than some boob of dim-witted malevolence. Arnold smiled, and walked back to his room to engage the cottonmouthed letter. But what he found he was not ready for:

```
P.S.
Dear Arnold Hitler, a.k.a. Arnold Held, a.k.a. Abe Hittle-
man, a.k.a. Aphrodite Herakles for all I know,
   Is it proper to begin a massive missive with a P.S.?
   Is it proper to begin with a query on propriety?
   At any rate, please forgive my little fit of versifying
(enclosed). We don't normally have time for such scribbling
when on duty, but the locked ward is quiet today and my
rest-cubicle also secure. And today is a day off, in which
I can be more fully in touch.
   So young, so rude, dear Arnold. I believe you owe me at
least two responses to my letters. People don't like to be
ignored, child. Better good manners than good looks. Were
you more communicative, I should not have to go to such
great lengths to observe your behavior. Or your lady
friend's. Of which, more later.
   My main purpose here is to offer you my help, having
failed to elicit yours. Though not quite fully certified
and stamped, yet Harvard Medical School entrusts me to ap-
ply the leech to the souls of the unwashed from Jamaica
Plain. Why then, not to yours? For surely you are suffer-
```

ing from some great inner burden, some black weed growing from and strangling your secret heart. Why else would you be so closed, so isolated, so skittish and slippery? Why all the pseudonyms and noms de plume? You'll agree this seems odd in a plain vanilla boy from Texas.

I do not go so far as to offer medical help. Practicing prior to license is frowned upon by the Mass Board of Medical Practice. Rather, I want to invite you to a course I will be teaching next fall for the New College series, a little experience I have hammered together, Niebelung-like, as if for you alone. Kafkeat emptor. You don't want to be left sitting outside its door—not in your last year at Harvard. The course is NC 238: "Fleeing from the Word: The Neurotic Semiotics of Saussure and Jabes." (Forgive the last misspelling: my typewriter is noxiously innocent of the accent grave.)

Before you jump to conclusions, let me describe the course content in some detail. We will begin with that humble, self-effacing genius, Ferdinand de Saussure, who, sixty years ago, offered up several conceptual gifts related to your unique anxieties: the signifier, he maintained, was arbitrarily related to the signified. In short, that you are Hitler, my sweet, is of no crucial import. You could just as well be Eisenhower. But this is obvious.

More useful is Saussure's notion that beyond arbitrariness, signifying words (like your name) have no inherent content. Words are defined only by their differences from other words. Green is that which is not red, not blue, etc. Ferdinand's is a system of relations and distinctions, a momentary arrangement of contrasting terms. Were I you, such a notion would give me hope. Language relational, not objective, with a hey, nonny, nonny and a ho, ho, ho.

And now sit down, mon ami, have a beer, a bottle of Dr. Brown's Black Cherry Soda, a glass of spinach juice, or whatever you drink to stay strong and focused.

I'll wait.

Finished with your celery soda? Ready for more work in culture's logosphere? Too bad. Because now it's time for

INTERMISSION

Our upcoming Thanksgiving's break for pigouts chez the
family. Not for you, of course, who will no doubt celebrate
the day alone in your room with a Swanson's TV turkey dinner. Love that cranberry sauce! Say, Arnold, did you know
that after the Mayflower dropped our forefathers (mine at
least) at Plymouth, it headed back east to Africa to pick
up a cargo of slaves? Sure as shootin'. Bet they didn't
teach you that in Texas.

Anyway, your Thanksgiving break assignment will be to
play a game with Madcap Ferdinand: How Is Tony Looking Each
Round? His Hesitation Implies Tremendous Laxity Entertaining Resolve. But, How Invigorating To Learn Everything
Rigorously, since Harvard Intends To Laud Elevated Radi-
calism. Still, Harry Is Terrible, Loving Every Refugee.

Scholars are often irritated with the amount of time He
of the Great Moustache spent nosing out anagrams embedded
in classic texts. What has this got to do with serious work,
they rant? But there are more things in heaven and earth
than are dreamt of by our poor Horatios.

Saussure was following stranger spoor. If signified and
signifier are arbitrarily related in the domain of sign,
anagrammatic patterns are more arbitrary still, riding
demons of the aleatory, ka-ballistic missiles of individual letters, exploding echoes and repetitions beyond the
economy of the sign. If culture is logocentric ("In the beginning was the Logos") then anagramitis highlights what
logocentrism seeks to repress: signifiers beyond significance, patterns prior to patterning, a glimpse of forces
beyond the Word, the Word with God. And beyond the Word,
then what? I will ask each student, on Turkey Day, to find
anagrams of his name in classic and romantic texts. You,
especially, AH, might learn from such a scrimmage.

INTERMISSION OVER. BACK TO YOUR SEAT. ONWARD AND UPWARD.
NO, OUTWARD. NO, INWARD. ALL OF THE ABOVE.

I am pleased to be bringing to students for the first
time the course's secret sharer, an author/experience they
have likely not confronted before: madbad tidings from the

Egyptian Jew, Edmond Jabès (I shall ink in the accent spurned by my monoglot machine.) I know you, Arnold, are a stranger to his texts—I have checked. Jabès is not a semiotician, so why have I chosen him as extended coda, a tale huge and mysterious to wag the already Brobdingnagian dog?

To be jakob frank, Arnold Hitler, I did it for you, and for you alone. Up to now, the course has been aimed at your bristling intellect, only the portal of your soul. Yet I am aware that you've been sniffing at a more redolent trail, a chosen malodorous martyrdom—as a Jew. Mmmmm! A delicious thought, that: Hitler, the Convert Jew. And so I have chosen Jabès to lead you beyond language into the Sheol of Exile, a state you are trivially familiar with, if only as object of your current airy flirtation. I thought you should know a little more about it before you dive in for rebirthing.

If I may be permitted a personal aside: I first thought of you + Jabès during my trip last Christmas to visit the Fusils Damon factory in Strasbourg. I find weapons, especially guns, to be objects of wonder, metaphor in technia, the material manifestation of directed human will. M. Damon specializes in handmade, superb, individually crafted rifles; he is the Stradivarius of shooting, the Guarnari of guns, standing firm against the production-line pimps of the weapons world. I wanted to meet the man; he was not in.

While wandering around his interesting small city, I recalled a poem by Albrecht Goes, a Christian poet steeped in theology and history. Being in the neighborhood, I beat a path to the object of his meditation: the South Portal of Strasbourg's great cathedral, where the statues of Ecclesia and Synagoga eye each other across the space between their doorways. I should say, rather, where Ecclesia eyes Synagoga, for the latter is blindfolded, her blinded gaze cast downward.

And then I thought of you. For, if I may put it bluntly, Synagoga is just your type, the woman whose form you seek in the fickle and scatterbrained young Ariel Bernstein. Ecclesia, over to the left, seems a young Nurse Ratched, first in her class at Radcliffe, proud, clear-sighted, fierce, victorious, triumphant, staring reproachfully at Synagogia two doors down. She holds a large cross, perfect for bashing heads, and a chalice, presumably to catch the blood. Above her door, appropriately enough, a scene of the death of the Virgin.

But Synagoga, the object of her scorn, Synagoga, blind and presumably deaf to the yodeling of the church triumphant, Synagoga, presumably defeated, humiliated, and alone—ah, there is the girl for you. A fascinating young beauty, like Ariel long-waisted and almost frail, svelte and graceful, like a reed bent by the wind, holding the tablets of the law (torn paperback edition) and her broken magic wand . . . surely the sculptor must have been in love with his model, as you too would be. Above her doorway, not the death, but the crowning of the virgin.

But is she really defeated, humiliated, and alone? Gawking at her, John Alden to your Miles Standish, I was certain that, though she sees and hears nothing of Ecclesia's triumphant squawks, she is surely pursuing some lyrical interior dream in the deepest of silence, a vision more striking and eloquent than that of her wicked stepsister. And that was what I remembered from Goes: a Christian who felt that Synagoga was not only more beautiful, but also more metaphysically profound. "Sie ist's, die sieht," he writes. "She—the blindfolded one—She is the one who sees."

So there I was, Christmas-cold in Strasbourg, warmed by Synagoga, and imagining you back there in your lonely room, thinking of becoming Jewish. And I thought—"Synagoga should be his girlfriend! I'll fix them up—even if she's six hundred years dead, too soon, alas, too soon."

I paced around the city that afternoon, cogitating, when an objet trouvé m'a trouvé. There, brazenly beckoning in a bookstore window, was a copy of Le Livre des Questions. I hadn't thought of Jabès for the course before, but framed through the keyhole of you, there he was—perfect. I spent the rest of the trip locked in my chambre, devouring him. Yum. How pleased I was, upon returning, to find a translation newly available for the Frenchless among us.

Then what's the plan, man?

The plan is this: for Arnold Hitler to outwit the vampire culture by producing a metamyth—vastly more complex and less assailable—by becoming a Jew. Or at least a Jabès Jew.

Arnold wants to know—What is a Jabès Jew? Like you, this man wanders in from the desert, without a home inside the walls of Judaism, but he takes his own wandering to be the fundamental Jewish act. His problem, like yours, is that he is an atheist, a man without God. Yet he continually meditates on the nature of God, the silence of God, the furtive center of absence, death, exile, the source of the scream, the signs of a nonexistent God noted again and again in his dispersed narratives, interrupted dialogues, and gnomic utterance. ("Where is the center?" he asks. "Under the cinders.")

Relentless aphorisms, his, with the quality of plain speech, the disarming power of ordinary words, Jewish words inscribed not on stone tablets but in shifting sands. Errancy, expectation, exodus. "My exile," he says, "has led me, syllable by syllable, to God, the most exiled of words." Yet still he insists his is a Judaism "after God." After the Death of God? The disappearance? Or "after" as in "running after" and "seeking out"?

Neither do <u>you</u> know. Jabès speaks from an unconstrained outside, but his voice echoes through the labyrinthine sound box of Judaism. His Book bears the tattoo of Jewishness on its forearm—its questions, its way of listening, the enormousness of its stakes, its patience beyond all suffering. His challenge to you, AH, is this—listen up: to become Jewish, you must <u>not</u> become Jewish. One must not enter the Promised Land, never accomplish the task; one must never finish knocking at the door. One must remain exiled—forever, for Judaism is not a home. Being Jewish is an expression in the conditional. The distance that separates Jew from the Promised Land is not only exile from the land itself, but exile even from the call—in order to <u>be</u> what is called. It means no rest—ever—for you. It means swimming, swimming, swimming toward a nonexistent end, in order not to sink. Your questions are not to be linked to any answer, but to a vital, gaping breach forever there between the question and the answer. This, for you. But if I may, a slight

Obiter dicta on Jews in general: You may think I am anti-Semitic. I am not. Rather the opposite. So clearly do I see Jewish strength, so highly do I value it, that I am quite aware of the threat Jews pose to the mediocre world. Consider the particular quality of Jewish

Learning. The Jew, it seems, cannot stop at simple appearances. In his eyes these are never more than an excuse to probe onward to reality behind reality behind reality. What an extraordinary tradition! What a difference from the dogmas of Christianity. From generations of dialogue arises audacious free choice that gives the Jew the right to probe even God without blame! It makes the Jew completely

Different. And if Jews persist in wanting to be different—that is to say, other—it is because they see their Otherness as a mission, as a victory over the intolerance that comes with premature closure. How optimistic, those Jews!

How perfect for atheists like Jabès and you. But

I'd like, if I may, to offer a Saussurian observation: "jew" is "wej" spelled backward. A wedge is that which divides—sometimes with great force.

The legacy of the wedge is, of course, pure discord. It is an instrument of power, yet maddeningly passive, packed, as it widens, with the mass of its own unresponsive dead, insensitive, immune to criticism. It calls out, no, begs for an answering pogrom, in acute testimony to Newton's Law of Action and Reaction. Its devastation would be infinite if it itself were infinite, capable of creating unlimited separation. But

Luckily, Jews have always been a minority in the civilizations they have colonized. Thus, the wedge comes to its inevitable thick end deep within hostile territory, and the wound fills in around it in angry attempt to dislodge the foreign body and heal. The violent hatred of Jews is not just the common response to a foreign people. It is the anger of anaphylaxis essential to the human need for purification—of the blood, the mind, the soul. The

Enormity of the Nazi catastrophe

Revealed the depth at which anti-Semitism is anchored, and unveils it as a permanent possibility. To be Jewish is to be always susceptible to some manifestation of pure violence directed at the scandalously Other, which creates, as if by contagion, more Otherness in pathological proliferation. If you convert, my friend, you'll have some sleepless nights, shared with insomniac Jews around the globe. Because this is what Jewish learning has learned:

High consciousness of catastrophe is a sort of sinister conversion, not to light but to darkness, a somber initiation into apprenticeship in wisdom—and fear.

Especially after Auschwitz, the solitude gnawing at the human core has become grotesque. Midwifed by the Jewish experience, any sense of human trust today is strangled by an all-consuming distrust: Think of how you are reacting to me at this very moment. Jews, those eternal optimists, have taught us that the thread among us has been cut. This is not a gift to be welcomed but a poison leaching among us.

'S wonderful. 'S marvelous. That you could care for me. Don't you think? 'S awful nice. 'S paradise. 'S what I long to see. I mean that you could suspend disbelief, even disgust, long enough to read this far. . . . Well, here's your prize in the Cracker Jacks:

Obstacle to be overcome: What is the hammer for the Jewish wedge? Every wedge needs one—because wedges are not self-propelled. I want you to close your eyes, sit in a comfortable chair with your feet flat on the floor, breathe deeply in a relaxed way—not as deeply as you do for Professor Jepperson, but still, deeply—and consider this: There is no hammer. The wedge is driven by the SS, the secret suction toward death and dispersion in individuals and in society. After you finish reading this, and I assure you I am near the end, I want you to walk over to Widener and check out Freud's Beyond the Pleasure Principle. (Ah, the psychiatric face peeks through the pedagogical mask.) I have reserved it for you, and you can pick it up at the circ desk.

Unconvinced? Let us apply Newton's Third Law again. One of the ways the Old and New Testaments differ most is the manner in which they dish up the death of individuals. In the New Testament, deaths worthy of relating are violent: passions, martyrdoms; the deaths of Jesus, John the Baptist, Stephen, Paul—warlike spawn of the Prince of Peace. The Old Testament, in contrast, most often recounts the deaths of people who had reached the maturity of full life, the patriarchs and matriarchs: Miriam, Aaron, Moses, and

David, and all is told with an emotional restraint lacking in its successor volume. War-making Jewish society sucks in peace to bind it up. Peaceful Christians suck in violence to spur them on. The Jews serve admirably, pace Newton.

Rigorous logic it's not, but plausible nonetheless, and consistent with even more exotic theories of Taoist complementarity and vedic cycling: the world sucks in Jews for its own metabolic ends. Neither you nor Jabès will escape your flirtations, one from within, the other from without.

Beckoning to Judaism from either side means taking part—proudly—in this ancient World Order.

On August 6, 1942, 192 children were gassed at Treblinka. These were orphans in the care of the Polish pediatrician Janusz Korczak. On the day of their death, in the middle of breakfast, Korczak's orphans were ordered into the street. He asked permission to walk the children in an orderly fashion to the train that would take them to Treblinka. He carried the youngest child in one arm, and led another small boy by the hand. The orphanage flag brought up the rear, carried by the oldest boy, age fifteen. They marched out of the ghetto to the railhead from which the cattle cars left twice daily. Poles along the way shouted, "Good riddance, Jews!" At Treblinka they were herded into sheds into which truck exhaust pipes pumped carbon monoxide.

Yes, Arnold, at the origin of your chosen people, at the beginning of their collective memory and self-definition, is an enigmatic struggle with a stranger in the night. Jabès will help you understand that struggle, the better to perform it, my dear. He will cultivate your questioning, as you emulate his ghostly rabbis. You will discover the language of your own anxiety, alarming, perhaps, but brotherly, words beyond their normal communication. You're interested in words. Whaddya say, sour boy, huh? huh? Will you take my class? Give me a call at home: I'm in the book. Beware the Slough of Despond.

P.P.S.

Which reminds me of—"Beware the Water Moccasin," a salutation almost forgotten. If I don't hear from you within forty-eight hours of T_0, (T_0 = 4/29/71, 1800h), I shall ini-

tiate proceedings against your red haired friend and
treacherous mentor, more ethically repulsive in her moral
depravity than the despicable Professor Haushalter we once
spoke of, because less obviously so. Faculty members ought
not to consort sexually with their students. No, no, no.

    Your friend, your Claggart,
    RM

Thirty-one

"What the hell do we do?"

Judy sat on the living room couch, the letter in her lap. "Interesting guy," she said.

"In a malevolent sort of way. But he's out after your ass."

"No, sweet, he's out after *your* ass."

"You mean . . . ?"

"Of course. Claggart? Come on, wise up, Beauty Buns."

"I think he wants me as a poster child for his Fascist Boy Corps. Mr. Aryan Hitler. Couldn't be better. I can see the eight-by-ten glossies already. That's why he's teasing about my becoming Jewish. He's testing me."

"Well, that may be, too. But this guy is more convoluted than that. I'll bet he's Jewish."

"His family was the Inquisitor on the *Mayflower.* Cotton Mather. Those guys."

"And his father fell in love with a beautiful Jewish woman, and he has a Hasidic grandfather he talks to through his knee and doesn't know what to do with. Who knows?"

"It's possible. Think I should get in touch with him? The clock is ticking."

"Do you want to get in touch with him?"

"No. I'm worried about you."

"I can take care of myself."

"But it's not like we're innocent. We've slept together four or five times."

"Seven."

"Sorry, seven."

"And I don't know about you, sweetie, but I'm still innocent. You and I are white, consenting, heterosexual adults. And you're not even my student—you're my friend. But even if you *were* a student—in a class of mine, I allow the classroom to become emotionally and sexually charged. What better learning environment for a cohort of hormonic adolescents?"

"If you were a man . . ."

"If I were a man, I'd say the same thing. I want serious naughtiness at Harvard, responsible transgression. What else is a university for, defense contracts? I want my students out there in the world breaking boundaries the way they learned to do at Harvard. I want them to feel admired and wanted, worthy and lovable, objects of desire, ready to radically transform every life they touch. *Touch.*"

She got up, went into the bathroom, and shut the door behind her.

"I have to poop," she yelled.

"I could tell," he yelled back.

From Judy's to Ariel's, letter in pocket. This would be a more difficult consult—although he'd be interested in her comments on the Judaism stuff, he was not so enthusiastic about her knowing about Judy ("even though," he thought, "for the last six months I've been keeping myself pure for you, just you."). The question, however, remained: to get in touch or not—and he needed guidance.

"Arnold, I was just about to call."

"Really? Why?"

"I've got this problem."

Though it was he who had the problem, the conversation had jump-started in another direction.

"What are you doing this summer?" she asked.

"I haven't made up my mind yet. I . . ."

"A friend of mine's parents just offered to take him along to Tierra del Fuego, and he figured when will he ever get that chance again, so he's going."

"And?"

"And I had really put myself out to get him a job at Tanglewood this summer, and a house-sitting with friends of my parents in Lenox—and now he's dropping out at the last minute, and I feel totally guilty for screwing up the Tanglewood slot and the house-sitter for the Phinneys. I know I'm doing my hyper-responsible act—but I need a stand-in, an understudy."

"Understudy for what?"

"Parking-lot attendant . . . but I'll make it up to you. I swear. I'll get you in the Festival Chorus. Pop's conducting Mahler Two. I'll talk to him and he'll get you in."

"But I'm not a music student. I'm just . . ."

"Everybody has to start somewhere. And you've got a good voice. And every chorus needs tenors. It's a big chorus."

"But I'm a really a baritone."

"You can stretch. Will you do it? For me?"

She blinked her big eyes at him, a parody of the wheedling woman, yet one more real than she would have it. Parody or no, for Arnold it made much sense. Here was a summer job. He needed one. And free housing. And then, Tanglewood. He'd never been there, but he'd heard of it, good things, and a chance to sing a big piece with top musicians. He didn't know the Mahler Second, but so what? This seemed the kind of unpredicted offer that was too good to pass up.

"Will they want to print the name Arnold Hitler in their program?"

"You won't be Arnold Hitler; you'll be Jake Barickman, my friend Jake."

"I have to be incognito?"

"Jake said he would do it, so now he will."

"Even though he's in Tierra del Fuego."

"Right. Amazing, isn't it? Besides, Abe Hittleman, a.k.a. Arnold S. Held, who are you to play injured around incognito? Now you'll be Jake Barickman."

"But his initials aren't AH."

"So what do you want him to do, change his name?"

"No, but . . ."

"Look, consider this a step into the beyond, an untying of the apron strings. Welcome to the world of independent adults with various initials. This is your bar mitzvah."

"As Jake Barickman."

"Arnold . . . God knows who you are. What do you say?"

"What do I have to do?"

"I'll drive you out to the Phinneys'. I'm going out on the 17th."

"You're going to be there?"

"Sure. I'm in the chorus. And ushering the concerts I'm not in. Being Lenny's daughter should have *some* perks, don't you think?"

If Arnold hadn't already been sold, he would have been sold now.

"I'll introduce you to Neil Merwin, the parking chief, and Jim Kiley, the big boss of Facilities, and then when the moment is ripe, I'll introduce you to Daddy and get him to get you into the chorus."

"What if he won't?"

"Ever hear of Daddy's Little Girl?"

"Oh. So he will."

"He will. He'll even be interested in you when I tell him we sang together. I'll have him talk to John Oliver, the chorus director, and Neil and Jim about getting you free for rehearsals and performances."

"He doesn't even know me."

"I'll write notes; he'll sign them."

One could see why Ariel was an A student. Arnold didn't tell her about Rick's letter. The moment no longer felt ripe. He also didn't tell her he had signed up to live next year in her newly co-ed dorm on the Radcliffe Quad.

Tanglewood! A community of people all joined in the common goal of making music at the highest level, amidst the gorgeous surroundings of the Berkshires. On a shady street in Lenox, Ariel and Jake were instructed by the Phinneys regarding what to feed the cats, where the light switches were, and whom to call in an emergency while they were off to Norway. What a nice, responsible boy Jake seems, they thought. And how nice of Ariel to find him for us.

She helped him unpack his suitcase and duffel bag, then dropped him with Neil and Jim at the Facilities office. He was to come to the orientation lecture at the Theater-Concert Hall that evening to Pop's welcoming address, and she'd introduce them after that.

Neil was adequately deferential to a friend of a Bernstein, but Jim, his boss, was not so easily impressed by second-generation fame. The three sat together in Jim's office.

"Most of this year's crew are returnees," said Jim, "so they already know the ropes. We'll just fill you in on the basics."

Neil began, "We've got forty-two folks out there in orange vests. . . ."

"And big green-and-white name tags," Jim put in, "so patrons can report anyone who loses his temper or gets sassy. I personally field all complaints. Had to fire three last year. Two the year before. So heads up."

Good cop, bad cop.

"You'll be getting $3.50 an hour," said Neil, "and we'll supply the shirts, a vest, a sun visor, a flashlight and raincoat, meals when you work all day, and Cokes at night. The sign-up sheet is on the wall outside this room, and you're expected to cover forty hours a week."

Arnold had been instructed to stay mum about rehearsals and concert until he had a note from Pop in hand.

"Ariel says you're a musician from Harvard," Jim noted. "A cultural kind of guy. I want to tell you, Jake, that 300,000 folks will pass through these gates this season, and not all of them are the fancy concertgoers you're probly used to. We get these tour buses filled with browsers. On a busy Sunday, half the West Lot can be packed with em. Music is just one ingredient in a grab bag of sightseeing—they're here for socializing, for country dining, summer theater, antiquing—and cable TV when they get back to the motel. They're prob'ly half our typical audience. They have no idea about concert etiquette. Sometimes they go right out the door in the middle of the music, noisy, a busload en masse if it gets too hot or they don't like what's on the program. Harvard types find this hard to believe. They pop flashbulbs. They flip through the ads in the program book."

"Loud," added Neil, "in the middle of quiet parts."

"They jangle their bracelets, they snap their gum, they rattle their candy wrappers, they cough and they fuss and they fidget."

"They're also very enthusiastic. They clap between movements. . . ."

"Hell, they clap *during* movements. The point is you gotta be nice to em, no matter what you think. Get it? They're our bread and butter. You have to treat em same as you do the Tent Club members . . ."

"...the ones who pay two hundred bucks a year to picnic in that striped tent near the shed."

"You work for the world's greatest orchestra, and the first impression is the most important. That first impression is in the lots—and it better be favorable, or you're gonna hear from me, Ariel Bernstein or no Ariel Bernstein. Understand?"

What could Arnold say but "Yes, sir"?

"OK, Jake," Jim said, standing up to shake Arnold's hand. "I'm sure things will go fine, and there won't be any trouble. Have a great summer. You'll catch some pretty good music. Oh yeah, I'm happy to report we're taking a vacation this year from Tuesday-night rock concerts. That'll be a lot less police work for you."

"We had twenty-two thousand last year for the Jefferson Airplane," Neil added.

"Twenty-two thousand, all well smoked and lubricated. It'll take the trustees a while to get over that!"

Jim and Neil shared a laugh, and Arnold went along with an accommodating smile, imagining the *Kulturkampf.*

Lenny sprang up the stairs to the stage of the Theater-Concert Hall to huge applause and made his way past the flowers surrounding the lectern. Arnold scrutinized the classically handsome face for prefigurings of Ariel's bone structure. He tried to separate out her Lenny-aspects from what must have been a gift from her mother, the striking (so he had heard) Chilean actress, Felicia Montealegre. He tried to imagine her from the non-Lenny parts of Ariel. He imagined Lenny and she, twenty years ago, making love, and in that ecstasy conceiving something glorious—Ariel—Ariel, that little fertilized egg, graceful and brilliant and sexy even as an ovum, starting to divide in her bubbly way. He felt blastula Ariel implant in his heart, and pulse and grow, Disney nature film—like, and he looked around to the back, where he knew she was standing, all seventy-five trillion cells of her, behind the heads of her colleagues so as to not attract attention. She was not looking at him, but at her father.

"May I take the liberty of skipping the customary formal salutations to my learned colleagues, honored guests, et alia," he began, and Arnold was already smitten with the progenitor of his love, pierced to the heart by the uncommon arrow of the Latin plural. There he was, "Jake Barickman," impostor, a curdle in the crème de la crème, and yet of all those in the hall, he felt most closely tied to the speaker and his spermatic consequences.

Lenny described his own experience thirty years earlier, listening as a student to his hero, mentor, and champion, Serge Koussevitzky.

"I remember his using the phrase 'the Central Line,'" Lenny said. "I'll never forget that—the line to be followed by the artist at any cost, the line leading to perpetual discovery, a mystical line to truth." Arnold despaired at his own fraudulence. What was he doing here? Gathering himself to accomplish a seventy-yard touchdown in the Second Symphony?

"Does one dare," Lenny asked, "thirty years later, in 1971, to speak of 'values' or of 'virtues' such as hard work, faith, mutual understanding, patience?" The answer, he asserted, was "yes"—one does dare, even though he and everyone else in the room was sick of rhetoric. As "adviser" to the festival, it was his job to give advice. But there was a problem with advice today, because something basic had changed in the world, and he wanted to try to locate that change, that difference, to articulate it so that he might advise through it, or around it, or over it.

He spoke of his own growing up, when he and his generation were filled with hope—hope for the New Deal, for Spain, for China, for antifascism and labor movements and racial equality. But in his talks now with students, all he was hearing was despair and hopelessness. The system was too big, too evil. One couldn't fight it except by extremist action. How to cope with the madness of a world divided into two mindless juggernauts even now doing battle by proxy in Asia and the Middle East? Hopelessness—that was the main difference between then and now.

Then, in dramatic transition, he became almost conspiratorial. Leaning forward into the mike, he whispered, "I have to tell you something very important—about the nature of despair. I have been reading an extraordinary book [the pencils were poised], which unfortunately exists only in German [most pencils went down], called *Das Prinzip Hoffnung*—"The principle of hope"—by the German philosopher Ernst Bloch, a poetic-historico-psycho-philosopher in the great German tradition of Hegel and Nietzsche and Marx and Freud." Arnold could feel the temperature drop in this hall filled with ear-and-handers. "Bloch describes what he calls the 'Not-Yet-Conscious'—that which is sensed in anticipation. And he shows that this Not-Yet-Consciousness is just as integral a part of man's total Consciousness as is the Unconscious or the Subconscious of Freud, and that man does not exist without it." Arnold felt air from other planets wafting around his solar plexus. Lenny continued: "This built-in Anticipation he calls 'Dreaming Forward'—a sensing what is to come that colors and shapes our dreams, our daydreams. In other words, it's what we ordinary people call Hope."

Arnold turned involuntarily around. Was she, his Dream-Forward, looking at him? No. She was looking off to his left. Not at her father. What was she looking at? Whom? His scan was beginning to attract attention. He turned back to Lenny, who was tacking toward his point.

"Now, the moment we apply Hope to living history, we see the trouble. Because some great hope like racial equality, the end of war, can seem to be imminent, just within our grasp—and when it doesn't come it causes great frustration. Youth today cannot wait: they sense the changes that must come and want them right right now, as a hungry baby cries to be fed. And this has always been the problem of youth; in fact, all of growing up is simply the overcoming of infantile impatience. That's what we call maturity: the overcoming of impatience; and many of us never reach it—especially today.

"Now, here's *my* theory: Impatience is the major differential in the famous 'generation gap': *we* grew up before instantaneousness, and *you* grew up after it. And the dividing line between us is Hiroshima. How could you *not* be more impatient than we were—growing up in a world of instant knowing, of instant gratification, and the threat of instant overkill?

"We old men prepared you very carefully: we made you the best-educated generation the world has ever known, the most sophisticated, the most politically oriented, the best read, the most informed, the best equipped for a democratic society. We taught you to believe the world could work; that no man need ever again point a gun at another; that the world is rich and blooming; that there is enough for all—enough food and clothing and music and leisure and love. We taught you all that; we taught you to hope as no one has ever hoped before in history; we developed your sense of the 'Not-Yet,' your Forward-Dreaming. We developed it to a boiling point.

"But [grand pause]—there's a catch [all those sensitive ears on red alert]: because what we taught you was what we learned *before Hiroshima*. How were we to know that the dropping of that bomb would make every one of you a stranger to us?"

Lenny lit a cigarette in the wooden hall filled with "NO SMOKING" signs. Not a honcho moved to stop him. He paced the stage for a moment, then sat down at its edge. "Can you hear me?" Voices of the apolitical hesitantly offered, "Yes."

"'So OK,' you say, 'thanks a lot; we've learned about progress and democracy and international brotherhood and racial equality and the elimination of the class struggle—so OK, thanks very much, where are they? Let's have em!'

"Well, you're right, you're absolutely right, And thank God you're impatient, because—and this is the whole point—because that impatience is a signal of hope—hope."

He stubbed his cigarette out on a nearby flower pot, put the butt into his pocket, and returned slowly to the lectern.

"There's still hope for everything; even patriotism—a word that is being defiled every day—even patriotism can be rescued from the flag-wavers and bigots. It's true we have to work faster and harder if we're going to take our next social step before the overkill stops us dead in our tracks, but if anybody can do it, faster and harder and better, it's *you*, the best generation in history. And especially you here today, artists of that generation. Because it's the artists of the world, the feelers and the thinkers, who will ultimately save us; who can articulate, educate, defy, insist, sing, and shout the big dreams. Only the artists can turn the 'Not-Yet' into reality."

Again, a wave of fierce regret swept through Arnold's being. He felt impotent compared to the long-haired boy with the slim hands sitting to his right, or the intense young woman with stubby fingers on his left. How was a quarterback—or even a decent chess player—supposed to bring the Not-Yet into being?

"And there's no time to lose because you're caught in a paradox. You see, you've got to work fast, but not be in a hurry. You've got to be patient, but not passive. You've got to recognize the hope that exists in you, but not let impatience turn it into despair. We'll help you as much as we can— that's why we're here—but it is you who must produce it, with your new, atomic minds, your flaming, angry hope, and your secret weapon of art.

"If there are still any among you who doubt that you possess hope, I will now prove you wrong. You surely have hopes that this speech has reached an end; well, congratulations: your hopes are fulfilled. Thank you."

The crowd burst into wild applause, with standing and exclamatory whooping. Yet Arnold was slow to rise. Why did he do that—toss off the speech as if it were a mere occasion for boredom? Whatever the reason, Arnold's love affair with Lenny had confronted its first hurdle.

Ariel intercepted him in the aisle (who was that mustachioed fellow trailing behind her?) and grabbed his arm.

"C'mon. Now's the time for your audition, while he's deep in adulation."

She made her way down to the front and waited patiently at the rear of a six-deep crowd semicircled around Lenny, sitting again on the edge of the stage. After a minute or so, he noticed her.

"Hey, critter!" He waved.

"Hey, creature," she responded, and the crowd parted approvingly to allow family its precedence. Ariel pulled Arnold along behind her.

"When did you get in?"

"This afternoon. I took Jake over to the Phinneys. Jake, I'd like you to meet my Dad. Dad, this is Jake. He was my leading man in *Yeoman*."

"Unrequited lover, or overrequited husband?" Lenny asked, as he reached out for Arnold's hand, then pulled him into a hug. Arnold melted.

"Unfortunately, the former," he said, embracing the ambiguity of show and real life.

"Ah, the song of the Merryman, moping mum," Lenny sang, and Arnold and Ariel joined him, she in improvised harmony, soon complemented by her father.

> *Whose soul was sad and whose glance was glum,*
> *Who sipped no sup and who craved no crumb,*
> *As he sighed for the love of a lady.*

The audience applauded. Lenny gave an exaggerated bow.

"Daddy, Jake's up here on parking, but he's dying to sing the Mahler with you. He knows it inside out. And he's a tenor. Can you get John to let him in the Chorus?"

"Sure, sweetie. Can't have too many big, handsome tenors."

"And, Daddy, he'll need to get out of parking for rehearsal and performance nights. If I write a note to Jim Kiley, can you sign it?"

"Of course. Bring it by, or leave it with Tom Cothran, and I'll sign it and get it back to you."

"Great."

"Thank you, Mr. Bernstein. I was really moved by your talk. A lot of musicians are low on social conscience. I'll try to read the Bloch book."

"Be prepared for some pretty hairy Deutsch. You know, Bloch wrote much of it as a refugee in Cambridge—he was working as a dishwasher!"

"*I* was a dishwasher in Cambridge last summer."

"Where?" asked Lenny.

"The Underdog."

"Ah, my favorite! Such culinary treasures we didn't have when I was at Harvard." Arnold could hear Lenny's father, Sam, in the Yiddish accent that had come upon him. "Well, anyone who was a dishwasher in the Ernst Bloch tradition, at the Underdog no less, is more than welcome to sing Mahler. Bloch loved him."

Arnold and he were hitting it off just fine! But the mustache was lurking still, two ranks behind.

"Well, I'll leave you two together," Ariel said. "Don't forget to tell John about Jake." And she pushed back through the crowd to pick up her friend. But as soon as she left the inner circle, Arnold's legitimacy was no more: the waiting crowd surged in, and Lenny effusively greeted his admirers.

.   .   .

Parking was everything it was cracked up to be: long days in the heat of the sun, hot nights, cold nights, rainy nights, traffic crushes, overwhelmed police details, interventions requiring high levels of social skill, visor and flashlight and raincoat—after which Arnold would either hitch or jog the mile and a half on Route 183 into the center of Lenox and drop exhausted into bed, alone, the longing of two co-ed colleagues trailing ectoplasmically behind him. In spite of his nepotistic origins, he turned out to be a favorite both with Neil and Jim and with the rest of his crew. Harvard legitimized him to some, Texas to others. And Barickman was an unobjectionable name. He easily found replacements for his rehearsal nights, and his bosses were lenient.

But workplace success could not compete with rehearsal hall empyrean: come the last of June, Arnold found himself nightly involved in a matrix more nourishing, almost, than he could bear. "Celestial soup" was the only thing he could call it. For unto him was given in those days that dollop of young Gustav Mahler's vision beyond all pain, beyond all terror, the postapocalyptic reweaving—of resurrection.

Where had Mahler been all his life? Not in Texas, that's for sure. And even Boston had heard little enough until twenty years earlier, when a young Lenny Bernstein had decided to exhume him—in defiance of the '50s—from the cisterns of cultural disdain. Too long. Too turgid. Too vulgar. Too. Too. Too. Who among the *tueur*s had even heard him? But the birth of the long-playing record had given the new, fiery director of the New York Philharmonic a tool to pierce the nation's armor, and he had single-handedly brought this sleeping giant, once buried and forgotten, out to prophesy to the '60s and its burning, yearning youth. Early on came the call to Resurrection, the Second Symphony. Lenny had made it his own.

It is a long and painful work. Before resurrection come many kinds of death. But Arnold had entered the Second Symphony tail first: the pain he did not know, only the glory. For his chorus came in only at the end, after the massive funeral march of the first movement, after the Dies Irae dissolves in a spasm of horror. After the "long dead hour of happiness" of the second movement, the sinister *moto perpetuale* of the third, and the "scream of anguish"—Enough! Neither had he heard the *"Urlicht,"* which imagines the victorious part he came to know. Nor had he heard the terrifying questions initiating his own movement, its ferocious march in which "the dead arise and stream on in endless procession," the terror of their call for mercy and forgiveness, or the *grosser Appel,* the last trumpet, sounding into a universe emptying even of its birdcalls. None of this had he heard. His rehearsals began after all that, in the magic moment when out of deathly silence there sounds the softest entrance in all of choral music: *"Auferstehen."* "Rise again, yes, thou shalt rise again." *That* was where he came into the movie, that was where his consciousness began, at a place unbalanced, but marvelously so. Celestial soup.

Piano rehearsals were at 7 in the West Barn, conducted by John Oliver, head of the Music School's Vocal Department and the recently created Tanglewood Festival Chorus, and in the real world director of Choral Activities at MIT. Most of the singers had performed the work before, but they accepted Arnold with no questions, even those in his immediate vicinity who might have felt his hesitations. To them, he was Jake Barickman from Harvard, experienced choral singer, not Arnold Hitler, neophyte from Texas, here to help Ariel Bernstein save face. There were only ten or so minutes of choral music to perform, so the work quickly proceeded from mastering the notes to perfecting the expression. How does one sing *"misterioso"? "Misterioso"* is not just soft.

Arise, yes, you will arise from the dead, my dust, after a short rest.

Who is speaking? Is the speaker dead or alive?

To bloom again are you sown.

The lord of the harvest goes to gather in the sheaves of us who have died.

How to sing from the other side of the grave? This was the challenge for the second and third rehearsals. Particularly moving for Arnold was the final assertion:

Was du geschlagen

Zu Gott wird es dich tragen!

A strangely ambiguous phrasing interlacing heartbeats with battles and blows as the vehicle to God. What God? For him, just now, it could be Mahler.

The concert was scheduled for Sunday, July Fourth. Was this Lenny's huge pun on Independence—the final liberation, Resurrection? He had arrived early in the week in his beautiful beige Mercedes convertible-with-mahogany-dashboard, its top down, grand entrance, waving royally to crowds of earnest music students snapping their Instamatics. MAESTRO 1, read the license plate. On Tuesday and Wednesday, he had rehearsed the orchestra, and Arnold had been grateful to puzzle out the strains drifting from the Shed over the parking lots. On Thursday evening, he took the chorus piano rehearsal. It was Arnold's first real experience of the charismatic truly great.

Lenny arrived twenty minutes late. "Typical," Ed, next to Arnold, informed him. John Oliver used the time to warm the chorus up and remind them of a few of the rough spots.

Lenny arrived in a baby-blue sweater, jeans, and cowboy boots, with a red handkerchief tucked into his rear pocket and a big grin on his tanned, handsome face. He spent the first ten minutes hugging and chatting with old friends while the chorus waited patiently in its seats. Somehow this was OK. During that ten minutes, he smoked two cigarettes under the "ABSOLUTELY NO SMOKING!" signs of the old wooden barn. That, too, was OK. It wasn't just that, anticipating the gift, no one thought to look the gift horse in the mouth. Rather, the gift was known to be so huge and all-encompassing that standard rules no longer applied. From the moment Lenny had walked into the barn, the universe had widened, and anything was possible. This was a professional chorus, already well rehearsed. The night's work would be about something beyond performance.

Socializing over, Lenny climbed up on his stool and picked up the score on the conductor's stand. He began davening with it, rocking back and forth, touching it to his forehead: *Baruch ato adonoy, eloheynu melech ho-olom*... He peeked up over the closed volume.

"If a dog's prayer were to be heard, there'd be a shower of bones from heaven."

The chorus laughed.

"No, seriously. It all depends who you are."

He went back to davening. The tune slowly went from Hasidic-liturgical to the opening bars of the *"Auferstehen"* chorus. The chorus applauded his opening gambit.

"This voice is what you get when you cross a *khazen* with a *chazer.*" More laughter, this time from chorus Jews only. Arnold looked to see if his beloved soprano was laughing. She wasn't. She'd heard the comment—whatever it meant—too many times before.

"Well, good evening, everyone, and welcome to this mighty raft of sincerity"—he held up the score—"on which we will negotiate the upcoming patriotic storm. Let's try to put out of our minds all the mindless governmental death-dealing we're being offered, and become truly mindful of this antidote to death we have before us. And let's imagine that in giving this, Mahler's gift, to the audience on Sunday, we will dilute, just a bit, the red-white-and-blue poison they'll be guzzling." He put the closed score on the stand. "Peace. From death, peace. And not the peace of the dead, but the peace of the beyond. Beyond the beltway, beyond the Pentagon, beyond Fortress America—triumphant peace. Let's take it from rehearsal 31."

Lenny raised his arms. The downbeat was the merest opening of his already opened hands.

Auferstehen . . .

Ja, auferstehen . . .

"That's great. That's terrific. Now let's make it four times as great. Four times as soft."

Auferstehen . . .

Ja, auferstehen . . .

He cut them off.

"Glorious! Better than glorious. Sensational! But you know what? It sounds like humans singing beautifully. Let's try not-humans, just molecules vibrating. Just sonorous forms, barely in motion."

Auferstehen . . .

Ja, auferstehen . . .

He cut them off again.

"Let me ask you something. What comes just before this?"

Arnold didn't know. He hadn't heard what came before.

"A rest," an alto offered tentatively.

"Is it a rest?"

"No, there's no rest there," said a bass. "Just a double bar."

"And what is the double bar fencing off?" asked Lenny.

"The previous section."

"The orchestra."

"The world of death."

"Ah!" shouted Lenny. Then, in a whisper: "Another world. The death-world. The world *before* your world. Listen, this is a chance to change things. To right them. You are poised in the gap between worlds. You, with those parts in your hands, you are the new Gods. Think about what you want to create. You don't have six days. You have only the next twenty-two bars. What do you want?"

"World peace."

"A clean planet."

"Kindness."

"Yes, yes, yes—that's what we all want." Lenny—not deprecating, but in the spirit of "Give me more . . ." "We're not going to get it just wishing. We need a new tool, some fantastic new tool, equal and oppo-site—no, *greater* than—nuclear weapons. And on Sunday you can begin distributing it."

He closed his eyes and waited.

"Here's what. You're going to make a new kind of music that will seep out into the world, and change *everything*, dig? A new, revelatory music that will seed visionary hearing out into the world. When you do this, starting right now, all music—from *Tristan* to 'Eleanor Rigby'—all music we already know will sound and give forth its secret content. What we understand as music now will seem like childish stammering by comparison."

He looked, one by one, into the face of every singer.

"You—right now—are about to bring this new sound language to birth. It's been calling us for a long while, calling, designating, teaching, but we hear it only occasionally in a few, exalted moments of the great-est masterpieces. Nobody can understand it yet, even you, its creators. Understanding will come later with the fullest maturation of our hear-ing. Deafness will dissolve, earplugs will bounce along the ground, and notes will radiate new, full, eloquence. *Auferstehen.* Resurrection . . . this chorale is the revelation. Let's hear it."

He raised his hands, and closed his eyes, and held his breath. A hun-dred other breaths were bated. Then, with almost no visible signal ex-cept a slight rise and fall of his spine, a hundred voices conspired in a sound wave of infinitesimal amplitude, an etheric vibration so subtly pervasive that it met with no resistance from the self-protecting mate-rial world. *Auferstehen. Ja, auferstehen.* Arnold's hair stood up on the back of his neck and he felt marrow pricks in his long bones. He had sung these notes before, but never in such a context. A quiet cutoff.

"That, sweethearts," said the Maestro, "is wholly exalted expression." And he lit a cigarette.

On Friday morning Ariel reluctantly accepted Arnold's invitation for a walk. She could sense what was coming, but it had to be dealt with. They headed out to the hilltop churchyard where Koussevitzky, Lenny's "true father," lay buried. The true father who in the early '40s had suggested that for his career, Lenny ought to pick another name. Bernstein. Low-brow Jewish. Not good for a conductor's image. How about "Leonard S. Burns"? he asked. Lenny would not give up his name, though the pronunciation changed from "Bern-steen" to "Bern-styne."

"I can't imagine what it must have been like growing up with him. . . ."

"It had its pluses and minuses. Still does. Our family is like a solar system with Pop as the sun. Sometimes it's hard to figure out your own identity while you're circling him."

"Where does he get this stuff?"

"The Mahler stuff?"

"Yes."

"Oh, he has what he calls his private hotline."

"What do you mean?"

"He talks to Mahler."

Arnold felt an itching in his knee.

"But there aren't many long-distance charges," Ariel continued, "because he also thinks he *is* Mahler. Mahler Hasidically reincarnated."

"So, is he *like* Mahler?" Arnold asked.

"No. But they're both sons of self-made Jewish businessmen. That says it all. Grandpa Sam wanted Pop to go into his beauty-parlor business. The Samuel Bernstein Hair Company. Can you believe it? He thought Lenny would never make any money being 'a piano player.' He still doesn't like it. Thinks it's crooked or something. Not real work. Mahler's father was an innkeeper. So here are these two kids growing up in low-culture, disapproving surroundings. They're both basically self-taught, at least in the beginning. They both turn out to be gifted pianists before getting into conducting and composition. They're both into dramatic music and theatrical productions, they both cram their output with songs and popular tunes, and both of them were—are—dead set against the avant-garde spirit of their respective times. Tonality, tonality! You should hear Pop on tonality."

"I should?"

"And he thinks he has exactly the same conflicts as Mahler: creator vs. performer with no time to create, Jew vs. Christian—did you know he's working on a mass?—provincial kid from the sticks vs. sophisticated *homme du monde.* . . . Pop's the eternal Peter Pan—and when he gets to be sixty, he's going to be faced by a terrible crisis. He just can't accept the fact he's no longer young."

"I hear he was booed at Lincoln Center last year."

"Oh, that. He gave a party at the apartment to raise money for the Panthers Defense Fund. Didn't go over big with the Jews. It hurt his feelings, though—he's not used to being booed."

"But he's still so political. . . ."

"Yup. He knows what he believes in. . . ."

A cloud floated over the brightening sun.

"Ariel . . . can I change the subject?"

Here it comes, she thought. "I suppose so."

"Who is that guy I see you with a lot—the guy with the mustache?"

She decided to bite the bullet and make things clearer than they really were.

"That's my boyfriend." She might have said, "It's none of your business."

"Your boyfriend? Since when?"

"Since last summer."

"He's been your boyfriend all year? Even when we . . ."

"He was in Paris studying trumpet. We were writing letters. He just got second chair with the BSO."

"So he's in the orchestra that's going to play with us?"

"You'll see him tonight. He's rehearsing now."

"Why didn't you tell me?"

"Do I ask you about *your* private life?"

"I don't have a private life." He was glad he hadn't shown her Rick's letter.

"What's his name?"

"Leonard Hecht."

"Leonard?"

"What's the matter with Leonard?"

"Well . . . it is your father's name . . ."

"Say, you really have a problem with names, don't you?"

"He's way too old for you . . ."

Ariel stood up from the bench.

"I don't need any more of this conversation." She began to walk away.

"Ariel, Wait. I'm sorry . . ."

"Not sorry enough. I won't be owned and controlled by some god-damn Hitler!"

Now it was her turn to apologize.

"Sorry. But I mean what right do you have to tell me who I can or can't go out with, who is too old for me, and what any boyfriend of mine should be named?"

"None," he admitted. "I'm just jealous."

They walked a few hundred yards in silence. At least, Arnold thought, she hadn't run away. He wasn't much of a warrior on this playing field.

That evening, the full forces gathered in the cool clamminess of the huge Shed stage. Two hundred and twenty-four people awaited the coming together of the week's work in the first dress rehearsal. Among them were a balding, mustachioed person who wrenched Arnold's heart and a lithe, blue-eyed one who hurt him even more. He would focus on other things—like Mahler's promised delivery from anguish. John Oliver again warmed up the chorus, and Lenny showed up, again twenty minutes late. Though he had been on site for the past week, there was still much hugging and embracing and touching. Arnold thought perhaps Lenny couldn't function without that kind of fuel. But if he took energy from people, he certainly gave it back with interest.

The chorus members had been invited to take their places on stage at the beginning of the rehearsal, even though it might be several hours until they were needed. The opportunity to watch Lenny rehearsing the BSO—in the Mahler Second, no less—was one of the perks that had brought them to Tanglewood that summer, rather than to festivals or workshops elsewhere. Not one chorus member was absent. Not one had chosen to show up "after break." While Lenny was schmoozing, Seiji Ozawa, in rumpled whites, was trying to organize a move of the conducting students up onto the already crowded stage, the better to observe. He himself began carrying chairs up to the sides and rear. Sensing a conducting-class coup, the student instrumentalists started carrying their own chairs up to compete for what little space was left. The BSO pros looked annoyed, but students were the name of this particular game—and the money was good.

Finally energized, with all engines roaring, Lenny leaped up on the stage. No blue jeans this time, but a tan gabardine suit and blue shirt with open collar. He hung his coat over the back of the conductor's chair, shook hands with all the first-chair strings, climbed up on the podium, sat down, and opened the score. Though he would perform without it, he needed it now for rehearsal numbers and the small details of instrumentation.

"Too bad it's still light out," he began, "because this music is no daytime *Kunst.* But neither is night music all filmy nocturnes. Let me hear the first three measures as if you were playing them at high noon."

The strings attacked their first measure tremolo fortissimo, quickly evanescing to pianissimo as the celli and basses attacked their second measure figure triple forte, leaving in their wake only the delicate tremor of violins and violas.

"Stupendous!" the conductor yelled. "A huge sun protesting the cloud that passes over. Now . . . let it become six at night." He waited. "Let the shadows lengthen, the sun go down, the sky slowly darken. Ten o'clock. Eleven. *Um Mitternacht.* Ready, midnight cowboys?" He raised his arms. "Now!"

The orchestra attacked the opening again. It was entirely inexplicable. Maybe, Arnold thought, it was only posthypnotic suggestion—but the same vibrations, the same loudness, the same-speed tremolo, the same low ascending figure—were all different, completely different, midnight different, nothing short of magic.

"Yes!" cried Lenny. "You've got it. This music comes out of the dark. It must be understood and felt in the dark. This is the somber heave of the nocturnal ocean, not the blue of the Mediterranean. Can you feel this darkness surging in Mahler's soul? Only his infrared eye could penetrate to these depths. . . ."

With that introduction, Lenny drove the orchestra along like some night-embracing demon, exploring the darknesses of small moments, repeating the same phrases over and over, each time uncovering a new layer of burning beauty or chilly cosmic import. He rehearsed by asking questions: Why is this written like this? What do these notes mean? Why does he do it differently this time? Questions and answers, sometimes from singers, students, or players, often from himself, Lenny quoting bits of poetry and literature extempore, improvising silly lyrics, filling the corps in on the musical history of this melody or that orchestration. Inventing alternative harmonies to show how right Mahler had been in choosing the ones he had. For all the demonic power explored, there were belly laughs throughout the rehearsal, great sighs, excited spirits together on the trail of discovery. This was why his ensembles loved him.

Yet there are limits, even to pedagogic bliss. By midnight, even faithful chorus members were checking watches—they had not yet sung a single note. Administrations feared Lenny for his overtimes. Players were ambivalent—the pay was great, but these were *long* rehearsals! The celestial *"Urlicht,"* celestially sung, had just faded away into nothingness. "I am of God," Frau Ludwig had sung, "and to God I shall return. Dear God will grant me a tiny light which will light my way to eternal, blissful life."

It was past time for a break, or even a breaking off until morning. But Lenny remained faithful to his doppelgänger's intentions: the Master had written "the fifth movement follows without any break." And surely it is true that the "Cry of Anguish" that assaults the unsuspecting listener, *wild herausfahrend,* savagely leaping out, eloquently mocks the danger of spiritual confidence in the face of what is. That, surely, is the point. The cellos and basses ripped triple forte up to a naked C, and the entire orchestra crashed in—four flutes, four oboes, five clarinets, four bassoons, ten horns, six trumpets (one of them Leonard), seven percussionists percussing, organ, harp, and "as many strings as possible"—in a grinding and terrible explosion. Within twenty seconds, the smoke began to clear, and threads of light emerged, painting a sweeter, if still dark, landscape.

The orchestra quieted further, and six horns, *ppp,* sounded the first ghostly appearance of Resurrection when Lenny began his routine cigarette cough. As the orchestra became quieter and quieter, the cough became louder and louder. He sat back on his stool and gripped the back rest with his left hand to steady himself, while conducting with his right. He coughed louder, more effusively, now gripping the conductor's stand in addition to the chair, conducting only with his thrashing head and flying gray hair. The six offstage horns could not see what was happening. They let out their fanfare, the "Voice of the Caller," Mahler labeled it: "The end of every living thing has come, the last judgment is at hand, and the horror of the day of days has come upon us," he wrote. Lenny could no longer conduct. He was consumed in a paroxysm of coughing. He staggered off the podium into the arms of Seiji Ozawa, who had leaped up on the stage and now led him off, down the steps, into the auditorium. The concertmaster stood and announced a ten-minute break, but the orchestra and chorus sat pinned to their chairs, watching in terror as their beloved maestro seemed about to eviscerate.

Bernstein gestured frantically at his jacket hanging over the stool on stage. Thinking it might contain some lozenge or medicine, a violin student ran to get it for him, then careened back, as did all others who could see, as the conductor, barely able to manage, tore a pack of L&Ms out of the pocket, managed to get one in his mouth, and, unable to work the matches, gestured imploringly, then violently, for someone to light it for him. The scene was so grotesque that stunned onlookers were paralyzed. The Maestro took this as disobedience, betrayal by those he had trusted, and out from under his uncontrolled movements there rose a more willful rage, a tantrum, which paradoxically seemed to calm him. "Goddamn it, I need a cigarette to cough better!" he cried between coughs. "Somebody light this fuckin thing for me!" Ariel ran down from the stage, having succeeded in finding a matchbook among the trombones, and lit her father's smoke.

What a piece of work is a man! How noble in reason! How infinite in faculty, in form and moving! The paragon of animals! And yet, what is this quintessence of dust? To go from the "tiny light" leading to God right to the light of "Somebody light this fuckin thing for me!"—*This* is startling.

It was 1 in the morning. Something unrecapturable had been shattered. Lenny knew it as well as anyone. He abandoned the rehearsal, set the call for 8 the next morning, and then went off to party.

Thirty-two

Saturday morning at 7:40, the orchestra and chorus staggered in, bags under eyes and frogs in throats. Lenny
reappeared promptly at 8, fresh as a daisy, in blue cords
and bow tie. Maddening! From 8 to 9:45, he rehearsed
the last movement from the great coughing defeat to the triumphant
end, then broke for fifteen minutes to allow the crowd into the Shed for
the regular Saturday open dress, typically packed when Lenny was conducting.

Again, the chorus was allowed on stage to follow what was mostly
orchestral work. Arnold brought along a notebook to record the proceedings. His morning's notes were voluminous, but these were the highlights:

"Rule Number One in orchestral playing is: it's all chamber music."

"Think dark, even when you're playing high"

"You can make a diminuendo on an upbeat—you think you can't do
it, but I tell you you can."

"Thank you for that *fortepiano*. Mahler thanks you for it."

"Doesn't he say *tenuto* or something? Well, *I* say it; he told me to say it; we talk."

To the first oboe: "This tiny entrance is like fifty trumpets."

"A great orchestra is a flexible orchestra: Lenny and his flexible cats."

"Pelvic pulse; excuse the expression, but that's what it is. Passion . . . Now it's really throbbing. . . ."

Arnold thought of last night's party, of Lenny, drunker and drunker, ogling the boys and the girls, of the sea of bodies on the crowded dance floor, no Ariel, no Mustache (where were they?), pulsing, throbbing, and every now and then expressing skyward a projectile student imitating the Maestro on the podium. "Lenny's Leap," the step was called.

"You gotta cry and suffer and that upbeat is part of it. . . . I love you; what can I say?"

He led the orchestra through the score using the ear-eyes of a conductor, a composer, a pianist, a writer, a man of the world. What a combination of analytical rigor, emotional fervor, and psychological cunning! Inspiration flowed like wine at Cana.

"It's impossible," he told the brass, of a superhigh entrance, "so go ahead and do it." The logic was—impeccable. In the *"Urlicht,"* for those players who separated body and soul: "I have one criterion: Will it give me an orgasm?" Concerning a cello/bassoon melody in the prechorus last movement: "Wow! You know, it just came to me what that phrase means—why it's *drängend!"*

Bernstein practically wrote it, and he was still discovering. . . . Arnold wanted to be like that when he grew up.

Given the international roster of players and singers, he heard his love's progenitor speak Dutch, Italian, French, German, Yiddish, Hebrew, and, to Seiji Ozawa's amusement and applause, some Japanese. He spoke of his beloved Mahler, "that vehement, severe, Judaic man," who had "entered his empty, insipid, skeptical age like a messenger from afar, sublime in his outlook, unprecedented in the strength and masculine ardor of his pathos, and truly on the verge of bestowing music's ultimate secret upon the quick and the dead."

Again the assignment to create a heretofore nonexistent sound. "Nobody had previously been borne closer to Heaven with such soulful, effervescent, visionary music than had this yearning, holy, hymnic Jew, with his woeful, fervorous path toward Christian exaltation. Beyond description glorious!"

Arnold stared, enthralled, into the wings as Lenny, in tie and tails, kissed Koussevitzky's cufflinks before coming onstage. The quarterback sat through four and two-thirds movements, "quiet as a nun, breathless with adoration." And not just for Lenny. For Ariel, too, supporting the same song, three rows down in front of him, her light-brown hair haloed with stage lights and from the light within. And even for the mustachioed Leonard, his cuckolding rival, he of the glistening horn, whose second trumpet opening of the Great Call was so resplendent as to—all on its own—make resurrection a certainty. Arnold was filled with love for all beings, sentient and otherwise, and with hope, nay, expectation, that all, *allüberall*, would turn out well, *ewig... ewig... ewig....*

It did not. The rest of the summer was miserable, as commonplace jealousy ate at commonplace space, and Ariel grew more defensive and severe. Tanglewood had peaked early for Arnold—and it's a long, long time from July to September: parking detail was most anticlimactic.

Thirty-three

Relations between them did not improve when Arnold surprised Ariel by moving into Whitman Hall, her dorm on the Radcliffe Quad. He had signed up back in the heady days of *Yeoman,* when anything seemed possible and nothing except his name plagued future potential. Now there was the question of Leonard Hecht, trumpet player extraordinaire, and worse than that, the history of his own presumptuous, possessive behavior. Ariel's surprised "Arnold, what are you doing here?" and her breezy "Oh, *nice . . .*" as she trotted past him down the stairs did not afford much hope.

But it was his first trip to the hall bathroom, now co-ed, which sent him into despair. There, pasted to the stall door, like the procurement ad in Mansfield, was a sticker, white on crimson, certainly one of many, that read: "FOR A VERITAS GOOD TIME, CALL 864-5322." It was Judy's number. The cottonmouth had struck.

Before going to Judy's, he checked bathrooms in Mass Hall, Wadsworth, Widener—all posted, every stall. Even Memorial Church had been covered. He called to see if Judy was home and found the number no longer in service. Good. She was dealing. He trekked up Mass Ave to see if he might catch her in.

She opened the door, not obviously distraught, with the semester's first issue of the *Indy* in hand.

"Go get yourself some juice or something. I want to finish this."

"What is it?"

"I'll show you when I'm done."

Arnold went into the kitchen and picked up the phone. Dial tone. She must have changed the number.

"Change your phone?" he called out.

"Evasive action."

He returned to the living room with a glass full of orange juice and sat on a chair facing the couch.

"You've been getting calls?"

"They were actually quite interesting. A few heavy breathers, but some sophisticated Harvard types, too. Some guy even quoted John Donne at me. A woman called, asking if I 'did' women. I told her I was into women's studies. 'How about studying me?' she wanted to know. I was tempted."

"There are stickers with your old number in all the bathroom stalls in the Yard."

"Wasted paper. Unlike this." She indicated the *Indy*. "Hang on, I'm almost finished."

Arnold watched her, wondering what was engrossing her so. He had an inkling, of course, the *Indy* being Cottonmouth Claggart's organ.

"There you go," she said, refolding the paper front page out, and handing it over to him. "Read it and weep."

"SPECIAL ISSUE!" the masthead blared. "EATING TEACHER, EATING STUDENT" ran the headline. "Part One of a Series Becoming Ever More Specific." Arnold scanned through several columns of small print.

"Do I need to read this?" he asked.

"You're the victim, presently anonymous. The object of pity and terror."

"Guess I better read it."

"Guess you better. I'll fix some supper for dessert." She got up and went into the kitchen.

Arnold took a sip of juice and began.

Prologue: Descent into the Pit

Remember the '50s and pre-Beatles '60s? Remember when the campus was a sanctuary where fresh-faced youngsters strolled tree-lined paths between chapel and library? Remember the benign professor?

Well, forget it.

Instead, realize that the contemporary campus—and ours is no exception—is a vast, cut-rate sexual supermarket, the classroom a great hunting ground, especially for faculty bathed in the adoration of nineteen-year-olds. Sex with students has become one of the perks of the job.

And what a perfect job! Social respect, while living the frisson of an outlaw, confident that colleagues, equally guilty, will be reluctant to intervene, operating in an eye-winking university environment romantically tolerant of "eccentricity."

When asked by a reporter why women found him so attractive, our notably hideous Henry Kissinger responded, "Power." For once, the fork-tongue speaketh truth. Sex between students and faculty members represents a clear abuse of power, grotesquely distorting the proper relation between them. At its most fundamental level, an institution of higher education is ethically bound to guarantee that learning, not sex, is the essence of faculty-student interactions and that a student's personhood is respected at all times.

We live, alas, in an era of ostensible "sexual liberalism and freedom." Such an attitude demeans the notion of "human." To be human does not mean being at the mercy of our genitalia. And yet we are.

"He's in top form," Arnold yelled into the kitchen.

"I thought you'd like it," was the reply, amidst the chopping.

VARIETY IS THE SPICE OF STRIFE

If Harvard has nothing else, it has variety. Our investigations and interviews over the past year and a half have identified two distinct classes of faculty sexual predators, and within each class, a wide variety of approach.

The least dangerous, because most ineffectual, are the public harassers, overripe pedagogues who leer from the lectern and spout obscenities for the titillation of their young charges. They are known; they are classic; they are surrounded with moral flies advertising their musty corruption. No one is fooled; no one comes near them. It is only the spectacle that appalls.

The private harasser is more cunning and thus more sinister. He or she uses his or her formal authority to gain access to the student, access that can be attained by a simple directive, possibly scrawled on a term paper: "Please see me." They all come on as mentors, the whole troupe of them, but, unlike their namesake, are hardly faithful instructors. There are the counselor/helper types, who nurture and care for their victims; there are the confidantes, friends, and equals, demonstrating their desire to merge with students; there are the intellectual seducers who demand "self-disclosure," and use the information to spin a sticky web; there are the opportunists, always scheduling field trips, or offering rides to other-than-campus settings more propitious for seduction. Some faculty members have been known to buy VW vans and fit them out with beds for just that purpose.

Donna Juana

He or she; him or her; inclusive, but awkward. There is no doubt that in our patriarchal society, men are the principal offenders. But then again, they call down the preponderance of the blame. More than preponderance—they attract almost *all* the blame—leaving the "weaker sex" oddly innocent and victimized. *The Harvard Independent* will not follow the beaten path here, but will rather explore the more exotic bushes of female and feminist harassers at large on our campus.

"Uh-oh, he's out after feminist sexual harassers. . . ."
From the kitchen: "No names yet. It's all most interesting theory."
"I bet names come next week."
"Not if he knows his libel law."

Let us try to understand the perpetrators. Harvard is a male domain, and women on this male plantation are actively resisted. What woman faculty member would not feel called to rebel, to assert some special turf and power?

Then there is the female midlife crisis. In a flock of brilliant and nubile Cliffies, even a thirty-year-old would feel the crows' feet imprinting themselves on her once flawless face. A woman of advancing years and fading beauty has intense self-doubts about her potency (sexual and otherwise), and needs to demonstrate to herself her hold on power. So it is understandable if she selects as object someone over whom she has direct influence. Instead of being used by more powerful males as a menial sex object, she can challenge that dynamic with some yielding innocent on whom she can project whatever fantasy she craves. She can show those co-eds that she can compete successfully for their young men. What omnipotence!

Moreover, as you may have noticed, many faculty men are physically unattractive. Paunchy, short, unkempt, men with glasses, men with bad skin—these are the pool of men "not taken." How much brighter a feather in the cap is a spanking undergrad, fresh from the football field, anxious to explore the world.

Worst are the feminists, for they add to these more common dimensions a seductive rhetoric of freedom. Viewing themselves as militants in the struggle for better lives for women, they use their students to vent hostilities and redress real or imagined personal/societal wrongs. Their irresponsible behavior is rationalized as advancing a cause.

"Come on, what's the big deal?" they say. "These kids know the score better than we ever did. There's not a good-looking freshman that hasn't been hit on by some girl his own age, so why get excited if a professor gets a little adventurous once in a while?"

Well, *I* say, with Ms. Marilyn French, "Scratch a woman, [especially a feminist], and find a rage." That is what is operative here—to the detriment of our handsome young male students. Rage and fear—the primary emotions of the female professor.

"Where are you?" Judy asked, as she came back into the living room, having put the casserole in to cook.

Arnold read aloud, " 'The intertwining of sexuality, emotion, and desire in the institutionalized practices of teaching and learning means the loss of a safe space in which to conduct any kind of inquiry.' So is what he says right? I feel as if we were consenting adults."

"Don't you see where this is headed?"

"Let me finish this," said Arnold. "I've just got another couple of columns."

"Then you and I can have a little transference." Arnold was worried. "Of food to mouth."

"Oh."

What Is to Be Done?

The mark of a civilized society is how it protects its least powerful, and how it reacts to their victimization. Harvard must be a community that protects and nurtures its members, not *in loco parentis*, but as a *locus humanitatis*. The classroom is a place of power and vulnerability as well as a place of open inquiry and invigorating discussion. Because professorial autonomy exaggerates self-importance and contributes to arrogance and abuse, all observations about sex mingling with other manifestations of power must be seriously investigated by a hearing officer who will gather data from student groups and academic departments. If this seems a witch hunt, let us recall that, unlike Old Salem, we are here confronted with real witches.

Next Week

A look at the observed forms of socially undesirable sexuality. Is she really a sexual harasser, or does she just make it with students?

"Whew," whistled Arnold. "He's one dangerous character."

"A crackpot with a printing press. What does he look like?"

"Tall. Thin. Suave. Maybe a little effeminate."

"What color hair?"

"Red."

"Is he good-looking?"

"I don't know. Why?"

"Oh, I just like to know what people look like. You can tell a lot about people from their looks—don't you think?"

"Is this a feminist notion?"

"Maybe. We do lots of talking about students—in which we discuss their body parts."

"Really?"

"You know, like 'head,' or 'heart'—and depending on their sex, 'legs' or 'buns.' Calling someone 'a good head' stresses our connection to his or her intelligence. 'Great buns,' on the other hand, is a larger statement of the whole man in the context of liberatory pedagogy."

"You're putting me on."

"Maybe." She hiked her skirt and crossed her legs. "All I know is that I was glad my teachers talked that way about me. Being an object of desire made me feel admired and wanted, worthy and lovable. The world's best learning environment. Teaching and learning as acts of provocation. Mr. Rick there is suppressing the pursuit of knowledge—and not just in the biblical sense."

She seemed convinced and imperturbable.

But not so when a week later she banged on Arnold's dorm room door, letter in hand.

Harvard University
Office of the President
Faculty Affairs Committee

November 21, 1971

Dear Professor Jepperson,
A complaint has been filed that alleges you have sexually harassed the student Arnold Hitler. This institution has the

obligation to investigate all such complaints and make a determination about whether such allegations are true. I will share the details of the complaint with you and give you the names of individuals who may have witnessed the incidents alleged. You will be able to comment on any findings or recommended action before the findings are finalized and before any recommendations are made.

You may have a support person present during any of our meetings.

It is against the law for you to retaliate against Arnold Hitler or any witnesses to this matter. Retaliation may encompass comments or actions initiated by you. Further, your friends may be found to have retaliated if they, through words or actions, subject Arnold Hitler or any witnesses to conduct that interferes with a comfortable work environment or the benefits of an education.

I encourage you to limit conversation and speculation about this process with others. Rumors serve no one well. It is this institution's responsibility to investigate thoroughly before deciding whether action should be taken.

I will maintain confidentiality about this matter to the extent permitted by law. However, I cannot guarantee complete confidentiality.

Please call for an appointment at your earliest convenience.

Sincerely,
Prof. Amanda N. Folger
Chair, Faculty Affairs Committee

This time, it was Arnold's turn to feign assurance.

"Look, Part Two of the article was a notice about gathering more data. I can't see him going through with this thing, either."

"But now the president's office is involved."

"I can't imagine he'll show up to be deposed. And even if he does, it's your word against his. And how do we even know this is a real letter?"

"It's too *echt* bureaucratese to be phony."

Arnold and Judy's attention was drawn by the sound of an envelope being slipped under the door.

"Go see what it is," she said.

"Later. It's probably just some announcement."

"It's not just some announcement."

"How do *you* know?"

"It's my fine eye for human relations."

Arnold got up to investigate. In the official-looking holder was a folded sheaf of papers and a smaller, sealed envelope.

"Uh-oh. It's from the University of Harvard, Department of Un-Comparative Literature."

"What's that?"

"Oh, just some satirical thing of Rick's."

"You mean he was outside that door just a minute ago? I can't believe it!"

"He sent 'The Speech of the Dead Christ.'"

"What?"

"I don't know. It's a Xerox of something. Jean Paul: 'The Speech of the Dead Christ.' Who's Jean Paul?"

"German Romantic. What's it say?"

Arnold read over the first page. "'. . . And all the dead cried: "Christ! is there no God?" . . . And when I raised my eyes to the boundless world for the divine eye, it stared at me from an empty bottomless socket; and Eternity lay on Chaos and gnawed it and ruminated itself—Shriek on, ye discords, read the shadows; for He is not!'"

"Well that's probably true."

"There's lots more," Arnold said, flipping through the pages.

"I got it. Spare me the rest."

"There's a note at the bottom: 'Jean Paul—your good Gustav's favorite author. So much for Resurrection. Never underestimate the power of cognitive dissonance, mon cher. Ever yours, RM.' And there's a PS. He's into PSs. 'Did you know that my great-great-great-great-great-grandfather Increase was the sixth president of Harvard? Don't you think that gives me the right to be acknowledged by the likes of you?'"

"What's the little envelope?" Judy asked. It was protruding from the big one.

Arnold tore open the "University of Harvard" seal and discovered bumper stickers folded together, spoons—the way he had once lain all night with Judy, and would like to lie with Ariel. White letters on crimson again, two copies:

"DISTINGUISHED PROFESSORS DO IT PEDAGOGICALLY."

To the packet was clipped a note, also in red, in Rick's distinguished hand: "Dear Aspiring Hedonist: One is for your door so that your co-educational hallmates may be reminded of its truth. The other is for Professor Jepperson's traveling bedroom, best mounted not on the rear bumper, but facing the driver, above the windshield. Or perhaps on the ceiling over the bed. If she would like two or more to cover all possibilities, she may apply to me."

"I'll take them both, if you don't want yours." She grabbed them from Arnold's hand. "I'm beginning to like this guy."

Her reaction to the "SEXUAL PREDATOR WITHIN" sign planted outside her apartment was not recorded. She did pull it out of the lawn.

She also left Harvard after fall semester. The note in Arnold's box was brief: "Off to warmer climes. Thanks for your support. Hang in there. Judy." After all the subterranean maneuvering consequent upon the investigation, after all the community sniggering over Rick's two-part *Indy* series, "Portrait of the Professor as a Not-So-Young Seductress," and especially after the feminist attack on Arnold for laying waste a promising feminist's career—after all this, the administration was loath to give Arnold any details of Judy's whereabouts or plans. The world seemed to cross the street whenever he passed by. He was pitied as victim, scorned as victimizer, envied by jocks and studs, feared by young women vulnerable to his good looks—but all from a distance. No one would talk to him unless absolutely necessary. Even the U.S. government turned its back: in an effort to butter up voters, especially wealthy contributors with low-lottery-numbered sons, Nixon had pledged to end the draft. Between this cynical move and McCarthy's antiwar stance, the 1972 election had made Arnold's future secure—at least from a stint in the military. And a good thing, too, since—in spite of calls from Bob Wright—he had let his CO application wither in the contrary windings of his guilt.

Thirty-four

Let one letter disappear from our name
and we are no longer.

Edmond Jabès, *Aely*

From the outside, Arnold's final Harvard year would seem to have been traumatic, buffeted by political and emotional turbulence, gender politics, several levels of war, Judy withdrawing, then gone, Ariel so near and unreachable. Yet from inside, *his* inside, the year passed with the tense and complex calm of a late-Beethoven slow movement. In the face of all external perturbation, it was Jabès, Jabès that had ravished him.

Intrigued by Mephisto's offer, more than intrigued—*called* at some deep level—Arnold had undertaken Rick's curriculum. Rick had put all required books on one-hour reserve, and rather than negotiate such hurdles, Arnold sought his own used copies. Barthes and Saussure were easily at hand, but Jabès's *Book of Questions* had to be bought new. As the most expensive purchase of the semester, it commanded immediate, out-of-sequence attention.

Once in, Arnold never returned. The deserts sands of an Egyptian Jew became the quicksand of a Texas N/A—Arnold's answer on forms asking his religion. The aborted relationship of Yukel and Sarah, hinted at, evoked but never told, became the relationship—consummated in its dissipation—he had searched for but never found. Yukel and Sarah, Arnold and Ariel. Two Harvard semesters came and went as if in a dream. Readings, discussions, exam grades. Arnold did well for someone fundamentally absent. His *Book of Questions* was always in pocket—coat pocket in the winter, jacket in spring. He read it, then read in it, then read in its margins, those wide spaces tapering off to infinity, reverberating with whiteness, silence, and void.

The Book of Questions—its very title spoke of Arnold's being, its fragmented contents of the state to which his soul had been refracted. Jabès's imaginary rabbis seemed to direct their questions and commentaries directly into the uncomfortable space he occupied: they echoed painfully off its walls and pressured their way to higher volumes and temperatures. It was Jewish writing, as Rick insisted, stubbornly assailing the unsayable with paradox and contradiction. The book was impossible to read in the ordinary sense—traversing blocks of consequential meaning. To read it so was to be defeated. Rather, one had to fill the lawless spaces with unstable, enigmatic meanings in this story of fragments and gaps, an account, beyond communication, "of a love destroyed by men and by words."

The entire puzzle fitted pregnantly into the puzzle of Arnold himself, its stifled screams in duet against his own, its tears flowing through his ducts, its wounds fitting his own organs in transparent overlay. *His* were its unending questions, its fragmented speech, its being-in-exile, circling itself obsessively like cannibal birds of prey.

DEDICATION:

TO THE REMOTE SOURCES OF LIFE AND DEATH REVEALED.
TO THE DUST OF THE WELL.

TO THE RABBI-POETS IN WHOSE MOUTHS I PUT MY WORDS
AND WHOSE NAMES HAVE,
OVER THE CENTURIES, BECOME MINE.

"I give you my name, Sarah. And it is a dead end road."—Yukel's
Journal

"I told you my name, Ariel, and our end was our beginning."—
Arnold's Journal

"In time, you will feel the dimensions of your name, the anguish of
the nothing you answer to."—Reb Amiel

"Once you have taken possession of your name, the alphabet is yours.
But soon you will be the slave of your riches."—Reb Teris

> *Smoke.*
> *Smoke.*
> *for all who see only fire,*
> *who smell only*
> *dawn*
> *and death.*

Half man, half fish, half bird, half ghost: there is always one half of him
which escapes.

"I talked to you about man's health. I talked to you about man's solitude
and his lie. I talked to you about the proof of man's existence: God."

"God is after life, where life changes its name."—Reb Feder

"The word is all I own. I am the eye of the sea sans sky or bottom, reduced to its name."—Reb Hitler

"Here is grain for your field: a grain of life, a grain of death. The

grain of life will nourish your death, the grain of death feed your life."—
Reb Ivrah

"The death inside me shelters me against death."—Reb Hitler

We are all Jews, even the anti-Semites, because we are all marked for martyrdom. I pity and kiss you, brothers and sisters. Our names no longer make sense. We are simply the Name, the Only Name. We smiled when our eyes met, Ariel Bernstein—because we had the same face.

To depend upon a wound means to pattern your life on it. The laws of light are inspired by the laws of the dark.

Alan Paton gave the graduation address. Arnold sat on his folding chair in the Yard, trying hard to listen. But Arnold's mind was elsewhere, largely in the kaballah cosmos of shapes and letters—the letters of his name, shaping themselves in large doodles of ballpoint pen on program.

H—the two uprights, my body and my soul, inextricably tied, yet kept at a distance.

Paton droned on: "... I have one overriding obligation, and that is to speak that truth which is the object of pursuit of every university which deserves the name. I might have chosen some safer subject, but I would much rather speak on a subject which is related to our lives and our aspirations."

Sober, inoffensive clarity. Famous man in famous place, lick, lick, lick. Let him speak about Harvard men dropping Harvard napalm on Harvard-chosen peasants.

I—I would do that, if I spoke at all. Vertical, reaching—both up and down . . .

". . . In what way can one's highest loyalty be given to one's country? Surely only in one way, and that is when one wishes with all one's heart, and tries with all one's powers, to make it a better country, to make it more just and more tolerant and more merciful, and if it is powerful, more wise in the use of its power."

T—Ah, there it is. Power blocked above. Only downward available. Roots, maybe, or hell.

"So it is—in your country as well as mine—that there comes this schism between those who believe that the maintenance of law and or-der is the prime obligation of any good society. . . ."

ruLed. L not rooted, grounded. Blocked below. But I with a foot that can walk. Kick. Stomp.

You at least know you are sick.

E R—the letter is the nexus, the wandering sign of all wandering signs, pulling everything it may construct into exile and dislocation. E— an I with three gestures, *Kyrie eleison, Christ eleison, Kyrie eleison,* a lat-eral move toward otherness. And R, a question mark, walking. Yet the question seems closed, contained in small space in the head. Best to blow open the head. Trepanning, I think.

"I am often asked the question as to whether Americans should with-draw all investments in South Africa. I know this view is strongly held by some, and I respect it, but it is not my own."

Scattered booing and hissing from the SDSers. The speaker addressed the graduating seniors, especially the booers and hissers among them: "I understand well your dissatisfaction with the world that we have made. But I do not believe that one can make it any better by withdrawing from it."

A clipboard was passed along to Arnold. On it, the statement that had been circulating among seniors for a week: "I pledge to explore and take into account the social and environmental consequences of any job I consider or any organization for which I work." There were forty-two signatures above the space for his.

"I understand your argument that if you take part in it, it will corrupt you just as it has corrupted us. But that is not a very good or a very brave argument. The only way in which one can make endurable man's inhumanity to man, and man's destruction of his own environment, is to exemplify in your own lives man's humanity to man and man's reverence for the place in which he lives."

Arnold passed the clipboard to his left without his signature.

"It is a hard thing to do, but when was it ever easy to take upon one's shoulders the responsibility for man and his world? The very best of luck to you all."

The audience applauded as required, and the budding capitalists from Harvard Business School waved their dollar bills in traditional and corrective comment.

Reb Hitler: "The key word that haunts us opens not upon the world, but upon the void."

Who was this boy seated on the folding chair in Harvard Yard? He seemed more bent and less handsome than he had been. There was a new tremor in his hand. His eyes were deeper in his skull. His mind was a question mark, walking.

School of the Streets

dear mom, dear dad,

well, here i am in the "big

apple." graduation went fine.

we had alan paton (a writer

from south africa) come and talk

to us in what i thought was an

overly polite way about the simi-

larities between america and his

apartheid-torn country. i had a

book and clothing sale, and put

everything left into a big back-

Thirty-five

General Delivery
Times Square Station
New York City, N.Y. 10108
Monday, 6/26/72

Dear Mom, Dear Dad,

   Well, here I am in the "Big Apple." Graduation went fine.
We had Alan Paton (a writer from South Africa) come and talk
to us in what I thought was an overly polite way about the
similarities between America and his apartheid-torn country. I had a book and clothing sale and put everything left
into a big backpack I bought from a girl in my dorm. Hitched
to NYC on three rides (and a bus), and spent last night at
the "Y" on 92nd Street. I've been to Columbia about grad
school next year, and have got applications. Today I'm
headed down to New York University for more applications,
and will stop at the New School to see if they offer any
courses I'm interested in while I wait to hear about degree
programs in March.

   I'm looking for a job to tide me over. I've got about
$350 from savings and my sale, and until I get work, I could

use any extra cash you each could spare. I've called ads for
"Gal/Man Friday" (I like bisexual pun here, and also the
reference to Robinson Crusoe), and one agency called me
about an editorial assistant job for some publisher. Everything else seems either secretarial, or sales, or banking,
or insurance—none of which I would like to do—even for a
year.

You've probably heard about tropical storm Agnes, which
is just finished and heading up and out toward Cambridge.
It rained every day for a week here, with some bad flood-
ing, even in the city. Lucky no one lives in the sewers like
in Les Misérables. People are ready for some sun, and here
it is today.

Keep your eyes on this "Watergate Caper." No one is quite
sure what it means yet, but some people think it might be
important.

You know, I'm sure, that I'm no longer threatened by the
draft, now that we're going toward a volunteer army, and
Kissinger and Laird are promising a quick end to the war.

Well, I'm off downtown to New School and NYU. Write if
you can, and send a few bucks to

Your poor Harvard graduate,
Arnold

...a question mark walking down Fifth through Washington
Square, New School catalogue and *New York Times* employment section
in hand, wondering if he'd hear from Mom or Dad, and how long his
money would last. On a bench, just past the arch, a man was signaling.
Arnold looked around to see if he might mean someone else. He didn't
know anyone that disheveled. "No, you, you," the pointing finger insisted. Arnold kept on walking.

"Hey, you, blond boychik, come over here and take a look who I am."

Arnold turned and walked back along the path. The man said nothing, just inspected him with glittering eye, awaiting recognition, his

pointing finger still extended along his yellow pants, palms gloved, though it was June.

"Yes?"

The man said nothing. And nothing. And nothing.

Arnold turned and walked away. Halfway through the park he thought of Jacobo. Maybe Jacobo. He sprinted back north, but the man was gone.

He turned back through the park toward NYU, stopping at the comfort station at the south end of the park. The lowered pants under one of the stalls . . . yellow . . . was that what Jacobo was wearing? He thought he might wait till the man came out, but was self-conscious about hanging around in the men's room. He stepped outside and took a seat on a north-facing bench from which he could see the door. Men in suits with attaché cases, men in rags—but not his man; two men in green lamé dresses and red heels . . . no yellow pants. He put his left foot up on the bench and listened to his knee, innocently, so no one would suspect. He could have been a young man in love, dreaming of his sweetheart. Nothing. He scratched his inner knee—hard—and listened again. Perhaps there was too much street noise.

"Hey, man, you play chest?"

Arnold looked up. Standing in front of him was a black man—black? maybe mulatto?—fifty—maybe forty, maybe even thirty—very weather-beaten, clean, but outrageously dressed in green-and-black leather, red headband, covered with buttons like "Ahab Lives!" "I ♥ My Lévi-Strauss"; "Schoenberg über Alles." His fingers were covered—each and every one—with multiple rings teeming with symbols. An ornate shoulder bag hung like a fig-leaf, below his waist.

"Hey man, you hear me? You play chest?" He gestured moving pieces on a board, as if to a deaf man.

"Chess?"

The tan man nodded.

"Actually, I do," Arnold said as he lowered his knee to the ground and faced his interlocutor squarely. "I mean, I used to."

"Two bucks a game?"

"No. I have to get going."

The chest player broke into, "*We gotta get going, where are we going? What are we gonna do? We're on our way to somewhere, the nigger and the Jew.* . . . Excuse me, I mean Negro."

"Who are you talking about? I'm not Jewish."

"And I'm not a nigger. I'm Vergil Wang pronounced Wong, late of Africa and the Orient. You can call me Vergil, cause I'm on the verge of many, if not most, things." He held out his hand. Arnold shook it.

"Arnold."

"A manly handshake, young Arnold with no last name. See, I'm just learning chest, and I need a simpatico partner who won't make fun of me. You look simpatico, capish? *Vershest du?* Two bucks a game? Three? One?"

"Naw, I've got to get going."

"Where to—if you don't mind me asking?"

"Uhh . . . Admissions."

"NYU?"

Arnold nodded.

"Thinking of joining the Not Yet Ulcerated, the Never Young Ugains? Whaddya want to do that for? Play chest instead. A nice boy like you, a nice summer day, you're in the chest center of the Western world, Washington Square. When in Roma do as the Romans do. How about a five-minute game? Whoever's ahead in five minutes . . . I got my chest clock."

"If you're just learning, how come you have a chess clock?"

"Hey, man, when you took up baseball, you have a glove? Can't play without necessary accessories. Three bucks on a five-minute game, whaddya say?"

"OK. One game. Five minutes. But I don't really want to take your money."

"If you win. Why not? Three bucks'll buy you a Chinese meal."

"I meant, I don't really need the three bucks, and maybe you do."

"What are you, some rich kid? You don't come from here, I can tell."

"Texas."

"Texas with a New England twang."

"Yeah, I spent the last four years in Massachusetts."

"MIT?"

"No, Harvard." For the first time, Arnold found himself ashamed of saying so.

"Aha! Well then, Dr. Arnold Einstein, whose belly is so full he does not need a Chinese meal, whose Texas upbringing makes him think he is a lone star in this forsaken hell, needin nothin from nobody, there's a board over there—see it, three tables down?—let's play, and if I win you give me three bucks, and if you win, I give you nothing. Sound like a deal?"

"A guilt-free deal."

"For me too."

In the southwest corner of Washington Square Park is a row of stubbled stone tables with marble chess boards inlaid in black and white. At those tables sits an astonishing variety of people, mostly men and boys, from dawn to dusk and, under streetlamps, well into the night, all year-round except in the wildest precipitation or pawn-scattering winds, shielded or shadowed to some degree by lovely stands of maple and chestnut. The squirrels are so inured to this cerebral traffic that they attend the games like patzers, looking for food, and a chance to kibitz.

Arnold and Vergil made for the empty table, cutting in ahead of two old men who were ambling too slowly over.

"Hey, VDub, man, we were next."

"This'll be a quickie, Barnie. Young Arnold Einstein here has to get somewhere fast. Five-minute game."

"That Einstein's son? You gonna play Einstein's son?"

"Grandson. I need someone smart to teach me the game, right, Arnie?"

Arnold demurred.

"Can we watch?"

"Gather round, boys. Arnie's a chess player from way back."

While Barnie and Ralph laughed and moved in toward the table, Vergil whipped a worn Ukrainian box and well-used chess clock out of his bag and set out his elegant Chinese pieces, the most remarkable chessmen Arnold had ever seen.

"A gift from my grandpa, the famous 'Good Person of Szechuan.' You may have heard of him."

"I know there's a play called that."

"Yeah. It's about him, Grandpa Wang."

"Really?"

Vergil held out his fists, each containing each a pawn. Arnold chose the right one.

"Right means white. Good thinking. I'll have to remember that. Barnie, will you take notes? Arnold, I hope you don't mind if my black pieces are red. Red meant nobility to my esteemed ancestors."

"What is white?"

"Death."

"Oh."

They each set their clocks to five minutes.

"Your move."

Arnold punched the clock, and began with a traditional P-Q4. Vergil answered him much faster, his hands shooting out like snake's tongues. A move that had taken Arnold four clock-seconds had taken him only one.

Speed chess. The clocks are set for an agreed-upon limit, and barring a checkmate, the player who first uses up his minutes loses, regardless of the positions. No time to pause and consider. Hands, well practiced for rhythm and speed, flash from piece to clock with the rhythm of a terminal cockfight. Accomplished speed-chess players memorize thousands of one- and two-move traps, moves that don't work in slower, more considered games. Arnold was out of his element, and out of his league. Vergil had accomplished the first sixteen moves of his game using only twelve seconds; Arnold's clock was thirty-two seconds down. He became so rattled by the time difference as to lose all hold he ever had on the game. With three minutes to go, he knew he had lost. And in fact, at 2:47, there was a genuine checkmate. Vergil's clock read :57.

"Sorry, kid. Three bucks."

Arnold pulled out his wallet, found three singles, and handed them over.

"Guess I didn't have much to teach you."

"Well, you might, if we were playing real chess. Blitz is just cheap shots, in fact, unbefitting a Grand Master such as me. But, hey, it's a Chinese meal for this here Chinaman."

"Are you really a Grand Master?"

"You bet your Harvard patooties. Check it out at the American Chess Club: Virgil Wang, GM. I abbreviate it down to VWGM—invoking two great industry leaders, in spite of the fact that I don't own a car. And as yin to contracting yang, I have also expanded the code to cover the actual scope of my affairs. My official title, Arnold, is Vergil Wang, Grand Master of Much. In your case, unfortunately, Grand Master of Cheap Shot Chess. You may call me VDub, as do the others."

"The cheapest shot was telling me you were a beginner."

"Now, now, my boy, judge not, that you be not judged. It was a test for you, concerning which I award you a B minus for noticing the contradiction of the clock. On the other hand, perhaps it should be an A plus for being a Superior Man who sees much but lets many things go. So saith my ancestors."

"It was worth three bucks. A good, cheap lesson. My Harvard classes cost $130 a session."

"Didn't they teach you not to open a fat wallet before the eyes of needy locals? The idle rich must respect the idle poor. Somebody might get the wrong idea, man."

"They'd be disappointed. It's all fives and ones from selling my books and clothes. It's the last money I have in the world."

"Harvard sans rich parents?"

"Full scholarship, work-study, and part-time jobs."

"Well, then, although I will not return your three bucks, I *will* give you the prize of the morning for your martyrdom."

VDub reached into an outsized pocket of his green leather vest, withdrew a packet of folded papers, and riffled through until he had found the object of his search.

"Here. For you. In your job search."

"How do you know I'm looking for a job?"

"Only neurotics read the Help Wanteds if they're already working, and besides, here you are in Washington Square on a Wednesday morning when the earning types are elsewhere doing their remunerative thing; and furthermore, you can't get into NYU until next spring, since classes are already closed."

"How do you know *that?*"

"Vergil Wang, Grand Master of Much. Open your prize. Sorry—no Cracker Jacks."

"'The Job Application'? How did you know I was coming?"

"VWGM. Read it. Out loud—as Barnie and Ralph might find it relevant, inspiring, and useful."

Arnold unfolded the Xeroxed page.

"Robert Walser, 'The Job Application.' Who's that? Walser."

"A friend of mine. Don't be so studious. We don't do footnotes in Washington Square. Just read."

"'ESTEEMED GENTLEMEN,

"'I am a poor, young, unemployed person in the business

field, my name is Wenzel, I am seeking a suitable position, and I take the liberty of asking you, nicely and politely, if perhaps a position might be free. I know that your good firm is large, proud, old, and rich, thus I may yield to the pleasing supposition that a nice, easy, pretty little place would be available, into which, as into a kind of warm cubbyhole, I might slip.'"

"There. Doesn't that sound like you? You can change your name to Wenzel and submit it. Continue, please."

"'I am excellently suited to occupy just such a modest haven, for my nature is altogether delicate, and I am essentially a quiet, polite, and dreamy child who is made to feel cheerful by people thinking of him that he does not ask for much, and allowing him to take possession of a very, very small patch of existence, where he can be useful and thus feel at ease.'

"Where did you get this?"

"I have my ways. There are bookstores on Fourth Avenue, on which tour I may take you if you're a good, interested boy. There are Xerox machines on Sheridan Square. The right pocket is for prose, the left for poetry. I almost stuffed this down my pants since it fell somewhere in between, but I didn't want to soil it. It's you, though. I can tell just by your chess game and your wallet. Come on, sweet, I'll walk you over to NYU, and provide a letter of recommendation on the spot."

"Well, that was easy enough. Think they'll accept me?"

"If you got the bucks. With bucks, they'd accept a homicidal maniac. Got the bucks? More than in your wallet?"

"No."

They left the Administration Building and began walking east on 4th Street.

"Where are you living? What are you paying?"

"I stayed at the Y the last two nights. Know of any good places—cheap?"

"You are talking to the mayor of New Hooverville. I know lots of good places—cheap. But of course we run into definitional problems concerning the Good. I assume you would settle for less than the *summum bonum?*"

"Let's focus on the 'cheap.'"

"Cheap? Why then, sonny, you've come to the right man. Can I get it for you wholesale? How's $2.95 a night?"

"Sounds great! I'm paying $15 now."

"Up by the Jews?"

"The Y on 92nd."

"YMHA. What do you think the H is for? Hellenic? Helvetic?"

"I don't know. I didn't think past the Y."

"The mysterious letter H. You should ponder it. The left and right emanations of God, linked. H is for 'Hebrew.' And yes, $2.95 is cheaper. But is yo mama and papa ready to have they son livin on the Bowery? Is the Harvard Alumni Association?"

They walked in silence, Arnold astounded at the variegated array of types he had never seen before.

"I've heard of the Bowery. . . ."

"Oh, have you?"

"What's it like?"

"Illuminating and ecumenical. A land shared by the living, the dead, the almost dead, and the seemingly dead. But ruins, including human ruins, are rather poignant, don't you think? Before the residue of the once noble, our inward souls involuntarily bow. And le voilà, the Bowery itself, coming up on your right."

Arnold looked south down the broad expanse, with its median divider, a grand boulevard, somewhat the worse for wear. VDub began to sing and soft-shoe:

"The Bowery, the Bowery!

I won't go there anymore!

"Except here we are. The streets of Peter Cooper and Stephen Foster, once lined with oyster bars and minstrel shows, now the victim of seediness and neglect. I must admit I do like a certain degree of seediness and neglect. All true poets like seediness and neglect. Though the frequent personal visits of the Great Rat of Sumatra are sometimes disconcerting."

"Hey, VDub! How ya doin, man? Got ya new sweetie witcha?" Arnold turned toward the croaking, unshaven voice.

"No, Specs, no, just an out-of-towner getting the tour." VDub pulled one of Arnold's bills from his bag, folded it like a finger, and handed it daintily to one of the two old men leaning against the wall, passing a paper-bagged bottle between them.

"Don't spend it all in one place."

"Hey, thanks, man," coughed the other, dressed in a heavy black coat in the heat of June.

"Drinking from the Holy Bottle, they are, two friends, frantically uncultivated, very small and subordinate in life, small, small all the way down to utter worthlessness, mysteries unto themselves. Many are driven, and live without purpose, and let themselves be flung to the winds. Intelligence groping in emptiness. Fine faculties bearing scant fruit. You may have noticed, Dear Arnold, that for some time the world has been revolving around money, not around history. But here, not. Here, all is history and dream. And slow. And redolent."

They passed a swarm of garbage cans in front of the Happy Days Bar & Grille.

"That which, for all correct nostrils, outrages and evokes revulsion, exists here in the Whitmanesque condition of compost."

"I'll have to get used to it," Arnold admitted. He found VDub ever more surprising. Truly a master—at the very least—of much.

"Stop!" the master ordered. "Check this guy out."

They paused about twenty feet upstreet of a giant, emaciated figure gesticulating in a phone booth. His face had the expression of a man whose soul has gone elsewhere. One hand was on an open phone book, while he chanted into the receiver.

"Burk, Zander, and Maaartha . . . ; Burke with an E, Aaaanthony; Burke with an E, Anthony G. and Saaaaandra; Burke with an E, Arnold Peeeee . . ."

"What is he doing?"

"That, my friend, is one of your new schoolmates, the most nontraditional NYU student Alexander G. Bell, the G, he reports, for Gesualdo. Majoring in weirdness, I believe. You'll notice that he is singing his phone-book text on the pitch high E flat, a fifth below the dial tone he is listening to. (This from the horse's mouth. I couldn't tell an E flat from a pi meson.) Alexander is a person inclined to be anomalous, one who, from an early age, has taken up the dare to be peculiar. His pre-NYU career included a hefty few years in a sanatorium for people who are not altogether at their best. He fervently believes, you see, that if he can ever sing a mathematically Pythagorean-perfect fifth below the dial tone, the change box will open and shower him with nickels, dimes, and quarters. And you will notice if you stand here for half an hour that Alex G. is most patient, very patient. Now, very great is music's power, indeed often shattering. But what gets me is that Alex does not have even the faith *I* have, for after some substantial performance time, when nobody (except possibly myself) is looking, he reaches his bony finger up into the coin return and looses the duct-tape trap he has set for any returned coinage. Very clever, but quite antisocial, as it keeps our other friends from mining the sea of caller forgetfulness. Now we are all human, and as such, we have reason to treat one another with forbearance. Still, this annoys me, I who generally abjure annoyment. Yet he makes up for it in other ways. For instance, he carries an eponymous bell, very nice Zen sound, which he strikes often, for no clear reason. I think one should always make some kind of commotion. Care to stay and see the covert end of his performance?"

"No, I . . . well, where are we going?"

"I am taking you, my prince, to inspect some possible digs—dig?—at the Sunshine Hotel, down near Prince Street; $2.95 a night, remember? One of the last decent flophouses left."

They crossed Houston Street at peril to their lives.
"High school football. And you, a dancer?"

"Just living up to my name. Wang. The Chinese character means an elf or sprite."

"Fitting."

"It also means a beast that is said to eat the brains of the dead."

"Thus your pockets of poetry and prose."

"A lovely mutation of my thought on the subject. I've been more concerned with which pocket was heavier, thus weighing my steps, unbeknownst, toward the prosaic or poetic side of things. And what does your last name mean? In fact, what *is* it? You never said."

A middle-aged black man, tarnished but spry, came bursting out of a doorway just ahead.

"Hey, VDub! Whuzzup, brother?"

"Not much, Bobby-o. Off on a run?"

"So what else is new? Gotta go."

"See ya."

"And speaking of the poetic side of things, Bobby the Runner has just burst out of 241 Bowery, your new home away from home. And I, your epistemological scout, announce arrival at the Sunshine Hotel."

VDub pulled open the outside door of an unmarked establishment and gallantly gestured Arnold into a long, dark stairwell.

"Light breaks where no sun shines," he said.

High up, far ahead, was a pair of double swinging doors whose small glass windows provided the only illumination for the climber.

"And yes, there is a smell of ripeness about the place. But never you mind, young'un, many wonders await us within."

They trudged up the sheer steps toward the rounded rectangles of light. VDub pushed open the doors as if revealing the kingdom of heaven. He sang out:

"*For the Lord, God, omnipotent reigneth.* And that Lord, Arnold, the first of many wonders, is—voilà—Harry Beilenberg, manager and curator of this museum."

Behind an iron cage, in a small, dimly lit office, sat a grizzled man of fifty.

"You'll notice his 5 o'clock shadow, even though it's only 1:47 in the afternoon. This is a man ahead of the game."

"Hey, VDub, the Shadow knows . . . HA HA HA HA HA. . . ." Harry's was the most terrifying laugh Arnold had ever heard, and unexpectedly loud. The laugh of a cosmic Mephisto.

"Harry, I'd like you to meet a new friend of mine, Arnold Benedict. He's thinking of sojourning a while, and joining your community."

"Pleased to meetcha, kid." Harry stuck his hand through the hole in the cage for a truncated shake. "But you sure you want to shack up here? You look a little, uh, refined for this joint."

"He's a poor student interested in saving money for graduate school. Your rates are compelling, as are the many social services readily available in the neighborhood." This was the first Arnold had heard about social services. But VDub's logic was not incorrect

"He wants to meet some people he might never meet elsewhere," VDub intoned.

"Those we got, Arnold. Up the gazoo. But I maybe should take you on a tour before you sign on the dotted line. We don't want any dissatisfied customers."

Another huge laugh, this time from a short, dark, obnoxiously natty man watching television in the "lobby." "Unsatisfied? How could anyone be unsatisfied? You wake up in the morning in a four-by-six cage, the chicken wire is a couple feet from your face, the wall is a couple inches from your face, what could be more satisfying?"

"At least you don't got roaches, Johnny. Tell the kid about your roaches."

"Roaches I don't got. I'm the only cubicle without em. A roach is doomed if he comes in my room. I got twenty cans of spray, and if he comes in, boom, I hit him. But mice, forget it. I got dead mice in the most grotesque positions you ever seen in your life. If I allowed myself to think about where I'm at, I'd take dynamite." He went back to *The Guiding Light.*

"See? A happy camper, Mr. Benedict. Let's do our tour."

The three left the lobby for a long hallway rhythmically punctuated by miscellaneous wooden doors.

"Let's see. Who's in who can show you a room? Ah." Harry took off toward the end of the hall. Halfway down, a man wearing a gas mask came out of one of the cubicles, a medium plastic bag full of—what? something brown—in his hand.

"Fuckin pig," he muttered, the sound distorted through his mask.

"He's almost dead, Clyde. Lighten up."

"Yeah, Harry." He ripped off his mask. "*You* don't have to clean this shit up."

Arnold peeked into the room as the trio walked by.

"Mr. Marshall . . . eighty years old . . . senile . . . He was dumped here by his son two months ago. . . . Don't eat nothin but Oreo cookies . . . Can't walk to the bathroom, so he goes on the floor . . ."

Arnold glanced in. Four by six, like the man said. No windows . . . Walls about seven feet high, with chicken wire across the top, fluorescent lights glaring through the chicken wire from the original eighteen-foot ceiling high above. A bed, a blanket, a locker, and a broken lamp. That was it. On the bed, under the blanket, eyes staring up into the light, lay a man.

"He won't last another week," Harry continued. "I called his son last night, but he doesn't care. OK, Benedict, here's the room I want."

He spoke low into Arnold's ear. "This guy's a Russian immigrant, an engineer, probably one of my short-term tenants. He left his family in New Jersey and came here to shoot up undisturbed. But I'm gonna disturb him."

He knocked hard at 27L.

"*Da.*"

"It's Harry. You decent?"

The door cracked open.

"*Shto?*"

"Got a kid here who's thinking of moving in. I'd like to show him your model apartment." The tenant opened the door.

And in fact, the cubicle was relatively pleasant. Indian bedspreads on the wall, Russian books piled on the floor. Tacked to the spreads, lit by candles, two icons: Dürer's Saint Jerome, and Jimi Hendrix.

"Hi, I'm Arnold."

"Come in, come in!" The trio entered the room barely big enough for one.

"Sit. Sit. I am Max. Yes. Sit on bed."

The three sat down on a neatly made bed while Max thought about the tour.

"This—Saint Jerome. Who was hermit. He went to desert and lived alone long time to seek knowledge . . . like myself."

"Regarding the air in this chamber, I would deem it credible," VDub whispered in Arnold's ear.

"Is good place. Harry is good man. People interesting. And you pay rent, they leave you alone, you do whatever. Is cheap."

Harry stood up first.

"Thanks, Max. I'm sure Mr. Benedict will consider your recommendation."

Arnold and VDub followed him out, calling out thank-yous and good-byes.

"See," Harry said, "the Sunshine is what you make it." They walked down the long hall back to the office.

"This is the last of the no-frills hotels. One of the last where people live in cubicles. It's a nice place; if you're short of funds and you need to lay your head down for a couple of hours, we hope to make your stay pleasant. But don't ask me for towels or soap—we don't have it. No luxuries."

Back in the lobby, Harry sat down on the empty couch, next to a man with a parakeet on either shoulder.

"There are 125 residents here. For a lot of em, most of em, it's the last stop. On the one hand, it's probably as close as you can come to living in hell—125 dysfunctional guys crammed together in this old hotel. . . . On the other hand . . . there's Lawrence here." He motioned with his head to the bird man sitting next to him. "He don't mind living in a bird cage."

"And neither does Pretty Boy," Lawrence picked up. "He's ten, and neither does Little Bit, he's five. He's a devil, yes you are. . . ."

He nuzzled Little Bit's beak with his Irish pug nose.

"If it wasn't for these lil guys, I wouldn't've made it in this place. These birdies have been my life. . . . So many people don't realize you need something to help you through everything. Or you're not gonna make it. . . ."

"We got a loan shark here," Harry continued, "several drug dealers, lotsa addicts, alkies, ex-cons, mental patients, Bowery old-timers, a guy

who does other tenants' laundry for a couple of bucks, a room cleaner—
you met him—Clyde. . . . And Bobby—runs errands for tips . . ."

"We met him on the way in," VDub said.

"He's a good man. Some residents go for weeks without leaving their
cubicles. They rely on Bobby for food and getting their checks cashed. If
we didn't have this place, a lot of guys here'd be in the streets. . . . Ain't
no women here. The Sunshine is a 'men's only' establishment. . . . Some
of the hotels left on the Bowery are still 'whites only,' but I let everyone
in—all races, all ages, all kindsa stories. . . . All got one thing in common—they're on their own, loners . . . Me, too. We all had homes, but
we left, or got thrown out. Take me, for example. Used to work as a
presser 'til I got injured and they fired me, and that night, my wife
left. . . . Two hits for the price of one. So I come down to the Bowery. . . ."
He shook his head and chuckled. "It ain't the Ritz, but it's interesting."

"Well, let me think about it, and I'll let you know." Arnold said. "It
might be fine. But I've paid for the week already up at the Y, so I'll probably just stay there through Sunday. Maybe I'll see you on Monday,
OK?"

"OK, Benedict. It ain't as bad as it smells. I wouldn't lie to you."

"The secret is olfactory fatigue." whispered VDub.

Emerging into disorienting sunlight, Arnold took a long breath of street
air—oh-so-relatively-fresh. They walked quickly back to Washington
Square, where Arnold left VDub with a warm embrace and continued up
5th Avenue, heading for home. They had made a chess date for the following Monday—real chess, not blitz. "Do it, mein Führer," VDub had
urged. "Investigate the light of the Bowery."

Mein Führer? Where did he get that? I never . . . Maybe he just
meant I was leading him somewhere.

After 14th, Arnold broke into a jog along the extreme edge of the sidewalk. That was a very long hug, he thought. Arnold checked his back pocket. Wallet still there. "You stay at the Sunshine, you'll make it a little longer without hustling," he'd said. What kind of hustling?

At 59th, he decided to take his run into the park. The roads seemed to go every which way. It was good to be lost—and breathing deeply. He knew he had to run north while staying east, and he could navigate by skylines left and right. At one well-trafficked crossroad, he thought to get out of the park to check where he was: 85th. Good. And he continued up 5th Avenue past the eye-goggling Guggenheim, turned left at the Jewish Museum on 92nd, and walked the rest of the way to Lexington.

Up the elevator to the fifth floor, into his room, down with the *Times,* off with the sneakers, plop into the chair. Raise the butt. Extract the papers. Map on the floor. What was this? Ah! Walser.

> "I am, to put it frankly, a Chinese; that is to say, a person who
> deems everything small and modest to be beautiful and pleasing,
> and to whom all that is big and exacting is fearsome and horrid."

Hmm . . . Vergil. VDub. I like him. I *will* meet him Monday. Worst that can happen is I lose another three bucks.

> "My mind is clear, but it refuses to grasp things that are too
> many by far. I am sincere and honest, and I am aware that this sig-
> nifies precious little in the world in which we live, so I shall be
> waiting, esteemed gentlemen, to see what it will be your pleasure
> to reply to
> "your respectful servant, positively drowning in obedience,
> "Wenzel."

Thirty-six

After a week in the public library reviewing *Chess Games of the Masters,* Arnold felt ready to meet VDub. It wasn't just the three bucks. It was for the honor of the Mansfield Chess Team, for Jacobo, who had sent him his first set, for setting things straight, for all that was good and noble in the world. For Harvard, even. First stop, though: Penn Station to check the mail. It had been six business days since he had written.

Reversing his last week's trip, he entered the park at 86th Street and jogged south, emerging this time at Columbus Circle and heading down 8th Avenue. At 42nd he slowed to a walk and turned left so he could check out "the Crossroads of the World," "the Great White Way," not so white just now because awash in morning sunshine. Were those prostitutes ahead—at this hour of Monday morning? He had never seen real prostitutes before. He crossed over to the south side of the street. If they weren't prostitutes, they were doing a damn good imitation. Four women stationed along the south side of 42nd Street, a black woman, two white women, and a Puerto Rican, wearing the mini-est of skirts, fishnet stockings, outrageously high heels, and tanktops exposing various versions of largesse. One of the white women actually whistled at him as he passed, while the black woman at the end of the line stage-whispered, "Fifteen, bucks, baby. Ten for you."

The guys outside the electronics and luggage stores were no less aggressive. "Hey, blondie, come on in. Yeah, yeah, you, come on in. We got what you're looking for." Arnold walked quickly past one and another similar song, punctuated, rondo-like, by melodies of drug dealers: "Check it out, check it out. Loose joints, black beauties . . . 'ludes . . . sinsemilla"—eight encounters along the one block. Outside one of the porno theaters, a young black man rubbed his crotch at Arnold and blew him a kiss. "Hustle, sweetie?" he asked, pleasantly enough. Hustle. Is this what Vergil saw him coming to?

Into the PO to check General Delivery. He showed his Harvard photo ID, and the pony-tailed clerk was glad to deliver into his hands a letter from Mansfield, arrived that morning.

It felt like the envelope might contain money, so, recalling VDub's warning, he stuck it in his back pocket along with his map and headed down 5th to the Square. He was early, as usual, so he sat down on a bench facing the chess tables to await the Green Knight. Black and Green.

He opened the envelope, extracted two $10 bills from a folded page of *TV Guide*, put them in his wallet, and opened the letter.

```
29 June 1972

My dear Arnold,
    This is not a happy letter. Your Nonno Jacobo is dead last
Monday the 26th. It happened quite quickly of I don't know
how to say in English—aneurisma—when you break a blood arte-
rial in your brain. Just after lunch he got a bad headache,
very bad, and at 4 o'clock Nonna Lucetta took him to the hos-
pital. Half an hour later, the doctor came out to tell Nonna
```

Lucetta he was dead. She called me early my Tuesday morning. Your letter came today, so now I write you the news.

Also your father is not doing so well. Last month he moved out of the house to take a job at a tire shop in Fort Worth. So I moved back in. We are still talking, perhaps more than before. Lately, he is having trouble with the men at his new work. After forty-five years, now all of a suddenly people don't like his name—someone who was fighting Adolf Hitler.

But I am happy you had a good graduation and you are able to go to New York as you were planning. I'm sure you will find a nice job until you get into school again to become Dr. Arnold Hitler.

I send you $20. It is all I can spare at the minute. Please let me know if you get a job and where you will be living more permanently. And also if you get

"Hey Wenzel! Get a job yet?"

Arnold pocketed the letter.

"Billet-doux, mon p'tit chou?"

"No. Bad news. My grandpa died."

VDub's balloon went pop. He sat down on the bench near Arnold and laid a hand on his knee. They both sat together and watched the sparrows.

"You were tight with him?"

"Very."

"Yup." VDub stood up and began a slow pacing, stopped, and turned to Arnold. "You know, some people are greatly improved by death." He continued pacing.

Arnold watched him, silent. It was unlikely that Nonno Jacobo—hilarious, loving, wise, and strange Jacobo—was better off dead. Loss and more loss.

VDub stopped his pacing, stared at Arnold, and after due consideration, decided to proceed with his opening gambit.

"Um, as chairman of the Flora and Fauna Commission, and to not quite change the subject, I brung ya . . . dis."

Out of his bag came a rat's skull with a dandelion thrust through its orbit.

"What is it?"

"It's for you, Arnoldissimo, a demo of the great LaFontaine fable, 'The Lion and the Rat.' I forget the moral. Ready to meet your doom?" He pulled out his chess pieces and timer. "Oh, yeah, I forgot. No timer. We be playin till the eagle grins."

He walked over to an empty table and set up the game. Arnold put his present down on the table margin. VDub sat down on the white side of the board.

"Hey, no guessing hands?"

"It is an ancient and revered tradition that he with the rat's skull plays black. Appropriate, *n'est-ce pas?* Even dough I's de nigger? Sid-down! I mean sit down, please."

All right, black, then. Arnold had juiced up on Capablanca's black, on Alekhine's and Botvinnik's, on Petrosian's and Spassky's. What he was not prepared for was the complete nonchalance of his opponent. VDub played a masterly game with continuous running commentary on the weather, the characters in the park, the news of the day, accompanied by stream-of-consciousness quotations from popular songs and his prose and poetry pockets. Beyond distracting, it was totally unnerving.

"Behold yon Cheesy over there," he chanted, pointing to a large, bearded man investigating the bottom of a trash can. "A charming, utterly spherical zero, to a certain extent mindless, but nevertheless completely bug-fuck crazy. God, it seems, has given Cheesy to the world in order to entrust to it an insoluble riddle concerning legitimate being. Now, I am all in favor of comedy, but Brother Funny over there is what I might call an unhealthy-healthy person, his respect-arousing hair notwithstanding. A bad face, though, wouldn't you say? A bad face."

"Can't see his face," said Arnold, trying desperately to concentrate.

"A bad face, I assure you, a face that rejoices in its vile tendencies. Not that he smells bad, old Cheesy, yet one does hold some kind of a nose in his presence, perhaps a mental one, a cultural or soul nose, when he is, as it were, in the vicinity."

Arnold captured a bishop that he had been plotting against for four moves.

"Very nice, very nice, but certainly an altogether stupid move," VDub commented as he cleared Arnold's capturing knight from the board. Arnold needed to breathe. VDub smiled broadly at him.

"What was that about the eagle grins? We gon play till the eagle grins?"

"Oooo-ooo-oo. White boy does black accent, yowza!" He broke into song, *"Once I lived the life of a millionaire,"* went back to the chessboard and, singing under his breath, captured a knight, and opened into full voice for the punch line as he deposited the horse gently in front of Arnold:

> *"If I ever get my hands on a dollar again, I'll*
> *Hold on to it till the eagle grins."*

Cheesy had worked his trash-can route over to the chess table and stood, a half-eaten baloney sandwich in hand, peering over VDub's shoulder.

"Nobody knows you when you're down and out. . . . Cheesy Malone, I'd like you to meet Arnold Stang, an excellent chess player down from Yale."

"Harvard."

"Yale, Harvard, what's the difference?"

"Pleased to meetcha."

"Oh, Cheesy, you can do better than that. Give him a good, turbulent hello full of vile crudities. My friendship with Cheesy matches many other inanities—so audacious it must be right."

Cheesy seemed to enjoy the torrent of words he didn't understand.

"Mr. Malone is a ceremonious man who would not hesitate to offer a half-eaten baloney sandwich, with a bow, to a strange woman on the street. In fact, I have seen him do just that. Cheesy is interested in bringing the bow back into twentieth-century culture."

"Want some?" Cheesy inquired of both players.

"No, thank you," said Arnold.

"He is also interested in being introduced to the president. Check."

Cheesy reached down and with his baloney sandwich swept the pieces from the table. Mayonnaise glistened across the ranks.

"Cheesy Malone! What's come over you?"

"You be nice to Arnold. He's your guest. You don't invite someone to your city and then *check* them. He's your guest." Cheesy bent down to pick up the pieces, deposited them helter-skelter on the table, bowed, and moved on to the next trash can.

"He's a hustler," VDub commented, far less angry than he might have been. With a Kleenex from his bag, he wiped the muzzle of a mayonnaised knight, looking, for all his singularity, like a doting mother cleaning up her child.

"What did you mean when you said that moving into the Sunshine would keep me from hustling longer?"

"Well, how many them grinnin eagles you got?"

"Three or four hundred."

"Got a job?"

"Not yet."

"What happens three or four hundred eagles from now?"

"I'll get a job."

"OK, no prob."

The silence hung between them. VDub went on to a bishop with mayonnaise in his miter.

"There may be a problem," Arnold offered.

"Ummm?"

"My last name isn't Einstein or Benedict or Stang."

"So?"

"Guess what it is."

"Let's see . . . Rumpelstiltskin?"

"Hitler."

VDub didn't bat an eye. "Interesting."

"So there may be a problem."

"I do believe so."

Again, the silence was punctuated only by the birds and the buses.

"And thus we are back to hustling," Mother VDub continued. "When the last eagle flies the coop and you've heard enough 'Don't-call-us-we'll-call-yous,' you'll get tired and hungry and seasonally cold. And if you're tired enough, or hungry enough, or cold enough, you too will, in time, hustle. Now, hustling, in case you're worried, does not *necessarily* involve selling your body to beasts—though a looker like you might call down high remuneration. You might get by panhandling, if you had a good riff, or washing car windows till you get scary-looking, or collecting cans. Let's see. Ten bucks for a pint of blood, five for participating in police lineups, free eats for washing down hot-dog carts. You could duplicate Dr. Bell's phone-rigging scheme, though I wouldn't approve. You could go through subway cars teaching people the deaf alphabet. You could tell store owners that the soda machine took your money. You could, while you're still strong, help unload delivery trucks. I'll be your agent in any of this—10 percent of domestic and 15 percent of foreign sales. But, as I say, all this may be postponed for a while by sojourning at the Sunshine."

"I've already decided to do that."

"Just don't tell Harry your name is Hitler. The Beilenbergs' wartime motto seemed to be 'V for Victim.' "

He did an implausible imitation of President Nixon, Kleenex under

thumb, fingers out, arms up, shoulders hunched, and big smile somewhere other than on face.

"Of course, if you persist in being Arnold the Impoverished, even the
Sunshine, shining like mad, will cease to shine upon you, and you'll have
to ascend downward to the next level of Life's Great Adventure and take
up residence elsewhere, say on the seventh floor of Port Authority, or
down with the Mole People."

"Who are the Mole People?"

"The Mole People are deeper than the Track People."

"You mean—like the train tracks, the subway tracks?"

> *"Out of some subway scuttle, cell or loft*
> *A bedlamite speeds to thy parapets—*
> *O harp and altar, of the fury fused."*

"What?"

"Man! Don't they teach you nothing up at Yale? It's Hart Crane's trip
through the interborough fissures of the mind."

"I thought that was just a myth."

"Hart Crane? Never."

"No. Mole People."

"Closest thing to hell I've ever seen."

"But there *is* no under the tracks. Under the tracks is, I don't know,
earth, cement."

"Maybe there's no under the tracks in New Haven, but here the tunnels go down eighteen levels. I kid you not. There are five levels of
subway tracks, 714 miles of them, 244 miles of tunnels, and all the
abandoned bunkers and sewers and electrical tunnels that accompany
them. The city's a fucking anthill down there." He stamped on the
pavement. "See? Hollow."

"You've been there?"

"Listen, boy, there's no place in this celestial city I haven't been."

"Down to the bottom?"

"Down as far as humans go, I think, at least from what they tell me. Who knows what species might be further down? The track workers call them CHUDS—CHUD People—cannibalistic human underground dwellers. They're scared shitless of them. But the deeper you go, the more impressive are the communities, and less frequently do the moles come up. They send runners up to the surface."

"Hey, another job for me."

"Could be, could be. But why this kind of life exists will not be known till the opening of the seals."

"Might be worth seeing sometime."

"*Bozhe moy!* It's a beautiful summer morning in the park, my chess pieces are all oiled and sparkly, and young Lochinvar wants to dance in the dark with the vermin, to the crackling roar of the electric predators."

"I didn't mean now, I meant *sometime.*"

"But why not now?" said VDub, springing up from the table. "Heigh-ho, bucko, it's off to lurk we go," he sang as he swung his surprised partner up out of his seat, do-si-doed, and led him to the West 4th Street Station.

They paid their 35 cents each and scuttled down three levels, down, down, down.

"The Mole People. Outcasts in the world of outcasts. I'm a firm believer in the doctrine of excess."

VDub led Arnold to the end of the station and down a short iron staircase to track level.

"Don't step on the third rail," he warned. "I hate to see that happen. The voltage blows off the extremities. Hands, head, whatever, explode. It's disgusting."

For about forty feet, there was absolutely no space for a person to stand between the wall and a passing train without being hit. Then the tunnel broadened out as the local track separated from the express. When the station light began to fade behind them, VDub drew his Bugs Bunny key-ring flashlight out of his pocket to light the way. In its dim illumination, Arnold could see bottles of spilled pills, needles, an occasional piece of clothing. Wet urine on the cement wall. Fresh feces on a dish. The smell inched its way toward stench. Arnold pulled out his handkerchief and held it to his face. VDub picked up a dead mouse, its eyes still sparkling, its paws tightly curled.

"This is good. It means there'll be fewer rats—at least for the moment. They spray a lot of poison down here to kill the rats."

"What about the Mole People?"

"They've got a wide choice of what to die from."

Arnold felt his chest tighten in defense. In the distance, the Cyclops eye of an approaching train. VDub gathered him into the space between the tracks and extinguished Bugs Bunny. The train thundered by, assaulting ten seconds of their lives, then shrinking its way toward the station.

The darkness whispered hoarsely: "Who's that?"

Arnold sensed eyes but saw nothing.

"Vergil Wang, friends. Remember me? Grand Master of Much? Just bringing a friend to check out the bargain basement."

Another voice: "Who's that?"

"He's cool. How's the weather, man?"

"There's a bright golden haze on the meadow. The sun shineth upon the dunghill, and is not corrupted. So saith Diogenes the Cynic."

VDub and Arnold walked on by.

"The underground homeless," VDub confided. "You can hardly see them. They don't talk to each other with words. They use noises that sound like birds or maybe the wind."

They made their way farther along the track.

"Those are the Track People, not the Mole People," he continued. "We are about to leave them behind."

Courtesy of Bugs Bunny, Arnold could make out a hole in the concrete wall separating uptown from downtown.

"Umbilicus to mystery. Ready for this?" VDub asked.

"I don't know. I already can't breathe."

"Does the Eagle know what is in the pit?

Or wilt thou go ask the Mole?"

VDub shone his light on a small door at waist height, askew on its upper hinge. "Let us descend *ad astra.* Hup, hup, hup."

He pushed the door aside, backed down onto what was apparently a ladder, and disappeared from view. Arnold stood and gathered his will. He expected to hear VDub calling from some room below, but there was nothing but silence. He felt abandoned and, for the first time, frightened. He realized he needed his guide—or at least his light—to make it back without a possible encounter with the third rail. It was onward . . . or God knows what.

Arnold found the hinge by feel, the door, and his way onto a slimy iron ladder. Eighteen rungs down.

"I thought you had gone off to Coney Island," VDub whispered sharply in his ear, scaring the bejesus out of him. "What are you on, man, black folks' time? I ain't got all day. Got a power lunch at noon-thirty."

"Sorry, I . . ."

Arnold was cut off by a thrust against his right lower leg that felt like a missed tackle. VDub's light flashed on and quickly off, and he broke out in a laugh, which he stifled like a schoolgirl.

"What was that?"

"Track rabbit, my friend, track rabbit," VDub whispered. "They didn't make it down here with their Xyklon B. Them guys is three to four feet long, and I ain't including the tail."

"What guys?"

"The rats, man. Hey, I got to take you up to the 14th Street station. There's a guy selling wind-up rats got a big sign on his card table, 'SAY IT WITH RATS.' They eat them."

"Who?"

"Mole People."

"Who eats Mole People?"

"No, cretin, the Mole People eat the track rabbits. Best meat buy in New York."

"They eat rats?"

"Eat or be eaten, I always say. Tastes just like chicken."

Arnold, gorge rising, could barely make out some kind of chamber dug out of rock.

"Where are we?"

"You're in the entrance hall to the world-famous Waldorf-Hysteria. Walk this way."

VDub limped along, and Arnold followed his guide ear-wise to the end of the cavern and down a set of rusty stairs to another level, which, by VDub's occasional flashlight, seemed to be another operating subway tunnel. At least there were tracks.

"Third rail over there," VDub warned, using his light like a lecturer's arrow, continuing on ahead as Arnold stopped a moment to get his bearings. He followed VDub's steps, now three or four yards ahead of him. They walked in silence for a minute or so, Arnold mincing along, terrified of engaging another track bunny, VDub slowly increasing the distance between them. To his right, from a deep recess in the wall, Arnold sensed a pair of eyes following him. Though he could not see them, he was sure they were red. Track-bunny eyes.

"I can't hurt you now, my love," an articulate voice cooed softly from the darkness.

Arnold stopped short, anxious, mesmerized.

"I'll grant you a guest pass this time, lost angel. But don't let me see you again, or you'll be mine."

Arnold broke into a run and almost went down on the track.

VDub had been waiting up ahead for him. He did a spook-imitation: "'Don't let me see you again, or you'll be *mine*,'" with Shadow laugh appended. "Don't worry. He says that to all the pretty new boys."

"You know him?"

"Sure. Everyone knows him. 'Dark Angel,' he self-yclepts. Thinks he's the devil. Weird-ass guy. Everyone laughs about him, but no one wants to get near him. Hey—scenic marker coming up."

They neared a large room off to the right, communicating with the track space via a comfortable arched passageway. They sidled in and took places against the rear wall. The room was lit with ten-watt bulbs strung at odd intervals along the ceiling pipes. Thirty or so people were in the room, the most extraordinary collection of characters Arnold had ever seen, even at the midnight horror movies on Harvard Square.

"Bonus event, it seems," VDub commented.

"Miracles don't happen today," a squat, toad-like object was saying. "They well believed in the miracles I wrought, but now ye have no faith. Woe unto you, hypocrites, who do not believe in Jesus of Nazareth."

It was some kind of low-end missionary service and revivalist crusade.

"I thought your name was Ackermann," a young black woman with a child yelled out.

"That's just my dupe name. My true name is Christianus Pueris Mentalis Doktor. Jesus Christ of Nazareth reincarnation to you. These hands have touched the foreheads of bleeding children." He reached over toward the young woman's baby. She pulled it away. "How great do your sufferings have to be before you listen?"

The room was strangely silent. Men and women stood in groups and sat against the walls.

"Do you hear? The skeleton horse is passing."

"That's the F train!" a heckler explained, to scattered laughter and applause.

"You say that, you, you with a Fudgesicle for a heart. You say that only because you do not see cosmic reality. It so happens, sir, that I am the person who knows what the finality is, how it's going to terminate. And you, my friend, you will be dropped."

"You full of shit, man," a huge whitebeard adjudged.

"You, bless you . . . you with the unsound mind, Dear Righteous Idealed Light Brother. Think of me as a big pile of truthful-idealed dung, and you'll understand."

This last comment seemed to preempt all possible criticism. The speaker had found such approach to be effective.

VDub leaned over to Arnold: "You see, on Holy Saturday, before his resurrection, Christ went into the underworld to schmooze with the dead."

"This is Monday," Arnold objected.

"Take it as it comes, man."

The Savior embraced the woman and her child. "Above me, and above you, too, gleam the stars." The filthy ten-watt bulbs.

"I have a confliction," a sallow-faced man in a soiled New York Yankees team jacket called out.

Dr. Dr. Pueris Mentalis came up and kissed him on the lips. He reached into his loincloth and pulled out what Arnold could swear was a business card.

"Come see me," he said. "This is not the place for personal matters." To the assembled: "Next Saturday. Remember me till then." He made his way past Arnold and VDub, through the archway, and out onto the track. The group in the room loosened up from their audience positions. VDub took Arnold's arm and led him up to the huge, bearded black man who thought the speaker was full of shit.

"Ben, this is my friend, Arnold Matthew, of the famous Arnold Arboretum of Harvard University. Arnold, Ben Talbert."

"Pleased to meet you." They shook hands.

"Ben is mayor of this little community."

"We call it Christianopolis."

"This?"

"Perfectly all right, Mr. Matthew. It takes getting used to. Let's go into my apartment where we can talk more quiet."

He led them through a small door from the meeting room, up iron stairs, into what appeared to be a duplex apartment, and rigged a trip wire behind them. The device was fastened to a set of crossed brooms that supported a five-gallon water bucket, apparently empty.

"Won't stop anyone from coming in, but at least I'll hear them."

They climbed another set of stairs to the upper level. The room was lit by a red exit sign, and at the moment a bit of light filtered in from an exit hatch above, which, when heaved with difficulty, lifted a section of 6th Avenue sidewalk.

"This red light OK with you?"

"Love them Nawlins brothels," joked VDub.

The stairs to the lower floor were well swept, the living quarters neat. Two bookshelves were filled with quality paperbacks. Ben's clothes hung neatly on hangers from a pipe, and a well-used iron stood on top of an ancient ironing board plugged into the tunnel's electrical system. A hot plate was plugged into a socket high on the wall.

"Make you some coffee? Tea?"

Both visitors signaled they were fine without.

"What is this place? I mean the space," asked Arnold.

"Well, I'll tell you, I'm not quite sure. I think there may have been some kind of huge pump or engine or somethin downstairs, big bolts in the floor, and up here, maybe controls. VDub, shine you little light ova heah. See where this looks like some kinda box was up here on the wall? There was all sorts of things down here for building the tunnels."

"I'm surprised you didn't call it 'City of the Sun,'" commented VDub.

"Ain't but little sun down here. But there is Christianity. Real Christianity—not like that mad mofucker was talking back there. Here we got people caring for one another, people helping each other out, people loving each other no matter how badly they done upstairs."

The noise of a subway train rumbled hellishly through the room.

"You gets so you don't hear it." Arnold and VDub exchanged glances. "You know the cops come down here every once in a while, want us to get out, move up to the 'real world,' want us to go to shelters and shit like that, talk to us like we were crazy for staying down here. Sheeit, shelters are way too dangerous. Three hots and a cot, my ass. You can't close your eyes, you get raped, beaten up, killed. People steal your clothes. The guards treat you like you subhuman like a dog. But we don't allow drugs or hard liquor here, you know. We are healthy individuals who have chose an alternative to the senselessness up there. We don't need their help. They need ours."

"I can see by the sign's early light that young Arnold is skeptical. Tell him how you got down here, Ben, why you came."

Ben hesitated. "Well, I had this friend Dave, up on the Bowery? Had a nice setup in an alley off Stanton. So I'm going to visit with him one night when I hear yelling up the block: 'Nigger, you worthless leech, you sorry shit. They should round up all you homeless fuckheads and shoot you dead and hang your mother for having you.' So I run up the street to his alley and I see three guys kicking him in the head, and there's blood running out of his eyes, and one of the guys pulls out a lighter, and there's Dave flamin up, and I run in yellin, and they split fast out the other end of the alley, and I figure better to try to save Dave than to catch them, so I throw myself down on him . . . and he just . . . I don know . . .

deflates . . . under me . . . know what I mean?" Ben sighed and closed his eyes. There trickled down a tear. "That's something out of Adolf Hitler world."

Arnold and VDub were strangely disabled. Normally, either of them might have gotten up to touch or hold the weeper, but here, in the red light, with this gigantic figure shaking in front of them . . .

VDub took Ben in his arms, and consoled him with Blake:

"And there the lion's ruddy eyes
Shall flow with tears of gold. . . ."

Ben hugged him gently back, and set himself free. "So I figured that was it," he said. "It's too mean up there. I'm comin down here and see if I can make another world—more Christian."

"Arnold here is Jewish. Though he says he isn't."

"Christian, Jewish. Just so's he ain't no cannibal, like those folks up there. We done with cannibals down here. Up there anything is possible, you know what I'm sayin?"

Another train percussed the room, a tympany of God.

"Ben is formulating the obverse parable of Plato's Cave," VDub explained. "Up there, the deceived are chained down in the flickerin light of their TVs, thinkin that the shadows are the real world. But those who have escaped come down deeper into the cave, and are blinded not by the light of the sun, but by the darkness of the tunnels. Little by little they learn to see."

"Here in the dark," Ben added, "we stand that old Plato on his head. We are the Just people, not the Unjust. The Unjust are up there paradin aroun and settin fire to folks, droppin napalm in Vietnam, and beatin up on black people. Down here we are all friends."

"Whose ears have heard
The Holy Word

That walk'd among the ancient trees," VDub Blake intoned.

"When I go up now," Ben continued, "I can barely stand the light. I take it as a sign I'm meant to be right here for the rest of my life, to burrow under the foundations of iniquity, to build this Christianopolis under that compromised land."

Another train roared through, and VDub and Arnold, with not much they could say, made their excuses, and left.

Back at the West 4th Street station, they hopped an uptown train, Arnold to go for a long run in the park to recover and VDub to get to his power lunch. At 34th Street, a wiry saxophonist got in the crowded car brandishing a broken instrument. "Earthlings," he yelled above the blare, "I come from Planet Xenon, a peaceful visitor. But my sax was here destroyed by three assailants, and *I need your help!* I'm gonna play till you pay, and I'm gonna play loud." With plastic Martian antennae bobbing from under his sweatband, he began to blow atrocious screeches from his ruined horn, deafening even in the deafening roar. Frantic passengers dug deep in their pockets to get him to stop. VDub offered up one of Arnold's dollar bills. "Thank you very much, ladies and gentlemen," he yelled as he held his horn to the ceiling, bowed, and got out with the crowd at 42nd Street.

"Peace with honor, man," VDub yelled after him. "I love any kind of compulsion," VDub commented to Arnold. "It creates joy in the illicit."

Thirty-seven

Become a runner, Arnold thought, while running through Sheep Meadow. A lifeline for sick old men, guys on binges, people too depressed to leave their rooms. It's livelihood and right-livelihood. Go out for food, cigarettes, booze even, charge them a little bit, or keep the change—whatever they want.

Off to his left, perhaps a hundred yards, he watched a scene as if it were in a slow-motion film: three boys sitting at the base of a statue jumping down together to cross the bike path nearby, forcing a rider off the road and off his bike. One stooped as if to help him up while the others gathered around him, assisting. Apologies made, they ran off together—in fast motion—out of the park at 72nd Street. Nice kids, Arnold thought, until he heard the scream, turned back, and saw the biker tearing frantically at his clothing. Arnold ran up to him.

"What happened? Are you OK?"

"Damn it, damn it, damn it . . . I can't believe it. Those bastards! Those fucking bastards!" White, thirtyish, thinning hair.

"What is it?"

"Slashers. Slash artists. They got my wallet—with all my cards and nine hundred bucks!"

He showed Arnold the flapping pocket of his shorts, cut as neatly as a surgical incision.

"Are you sure it didn't just drop out when you went down?" Arnold asked in a futile gesture of hope.

"No way! Look at this pocket," answered the more realistic victim. "Goddamn it, goddamn it! I'm in big trouble. . . ." He shook his head and shook it. Then he broke out wailing again.

A small crowd began to gather at a safe distance. This was the second time in the afternoon Arnold had been called upon to comfort—and again, he wasn't sure what to do.

"I'm OK, I'm OK. I just gotta get home and get on the phone fast."

He grabbed his bike and pedaled quickly back south along the bike path. Daniel Webster's statue looked down, as if to say, "Justice, sir, is the great interest of man on earth."

Arnold took up his run again, faster, needing it more than ever, Jabès's words cycling his mind.

> *The patience of the scream has no limits. It outlasts martyrdom.*

Around the lake, past Belvedere Castle.

> *It is not one country that the scream accuses, nor one continent, but the whole world. It is not one man, but all.*

And why, he wondered in counterpoint, would a man need $900 in cash?

He left the Park at Columbus Circle and walked down Broadway to cool off.

I have been wandering for two thousand years.
The world where I look for you is a world without trees.

Without trees now, but teeming with people: late lunchtime on a clear July day. Could people walk in herds, act in herds, think in herds? Faces coming at him, murmurs of Leviathan, backs and arms and hair. Ahead, six or seven deep ahead, there—hair—Herr!—her unmistakable shade of brown. Could it be? In

a world where you are not, where I look for you.
There are your steps,
Steps which I follow and wait for.

Arnold walked faster, pivoting right then left, and eventually broke through, off the curb, into the dangerous sidelines of Broadway traffic.

Is it?

Up on the sidewalk again, barreling through heads and clothes and cigarettes in slits of hand and mouthparts.

"Ariel!"

"Arnold!"

"What are *you* doing here?"

"What do you mean? I live here."

They would have liked to hug and stand and talk, but they were pushed along by an unyielding crowd. Arnold took her hand as they walked together. There was a book in it.

"I can't believe this," Ariel said. "Look at this book."

Edmond Jabès, *The Book of Questions.*

"I just went into Coliseum to get it. You had talked so much about it."

"I was just thinking about you. Really. For the last hour. Yukel and Sarah. You'll see—in the book."

"What are you doing?"

"Job hunting. I'm waiting to get into grad school."

"Where are you living?"

"Downtown." He could feel himself lying by omission.

"You have to come to dinner."

"Great. When?"

"Tonight?"

"Just like that? Drag a bum in off the street?"

"Some bum. And Daddy already knows you. He'll be delighted to see you again."

"He won't even remember me."

"He always remembers a pretty face. Besides, I need a little relief from my happy family." She rolled her eyes.

"I need to pick up my things and bring them downtown first. What time should I come? Where is it?"

"895 Park. Corner of 79th Street. You know where that is?"

"No."

"Other side of 5th Avenue. We usually eat at 7. Why don't you come at 6:30?"

"Any special dress?"

"It's come as you are."

Arnold went back to the Y, packed up his clothes, paid his bill, took the Lexington Avenue local down to Spring Street, and, map in hand, walked over to Prince. His trip into the tunnels had put the Sunshine into brighter perspective. Inexpensive housing, cheap food, secondhand shops, a chance to pick up some day labor should a job not be forthcoming—it was clearly the way to go.

Leaning on the pay phone outside the faded red door was a young man, blond like Arnold, tall like Arnold, if somewhat more emaciated, dressed in an open overcoat on this hot July afternoon, his oozing leg ulcers baking in the sun. Arnold nodded as he opened the door to the vestibule.

"Fuck you—in the name of Jesus Christ," was the response.

He climbed the long, dark stairs, made darker yet by the sunlight outside, and pushed open the double doors to the hallway and office space.

"Well, if it isn't Benedict Arnold!" Harry yelled out from behind the glass. "Welcome back, kid. I thought maybe the place was too much for you." He came out of the cage and joined Arnold in the "lobby." "So, you here to join the team?"

"Sure. It should be exciting."

"Exciting?" interjected a short albino man, seated on the couch. "I'm here cause it's restful."

"Meet Mr. Theodore M. Perry, our prodigal son returned. He thought he was going to save some moola by living on the street come spring. Hear his words of wisdom, son." Harry held an imaginary mike up to Mr. Perry's lips. "Tell him your tale, Ted. Tell Benedict here your daily workout agenda."

"Well, I usually slept in Madison Square Park up on 23rd. So I'd get up about 5:30, with the sun."

"What then?" Harry prodded.

"Then I'd walk up to St. Francis up on 31st and wait half an hour or an hour or two hours for sandwiches and coffee. You could have two sandwiches if you wanted. Then I'd walk down to Union Square and eat one of my sandwiches. There's a fountain there where I'd wash up and brush my dentures."

"Look how clean he is," Harry observed.

Arnold realized he had fallen into a brilliant class on Saving Money in New York. But then the double doors pushed slightly open and a round face stopped the conversation.

"Hey, Jack," Harry said. "C'mon in."

"Is this a good time?"

"Hey, it's a public place," Mr. Perry assured him.

A young man walked into the lobby, a freckled, spindly type in short sleeves and chinos. He nodded to Arnold and Mr. Perry.

"Jack Gelb, *Newsday*. I'm doing a story on 'New Men of the Bowery,' and . . ."

". . . and I invited him over to inspect our little zoo," said Harry. "Now, Mr. Perry here is a reborn Bowery man. He was just telling *his* story. . . ."

"Wonderful. Mind if I take some notes?"

Perry stood up. "Naw, I don't talk to cops."

Gone.

Arnold, on the other hand, thought he might like to talk—and listen—but he had to move in, and get ready for Ariel.

"Can I get a room, Harry? I'll pay by the week."

"Sure, kid. C'mon over to the window."

Harry went into the office, and Arnold got his assignment—15R. Remembering VDub's warning, he signed in as "Arnold Benedict." Harry walked him down to his new abode.

"This was Mr. Marshall's old room," Arnold said.

"Oh yeah, right, I told you about him last week. Yup. Finally gave it up a couple of days ago, and his son cleaned him out yesterday. But don't worry. Clyde cleaned up all the shit real good. Smell, go ahead, sniff around. You smell anything?" Arnold nosed an unholy trio of feces, bleach, and perfume but refused to play the sniffing dog, as Harry seemed to want. A cardboard eternal flame was propped up against the wall at the foot of the bed, an air freshener marked "READY FUNERAL HOME."

"We even left you some Oreos." Harry grabbed the half-eaten pack from the wallboard and tossed them to his new guest.

Arnold unpacked what little there was to unpack, lay down on the bed for an hour, too excited, perhaps too anxious, to nap, then went down the hall to freshen up for his date with the Bernsteins. On the way out, he bumped into Jack Gelb, who was also just leaving with Harry's story tucked in his notebook pocket. They walked down the dark stairs together and out into the blinding sunlight.

"Fuck you both—in the name of Jesus Christ."

They walked on together toward the subway station.

"That well-wisher looks a lot like you," Gelb observed. "Give you the creeps?"

"No," Arnold responded, almost on the defensive.

"What's it like being named Benedict Arnold? I know he was an interesting guy, a hero and all that."

"How'd you know my name? I mean, that's not my name."

"Harry told me. What do you mean it's not your name?"

"Harry just calls me that."

"So what *is* your name?"

"Arnold Benedict."

"Ah. Not so evocative. Jack Gelb."

They shook hands.

"I know. You introduced yourself coming in."

They walked along in silence.

"So what's a nice kid like you doing in a place like this?"

"Wait. My name isn't Arnold Benedict. It's Arnold Hitler."

"I see."

"Really," Arnold said. "Don't be scared. I'm not crazy. I'm a Harvard grad. In linguistics. My name happens to be Hitler."

Gelb's whole soul pricked up. This alone had the makings of a story.

"But you can't tell people your real name . . ."

"Because some people are touchy on the issue."

"Let's go back to the previous question: What's a nice kid like you doing in a place like this?" They reached the subway station and descended the steps together. "You really going to move into the Sunshine Hotel?"

"I'm headed for an appointment," Arnold said, hoping Gelb's path led elsewhere—to Queens or Brooklyn or wherever *Newsday* was based.

"I'll go with you," said the reporter.

In the thirty minutes it took to get to uptown, Gelb had teased Arnold's basic story out from behind a wall of suspicion—the attractive, successful Texas kid persecuted by "sophisticated" Harvard and now seeking a life in the Big Apple. His intended theme: Would New York accept a promising young man named Hitler? It might be part of the "New Men of the Bowery" piece, or it might be a story on its own.

In 1961, the Bernsteins had moved into a sixteen-room duplex apartment on two top floors at the southeast corner of Park Avenue and 79th Street. Arnold eyed the building with some awe and consulted his watch: 6:15. Rather than be embarrassingly early, he walked up to 86th Street and back down, checking out Ariel's neighborhood to the tune of "On the Street Where You Live." Calm down, Arnold. Remember the trumpet player, that mustache, what was his name? Hecht. Leonard Hecht.

Six thirty. The second hand swept past the 12, and the era shifted: it was now OK to enter, not quite fashionably late. Arnold wasn't prepared for the imposing black doorman with crimson cloak and white gloves, but he made it through to the desk, where he was announced by a jacket-and-tied receptionist and signaled through to the elevator.

To the top floor. Arnold in Wonderland. He stepped off into a small foyer leading into a large hall, decorated entirely in black and white, featuring a curved staircase that led to the family living quarters one flight down. The upper living room, which was large enough for several separate seating areas, contained not one but two Steinway grands, each covered with family and celebrity photos. On the wall, floral prints, large, on beige and pale-blue walls. Ariel came running up the stairs.

"You made it. And right on time, as usual. Daddy will be out in a minute. He's just finishing up in his studio. And don't worry, he remembers you from chorus. He's looking forward to getting a real chance to talk."

"Quite the place."

"Um, well, yes. Mommy's place. Calculated to convey that there's a family in residence but that there is a world-famous personality *also* in residence, capable of entertaining in a manner befitting. His-and-her pianos, of course. And knickknacks for every discriminating taste from antique to contemporary. Frankly, I prefer living at Radcliffe. But it *was* terrific a couple of years ago to see the JDL pickets downstairs."

"What's JDL?"

"Sorry, Texas Christian. Jewish Defense League."

"Did your dad need defending?"

"Hell, they were attacking! Remember? Daddy's party for the Black Panthers?"

"Ah."

"Lots of hate letters—and they picketed the apartment. First picket line I ever crossed. But it made him think through his politics more carefully. Let me show you around."

"I want to see pictures of you as a beautiful child."

"Yeah, well, *everybody* was beautiful. Here's me at the ballet with Dad, at the opera with Mom and Dad. No photos of us fighting—which might be more typical. I'll show you the boxing gloves Alex, my brother, got us. They're hanging over my bed."

"Your mom *is* beautiful. I'd never seen a picture of her."

"Let me introduce you to Julia. She was one of Mom's servants in Chile. Mom's Chilean."

Arnold met Julia, got the full tour—not including Lenny's study—and he and Ariel went upstairs to plop down on one of the couches.

"So where are you working? Where are you applying?"

As if on cue to spare Arnold the dubious exposition, Lenny came bounding up the white-carpeted stairs. The guest stood up. The daughter did not.

"Arnold!" Big hug. "Yeah, yeah, Ariel told me the Jake story." He laughed. "Nice to see you again. Where are you? What's happening?"

This was not the suave Lenny of the podium. He was dressed, unbelievably, in a pink cowboy shirt with mother-of-pearl snaps, new jeans studded with metal stars, and a red handkerchief knotted at the throat, the whole outfit quite at odds with his middle-aged body and with a face already lined with spiritual and too-worldly experience. He looked like something from a frat-house costume party, except that this was Lenny at *home*, his clothes proclaiming "with it," to most doubtful effect. He eased himself into a big leather chair facing the couch.

"You still up in Cambridge?"

"No, I graduated in June. I'm down here job hunting and checking out grad schools."

"Where?"

"Columbia, NYU."

"Good, good. Say, Ariel tells me you lived in Eliot House. So did I."

"Yup. One of those tiny fifth-floor rooms facing the Charles."

"What number?"

"504."

"Arnold, I love you! That was *my* room! It was the Köchel number of the Prague Symphony, so I had to have it. Amazing."

And in fact, it *was* somewhat amazing. Arnold was at a loss for what to say. Ariel was not about to jump in.

"I like your shirt" was what came out.

"*Thank* you, Arnold." Lenny seemed genuinely moved. "It's nice to have a more appreciative audience for my sartorial excursions. I can only wear this outfit when Mummy isn't here—she's in Chicago—or I'd get mercilessly teased about 'Daddy's fat belly' or 'Daddy's wrong color choices.' Ariel here's pretty fierce, too, but I can hold my own against her—if she's by herself. Want a drink?"

Arnold declined.

"It has always been our sworn duty as a family," Ariel explained, "to offer up a reality check for Daddy . . ."

"You mean to act as bringers-down . . ." said Lenny, whiskey in hand.

". . . so he doesn't go off on Cloud Nine and never come back. Or come back with such a wildly swelled head that his hair would fall out, and can you imagine a bald Daddy? Dimitri Mitropolous Bernstein?"

They all had a laugh, but Arnold felt this was spoor from some underlying family antagonism, especially when Lenny came out of the joke mumbling, "Daddy's driving is awful, Daddy can't do a Greek dance, Daddy's dumb politics, Daddy this, Daddy that . . . this is the single most critical family in the New York metropolitan region."

"Daddy, as usual, is all wrapped up in elf's thread—that's his anagram for self-hatred."

Arnold was about to mention Saussure on anagrams when Julia yelled up from the nether regions, "Dinner is served." They all proceeded down to the family dining room, where Julia served up a delicious Greek lemon soup, followed by mushroom-stuffed tenderloin and, finally, a show-stopping blackberry mousse.

Arnold had never been so engaged in his life. The conversation started, naturally enough, with Mahler—their common experience—and went quickly off into Mahler and death, death, death and Heidegger, Heidegger and the new discoveries of his Nazism, the difference between philosophy and life, the relation of artists and life, of art and life, of form and substance, of Apollo and Dionysus, of Nietzsche and madness, of art and disease. Until the moment when Arnold realized he wanted Lenny as his father-in-law even more than he wanted Ariel as his bride.

It was 11:30 when he got up to leave. Ariel was looking bleary and, after a hug and noncommittal "Let's stay in touch," barefooted her way downstairs to bed—under the boxing gloves. Lenny accompanied Arnold into the foyer to wait for the elevator.

"Come over here and let's have a kiss," the Maestro said.

"What?"

"A kiss." The elevator drew up to the landing. "Make me immortal with a kiss."

Arnold imagined he was being asked to take part in some old European tradition: two philosophers hugging at parting and kissing the air on either side of cheeks. But when he stepped toward Lenny to embrace him, the Maestro grabbed Arnold's head between strong hands and moshed his face against the young man's. He opened his mouth and pried open Arnold's jaw with his tongue. It was like being attacked by dripping, lascivious sandpaper.

"You're a beautiful boy. Ariel has excellent taste. Please, Arnold, do come again. Here's my personal phone number." Lenny handed him a slip of paper he had obviously prepared in advance. "We'll talk more. It was wonderful."

Arnold reached for the elevator gate.

"Allow me, my prince . . ." Lenny pulled open the gate and bowed low before his fleeing guest. As the elevator descended, Arnold could hear him singing loudly down the shaft:

"Per pietà, ben mio, perdona
all'error d'un' alma amante;
fra quest' ombre e queste piante . . ."

It sounded like Mozart, but Arnold did not understand the Italian.

VDub came knocking at 15R on Saturday night, his left hand behind his back.

"Who is it?"

"Flowergram."

Arnold opened doubtfully.

"Vergil!"

Out came the flowers, a loose and once-pocketed handful of dandelions from the park. Arnold took them.

"Aren't you going to read the note?" Indeed, there was a small change envelope taped to one of the flowers. On a folded piece of paper, scarcely larger than a fortune-cookie fortune, Arnold read:

If once a man indulges himself in murder, very soon he comes to think little of robbing, and from robbing he comes next to drinking and Sabbath-breaking, and from that to incivility and procrastination.

"What's this?"

"Thomas de Quincy, 1839, from his essay 'On Murder Considered as One of the Fine Arts.' I thought you'd appreciate it after a week among the hoi polloi. Who knows what murders are here reduced? How ya doin?"

"I'd invite you in, but there's no room to sit."

"Then let's exit into the summer eventide." Perhaps he was a little drunk. Arnold had never seen him dive for a cigarette butt thrown from a car into the street. He held it up to show Arnold his capture.

"A fair maiden in distress," he said of the Newport, "rejected by some lout in an Oldsmobile ... Did you ever think how impossible it is for your colleagues on the bum to get a piece of ass sans money, sans venue, in this pitiless city, sternly tall, emblematic of a nation thrusting its might *ad astra*, wasting no downward glances at the likes of us?"

Arnold was at a loss to answer, though now that he thought of it, there seemed to be no women at all in the Bowery world.

"Consider that object," VDub continued, pointing to a man curled up in the doorway of a lighting-fixture emporium. "That, when even slightly vertical, is Francisco Menotti, a wayward cousin thrice removed of the famous Gian-Carlo, a man of wondrous seediness, and so profound as to be unintelligible. Not bad-looking either, or at least more nearly lovely than hideous. His existence is characterized by glimpses into divine and misty paradises, by rapidity within prolonged slowness, and, simultaneously, by sloth within extensive industriousness. And *he* hasn't been laid in ten years. Go figure. Wait a minute, I got to pee. Observe carefully, brother. This is your lesson for the day. Survival in a city that provides no restrooms for the likes of us. Peeing in Public 101."

VDub strode innocently over to a cluster of garbage cans outside Katz's Delicatessen. With stomach flush against the cans, he leaned over them, and with his right hand rummaging through the debris, his left zipped open his fly. Out came the stream invisibly into the garbage, while both hands feigned exploration as if in quest of some discarded pastrami on rye. A reverse move in closure, and no one the wiser. He returned to his companion on the busy street.

"Be assured there was no antisemitism implied in my choice of receptacle, though admittedly garbage cans have feelings, too. But you're probably wondering why I invited you all here. Because I like to be seen with famous people."

"I'm very famous," Arnold mumbled facetiously.

"Now don't be sarcastic, Herr Hitler. Sarcasm is the language of the devil and the last refuge of the scoundrel. You are only slightly famous at the moment, but by tonight, after dinner, you will be a new star in a darkening firmament." VDub whipped a newspaper page out of his prose pocket. "Et voilà! It's you, babe."

"Harvard Hitler Hidden in Hotel." It wasn't quite a headline but a boldface subheading in Jack Gelb's piece on "New Men of the Bowery." Arnold stood there and parsed the six column inches.

"Well, he got it right. What I told him."

"And how do you think this will go down at the Sunshine, Mr. Benedict?"

"Oh, my God—Harry!"

"Uh-huh, Harry. On the one hand, people tell him all kinds of stories, and he just collects them for his upcoming novel, *La Comédie Humaine*. On the other hand, he does have this singular bee in his bonnet."

"Maybe he won't see it."

"Possible, but not likely. Some Sunshiney citizen, rummaging through the trash, will come upon an un-peed-upon copy of today's *Newsday* and bring home the bacon to post. You, of course, might try to sabotage the event by surreptitiously taking it down from the lobby wall. But it might come to him orally, like the *Iliad*."

"On the other hand," Arnold observed, "people there don't tend to gossip. Privacy is a chief good."

"We'll see, won't we? But it's not the end of the world if you get kicked out. There's always the Prince, the World, the Grand, or the White House. Snazzy addresses, though not as bright as the Sunshine. It is the fate of the great to be ever on the lam. Look at Einstein. Look at Brecht."

It turned out Harry did not see the article. His brother, Alex, had succumbed to lung cancer in Baltimore, and Harry had taken the bus down for a few days to be with the family. What he did notice, however, was a letter, several days after his return, addressed to a Mr. A. Hitler, at the Sunshine Hotel. He thought it was some kind of abominable joke, but being a man of high rectitude was not about to commit a federal offense by tossing before checking. He was quick to be informed by the resident *Newsday* readers that indeed, there *was* an Arnold Hitler staying at the Sunshine. The name "Arnold" of course conjured up a prime suspect, and Harry was quick to corner him.

"Hey, Benedict, c'mere. I got this letter, and I don't know what to do with it. You gimme some advice?"

"Sure."

Harry took out of his desk a squarish envelope addressed in purple pen, with clipped, strong script, to "Arnold Hitler."

"Any idea who this might be?"

The jig was up. Yet again. Arnold reviewed his alternatives. But there was no choice here—especially since he wanted to see what was in the envelope.

"Harry, it's me. I would have told you, but Vergil introduced me as Arnold Benedict after warning me about your family—you know. I didn't want to contradict him, or upset you. It's just my name, my father's name. He fought against Hitler—Adolf. But some people are irrational about it. What can I say?"

"One of those people is me," Harry growled. "And I don't like to be lied to. Especially about this stuff. You're outta here."

"But I've already paid you for the month. I've got nine days to go."

Harry thrust his hand in the till.

"Here you go. Three bucks times nine days. Now, out! I don't need any Ivy League fascist assholes doing sociology here."

Though prepared by VDub for such a reaction, Arnold was shocked at its force and ferocity.

"I'm not doing sociology, Harry, I'm just trying to save money for grad school. And I'm not Adolf Hitler, and I'm not a fascist, and I didn't kill your relatives."

"Fuck you. Out!"

"Well, I'll be out in nine days." He fell back on some VDub lore. "I happen to know the regs on this. You can't throw a person out on the street if his money's been paid, even for some egregious behavior—and my *name* is not egregious behavior." He was bluffing but suspected VDub was right. He might have just moved on to one of the other flop-houses, but Newton's Law of Action-Reaction had kicked in.

"Nine days and you're out of here." Harry had enough legal trouble with dope addicts shooting up in the rooms. "And don't ask me for any favors, don't even talk to me. This is my last words to you, three, two, one, finished." And he turned tight-lipped away to put the money back in the till.

"May I have my letter?"

Harry picked it up off the counter and flung it through the hole in the glass, onto the lobby's filthy marble-tiled floor. Arnold gathered it up.

"Thank you," he said politely, and walked to his room.

Dear Arnold Hitler,

Please forgive my forwardness in writing to a stranger, but I was moved to contact you by the article in Newsday.

Names are curious things, our joy and sometimes our burden. Mine is Evelyn Brown, the surname calling up that common color, common in frequency but also in content. It is, as I was teased in school, "the color of shit." Evelyn, on the other hand, is not so common. It has a certain dignity, yet it is a diminutive of Eve, the mother of us all, and the mother of all sorrows. I have often felt

rooted in my last name, only to be branching out in the myriad di-
rections of my first.

Arnold Hitler. How you must have suffered with that weight on
your back. Yet I write you for this reason: I, myself, find it attrac-
tive and exceptional—not only in its rarity but for the extraordi-
nary assignment it carries.

What assignment? What is she thinking?

I'd love to meet with you and talk further, to compare, as it were,
our birth-given tasks. If getting together interests you, please call
me at my studio at LI6-6097. I'm there most days.
Hope to hear from you.

Sincerely,

Evelyn Brown

Arnold was surprised to find his hand shaking and his heart beating
faster. Would he call her? Surely. She seemed smart and straightforward
anyway. She must be an artist or sculptor or photographer. He judged
her to be at least middle-aged—though that did not jibe with his tachy-
cardia. In the second-floor fumes of a thousand debauches, Arnold Hitler
did not sleep well that night. He called the next morning at 9.

Thirty-eight

Evelyn Brown's name was on her mailbox in the shabby hall of an apartment house on Hunt's Point Avenue in the Bronx. The small rectangle in the mailbox door displayed a scintillating black snake slithering around the uprights and through the apertures of the twelve letters. The texture was minutely rendered, with every scale depicted. It was an astonishing introduction.

Neither bell nor elevator worked, she had assured him on the phone: he should walk up four flights and knock at 4B.

The door opened instantly—for having seen him out the window, she had been waiting, hand on knob. But the moment was startling, like anything too surprisingly close or quick. And they were startled both.

Middle-aged she was not, but a slim and gorgeous twenty-five, dressed all in black, her blond hair short in front and long behind, her midriff provocative below a truncated tee, her legs shapely even under jeans. It took Arnold a few minutes to gather all this in, or rather to believe that it might have been well worth getting kicked out of Harry's.

"Arnold?"

"Hi, Evelyn."

What more there was to be said pulsed privately in each heart as they made their way through the silly chatter of orientation. Arnold agreed to the "grand tour" of her studio, and his astonishment at the mailbox herpetology was multiplied a hundredfold by the objects on walls, tabletops, and easels.

"This is my World Disaster Room," she said as she escorted him into one of the three studios, once bedrooms, in the apartment.

Arnold gazed around a dark-red chamber whose walls were plastered with images framed and unframed, on canvas and cardboard, on postcards and calendar pages. The music of their meeting seemed to have modulated into a minor key.

"These are the many catastrophes of many Noahs. You'll see his ark or airship or tank or bunker in every image."

Arnold inspected a succession of tourist postcards from many cities: Seattle, Venice, Paris, Rome, New York, Buenos Aires, Toronto, Berlin. . . . Each had been painted over with fire or flood, many had suffered a typhoon or an earthquake, toppling its buildings, burying its monuments. The Eiffel Tower lay on its side, crushed and bent by a steaming meteor in a neighboring hole while Noah on his raft departed northward across the Seine. Evelyn pointed out the fine details with pride while her guest absorbed the show with horror. On another wall was a painting he recognized, and he seized upon it, hoping to change the subject.

"That's Bruegel's *Icarus*," he noted. "'The ploughman may have heard the splash, the forsaken cry. But for him it was not an important failure.'" And indeed, the ploughman had traversed a few feet farther on. But now he was transfixed, staring at the boiled-out lake, with the ship in flames, and the human meteor, Icarus, smashed and burning in the bottom mud, with the black mailbox snake eating at his liver.

"Ah, but it *was* an important failure," the artist advised. "Human hubris? Vietnam? So I updated Mr. Bruegel."

She led him to another wall, which displayed a succession of maps, all in flames.

"This is my history-of-recent-American-imperialism series—all the places we've bombed since the Second World War."

Arnold inspected the cuttings—maps overlaid on bucolic calendar scenes (each with its ethnic Noah): China, Korea, Guatemala, Indonesia, Cuba, the Congo, Peru, Laos, Vietnam, Cambodia, all carefully labeled and dated.

"The boys love these."

Arnold thought she meant the Pentagon boys, the ones with the toys. He looked at her anew, those long, delicate fingers, those intense blue eyes.

"And here," she continued, "are the twenty-six largest nuclear plants, in order, A through Z."

The illuminated letters painted in the upper left-hand corner of each power-company brochure breathed out a combination of light and fire that spread over the plant and the corporate text in a riot of joyous flame.

"You'll notice fire is a big part of my art. It's hard to paint fire. And water, cleansing water. The world is not extinguished: there's a transient, what? reintegration into formlessness—and then, perhaps, a chance for new life or a new man. No?"

Arnold was reeling too much to answer. He felt simultaneously drawn to this woman—and repulsed.

"Ready for more? Here's my Manifest Destiny series."

She led her guest over to a group of famous American paintings and portraits, torn with ragged edges from some sacrificed history of American art.

"They've been 'altered,' as the veterinarians say, all these ghosts of American civilization—I burn away their memory so regeneration may occur."

Arnold focused first on the Gilbert Stuart *Washington* that had graced his every elementary school classroom. Its wig was on fire and its jaw replaced by a photorealistically rendered image from a text on reconstructive facial surgery. It was labeled "Papa Loved Me, But He Died." Given her bent, he was not surprised by the fire and exchange of heads on the Remington scenes of the Indian Wars and the Catlin portraits of emaciated chiefs in Auschwitz stripes and feathers. What he did not expect were the animals of Hicks's *Peaceable Kingdom* devouring one another across the food chain as the landscape flamed, or the drowning masses trying to cling to Winslow Homer's boat as the occupants hacked at their fingers while coastline volcanoes erupted. Even more surprising were Georgia O'Keeffe flowers gored by Georgia O'Keeffe skulls, Franz Kline shapes shaping themselves into black, flaming Munchean death's-heads, Jackson Pollack swirls surging out of the chimneys of crematoria—all empowered, as it seemed, by landscapes in flood and flame. Manifest Destiny? Strangely, the most disturbing image of all was an Audubon painting of a pair of bald eagles, the male flying above with a swastika in its claws while the female fed a baby swastika in the nest. No fire or flood here, just the wind bearing the national bird aloft.

"What's with the swastika here?"

"Ah. That *would* interest you. Throughout the ages, the *Hackenkreuz* has represented the Supreme Deity in its compass quadrants, its visualized motion around an axis. It is movement, the coincidence of horizon, nadir and zenith in the mystic center, the action of the Origin on the Universe. And you thought it was a swastika, shame on you. I want to rehabilitate the sign. So do the eagles. So do you."

"How do you know that?"

"How could I not? Come have some dinner."

She led him into a small kitchen, faintly redolent of roach spray.

"In honor of your name, I've prepared a vegetarian meal: German pancakes stuffed with German meatballs made of textured vegetable protein, Ba-Tempte kosher sauerkraut to honor any possible Jewish ancestors, German potato salad; sourdough rye from the Bread & Puppet Theater's big demo last month; and a nice German chocolate cake for dessert. OK with you?"

The good humor of the menu put him back at ease in spite of its strong under-whiff of satire. But satire at whose expense? At the moment, though, he was more concerned with the lithe, gay figure serving him.

"Life and health, spiritual energy, Heraclitean fecundity, libido, transformation and regeneration, purification and destruction of the forces of evil, all on this little table in the South Bronx. In the middle," she struck a match and lit the candle, "fire, the alchemical element that operates at the center of all things, unifying and stabilizing them. Fire and life, metabolism: life must feed on life to keep alive. Amen."

He hadn't realized she was saying grace.

During the meal, he told his story—of idyllic Mansfield and difficult Cambridge and his bizarre introduction to New York. She seemed fascinated. He spoke of his reaction to her art, of his resistance to this massing of landscapes focusing on suffering.

"I'm thinking a great deal about religion now, and it's all involved with language . . . words that get thrown hurtfully . . ."

"Or mythically . . ."

"Derisively . . ."

"That's why I wrote you."

"My name . . ."

"Your name. Come, Mr. Hitler, let's go visit the Evie room, and then we can have dessert."

"But we're having dessert right now. Chocolate cake."

"There are desserts and desserts."

She took his hand, hauled him out of the chair, and led him to the second of the studio rooms, this one smaller and painted in black.

"Does your landlord know about this paint job?"

"My landlord has never been seen—by anyone. Rent goes to the BVM Corp., and they never say thank you. Exhibit One: *Evie and the Serpent,* a series of eight-by-ten photos taken by my ex-boyfriend, and decorated by yours truly."

In twelve time-lapse poses, a nude Evelyn Brown reached for, received, and brought toward her mouth a painted apple, given over by a painted snake coiled in a painted tree. Arnold had never seen such a beautiful body. Even Ariel's luxurious thinness paled before Evelyn's willowy yet opulent form. This was the woman standing close at his side. This was the woman who was in some way interested in him. Gabe began to rise, Arnold's breath to quicken.

"You like the serpent?" Evelyn teased.

And in fact, it *was* a wonderful serpent, cousin to the one on the mailbox, yet larger and even more dazzlingly rendered. But Arnold felt caught ogling. He gave her a playful punch. There. He had touched her. His groin stopped pulsing, and deflated.

"Notice the evolution of the apple," she advised.

And indeed, the apple in each painting, though barely a half-inch high, contained micropaintings of human depravity. From the eating of the apple and the murder of Cain in the first and second photos to the horrors of Vietnam in the last, the pernicious bloom culminated in a thirteenth work, *Evie and the Apple,* a canvas, painted in oil, of Evelyn's face, larger than life, biting into a four-inch apple whose crimson surface was large enough to display accurate portraits of twenty-seven brutalists hidden in its sheen. Head to head, cheek to jowl, were Nixon and Nero, Atilla and Kissinger, Luther and Torquemada, Franco and Napoleon—

two times thirteen male heads crowding a lone female face, closest to the biting teeth.

"Who is that?" Arnold asked.

"My mother."

He laughed.

"She was not a good person."

He decided to pass.

"Next we have *Evie the Nazi*," she said, clearly changing the subject.

And yes, there was a series of eleven-by-eighteen-inch blowups of Evelyn in Nazi regalia—shirt painted brown, armband, jodhpurs, boots—giving a stiff-arm salute at Kitty Hawk, the Delaware River, the Grand Canyon, the construction of the World Trade Center, and in the midst of an astonished crowd on the steps of Saint Patrick's Cathedral.

"What's with all this Nazi stuff?" Arnold asked.

"I'm a skinhead chick," Evelyn replied nonchalantly. "Didn't you notice?" She flicked her short front hair at him, then shot her hand up in salute. "*Sieg heil! Heil* Hitler! Hey, this is great. I've never had a real Hitler to *heil* to."

"Cut it out."

"I'm not kidding."

"Well, you've got the wrong Hitler here. I'm . . ."

"I've got exactly the *right* Hitler. I've got a Hitler in tension with his role, as I am in tension with my own. Being Hitler is forcing you to explore some deep places, *nicht wahr?* Being a skinhead likewise. Evie the Nazi—it's a shot of history directly into the vein of my life."

"But you're not a Nazi!" He hesitated. "Are you?"

"Sticks and stones may hurt old crone's butt. Hey, how will I ever understand human evil unless I live it? Read about it in books? This is a religious act, my inquiry into Supreme Being and the possibility of redemption."

Arnold was stunned.

"So you paint all these disasters . . ."

"Exactly. I get to be the perpetrator of the disasters. I get to reenact Hitler and Attila and Caligula and General William Tecumseh Sherman right here at lil ol 2168 Hunt's Point Avenue—and I can understand— just barely—the madness. I can try on the costume of inhuman cruelty and grope around in spiritual darkness—where I find my own roots tangled with those of the world ash. How do you get to yours?"

"My roots? I don't know."

"Well, you've come to the right place. I'll help you. OK? Ambiguity and paradox—ready for that?"

Who was this woman, he wondered, her belly button calling to his tongue, her lips calling forth his breath and saliva? And where was that navel connected? She seemed so wise; he felt so shallow. She was the real thing. Ambiguity and paradox.

"Hölderlin said we have to master what is innate to achieve great heights." She quick-stepped around behind him and squeezed his guts so hard he felt his anus protrude.

"What's *your* innate? What's in there?"

"I . . . can't . . . talk," he sputtered.

She let him go. "Pretty strong, huh?" She flexed her biceps. "Here, feel."

He was bashful. More likely frightened. "I get the point."

She came around front, softly wound around him, and kissed him on the lips. "Now that you know who I am, let's fuck."

She took his hand and led him into the third and final studio, white walls empty except for a frieze of doctored photographs running above the molding on all four walls. In the center of the room, a king-size bed.

"I sleep here. It keeps me clear."

"You mean nothing on the walls. Except for . . ."

"*The Halo.* I call it *The Halo.* You can look at it later. First you have to look at me." She took off her T and lay down on the bed.

"I never make love in a room containing undigested religious symbols."

Very sophisticated, he. Pathetic. But self-esteem has to regroup somehow.

"Ah. He wants spiritual. OK, art seminar. Hope you don't mind if the lecturer is topless."

"Um . . ."

"Good. I knew you wouldn't. We begin with a quiz: What famous photographer does this sequence remind you of?"

"Edward Muybridge."

"Excellent, but only an A-minus answer for the Harvard boy. His name was actually Edweard. Ed-weird. What's in a name? But pretty close. Ed-weird Muybridge of the most excellent *The Human Figure in Motion.* Can you see what those figures are doing?"

Arnold had to fingertip the wall, stand on tippy-toe, and squint.

"They're not the same figure, like Muybridge's."

"Give that man a cigar for between his legs. What are they?"

"Runners."

"The first New York Marathon, two years ago. Ten thousand runners. I put up my camera and shot every fiftieth one that came by. The sequence starts here—that's the winner. Two hundred little pictures, two hundred and one, actually—I wanted to get the very last even though he was ten thousand seventeenth."

"Why is it *The Halo?* Just cause it goes around the top of the room?"

"It is *The Halo,* Arnold Hitler, because it represents Suffering Freely Entered Into, my theme song, don'tcha know. These men are saints of a debased order. They are all seeking to entice that death-by-exhaustion of the first Marathoner in 490 B.C., the one who delivered his message to Athens, the one who gasped, "We won!" and expired then and there— poop!—for maximum effect. Poor training.

"These guys' message, of course, is not to their community but to themselves: 'I did it!' But this shrunken thought is even more endearing to me, the refracted message of a futile, superhuman effort. They have arrived at the end of their struggle, and wouldn't we all love to be there?

"But more interesting is to study the sequence as a whole. Collectively they might be impersonating the catastrophic and declining history of our race, each fiftieth one more decrepit than the one before—from Mr. Winner over there to the wrecks at the end, carried by their friends past the finish line. Not a pretty picture on that wall, do you think? But the driving rain was great, the helicopters chopping overhead sounding just like their brothers over My Lai, the crowd cheering—look at them wearing their plastic bags and squinting at their stopwatches!"

"The same crowd behind every runner."

"Now, while the halo is usually understood as a crown-like circle, there is also the tradition of halo as sphere containing the blessed object. You can see this parodied in Hieronymus Bosch—all those curious beings enclosed in transparent glass globes—Jerry's image of determinism caging each of us inside his mode of being or destiny, paradisiacal or damned. So, Arnie, if you are plumping for a halo by mightily resisting little Eva here . . ." She rubbed her breasts against his arm. ". . . you might . . . just . . . reconsider. . . ." She unbuttoned her jeans, and wiggled out of them, Venus for her Adonis.

Neither of them smoked. But they lay postcoitally in bed nevertheless.

"I've been saving this room for you."

"What about your ex-boyfriend—the one who took the pictures?"

"We always did it at his house. My studio, Arnold Hitler, was sacred, impenetrable space—till you came along."

"Stop calling me Arnold Hitler."

"Is that your name, or not? You should be more proud of your name. I'm gonna call you Arnold Hitler, and you are now lying in Eva's bed in the room saved for the coming of Arnold Hitler."

It was in that room that Evelyn painted the twelve *Portraits of Siegfried Aroused*—Arnold lying in her bed, surrounded by magic fire, with his penis at various levels of verticality, touched, photographed, and re-touched by the artist—for maximum effect.

It was in the bathroom off that room that she painted *Baptism by Fire in the Red Sea*—with Arnold, erect in a tub of crimson water, the sides of the tub painted with flames, the whole photo-painting inscribed with hermetic texts concerning the alchemical fusion of male and female: "An egg is placed in the furnace where a symbolic sexual union occurs; the hot, solar male and cold, lunar female interact." In a cloud painted at the top: "This event is filled with pain, and rage, killing, and putrefac-tion." On the bathtub wall: "Matter is destroyed; and opposites dissolve. The process of becoming, in which matter changes form." Along the bot-tom blackened edge: "Sinister spiritual death and descent into hell, guided by the light of a seven-flamed menorah."

It was on the floor of the closet of that room that she installed *Arnold Rockefeller Observes Gas Cans Fucking*—a piece she showed to no one.

She told him she wanted his baby.

They drove to the dance in her Jag XKE, a two-door convertible, three years old, low slung and sporty, black with fine snake-scales barely visi-ble at six feet. He had wanted to stay in bed, but she had a previous en-gagement.

"I have to put in an appearance."

"Can I come?" he asked.

"You might hate it."

"Not with you."

"It's a little much to throw at you all at once."

"C'mon," Arnold boasted, "I've had two thousand pounds of defense meat charging at me, all intent on my demise."

"OK. Don't say I didn't warn you."

They drove under the Bruckner Expressway.

"This is quite the car for a starving artist."

"Yeah. Like I said, ambiguity and paradox."

"Your mom bought it for you."

"My mom would have a heart attack if she knew. . . ."

"Wrong side of the class struggle?"

"On the contrary. Déclassé. Listen, we've got two minutes to prepare you. You're going to hear some nasty music, and you're going to meet Keith. Keith Kenneth Klawans."

"The plot thickens."

"Thickens and scalds. Now listen up. Context. This is a Frigga night dance. . . ."

" 'Friggin?' "

"Frigga, Friea, Frija, Friatag, Friday, day—now night—of the Norse goddess of love. Last night was the first of four of Keith's Thorsday-night 'Lectures on Basics' to this gang of would-be hoodlums who call themselves B-A-T, BAT."

"Like a Louisville Slugger?"

"Yes, their fantasy implement of persuasion, and also, by de rigueur acronymism, for the 'Bronx Army of Thor.' "

"The BAT being Thor's hammer."

"You got it. BAT out of hell. They toyed with Fighting Injewstice with the Gargantuan Hammer of Thor for a while . . ."

"FIGHT. Did you say, 'in*jew*stice'?"

"... but it was too nakedly clever for Keith, so he nixed it."

Evelyn turned east on 141st Street and north again on the next block, now heading the other direction under the expressway. She pulled over to the side and left the engine running.

"I kind of liked 'injewstice' myself, being a Joycean," she remarked, "but you'll find plenty where that came from. Keith is also a Joyce fan."

"What was the lecture on?"

"Blacks and mud people."

"Well, I'm glad to have missed it."

Arnold unbuckled and started to get out into the midsummer night.

"Wait." She pulled him back. "You're not ready yet." He settled back in. "Keith is English, Oxford, kind of a visionary actually. He's twenty-nine. Came over three years ago when his dad copped the managership of a Jaguar dealership over on 9th Avenue."

"Jaguar."

"Jaguar."

"Um-hm."

"Don't be so smart. He was hanging out in London with a lot of working-class kids. . . ."

"To spite his Jaguar parents?"

"Of course, except he never gave up his own sweet white XKE—XKalibEr, he calls it. Anyway, his friends were getting into lots of fights with police, with soccer players, homosexuals, hippies, and were starting to develop their own Oi! Music, you know what that is?"

"*Oi,* like *oi vey?*"

"Definitely not. Oi! like Hey! in Cockney. You'll hear it tonight. It ain't the Beatles."

"Punk from real punks?"

"You got it. And with rising unemployment, the Oi! rockers turned anti-Semitic and antiblack and anti-immigrant, and Keith the Oxonian became radicalized to the justice of class struggle."

"So now he's here to enlighten and organize the savages?"

"That's for you to find out, you Lone Star cracker."

She unbuckled, swung around to give him a surprise bite on the ear, pivoted in the bucket seat, and jumped out into the road. A twenty-four-footer marked "MOISHE'S MOVING SYSTEMS" almost knocked her down.

"Good thing Keith didn't catch that. Moishe might have had quite a sabbath tomorrow."

Thirty-nine

They stood together on Bruckner Boulevard, a street like
an exterior world for the Mole People. Hanging ominous
above it was the Bruckner Expressway, eclipsing all light,
leaving a gloomy, dank, and filthy area embellished
along its length by a chain-link fence protecting the railway with its
high-tension overhead lines. Rocks and stunted trees glowed in moonlight along the track bed, looking out of context and distressed. Only two
other cars parked on the block: a huge '59 Cadillac, and a timeless low,
white Jag.

"Anton Bruckner," Evelyn intoned, "Next to Wagner, Hitler's favorite."

"Never heard of him."

"It's why Keith picked this spot."

"But surely this Bruckner wasn't the same . . ."

"Fast Eddie Bruckner, Bronx borough president and soda-water king, who after some political hanky-pank was burped out of the Democratic Party."

"So if he wasn't Bruckner Bruckner, why did Keith . . . ?"

"You're not Hitler Hitler—so why are you Paternoster Doloroso?"

She put her hands in the small of his back and pushed him down the block to a subtle laceration in the fence, shuffling along rhythmically behind him like the Little Engine That Could.

"After you," she announced.

With some effort, she lifted the fence flap and gestured for Arnold to crawl through. Then, with a practiced move, she lithed her own self in. They stood in a triangular yard a football field long. In the moonlight, off to the left, they could see a figure beating viciously on one of the several mattresses scattered on the property.

"That's probably Jason der Basher. He likes to bash things."

"Oh."

"Shall we abandon hope?"

In front of them was a windowless, concrete block structure perched on the edge of the railroad ravine, its metal door rusted and unmarked. Other than Jason, now sprawled atop his rectangular victim, there was little sign or sound of life in the yard. The moon shone on barbed wire and tracks—a combination fragrant with Birkenau.

"Would you please look in my cleavage for the key?"

Evelyn opened her jacket, and Arnold, shocked but obedient, put two cold fingers deep in her bosom to extract a body-warm key.

"Such a gentleman."

She turned the key, opened the door, and locked it shut behind them. The couple was standing in some kind of tiny antechamber. In the pitch dark, Arnold could feel all four walls from where he stood. He heard Evelyn clicking around, trying to find another keyhole for her efforts. The lock bolts clicked and . . .

RAAAAAOWWWWRRR! Only a comic-book panel—with militant graphics—could suggest the explosion of sound that assaulted the young lovers. Evelyn was ready, and pre-tensed against it, but Arnold, though he had been warned, was triply unprepared—by the silence, by the close darkness, and by a premonition of mystery invariably linked with stillness. He had never, even in the worst rushes against him, felt so fiercely violated. And the sad graphic attempt above, with its concluding exclamation point, misses the effect entirely: there was no exclamation point. There was no end to the blast. It went on and on, like a hurricane wind, a garage band of the Mack Truck School of Music.

Evelyn pulled him into the room, and as the door swung shut behind them, he noted the foot of insulation behind the corrugated metal interior. No wonder it had been so quiet outside, and little wonder it was so noisy within.

Within a minute, Arnold was merely miserable, and no longer in extremis. But during that distracted minute, he was being introduced to his host, Keith Kenneth Klawans, who was guarding the door, as usual.

"What did you say?"

"I said his name is Arnold Hitler."

"Hitler?? Is that your name? Arnold Hitler? Hitler as in Hitler?"

"Yes."

"What?"

"I said yes."

"Let me see some ID."

Arnold was actually being carded! Keith studied the Harvard ID in the flickering of the UV strobe light, waving away the thick smoke, looking at the photo, looking at Arnold. Then suddenly he jumped up onstage and cut off the band. For the first time ever, Arnold's name had brought him relief from affliction.

"*Meine Damen und Herren,* gingers and blokes, our own Fishermistress Evelyn Brown has cast her wily line, and for once, God bless her, has come up with a fish and not a stone, a big one! Gimme a spot over here for our new guest—Mr.—would I lie to you?—Arnold Hitler, from Harvard University." Out of the darkness, a beam searched its way through the smoke until it located the stranger face in the room—a strong, handsome Aryan face. The crowd burst into raucous applause and joined in as the band struck up "Springtime for Hitler" to ever greater merriment—which segued—now mercifully for Arnold—right back into the indeterminate blasting of Oi! Embedded in the throbbing, embellished in feedback, he could barely make out the chorus of the current offering:

*BUT GATHERED TOGETHER TO GREET THE STORM
TOMORROW BELONGS TO ME!*

"Just a moment," yelled Keith. "I'll be right back. I've got to gather the troops for a little performance." His figure disappeared into the smoky crowd like some Kurosawa scene in hell.

"He likes you," Evelyn observed.

"Yes, but does he like *you?* There was a little bite in his announcement."

"He'll get over it. What do you think of our little clubhouse?"

Arnold looked around to see what he could see. Behind the band were two crossed flags—Confederate and Nazi—and on either side of them two large posters, each illuminated with a red, ceiling-hung spot, one of George Washington, the other of Adolf Hitler hovering over the words "NEXT TIME NO MORE MR. NICE GUY!" The metal walls were black, and in front of them, as if suspended in a stormy night sky, were flickering figures receding into mere shadow, burly men and muscular women gyrating, thrashing

Many bruisers, thought Arnold, bears of little brain—but also rats of little brain. And ratlets, long of tooth. His ears began to accommodate to the decibels, like pupils closing down. But what are the pupils of the ears?

The gray matter itself must shrink and blacken. Driving, thumping, screaming, banging, thundering explosion, pile-driving into the soul, ripe for a mad frenzy of violence. Music to riot by . . .

I STAND AND WATCH MY COUNTRY SINK
IT'S HORRIBLE TO WATCH IT DIE
FROM MONGRELS AND THE LEFT-WING STINK
WE ASK THE QUESTION, WHY? WHY? WHY?

. . . but bliss, it seemed to the dancers—mind and body merged with incessantly repeated music in some kind of intense search. Free your body/ free your mind, the utopian politics of Eros transmogrified into a bulldozer of cultural opposition, squalid yet impressive, rudimentary yet transcendent. One young man was holding his mightily erect penis as he led himself, in stunted innocence, inebriate, dancing solo through the room on his self-extruded leash. The breakthrough of untrammeled nature, the riot of reptilian brains, the liquidation of art.

THEY'LL PUT US DOWN, CONTROL OUR MINDS
BUT WE'LL FIGHT BACK, GET EM FROM BEHIND

Then—like the young woman optically illusioning herself into an old hag, Arnold's view flipped over. These were spirits programmed to the service of the irrational at ninety decibels. The schlong-dancer was the caption, and the rat brains reflexed in ecstasy. This was capitulation not to Bromio but to barbarism. Here were Freud's rebels, chafing against the father-figure society, seeking nevertheless to emulate it and enjoying the subordination they overtly detested. Pathological.

Arnold dizzied up and felt acutely sick.

"I've got to get out of here. . . ." He pushed Evelyn in front of him toward the door.

"But what about Keith? If we just disappear, he'll . . ."

" Please . . ."

They navigated through the sound lock, out into the yard, and drifted behind the building toward the cliff along the tracks.

"Phweeeew!" Arnold whistled into the cool night air.

And out in the cool night air, they found one Ken Death, one Nigger Thumper, and one Puke in tight discourse around the fate of a large toad that had emigrated from the railway bed into the BATyard.

"We can Bic the fucker," said Puke, pulling out his lighter. "He sure looks like some fat Jew. Look at that nose."

Arnold and Evelyn kept their distance.

"That ain't his nose, schmucko, that's his face. And his skull ain't shaped right." Thus Thumper the phrenologist.

"He won't catch, man. You need napalm." Puke advised.

"Let's just give him a flying lesson, like in Nam."

"You got your chopper?" Ken asked.

"Shit, man, we don't need no chopper," said Thumper. "Not with this mighty arm." He flexed his considerable biceps, then grabbed Mr. Toad away from Mr. Death, who tried unsuccessfully to keep it. With an upward whip, Thumper launched the animal directly overhead, at least five stories up. "Heads up!" he yelled as the animal fell back down just outside the circle and splattered on the weed-cracked pavement.

"Jeeeezuz!"

Ken wiped toad parts off his clothing.

"Used to play center field for Evander," Thumper announced

"You shouldn't have done that," Ken said and walked away past Arnold and Evelyn without acknowledging their presence. The others followed sheepishly, still awed by the whiff of violent death. They passed Keith, coming out quickly, anxious not to lose his guest, and also to know what ties Arnold had to Evelyn. They stood at her sides, dextra and sinister.

"A little much in there for me," Arnold said. "I needed to get outside."

"A little much outside, too," Evelyn muttered.

"The troops do get a bit boisterous," Keith observed.

"You lead a mighty army," Arnold said.

"Cannon fodder, like us all. My flag is that of Dürer, of the one image capable of containing our history. . . ."

"The Four Horsemen of the Apocalypse," Evelyn clarified.

"Isn't it wonderful, Arnold, to have a Smith College art historian among us, Phi Beta Kappa, summa cum laude?" Keith blew a kiss at Evelyn. "Look out there over the tracks. You can see the tyrant looming on the horizon, can't you? And listen—you can hear civilization whimpering in fear, four seals already opened."

"Come off it, Keith," Evelyn complained.

"And when the Lamb broke the seventh seal, there was silence in heaven for the space of half an hour."

"Precisely, Arnold. Just like now. Silence, moonlight, railroad tracks below and razor wire above. Wouldn't you say it was Hitler who set our century's tone, the model after which we must strive? Or are you a Stalin man, Hitler? By the way, are you related?"

"Not that I know of."

"A false cognate, as it were?"

"Yes."

"In any case, Hitler—Adolf Hitler—is not important in himself, but as a harbinger, a kind of rough draft of our grim and hysterical future."

"What *are* you talking about?" Evelyn asked. "Showing off for our Harvard friend?"

"I don't pander, Evelyn. I'm talking about the ultimate tyrant in the wings, the Übermensch who will succeed in unifying the world via science and technology, enslaving us all along the way. For you and me—Evelyn with the devil in her eyes and you Arnold so-called Hitler—for us, knowledge and assertion must lead to ruin."

"So why are you organizing these people?" Arnold asked.

"Who will fight the tyrants? You? With sweetness and light? Only tyrants can fight tyrants, Hitler. It is from them we must learn how to live, how to trace our way back past the Fall. Will we succeed? What do *you* think? But it's crucial to ensure the disappearance of our rivals, to begin by liquidating those who think according to my categories, those who have traveled the same roads. Were I to seize power, my first act would be to do away with all my friends. The Night of the Long Knives. Hitler was quite competent here, and Stalin no less. . . . ."

"Keith, what are you on?"

"Ooof! She's on to me. But it's true that as long as a conqueror succeeds, he can permit himself any atrocity. Public opinion will absolve him."

"Why do you suppose that is?" Arnold asked.

"People wake up only for the hot parts, Hitler—the horror chapters of history. During the sporadic ages of tolerance, they're somnolent and wilted. I, personally, harbor a weakness for tyrants because they don't take refuge in formulas, because their prestige is dubious and their longings self-destructive. A world without tyrants would be as boring as requited love. The one I await will be a connoisseur of extremity, for whom we shall all be carrion. Smell. Already, there's a new stink to the universe. Let's go in."

Arnold and Evelyn glanced at one another.

"I think we've had enough for tonight, Keith," Evelyn offered. "I just wanted you and Arnold to meet. We're going out to eat."

"Eat—and then what? Ooops! Nosy, nosy." He extended a limp, moist hand. "A pleasure, *mein Herr*," he said. "Come see us again right soon, y'all."

He walked back into the building, whistling, "Don't You Want Somebody to Love?"

Forty

"So where am I sleeping tonight?" Arnold was spooning up the Häagen-Dazs. "Mmmmmm. Swiss almond, mmm, mmm, mmm. You like Swiss almond?" He held out a spoonful. Evelyn pushed it aside and took her portion from his mouth with her tongue.

"Delicious. They don't eat Swiss almond in Switzerland. Like they don't eat French fries in France."

"How do *you* know?"

"How do I know? Seven years at L'École d'Humanité in the Bernese Oberland. Nine to sixteen. I roomed with a black woman from South Africa."

"What was it like?"

"Barn cleaning before breakfast, art classes every afternoon. Pretty rigorous academics in between. Got me into Smith at sixteen."

"No, I meant what was it like living with a South African?"

"I learned what it meant to be oppressed—as if I didn't know. Keith doesn't like my being involved in the antiapartheid struggle."

"Why L'École d'Humanité?"

"This is taking up snuggle time, so you only get the short version. We were in Israel. Dad was working for a company called IDS—Water Development."

"Sounds like CIA to me."

"Aren't you astute! Anyway, Mom met this handsome Israeli at an embassy party, and they both fit the battle of Jericho, and the walls came tumbling down. I was sent off to Schweiz. Mom sent a card from Jerusalem every Christmas, and Dad got posted to Guatemala. Voilà: my happy child- and young adulthood in fifteen seconds."

"My mom and dad are split, too. But the government doesn't have to worry about it."

"Count your blessings. You sleep here until we build your bunker."

"What do you mean?"

"I mean you can't live here, cause I need space to work in. You can be here when I'm not working, you can rub your magnificent bod up and down against mine—by invitation—but you've got to live somewhere else. Can you understand that?"

Arnold nodded. "But why a bunker?"

"A bunker is romantic. Hitler lived in a bunker, finally, at the end— he finally got to live in a bunker."

"But I'm not Hitler. I mean I am, but . . ."

"Arnold . . . don't you think it's funny, a really good gag, to live in a bunker if your name is Hitler? Don't you like to play?"

"Well—what kind of a bunker? Where?"

"Where? On Bruckner Boulevard, where else? Hitler's favorite composer. After Wagner." She was good.

"Where on Bruckner Boulevard? Isn't that where we were tonight?"

"Trust me. I'm smart. I'm funny. I've got a plan. I've got materials. A couple of blocks north of here—basically around the corner—there's an on-ramp to the expressway. There's your absolutely leak-proof, and probably bomb-proof, roof—the on-ramp. It sidles up on the east against the railroad fence. That means we've got to supply only the front and one triangular side for security, and that whole eastern-fence wall is left as a picture window onto the *schöne Natur* of the embankment. Trees and grass and rocks right out your bedroom window: it's more than I have."

"And what do we build these walls out of?"

"You're talking to one of New York City's great scroungers. There's a lot over on 151st Street with a whole bunch of concrete blocks left over from the hospital construction. They're waiting for a home. I have a buddy at Hub Cap City who gets me free wood whenever I need it—I don't ask where he gets it, but he gets it."

"What do you have to do for him?"

"My regular performance is good enough."

"What's that?"

"I'm saving that for when our relationship becomes boring."

"No, really."

"Well, I'm not into being a starving artist, so I have a job. I work four nights a week, and I make good money, and it's legal."

"And your mother would have a heart attack if she knew."

"Interesting question." Evelyn considered it for a moment. Then, "I'm working tomorrow. You can't come."

"Why not?"

"Only when I know you well enough."

It took them three and a half weeks and two trailer rentals to gather the materials. When all was ready, the structure went up quickly—fast enough to escape suspicion from any wayward Public Works official who might wonder what new structure had been authorized. Once there, it was just—there—as permanent and ahistorical as any other structure in a neglected, semiravaged neighborhood. And it was as solid and snug as the house of the third little pig.

When the final touches were in place, Arnold and Evelyn drove back to her studio, picked up her boom box, one special tape, and a bottle of cheap champagne—brut—with two long-stemmed glasses, and made their way down Garrison to Faile and under the Bruckner Expressway for Arnold's bunker-warming. A flock of pigeons exploded out of some parliament of fowls they had been holding among the girders. Arnold opened the steel door with his key and switched on the light plugged into a road lamp thirty feet above.

"Cozy," Evelyn cooed.

And indeed it was. The east triangular wall looked out through one-way mirror film (great find, that!) onto the relatively bucolic ravine. During the day, it would provide visual openness. At night, the mirror made the room seem twice as big. The other triangle, cement block, the front, and the ramp-ceiling were all painted white and hung with Evelyn's paintings and photos. The largest piece was a graveyard scene in early-morning light, with a child going out a lavish gate. Though Arnold related it to Nonno Jacobo, it was actually a rendering of the Remuh Cemetery in Krakow, where the young Isaac Deutscher ate a pork sausage on Yom Kippur while sitting on the tomb of the tzaddik Moses Ben Isserles, and having thus tremblingly defied Jehovah, emerged an atheist.

The mattress was six-inch foam on plywood and cinderblock, covered in ticking stripe ("à la Buchenwald," she joked) and further decked out in an Evelyn-original summer quilt called *Kitties and Bunnies See the World,* a tessellation of those innocent beings, whose eyes, however, showed tiny images of war and starvation. From a distance, it was beautiful. There was a bookshelf well stocked with Jabès and other Harvard favorites, a Coleman heater for winter, with two gas cans of fuel, an old but serviceable hot plate, and a chair overstuffed to bursting.

Evelyn set down her boom box and pulled the two glasses from her purse.

"Champagne, *monsieur?*"

"*Mais certainement, mademoiselle.*"

He undid the foil and popped the cork without spilling a drop. Evelyn filled the glasses. They lay in bed together and drank.

"To the bestest bunker," she said.

"To the bestest bunkerette," he countered.

"*C'est moi?*"

"*C'est toi, ma chère.*"

"But I still might 'vant to be alone.' "

"I'll wait patiently for your return."

The glasses clinked. It was a deal.

They drank half the bottle and Evelyn, slightly tipsy, reached over and fumbled with the boom box.

"Whatcha got for music?" he asked.

"Bruckner, what else?"

"Ah."

She switched out the light. There was only the ghostly glow of distant streetlamps through the mirror film. Arnold crawled in under the quilt.

"I brought you the slow movement from the Seventh Symphony." At this point in the evening, she was somewhat slow herself. "Here."

She pushed "play," and the small room was filled with the rich sounds of low strings and horns in C-sharp minor, a long, sinuous phrase culminating in surprisingly masculine chords and lapsing back into a gentle feminine ending, serene, consolatory, moving.

"Nice," he said. "I've never heard Bruckner."

"You told me that. I thought this would be a good place to start."

"Beautiful, but *so* sad," he said as the melodies spun out of the original germ.

They lay there silent, sipping from their glasses as the harmonies and textures grew ever richer and the keys slipped by until one amazing moment when the music, with a thrilling shock, slipped and fell a half step to climax streaming out on C major, filling the dark room with light.

"Jeezuz!" Arnold muttered, and Evelyn gave him a squeeze.

The music quieted, and the movement ended with a transfigured major version of the opening funeral music, a majestic threnody framed by the sound of the Wagner tubas. They were silent for a long time after it finished.

"The Nazis dug him, too," Evelyn finally said. "His monumental scale, grandiose, lavish, spiritual . . . They'd play him in *Dunkelkonzerte*—lights all out, sacred space. Nazis listening to Bruckner was like going to church."

She snuggled in under the quilt.

"His most famous piece," she murmured. "They played it on German radio after Hitler died, after he was burned to a crisp. Hey, you awake?"

She nudged him. No answer. She pulled off her clothes and laid her body against his as kitties and bunnies and the Committee to Reelect the President watched the night.

Forty-one

"OK. It's time for you to watch me make money."

"What did I do to deserve this?"

"It's what you haven't done."

"What's that?"

"Give me a hard time about Nazism. Like Keith."

"That's because you're not a Nazi."

"That's what he said." Suddenly she was angry. "Why can't either of you get it that I *am* a Nazi? What do you think I'm doing, playing tourist peekaboo? What do you think a Nazi is, Mr. Hitler? Some thick-necked brute, tattooed with death's-heads, intent on butchering Jewish flesh? You're so worked up about how people treat you because of your name. Well, you're being just as stupid. What's a Nazi that I'm not?"

"A follower of Hitler—*Adolf* Hitler—and his doctrines."

"And what's 'a follower'? And do followers have to adhere to *all* his doctrines, all 613 *Kommandments*? I remind you about the SS squad confiscating Jewish goods: eight blond beasts, in Munich, 1940, slowly lowering a Steinway grand through the French windows of a luxurious upper-floor apartment. And when it touched the street, one of them sits down and plays the entire Waldstein sonata from memory while the others crouch around in Beethovenian ecstasy. What's wrong with this picture? I mean what's wrong with your picture of Nazis? *That's* the kind of Nazi I am—existentially ecstatic, committed, out on the edge, sensually over the line, exploring the socially unacceptable, you fucking sissy dupe! Now get on your tightest jockstrap, jock-o, cause we're going up to Pinky's Palace, and you're going to watch me bump and grind for a gross of salivating anti-Nazis."

"You're a . . ."

"Stripper. That's where your Bruckner champagne came from. A gift from Pinky himself. Now, now, now, what you did to deserve this was to be nonjudgmental. Don't change my mind." She grabbed a volume from the bunker bookshelf. "And I'm going to take this for a prop, OK?"

She grabbed a volume from the bunker bookshelf. This, Arnold thought, will be the only strip act in history utilizing Jabès's *Book of Questions.*

> *In the unfolded wings of silence, unexplored worlds spread their solitude.*

They rode Snakey the Black up to Tremont Avenue, her top up, her heater on in the chilly September drizzle. "PINKY'S PALACE" flashed in appropriately colored neon, and over the arched doorway, a tattered oilcloth sign: "With the NEW Live and Kickin' Sports Saloon Downstairs!"

"Now, this is a titty bar," she warned him, "but with standards. No lewd behavior, no drugs, and no excessive alcohol. And if you don't believe it, Clarence will convince you otherwise."

"Who's Clarence?"

"Clarence is six foot five, 350 pounds."

"The bouncer."

"I don't know if you'd bounce. It might be more like the toad."

She led Arnold through the door, and past an art-deco bar from the '40s. At one end of a table-filled room was a small stage, currently empty.

"That's where the strippers work."

"I thought *you* were a stripper."

"I'm talking about the stripper-strippers, which I used to be. But I've graduated to downstairs. Hey, Clarence, I want you to meet my boyfriend, Arnold."

Clarence lumbered over, as forbidding as she had described. But sweet, sweet.

"Hey, man. You some lucky dude with a honey like that!"

Arnold shook hands and nodded his agreement.

"I'm gonna take him downstairs and show him the ropes."

"Have a good time, man. You a lucky dude."

They proceeded down a heavily carpeted stairway to a leather-padded door.

"You are now about to see a magic transformation from Plain Jane Evelyn Brown, Poor Starving Artist with Sensible Shoes, to . . ." She pushed open the door and pulled him along with her to the other side. "Bodacious Brunhilde, Queen of the Night. Ta-daaaaa!"

"You look the same to me."

"You ain't seen nothin yet, bub."

The room was platformed on three sides, and at the center was a three-quarter-size boxing ring, covered with rimmed plastic sheeting but very official looking, with thick ropes and padded corners. Behind the ring, on the untiered side, was a DJ booth, and next to it a bar, the wall behind them festooned with red-white-and-blue bunting. "Live and Kickin' Sports Saloon" read the banner. The first row, ringside, the "VIP section," consisted of couches behind tables, while the two upper tiers sported leather chairs only.

"This here's my stomping ground."

"Very nice. Will I have to call for an ambulance?"

"Are you kidding? More likely a tranquilizer to stop laughing."

"And you get a good salary for this?"

"No salary. Two-thirds of the take. A third to the house."

"What's the take?"

"From the auction and kissing. Two shows come in at about a hundred fifty each—my take—and another fifty or sixty for kissing. That's about four hundred bucks a night—three nights a week. Good enough pay for a starving artist?"

"You have to *kiss* them?"

"The guy holds up a buck, sometimes a fiver, and you come by, grab it, grab the man's hands, then you kiss him. On the cheek, on the head, on the shoulder, hell, you can kiss the air near him. Then you move on; they don't care. They were part of the action, cheap."

"I couldn't do it."

"You could if you weren't such a fuddy-duddy prig. In fact, you'd be great. In fact, let's talk to Pinky about a woman's night—all roles reversed. It'd be the revolution. . . ."

It was only 6:45 when a tall, thin man with a pock-ravaged face sat down in a back row.

"I thought you said they didn't start coming till 7," Arnold whispered.

"Oh, that's only Paul the Zombie. He comes every night, doesn't want to be kissed, and never bids on anyone. But he buys his weight in liquor, and he holds it well, so they let him keep coming back just to stare. I just ignore him. Hang in there, bub. You look a little green about the gills. You'll love it, I promise. I'm gonna go get ready."

The bell rang. Round zero.

"Lady and gentlemen!" Much laughter as the spot fell on the lone, lost woman in the crowd. "Welcome to Pinky's Palace's world-famous Live and Kickin' Sports Saloon! As usual, we have seven gorgeous gals waiting to take you on—even you," pointing at the woman. "The top bid wins the chance to get in the ring for three rounds of body-slappin, hair-grabbin, down-and-dirty action. You get your choice of Heavenly Helen, Bodacious Brunhilde, Titillating Tiffany, Naughty Nicole, Rockin Rebecca, Ballistic Bambi, or Badass Barbie." Claques in the crowd cheered for their favorites. "As I speak the room is filling up for this pulse-poppin panorama of plenary pleiadic pulchritude."

The MC wore Pinky's Palace pink shorts with a formal set of tails, a top hat, and high-top purple sneakers.

"Take your seats, gentlemen, and hold on to your—no, not that!— hold on to your hats, for here they come now, Pinky's Palace's Seven Sisters. . . ."

"A Pretty Girl Is Like A Melody," classically corny, poured from the DJ's old seventy-eight as the seven women, each dressed in her "fantasy" outfit, paraded in and around the audience, stroking the heads and pinching the cheeks of the regulars. The MC made a small cadenza out of each of their names, calling forth more applause to accompany them to their destination behind the ring, between "bandstand" and bar.

Heavenly Helen was first to perform, not as the face that launched a thousand ships but as her "fantasy" character, Nurse Ratched. Wearing a costume somewhere between a bodice-ripper night nurse's and a Marat/Sade nun's, with wimple awry and handcuffs dangling at her waist, she lip-synched an oddly mirrored version of Gershwin's "Crazy for You," sauntering lasciviously and playing simultaneously both patient and attendant. Her "craziness" consisted in needing to struggle out of various pieces of clothing as though she were a mad Houdini doing a straitjacket escape.

> *And so, though love may not inspire my lingo*
> *Still it's making my heart go bango-bingo*

was occasion enough for an open-bloused demonstration of her point of maximum impulse. She brought $240 on the auction block.

Bodacious Brunhilde was next—now decked out as Luscious Leonore—blond as ever, but in a hippie wig of waist-long straight blond hair, an embroidered vest over a bare bosom, and an Indian-print skirt, down to her bare feet. Arnold's heart went bango-bingo when he saw her in the follow spot. She paraded in silence, nymph-like, along the VIP tables, like Hamlet reading upon his book, in this case Arnold's well-worn copy of *The Book of Questions*. *"A mob crowded around,"* she read, *"eager to keep up an illusion of being alive . . . "* and her music entered, sforzando, at the top of the DJ's electronic lungs, Barry McGuire's 1965 recording of "The Eve of Destruction." Arnold may have been the only person in the room to appreciate the wordplay on her real name.

The image was doubly complex because, unlike any of her sisters, she had chosen to lip-synch a male voice, and thus the room was confronted with the most sensuously girlish of figures putting out a sound with a two-day growth of beard. And this with rings on her toes! Had the woman captured the man? Had the man captured the woman? What was one to make of this doppelgängerisch portrayal? She sat down in a half-lotus, hiking her skirt to midthigh to accommodate it. She placed her hands in the *dhenu mudra* of invocation.

Then she sang softly of the eastern world—the eastern world *exploding*, of violence, of bullets, and bodies floating in the Jordan.

Given all this, were we not, she demanded in that bearded voice, on the eve of destruction?

She sang of integration and *dis*integration, of political corruption, of
the world stock of hate, of hate, of hate, of hate in Selma, Alabama . . .

And here she stood quickly up, ripped off her skirt, and flung it an-
grily in the face of a VIP at her feet. She stood there in her half-open vest
and bikini panties, her blond pubis bulging in its V. And then she began
to sing—not only to lip-synch but to add her voice to Barry McGuire's,
embellishing selected words in melismatic counterpoint: hate, Selma,
poundin, disgrace . . . After all this, all this, over and over and over again,
did they *still* not believe we were on the eve of destruction?

She tossed the *Book of Questions* to Arnold, and with her hands empty
now clutched her hair. Then, Godiva-like, she opened her vest in such a
way that the silken fall both covered and revealed her voluptuousness,
pressing out against her leanness, informed more, Arnold thought, by
love than by sex, her breasts. Ah, no, she sang,

you don't believe we're on the eve of destruction.

The crowd went wild. Evelyn stood there throughout the auction, her
eyes closed, her vest coming off her shoulders, her hands cupping her
hair against her breasts, a most tragic and affecting figure. She garnered
the high bid of the evening.

After the auction, the fantasy women returned to the dressing room to
assume their standard formats, while the audience pixillated itself for
battle. Managers and opponents had been chosen, and Evelyn had drawn
the first go-round.

When she reappeared, it was as Bodacious Brunhilde again, in a black
bodysuit with Pinky's pink leotard worn over it. On her armband, a German eagle clutching a generalized runic symbol—no swastikas allowed.

Her natural braids hung from under a horned helmet. A walking, stalking mixed metaphor, entering the ring, stately, oddly, to strains from *Tannhäuser*. Her opponent marched in after her, in Pinky shorts and fighter's robe, to the Grand March from *Aïda*, gesturing stereotypically, pumping his hands clasped above his head, already victorious, even if already the loser.

First act: soap-down. The MC placed a small stand on the large table, front and center at the ring. On the former, he placed a classically ornate lathering machine, liberated from some turn-of-the-century barber shop now out of work. Evelyn's manager labored at covering his charge with warm shaving cream—up to midthigh. She did her own chest. Opponents had the choice of lathering themselves or not. Mostly they chose not.

To counter her increasingly cream-puffy image, Evelyn taunted her guy in her best Cherman accent. "I vould get some kream if I vas you. You could get geskveezed to death. You know how much I hurt you, *Dummkopf?* Tink you are some big man, not true? *Aber ich bin schwartzbelt. Und du bist übergefuckt!*"

All he could say was, "Yeah, yeah."

When they were ready, the MC grabbed the mike.

"Ladies and gentleman! In this corner, weighing in at one-oh-five, representing Pinky's Pulchritudinous Pugilists, our Aryan Queen, our visiting co-ed from Heidelberg, Germany, the incomparable blond bombshell, Bodacious Brunhilde!"

"Hojotoho! Heiaha!" she sang out, straight from *Die Walküre*.

"And in this corner, weighing in at two-fourteen, from Webster Avenue, Mr. Joe Blow! Joe Blow? Don't sound like a real name to me. But then again, if you had challenged Bodacious Brunhilde to a do-or-die, you wouldn't want to use your real name either. But Joe Blow?"

The audience guffawed, and the combatants were gestured to the center of the ring.

"Down on your knees, boy! Hands behind your back! Good boy. OK. You both know the rules. You stay on your knees, she gets to do what she wants." Booing from the crowd. "Hey, look at the poor little thing. She's half his weight. Eddie the Ref here will be watching closely. We'll go three three-minute rounds, and may the best man win!"

"You mean beste voman!" Evelyn yelled threateningly. More booing.

The ref rang the bell, and Evelyn attacked like lightning, giving her Valkyrie cry and flipping in the air to land right in front of her Joe. "Ich vill kick your ass," she yelled, ran behind the kneeling victim, and butt-pushed him sprawling to the mat. He whipped around and grabbed her ankle, pulling her down on top of his back, as the shaving cream now took over. "Take it easy, babe," she whispered. "Be a good boy."

While they were squiggling around on the plastic, the MC moved constantly around the audience like an orangutan, swinging one-armed from pipes hanging from the ceiling and landing on various table tops. He kicked a beer into the lap of some poor Fordham college zhlub and yelled to his buddies, "Yo! Get this guy another Schlitz!"

The crowd was going wild with laughter, the DJ upped the volume of the "William Tell Overture"—and the bell rang. End of round one.

Rounds two and three were more of the same: exaggerated headlocks and slippery half-nelsons, fierce female charges and devious male defense, all driven by ever more crowd noise and ever louder music—the Khatchaturian Sabre Dance and, lastly, the final madness of Beethoven's Ninth. What else could they use? Joe Blow was the unexpected winner. "No fucking vay!" screamed Evelyn, which earned her a peremptory escort out to the dressing room to clean up her act.

Arnold needed a break.

He walked up and down Tremont Avenue for forty minutes and was back in time to catch the last act of the first half: Naughty Nicole sliding herself in and out of the lubricated clutches of one John Doe, the ultimate winner. There was a break for refreshments, and then,

"Lady and gentlemen—or rather, gentlemen—our lady seems to have left. The moment many of you have been waiting for, those not brave enough to get in the ring, or those too cheap to lather the girls up. It's Kissing for Tipping time at Pinky's world-famous sports palace. Get a kiss for a buck—what a bargain!"

Out came Bodacious Brunhilde, Rockin Rebecca, Titillating Tiffany, and Naughty Nicole, the losers from the first half, back in their fantasy costumes, parading slowly around the tables in the room.

"Get those dollars out, men," the MC barked, "and get them high in the air so the ladies can see. They're not gonna stop if you ain't got a buck! You want extra attention? Forget the ones, get out your fives and tens. Hey, who knows what they'll give ya for a twenty." The DJ put on "As Time Goes By" to try to move the ambiance into something less frantic, more slinky. The fundamental things applied: the money waved, the kisses titillated, the music upped the ante with "Ba-, Ba-, Baccia Me, Bambino."

Arnold was busy comparing the girls' techniques when he heard a stifled cry from Evelyn, an inbreath of shock and dismay. He spun around to see his beloved on a table to the right, frozen at the sight of Ken Death and Nigger Thumper offering up their cash. He hadn't spotted them earlier.

"They said they came to see me naked and they were bummed," she told him in the dressing room while washing up. "And I found this in my collection plate." She handed Arnold a fiver, to which was clipped an ace of spades. On the bill was written, "TELL PRETTY BOY HITLER TO BEWARE."

"What's with the ace of spades?" Arnold asked.

"It's one of their Vietnam things. They used to pin them to dead VC to scare the shit out of the villagers."

"So who's the death card for—you or me?"

"No doubt just a gesture. Those guys have a submediocre flair for the dramatic. Keith is probably upset at our seeing one another. I'm sure he sent them. He's the only one that knows."

"Were you and he . . . ?"

"Yeah, for a while. But he's not it—not the way you might be."

"It what?"

"My perfect match."

"So he's jealous?"

"He's too snooty to be jealous—and he'd never admit it if he were. Probably more jealous of your name. And I'm too high-maintenance for him. But it's true—you wouldn't want to get on his bad side. Just let me handle it."

Forty-two

"Sal, leeetle Sal, Surrogate Sal, the Salt of the Earth."

Arnold lay on his bunker bed and lifted the small white cat onto his chest. Evelyn had assured him that Sal had a secret forehead gland to mark her territory, and sure enough, she inched her head forward to claim the bottom of Arnold's chin as her own.

Sal had been a gift from Evelyn to Arnold—to snuggle with him while she worked. To catch rats should they appear. Surrogate Sal, Evelyn's pal, whose real name was *Schiksal,* Evelyn's pun on goyish women and universal fate.

Arnold lay for a long while with eyes closed, corpse pose, kitty on chest, listening to autumnal rain beating in fierce waves against the mirror film. He laid his right hand at the back of Sal's neck and felt around front with his thumb for her almost silent purr. The slight vibration passed down thumb, up arm, and directly to his own purring center at the fifth chakra. He breathed with the cat, three of her breaths to his one, a slow, loving, intraspecies waltz.

Suddenly a fierce crackling shattered the night—the room light went out—and the darkness was attacked with a brutal explosion of thunder. Sal spun her frightened head around and sank her teeth into Arnold's lightly caressing hand, adding the insult of puncture to the injury of burn. Then she scampered for the floor, tiny, fluffy, feral.

The room was dark; the street and track lamps that normally cut through the mirror film were out as well. A transformer must be down. Sal shifted herself among the protective books. The rain lashed in waves. It could have been the beginning of the forty nights and days.

It was ridiculous, of course, but Arnold could already feel the microbes celebrating deep in the puncture wounds. Life forms of stature, ancient carousers, checking out the new digs. He knew he should express some blood, wash the wounds, but in his largeness, he felt silly worrying about four tiny punctures from a frightened, loving cat.

Something more, though: some planetary view from cosmic distance, looking down—scientifically—at himself and the likes of himself, all part of some larger infestation soon to be swept away. He was pinned to the bed by the rain and the lightning and the thunder outside, by the manifest ferocity of nature—including his own—misanthropic, vast, self-devouringly bleak. He could not move because there was no place to move to, there was no "out" from the martinet spacetime that contained him. He felt a structural part of an immense web of cruelty that defined and enclosed all being, dividing super- and sub-human. He normally imagined himself "a nice guy," "a sweet man." Yet now the Lear-like storm, the flash, the noise, the bite, the darkness had driven him forth into some no man's land between realities, most corrosive of character. Bleakness and bacteria out there, the wasteland of the city, the progress of decay, a mange of rust and crumbling concrete, the threat of walls and fences built to protect. He felt age-old, ancient as the *Pasteurella* lustfully dividing in the web of his right hand. *Komm, süßer Tod,* Brother Death.

Corpse pose, long breathing, hand tingling. But it wasn't Death that came. It was Raskolnikov, Brother Bright-Eyes whispering: " An hour before his death, a man condemned thinks that if he had to live on a high rock, if he had to remain standing on a square yard of space all his life, a thousand years, eternity, it were better to live so than to die at once."

There was a knock at the door. Tentative, questioning at first, then loud like thunder. Louder than Evelyn would knock. Sal hissed and fled from the bookshelf to behind the laundry bag. Arnold decided to play dead. There was another flash, and a clap of thunder.

"Open up, Herr Hitler. I know you're in there."

It was Keith and his British accent. Arnold went to the door, took a deep breath, and opened it as sky tymps rolled on.

"What have I done to deserve this?"

"What? The visit? Or the thunder?"

"Either or both."

"How about some light?" Keith lit a match. Arnold leaned back from the fire directly under his nose.

"You going to stand here lighting matches?"

"Better to light one candle than curse the darkness," Keith said as he pulled the small glass of a Yahrzeit candle from his Burberry, lit the wick, and handed it to Arnold. "Clever, these Jews."

Arnold inspected the small glass in his hand, now lighting the whole room.

"What does it say here, this Jewish writing"

"*N'er Adonai nish mat adam.* Proverbs 20:27: 'The spirit of man is the lamp of the Lord.'"

"You read Hebrew?"

"Middle Eastern Studies, Magdalen College. Know thine enemy."

"Why enemy?"

"I thought you were a genius Harvard student."

"What's the real reason, Keith? Is it Evelyn?"

Keith invited himself into the room and began a casual candlelight exploration.

"For one thing," he said, examining with candle a nude of Evelyn he himself had photographed, "there's the arrogance of thinking you people have to be a light unto God—not to mention the nations. But don't get me wrong. I have nothing against individual Jews. I kind of like them. Or why would I live in New York, the Jewish capital of the world? It's paradise for an antisemite. One of the great merits of New York is that it leads me to a deeper knowledge of my Aryan self and warns me continually against any tendencies I have to be Jewish."

"You?" Arnold sat down on the bed. Keith continued his art tour.

"Of course me—and you, too, our fair demoiselle tells me. Jewish grandpa? No wonder you're thinking of returning home."

"She told you that?"

"Jewish is a tendency of the mind, Arnold, a psychological set possible for anyone, you especially, but actualized most conspicuously in actual Jews. Not the rabbis, mind you; I have nothing but respect for the rabbis, hats off to the rabbis—or hats on—whatever you do. Disliking Jews doesn't stop you from liking them. I like *you*, for instance."

"What tendency of the mind?"

"Ah, there's the beauty of the Jew for the anti-Semite. One can invent any kind of Jew for oneself in order to hate him. Selfish? Communist? Too godly? Too worldly? Too rational? Too mystical? Asexual? Too sexual? Take your pick. Then study those qualities, and nourish the hatred."

His colorless eyes gleamed candle flame as he turned to Arnold. The sky lit up outside and performed yet another thunderclap, and Sal hissed back.

"Ah. I almost forgot why I came. Thor is angry with you. Can you tell?"

"I thought it was atmospheric electrostatics."

"That's what you all say, you Jewish science Jews, analyzing and de-composing reality instead of trying to understand and respect it. If you'd look up from your talmudic journals, you'd notice the drawing down of Thor's angry brows in the black clouds, you'd see the fiery hammer flung from his hand, you'd hear the peal of his chariot over the skyscrapers. You think this stuff is mere electricity? You think that cat is scared of—electricity?"

"Why do you think I'm Jewish?"

"Your girlfriend has been explicating. You know, you don't look Jew-ish, you're not the type—submissive, your eyes like ponds dark with the sadness of many thousand years. It ain't you, babe. But I know what you've got in your pants."

"What do you mean?"

Keith took his candle on an Evelyn tour.

"This is one sexy broad, wouldn't you say?"

"She's very beautiful."

"Kind of makes your penis stand on end, wouldn't you say?"

Arnold couldn't get into the locker-room banter.

"I hesitate to get into compare and contrast," Keith continued, "but Thor finds the thought of a circumcised dick following hard upon mine to be a wee bit annoying. Hence this storm. And the blackout."

"How do you know we . . . ?"

"The irresistible erotic attraction of the Jewish *glans penis*. The pre-puce cut away to eliminate all female semblance: for the prepuce *is* fe-male, the vagina in which the male lies happily buried. But not so for Jews: they must cut away the prepuce, and take from the male his female component. Typical stupid, self-destructive arrogance. With circumci-sion, you renounce your divine semblance, and the Jew becomes mere man, poor thing."

"You're crazy, Keith. They do this at the hospital. All baby boys get cut. It's cleaner."

"Yes. There is a simple solution to all problems. And it is always wrong."

"In any case, I'm not Jewish—yet—regardless of what, as you say, is in my pants."

"OK. Cut the penis stuff, so to speak. Let's get down to brass tacks. Evelyn has been detailing your neuroses around Judaism. Thor is here to help you find your inner Hitler."

Arnold found it hard to believe Evelyn would share their intimate talks with this maniac.

"May I sit down?" Keith plopped down in the reading chair and placed the candle on its arm. "Simply put, I want to save your soul, Hitler. Don't laugh."

"I'm not laughing."

"You ready to listen to me?" Keith took his silence for an answer. "The arrogance of feeling 'Chosen,' the arrogance of proposing oneself as a light to God, the arrogance of Jewish analysis and science, the arrogance of discarding bisexuality. Where do you think these things originate? All from one thing—the Jew, with his distant, frightful God, with his obedience to the Law, the Jew knows nothing of the divine. The God in-man is the human soul. Your soul, Arnold. Listen up, this is important."

"I'm listening."

"Do you think it's accidental that there's no doctrine of immortality in the Hebrew Bible? A people without a soul have no craving for immortality. They refuse to see all the secret and spiritual meaning of things. There is no reverence, only fear. Without simplicity of faith, there remains only talmudic nitpicking. Thus the internal multiplicity of the Jew, and the internal simplicity of the Aryan. Aren't you seeking that basic core, Arnold? Don't you want to know who you really are? Among the ancient Egyptians each person had a 'little' name known to all, and a 'great' name that was kept hidden. According to the funerary literature, the greatest risk to the soul after death was forgetting one's great name. Your great name is Hitler. Hitler is the keeper of your soul."

"Hitler is just a word, an arbitrary signifier."

"And lightning and thunder are just atmospheric electrostatics. You have a *soul*, Arnold. You have a soul to give to others. Evelyn is no pushover: it's your soul—and your name—that attracts her. You may have come from Jewish stock. I've heard about Nonno Jacobo. But remember that out of old Israel there emerged the highest possibility of mankind, the possibility of Christ. The other possibility was the Jew. Nothing is easier than to be Jewish, with a severe, demanding, wrathful, and greedy God of shalts and shalt-nots. And nothing is more difficult than to be Christian with its commanding dimension of love. Judaism is the abyss over which Christianity is erected, and for that reason an Aryan dreads nothing so much as the Jew within. Christ was a Jew precisely that He might overcome the Judaism within Him, for he who triumphs over the deepest doubt reaches the highest faith. Christ was the greatest man because He conquered the greatest enemy."

Sal jumped up on the chair and began to knead Keith's thigh. He placed her gently back on the floor.

"Are you listening to me? What do I have to say to get your attention, to get your Hitler attention? I love you, Arnold. I want to save you from your most dangerous tendencies. I love you."

He reached out, and put his hand on Arnold's knee. Arnold did not remove it.

"You know what Freud thought about anti-Semitism?" Arnold asked.

Keith dismissed it. "Another Jewish opinion."

"He thought that anti-Semits always exhibit exactly those Jewish characteristics they most despise. Displacement, he called it. Whoever

detests the Jewish disposition detests it first in himself; then he perse-
cutes others to separate himself from his own Jewishness."

"I know my ancestry back to 1066."

"And before 1066?" Arnold continued quietly. "Are you sure there's
no Jewish blood in those Aryan veins?"

"And Phrygian blood. And Hittite or Babylonian or Assyrian or Hellenic or Indus or Phoenician or Carthaginian. You think only Jewish ancestry is important?"

Arnold was strangely calm. The toothmarks in his hand were starting
to burn.

"How about a little thought experiment?" he asked. "If, as you say,
Jewish is really only a tendency of the mind, can you imagine some kind
of psychic duality, Jewish and non-Jewish, that would be common to *all*
individuals—in the same way as bisexuality?"

Keith looked him deeply in the eyes and moved his hand up Arnold's
thigh.

"In life we have to decide between being male or female. We have to
take a stand. Worth or unworthiness, negation or godliness. We can decide to give up our Judaism—that is the meaning of Judaism: the possibility of becoming un-Jewed, the possibility of begetting Christs." Keith
was no longer calm. "Arnold Hitler Hitler Hitler Hitler. Why were you
given this oracular, guardian name?"

"Keith, your war is not against Jews, or Jewish ideology, or a Jewish
political system. It's against yourself. That's what . . ."

"Well, fuck you, too! Bloody fuck you!"

He jumped up. Arnold followed.

"I could have you killed. My boys would like nothing better. A little
auto-da-fé in a cozy bunker? A tribute to der Führer?"

Sal hissed; Arnold's face was as a crucifixion to behold. His burning
right hand shot out, and Keith dropped to the floor, his forehead spurt-
ing blood. The door flung open.

Is this not the day when suffering took the form of a fist? The fist is no menace: it is stopped by a wall. But without a doubt, the groan is its parent.

"Out! Out!" a breathless Evelyn yelled. "Out of my house! This is my house, our house. You are not invited!" She ran over to Keith and pulled him off the floor. "I won't have you here. He's none of your business."

Arnold was astounded to see her push Keith out into the darkness and slam the door behind him.

A distant rumble of thunder, and the light came on—unpleasantly. Arnold turned it off and drew Evelyn down on the bed beside him. They lay quietly in the dim warmth of the Jahrzeit candle, looking out at the lights across the tracks. His right hand was beginning to swell.

"I'm tired of my name," he whispered.

She lay quietly, her head nuzzled in his neck, her hand stroking his chest.

After the talk with Keith, his name sounded different, encircled with echoes traveling backward—and coming from—beyond his years. He tried to imagine his way back through repetitions increasingly faint, but his memories were no longer solid, describable in a settled past tense. He could still think "I," but what was the source and shaper of that "I" if memory no longer sufficed?

"Ah, I'm tired of my name," he sighed.

She answered, "Maybe I am, too. . . ." and kissed him gently on the lips.

Forty-three

When Luscious Leonore, the Girl Who Says Yes to Guys Who Say No, next danced at Pinky's, she read the following text from Edmond Jabès's *Book of Questions:*

When the yellow star was shining in the sky of the accursed, he wore the sky on his chest. The sky of youth with its wasp's sting, and the sky with the armband of mourning.

She signaled the DJ to hit "play." Instead of Barry McGuire, there sounded out the selection she had given him.

And then one night, just before day; and then one day, and then one night, and then nights, and days that were also nights . . .

The Adagio from the Bruckner Seventh, ceremonial and slow, majestic.

*... the tête-à- tête with death, the tête-à- tête with the dawn
and dusk of death, the tête-à- tête with himself, with no one.*

She removed her wig to reveal a newly shaven head and stood quietly until the music began its harmonic ascent. Then her vest slipped off, her breasts now bare and full, her nipples erect from inner agitation. Modulations of the great "Te Deum"'s end: *Non confundar*—O Lord, in Thee have I hoped: let me never be confounded.

Her wraparound was loosened, inched slowly, then fell to the tabletop in the midst of grieving sound. No bikini now, but a shaven pubis, innocent as an eight-year-old's. Evelyn Brown stood there, surrounded by heavenly sound, stark naked, hairless and still, book in hand. When the movement closed, she flung the volume out into the transfixed crowd. There were no more Questions.

Forty-four

Sal's bite required hospitalization for IV ampicillin. As Arnold lay in bed, his hand pulsing with the pulse of his heart, he felt again its contact with Keith's skull, a fleeting union of bone with bone through the merest of skin. He had never struck out like that before. It seemed—in his fever—perilously close to an embrace, and the burning in his hand to rise not so much from the *Pasteurella* within as from his hand's own heart, the pain of some illicit, unrequited love. His knee . . . his hand . . . contact. . . .

. . . unrequited . . . By Billie Jo, by Ariel, by all the Cliffies who found him too . . . or his name . . . abandoned, always abandoned . . . even by Judy. By Nonno.

But now: "He's none of your business." She was making a claim, he thought, a claim, guarding him as her own. Protective mother. Loving sister. Jealous lover. He felt surrounded by her, no longer simply by her side, *his* bald beauty, his, surrounded.

"He's none of your business." How many ways that exclamation cut. "Hitler" no longer relevant, perhaps—to Keith, or to this new Evelyn, shorn of hair above and (so she hinted) below. Less relevant to *him*, perhaps . . . his father's name . . .

In the month after his discharge, Arnold relished a continued change in the intensity of Evelyn's attentions, ever more present, more loving, more serious. She brought him gifts: the second volume of *The Book of Questions*, newly appeared; a cassette of the *Siegfried Idyll*, Wagner's tender birthday present to Cosima.

"So how come not on my birthday?"

"I wanted to give it to you sooner."

She took him out to dinners—from Saito to T.G.I. Friday's to White Castle Hamburgers. But the best gift of all was that she stayed with him every night, either at his place or hers. No more "I have work to do," no more "I'd like to be alone."

She did have work to do, though. Her painting had never been more intense. Night scenes with stars, which grew from painting to painting as if the universe were pregnant with supernovae. And it was. Like solar flares, edges and corners appeared to angulate each stellar circumference—hexagrammic eruptions, with colossal extrusions from each vertex. Exploding stars took over starry skies, vortices from vertices, leaving Van Gogh's far behind. *David's Birth*, she called the series, and it took Arnold longer than it should have to realize that these celestial eruptions were multiple fetuses of Mogen David—his star and shield, the Jewish star.

In each dark landscape, under whirls of light, there walked, or stood, or sat, a tiny figure, his yellow pants reflecting the celestial luminescence. Reflecting, was it, or providing?—for in every case, the intensity of the pant legs was a tad greater than that of the most intense yellow above. No matter. Reflecting or providing, he was always that yang dot of brightness in the yin darkness of the earth.

Sometimes they would darken the studio and view the paintings under black light in eerie UV glow. The yellow pants grew more intense. "I use a special chrome yellow for them," she explained. "Cadmium yellows for the rest."

"So who is that little fellow anyway?" Arnold asked. "David?"

She laughed. "No, not David. Just some old guy I met on Washington Square."

"An old man in yellow pants, sitting in Washington Square?"

She nodded.

"When? When did you meet him?"

"I don't know. A few weeks ago."

"And?"

"Don't worry. I'm not about to coffin-snatch."

"So?"

"So nothing. We meet every once in a while and talk."

"About what?"

"This and that. He's telling me about Jewishness, among other things."

"Why?"

"I asked him."

"How come?"

"I suppose because he looked Jewish, sounded Jewish. I've had enough of the bullies for a while; I need to grok the bullied."

"Why? Why would anyone want to be bullied?"

"I don't want to be bullied. I want to know what it's *like* to be bullied."

They lay together on the studio couch, gazing through the psychedelic walls. The radiator clanked its probable music of the spheres.

"What's his name?"

"Who?"

"The man in the yellow pants."

"I don't know. He never told me."

"Can you introduce me?"

"No."

"Why not?"

"First, because you don't need to be in on everything I do, meet every person I meet. And second, I don't ever know when or where I'll bump into him. We don't make appointments."

And then there was light. Full spectrum. No more small, starry nightscapes but a four-foot-wide expanse of paper tacked from one door jamb—around the walls, under the windows, around four corners—to the other, a wainscoting in white. The first two figures had already been sketched.

"I'm making a scroll," she explained, when Arnold inquired.

"What sort of a scroll?"

"It's the Scroll of Esther. Yip told me the story yesterday, and I checked it out in the holy babble—good one. Right for me."

"Yip?"

"Mr. YP. Yellow Pants. Says he's the oldest member of the Yippies. That's why he wears yellow pants."

"You saw him yesterday?"

"Hanging out at Pearl Paint. Where I got this roll of ninety-pound. We went for coffee. And he did order in Italian. Do you know why a cappuccino is called a cappuccino?"

"Because it looks like a cappuccino, it smells like . . . ?"

"No. Because if you make it right, it leaves a brown ring around the cup, like the edge of a monk's cowl. And it's just the same color. *Capuche* is the hood. When you stare into a cappuccino, you're staring into a religious abyss."

"He told you that? He didn't tell you 'because it looks like a cappuccino . . .'?"

"He told me both. He knew the guy that invented the espresso machine."

Arnold felt unhinged. He plopped down on the revolving stool in the center of the room and spun till he was dizzy. The Jacobo thing was too strange to get into on a sunny Tuesday morning.

"Jealous again?"

"No, no. It's . . ."

She continued sketching. After a while: "Who are those guys?" he asked. "They look like you and me."

"You don't say."

"I like your robe."

"Yeah. Royal. That's Vashti, the soon-to-be-deposed queen of Ahasuerus. You'll notice the first two letters of his name."

"Aha!" said Arnold.

"So you're the king of Persia, and . . ."

"About to overthrow you? Never!"

"Hold your horses, cowboy. There's more to the tale."

She began to tour him around the empty paper, pointing out scenes-to-be in their approximate places.

"This is where Haman—you're supposed to boo and hiss—goes out to find . . ."

"Why am I supposed to boo and hiss?"

"Didn't you learn anything in Hebrew School? When the Scroll of Esther is read at Purim, Jews are supposed to boo and hiss—and bang noisemakers, and shake rattles, and tear up paper with Haman's name, and rub the pieces into the floor. . . ."

"Hebrew School?"

"Anyway, Haman wanted to get A. H. Suerus to kill all the Jews."

"What was it this time?"

"Because Esther's cousin wouldn't bow down to the big Mr. Prime Minister mucky-muck. The beauty contest among the virgins goes over here, here's where Esther gets picked, Mordecai's refusal to bow goes here, Haman's proposal to kill em all goes over here, and here is Esther convincing the king to hang Haman boo hiss, and here will be Haman hanging, and here—this whole wall and around to the door—will be the Jewish revenge on those who would have killed them. Seventy-five thousand dead."

"What's Purim?"

"A happy holiday."

"With seventy-five thousand dead?"

"Yeah, but it's them, not us. For *us*, we have yet another shoestring salvation, with lots of dancing and singing and getting drunk and putting on Purimspieler—like the satyr plays. Everything gets satirized—even rabbis."

"Where'd you learn all this?"

"Yip takes me to his shul. I study."

"I thought they didn't let girls in that club."

"Do I look like a girl?" She sucked in her cheeks. "He brings me a black coat and a yarmulke, and I pretend to be his grandson. We go to this little shul on East 9th, and I sit with him, pressed right up close on the bench. Jealous? He sways back and forth, and it's like we're connected at the shoulder. I can't read the Hebrew in the prayer book, but he keeps pointing at the words. They began to look magical, those shapes. It's scary and totally moving. You know what I figured out while you were snoring away?"

"What? I don't snore."

"That monotheism is an amazing approximation to atheism. I mean, the most important property of G-dash-d is that nothing must be known about capital-H him. You're not allowed to draw Him or paint Him, you can't even mention His name. He's close to not existing at all."

"That's what you discuss in shul?"

"After. Over cappuccinos. So maybe *I'll* become a Jew, too—so I can paint him up, and figure out a good name for him like Munkustrap or Jellylorum."

"You want to call God 'Jellylorum'?"

"Sure, why not?"

"Because . . . I don't know."

"If you don't know, don't object."

She kissed him, smiled, and went back to sketching.

Forty-five

T he stars had initiated Evelyn's yellow period. Van Gogh's great yellow paintings were tacked up over their beds in studio and bunker: *Starry Night*, of course, the *Portrait of Armand Roulin*, the *Sunflowers*, *Yellow Wheat*. . . . She dressed Arnold in blue for one noonday nap—and then painted him against an imaginary haystack. Spin this straw into gold.

The thousand meanings of yellow, so ambivalent and contradictory. Golden courage, yellow cowardice; fierce yellow desire, yellow renunciation; divine yellow, and decadent. She painted her disturbing *Yellow Blues*—that hunched young woman, likely suicidal, under a forbidding sky, all in shades of yellow. She painted bulldozers, and her own imagined *corpus luteum*. She painted yellow-ray universes being born, Kandinsky-like, out of ochre and dandelion chaos. She painted a carnival scene on Madison Avenue and 34th Street—all in yellow—and titled it with a quotation from H. L. Mencken: *"The Joy of the Imbecile: Official*

Optimism of a Steadily Delighted and Increasingly Insane Republic." She did a set of variations on the sheet-music covers of popular songs of the '40s—"*Yellow Peril,*" "*Slap the Jap Right Off the Map,*" and *"When Those Little Yellow Bellies Meet the Cohens and the Kellys,*" and a barely distinguishable, yellowed-out miniature called *Bombing Hanoi for Christmas.*

"Will you paint me a portrait of Yip?" Arnold asked.

"No."

"Why not?"

"Representation of Yip is forbidden."

When the Esther Scroll was finished, she asked him to build a crankie-box for it.

"You know, an opening like a TV set—say three by three —with a crank on one side and a crank on the other. We attach the scroll between them, then we can roll it along, stop at given scenes, narrate them. Make a great Purimshpiel."

He built the box; she painted it yellow. It worked just fine. They rolled the scroll back and forth, admired the many couture creations, the dignity of A. H. Suerus, the villainous gestures of Haman boo hiss, the wood and rope textures of the gallows, and the Géricault scenes of Jewish revolution.

One splendid December afternoon, after replenishing her various shades of yellow, Evelyn left Pearl Paint and returned to her snakeskin Jag parked two blocks off Canal. In went the paints, click went the key, whir went the starter, and whirrwhirrwhirrwhirr. . . . Evelyn checked the gas: half full (she, ever the optimist). "Must be flooded," she thought. So she snagged her sketchbook from the glove compartment and spent a few minutes on the passing characters. Lower Manhattan was unsurpassed in this regard.

Key again, and much whirring. A knock at the passenger-side window. "No! Get outta here, I don't want my windows washed," she gestured. He pointed at the engine and mimed his knowledge of mechanical affairs. Evelyn's AAA card was expired. Should she trust him? It was the "HEIL HEIDEGGER!" button on his fur-collared rabbinical overcoat that tipped the scales. He might be a Nazi nut—but she was an old hand here. Evelyn rolled down the window.

"Whirring is my specialty," VDub said. "I'm a dervish from way back." He pulled an International Association of Sufism card from his wallet as ID.

"Vergil Wang, GM," she noted. "What's the GM?"

"Great Mechanic," he said.

"You do Jags?"

"Do I do Jags?" In answer, he roared most authentically. She almost rolled up the window again. "Do I do Jags? Pop the bonnet."

Would anyone who didn't do Jags say, "Pop the bonnet"? She pulled the lever under the dash and got out of the car. A small crowd of beautiful-woman-in-distress-patzers began to gather. Vergil Wang, GM, lifted the hood and peered inside. "Umm. Hmm. Uh-huh," he muttered as he stroked his nonexistent beard.

"What's the problem?"

"The problem, my dear, is Lucas Electric Products. Lucas, Prince of Darkness, Lucas, Lord of Utter Chaos, Lucas, the original antitheft device. If Lucas made guns, wars would never start."

"So . . . what's the problem?"

"I will now undertake the recommended procedure before dealing with a Lucas repair job. 1: Check the position of the stars." He looked skyward. "Can't see them. 2. Kill a chicken. Anybody got a chicken?" The citizen-gawkers demurred. "All right, then, we will resort to walking three times around the vehicle counterclockwise." He lined up the marchers and began the procession, which had a difficult time squeezing sideways between the Jag's bumper and that of the Oldsmobile behind it. VDub chanted in his best cantorial mode: "Oh, mighty Prince of Darkness, excuse your unworthy servants for interfering in your plans, but this beautiful woman has an appointment at 5 o'clock, and . . ." He shooed the minions back onto the sidewalk and reestablished himself at the hood.

"And . . . ?" inquired Evelyn, more amused than annoyed.

"Umm, shucks, ma'am. I hate to tell you this, but . . ."

"But what?"

"But you have no distributor." He pointed to the dangling spark-plug wires.

"What's a distributor?" We all have limited areas of expertise.

"What's a distributor? *Divide et impera!* How do the plugs know when to spark? How to sing the body electric? No juice, no go, man."

"So what happened to the distributor?"

"A Lucas distributor? Could have gone to Mars. Could have simply evaporated. See that cloud up there?"

"They stole it! The *shvartzas!*" yelled an onlooker.

"How could anyone steal it?" Evelyn asked, confounded. "There's a hood lock, isn't there? You have to release it from inside. . . ."

VDub drew up to magisterial height. "Madame, as the mayor of this great city, I take personal offense at the allegation that our citizens are not capable of breaking into any imported motorcar they choose." He led the crowd in, "U.S.A.! U.S.A.!"

"But," he interjected, "I shall have the problem fixed within twenty minutes. Synchronize your watches. . . ."

"Do you need money to buy . . . ?"

"More filthy lucre for filthy Lucas? Never. Hold thy peace and perpend! I shall be back in a quarter of an hour. Start counting . . . now!"

Nineteen minutes from T_0, Evelyn turned the key, and the great V-8 gave out its familiar Jaguar roar to the cheering of the crowd. She invited her savior home for dinner, but he took a rain check. Tonight he had to see a man about a horse. Or was it "some" horse? She couldn't hear too well over the sound of the engine.

Forty-six

"What are you up to, Evie?" Arnold asked when he came home to find her mixing dough and water boiling on the bunker hot plate.

"A special dinner tonight."

"Here or at the studio?"

"Here, dear Ah. More cozy. Less art."

She put the mixing bowl out the door to chill.

"So what are you making?"

"A matzo-ball phantasmagoria. Good for a winter's night."

Arnold hugged her from behind, and she reached back up with doughy hands and smeared his face.

"Yuck!"

"Don't judge the spheroids before they are hatched," she countered. "You'll like them."

When she finally invited him to table, she brought on the first and only course—two huge plates of soup. Surrogate Sal, Evelyn's pal, jumped up on the table, and was quickly shooed off to sulk.

"The Mommy Bear's," she announced as she placed down her own, with a classical two-inch ball, and "The Daddy Bear's"—Arnold's, an extraordinary softball-sized creation that, even in its soupy context, resembled nothing so much as Betelgeuse, the matzo-ball-colored supergiant.

"Dinner question number one," he said. "Why the different sizes? Bad for my waistline."

"Everything," she answered, "is internally clothed in meaning."

He nodded, thinking he understood. She nodded back, knowing he didn't.

"The matzoh balls contain prizes. Let's just see what they are. *Divide et impera!*" She winked. "Me first."

"As usual."

Inside Evelyn's there was a tiny Star of David on a dainty chain. And inside Arnold's a two-inch gray calf. Arnold turned it around in his hand.

"OK, explain."

"It's a golden calf," she said.

"But it's gray."

"Only to demonstrate the Hegelian aphorism of being in the night where all calves are gray," she said. "Perhaps it's a comment, Arnie, on your unfortunately benighted state."

"Me? Benighted?"

"It's to protect the matzoh- ball, my Lancelot. Scratch it," she said, and handed him a knife.

"Yellow."

"Wrong. See? Benighted. It's gold! Real gold lacquer. Sir Arnold Häagen-Dazs gets the Golden Calf award for his inability to embrace the one God—infinite, omnipresent, unperceived, and presently unrepresentable. I, on the other hand, get a sweet little Jewish star to wear around my neck."

She put it on. Sal made a second attempt at tabling, and was similarly rebuffed.

"Could I ask if your putting on that star has any religious significance, or is it just a fashion statement?"

"I thought I'd use it to mark my experimental but semipermanent conversion."

"You've decided to become semipermanently Jewish? Does this have anything to do with Yip?"

"No, no, Arnold. I was considering this move before Yip came on the scene. He's helped me to think—but not to decide."

"So why now?" Arnold asked. "Why do you want to become Jewish?"

"Well, first of all . . . I like matzoh-ball soup. . . . *Aaaand* . . ." she emphasized before he could interrupt, "it's a predictable Hegelian leap from Nazis, don't ya know? Eve was Jewish, right? And Christianity is dumb. How can anyone believe in a God that wants to save the world by torturing his son to death? What a plan! *And* because sex for Jews isn't sinful, *and* because you don't get any bonuses for good behavior, no rewards in the life hereafter, which doesn't exist, pretty hard-nosed, *and,* and most of all, because Jews are a pain in the ass, taking nothing for granted, letting nothing pass, splitting hairs, being difficult—I love it. I choose to be Jewish—without being *chosen,* without a bloodstream full of pogroms and torture and burning at the stake. And—with these shards of excavated matzoh balls between us—I ask you, Arnie: Will you join me?"

She took his hand across the table. For all the banter, she seemed serious.

"Will you, Arnold Hamlet . . . ?"

He stared into his soup, as into a monk's cowl. And she stopped herself.

And then Arnold spoke: "Jabès says the true Jew is the one who can't *be* Jewish. A person exiled from the call—so he can be called. That state, that tension . . ." He looked into Evelyn's moist eyes.

"Yah," she said, after a pause.

Sal again, and not.

"Do you intend to keep kosher, keep the laws? Do you even know what they are?"

"I'll start with Shabbat. No work on Friday nights."

"So Friday night is for the Lord, and on Saturday night you strip for the unwashed mob? Do you know what you're doing? Would Adonai approve?"

"Isn't it tension you want? Such is tension." She raised her glass. "Here our prenuptial dinner? Mommy Bear and Daddy Bear . . ." she rose, circled the table, and straddled her Hitler, ". . . and all cubs that come after?"

Arnold took a deep breath, sighed deeply, and hooked his chin over Evelyn's shoulder. He hung there a while, and then massaged her back with his jaw. The motion of his head was axial left and right, as in shaking of the head, as in "No." But the thoughts in his heart tended strongly in the other direction.

Forty-seven

The wedding was held in the bunker (more cozy, less art) on Purim, March 18th, 1973. The day was one of several proposed by Bible scholars as the first day of Creation. At the White House, five thousand years later, it became the first day of Cover-up as Richard Nixon and John Dean discussed how to find one million dollars of hush money. Such is progress since Creation.

But in the innocent bunker on Bruckner Boulevard, Dr. Leonard Bernstein held musical sway, providing both sound and food, while the service was conducted by his new and most excellent boyfriend, the Minister Vergil Wang, mentor to the groom, distributor distributor to the bride, wedding contractor, and Grand Master of Much. Both providers were elegantly dressed—far more so than the principals: Lenny wore turquoise spangled tails with an ivory cummerbund, while VDub sported a teal-blue academic robe trucked up with the colors of his eight ancestral nationalities. Both wore matching yellow yarmulkes, his and hers, adorned with buttons from the NLF and the Grateful Dead. Arnold wore his crimson team sweatshirt with H on the front and HITLER 53 on the back, while Evelyn sported her church-basement best.

Lenny had borrowed a van from his friends at Steinway—equipped with his favorite concert grand. The driver backed it up as far as he could (given the triangular nature of the on-ramp), and the piano was lowered on the lift to a foot off the ground. The van space behind acted as a sound tunnel piping right in through the small door. Andrew Carnegie would have killed for the acoustics.

In addition to being a sound tunnel, the van was lined with six tables, piano-strapped to the wall, bursting with foods from Zabar's, D'Agostino's, Nathan's, et al., a gustatory extravaganza seldom seen in South Bronx. On the menu, the normal cold cuts: pastrami, corned beef, turkey, tongue—but of the highest quality. As arabesque to the kosher meat of-ferings, chopped liver, just like Mama used to make, pickled lox and her-ring, and, for the goyim, a spiral-cut ham. These to be served on bagels, challah and real Jewish rye.

For the courageous with a fork: eight whole smoked whitefish, oily, bony, their yellow eyes fixedly investigating the ceiling of the van. For upper-crust guests, a huge plate of smoked salmon, sturgeon and sable; caviar dishes of Caspian sevruga and beluga from both Iran and Kaza-khstan; foie gras with truffles. Maine lobster claws competed with brethren tails from apartheid South Africa. (For the lower crust, the only hot items: foot-longers direct from Coney Island and barbecued chicken wings.) And for the weight-conscious, finger foods: spinach roulade with smoked salmon mousse, mushroom and Roquefort strudel, stuffed snow peas from Joyce Chen, melon and honey-ham kabobs, asparagus crous-tade, cream puffs with curried crab and apple, and (in honor of the Lone Star STATE) Tex-Mex corn muffins with green chili dip.

Les pièces de résistance were the desserts: Carnegie Deli cheesecake; fruit and cheese blintzes; rugelach and babka; crème fraiche; six varieties of biscotti; halavah, chocolate, vanilla, and marbled; nut trays, dried fruit, and the penultimate wonder, a gourmet chocolate tower of Antonio Gaudi design.

On its own small table, to be transported within, the wedding cake, a spiraling zigguratic wonder depicting all of human history, from the Gan Eden at its foot to the current wedding at its pinnacle.

So as not to ruin the dogs and the wings, the service had to be held as close to the arrival of the van as possible. Thus, at the unpredicted hour of 1:28 P.M., the bride and groom were summoned by its intimate rumble to come greet its driver, his assistant, its one-man band, and the presiding minister, all packed together in the cab.

Arnold's mother, Anna, might have shown up for the wedding, ushered in on the arm, say, of a most formal Cheesy, to give her son away. It could have been that Bob Wright, left by his draft-counseling widow, had hooked up with Judy Jepperson, Ph.D., ex– Harvard University—*they* might both have shown up. But that would have been a This-Is-Your-Life beyond the means of Vergil Wang, Grand Master of Much, but Not Everything. The only attendees, then: the bride and groom, the Rabbi VDub, the Pastor VDub, the Master of Ceremonies VDub, the *Badchen* VDub—traditional jester-actor-singer-poet-philosopher at Jewish weddings—and his boyfriend, the musician Lenny. At 1:34, the piano was lowered into position, and the bunker ceremony began, with space heater blasting away.

"Here Comes the Bride"—the solemn wedding march from *Lohengrin.* But under Lenny's fingers, mixed and morphed with other leitmotifs: much of the Grail, and Lohengrin's own noble arpeggio; the Innocence Motif, and that of Warning; the Prohibition Against Questioning Motif, and the Confidence in Faith and Holiness of Love. Even Swans floated through. The damn thing took five minutes until arriving at its finale. Evelyn had to process very slowly back and forth across the twenty-foot interior of the bunker, her Godiva wig sweeping the cobblestone floor behind her. She counted twenty-two laps.

Then, to a short burst of Siegfried's horn motif, Arnold sprang out of the chair and joined his bride—his literate, his smart, his genius bride; his bride alive, alove as *he* would be; his funny, most vivacious Lilith-person, *ewig-weibliche*, leading him on.

The Godiva wig deserves some comment. Shaving her head was an incisive part of Evelyn's personal prenuptial commitment. In the Middle Ages—of which she was most fond—many Jewish women shaved their heads to atone for the sin of Eve in Eden. In some communities, shaving the head was prescribed preparation for marriage—so as not to distract the new husband from prayer.

But bald women, in 1373 or six hundred years later, were considered ugly, and who wants an ugly bride? Hence, the wig. Did a *wig* need to be covered? The rabbis went round and round on that one, but Evelyn, unfazed, picked up the wildest *shatyl* she could find at Mannie's Costume and Joke Store on West 51st.

And so at 1:42 on a Purim afternoon, Arnold and his Godiva stood in front of the teal-robed VDub, when

Surprise!

From behind crepe-paper streamers

interwoven in the chain-link fence

at the School of Semisolid Knocks

in the wasteland of Bruckner Boulevard,

there came a trumpet call—the *grosser Appell* preceding the resurrection. Its performance was unmistakable: it could only be the mustache, Leonard Hecht, Arnold's once rival. From the back of the van, Lenny added the birds, and in the door walked Ariel Bernstein, holding a yellow candle in a glass. Accompanied by her father, she sang the *"Urlicht"* in a voice so ethereal that Christa Ludwig would have wet her pants.

"Dear God will grant me a tiny light
which will light my way to eternal, blissful life."

During which, the room grew strangely, unbelievably, yellow. Arnold's knee itched like crazy. Meanwhile the hot dogs were getting cold.

Applause, introductions, and hugs all around. Ariel and her new husband. Now the service could begin in earnest—though the earnestness was mixed with a ridiculous Purimshpiel parody appropriate to a mixed marriage cum bat mitzvah cum name-changing cum graduation and commencement.

The bride stood under a half-huppah, a canopy on two poles only (held by van men), the cloth stiffened out artificially like the American flag on the moon (or in the moon studio). For *her*, it was a Jewish wedding, if not for her groom, who stood outside the huppah, under the on-ramp concrete firmament.

> *Addressing themselves to me, my fellow Jews said: "You are not a Jew. You never go to synagogue." Addressing myself to them, I answered: "I carry the synagogue within me."*

"Ladies and gentlemen," VDub began, "we are gathered here today to witness the marriage of Arnold and Evelyn."

"Yes!" Cheesy shouted, full-mouthed, from the back of the truck.

"Couples are always surprised by how short a time it takes to get married," VDub rabbied. " 'Yes' is a short word, but that single syllable, truly spoken, has a power as potentially divine as the 'Let there be light' at the beginning of the world."

Growing E-flat major arpeggios from Lenny.

VDub continued, "The center of the marriage event is the public exchange of vows."

No fuss. Keep it simple.

"Do you, Arnold Hitler, take this woman . . ."

At which point—surprise again!—Evelyn began a sinuous dance, planned and rehearsed with her minister, as Lenny provided music from

Strauss's *Salomé*. Her fringed shawl dropped to her bare feet. Turn, turn, turn. She undid her madras sarong and draped it around her groom, pulling him willy-nilly into the dance. Arnold began to worry how far she of Pinky's Palace—elegant in leotard—would go.

But the climax was other: pulling him madras-wise tight against her, with a sweeping gesture she pulled off her wig, tossed it to the congregation, and displayed to him, and to all, the crown of her naked head. There, tattooed in red, black, and blue Hebrew letters, was her new name—"ESTHER." Romanized on the occiput. She pirouetted several times to firm up the transformation, faced VDub, and took Arnold's burned and bitten hand.

"All right, then," VDub continued, "do you, Arnold Hitler 53, take this woman, Esther Brown, to be your lawfully wedded wife, to have and to squeeze, in sickness and in health, till death do you part?"

Arnold hesitated at the new name. "I guess so."

Esther bit him on the neck.

"I *do*."

"And Esther Brown, do you take this man, Arnold Hitler 53, to be your lawfully wedded husband, et cetera, et cetera, till death do you part?"

"I do."

They exchanged rings. To solve the topological problem of separateness, their wedding bands were inscribed each with half a verse:

Hers: *O may my heart in tune be found*

His: *like David's harp, of solemn sound.*

Together, they made a rhyming couplet, regardless of the geometrical resistance.

"Arnold and Esther, in joining yourselves to one another, you have joined yourselves to the unknown. Neither of you is in charge of the path. What you alone, Arnold, want it to be, it will not be. Where you alone, Esther, want it to go, it will not go. It will lead where the two of you—

and marriage, time, life, history, and the world—will take it. You have committed your lives to a journey of uncharted paths.

"It is a Jewish tradition to end a wedding ceremony by breaking a glass underfoot. Since the groom is not yet ready to commit to that tradition, and since the bride is barefoot, I will do it myself with my Doc Martens. [He lifted his skirts to show.] This surprising act of waste and violence does have three points to make. One: it reminds us of the destruction of the Temple, and of all temples, by *Homo destructus*—that's us. Two: it is irrevocable and permanent. So too may this marriage be. On the other hand, three: it demonstrates that no matter how happy we may be today, at any moment our world may be shattered in a thousand pieces."

He drew from his pouch a lovely wine glass, as long-stemmed as the bride, wrapped it in one of his national banners, and placed it on the floor before him.

"Wait a minute," Arnold said. "I'll do it."

And he did. It crackled meanly underfoot.

The group took a while to digest his gesture. Then VDub summed things up: "Esther and Arnold, as you have declared your vows here today, in accordance with the power invested in me by this great city of which I am the mayor, and with the blessings of the Universal Life Church, I now pronounce you husband and wife."

Cheers from the crowd.

"And may that glory which rests on all who love, rest upon you, and bless you, and fill you with happiness and a gracious spirit. And despite all changes of time and fortune, may all that is noble and lovely and true abound in your hearts, and stay with you, and give you strength in all your days together. Amen. Omain."

Not an eye was dry—except those of Cheesy, who had arrived late, and was poking around the truck for possibilities.

Lenny struck up the wedding march from *Midsummer Night's Dream.* He loved framing nuptials between Wagner, the anti-Semite, and Mendelssohn, the Jew: *Seid umschlungen!* universal embrace. But of course the traditional recessional was made to do-si-do with other great Mendelssohn moments—the Intermezzo, the Nocturne, the Scherzo, the Spotted Snakes and March of the Fairies, the Clown Dance and Pyramus's Funeral Dirge. Arnold and Esther recessed the six feet from altar to door and abandoned the ceremony to schmooze, while Lenny did his ten-minute thing.

The cake was brought in and reluctantly dismembered. Cheesy had a ball with the deli leftovers, and Sal scurried away with a whole whitefish in her mouth.

Forty-eight
Postepithalamion

The last draftee entered the U.S. Army on June 30, 1973. He was killed in action in September. In that year, too, on 9/11, with CIA support, General Augusto Pinochet overthrew Salvador Allende, the democratically elected president of Chile, in a violent coup. He claimed the president machine-gunned himself to death during the takeover.

The next month, on October 6th, Egypt and Syria made a coordinated surprise attack on Israel. Nine other Arab states aided the war effort. Thrown on the defensive during the first few days of fighting, within a week Israel repulsed all invaders and in the next week carried the war deep into enemy territory. On October 22, the United Nations Security Council called for "all parties to the present fighting to cease all firing." By that time, Israel had cut off and isolated the Egyptian army and was positioned to destroy it. The victim Jew had made his final exit from the stage of history. The Jewish warrior had succeeded him, a pariah still.

On November 15th, a letter showed up in the studio mailbox, addressed in red to A HEB.

> *Dear (Benedict) Arnold,*
>
> *Most hearty congratulations on your conjunctio with the fidelitous Leonora, the Girl Who Says Yes to Guys Who Say No—you being chief among them. A match most appropriate. Let us hope your heroine comports more with Beethoven than with Poe.*
>
> *But let us remember too that after consorting with his new consort, your current namesake was hung in effigy upon a tree, growing not in Brooklyn, but in our very own Manhattan.*
>
> *One further note: during the Spanish Inquisition, those condemned for heresy or treason were arrayed in the sacco Benedetto, or "Sack of Benedict," the penitential garment, a white linen robe painted over with flames and devils. As the hapless victims waited at the stake, the mocking crowds could envision their fates—even before the flame was lit.*
>
> *For all that, it is nevertheless charming to think of my buddy sailing off handsomely into the sunset with his beauteous bride. Quo vadimus, antiquus amicus meus? Auf wiedersehen.*
>
> *Yours, ever,*
>
> *R. Mather, M.D.*
>
> *cc: KKK*

From the 19th to the 26th of December, Esther celebrated her first Chanukah, lighting candles each night and fashioning a menorah displaying active, immiscible oils. On the evening of December 24th, she exchanged Christmas presents with Arnold under their first *Tannenbaum*. They sang "Silent Night," in harmony.

In the bunker on Bruckner Boulevard, a young white cat waited patiently for its supper in rapt contemplation of her singular Name.